PARADISE U

Also by Annie Dawid

Put Off My Sackcloth: Essays. The Humble Essayist Press, 2021.

Anatomie of the World: Poems. Finishing Line Press, 2017.

And Darkness Was Under His Feet: Stories of a Family.
Litchfield Review Press, 2008.

Lily in the Desert: Stories.
Carnegie-Mellon University Press Series in Short Fiction, 2001.

York Ferry: A Novel. Cane Hill Press, 1993.

PARADISE UNDONE

A Novel of Jonestown

Annie Dawid

First edition published in 2023 by Inkspot Publishing

www.inkspotpublishing.com

ISBN (Paperback US) 978-1-916708-02-0
ISBN (Paperback ex-US): 978-1-916708-00-6
ISBN (eBook): 978-1-916708-01-3

Printed and bound in Great Britain by Clays Ltd, Elcograf S.p.A

Cover Image: Joe Samuels

For Christine, who refused to submit.

This novel is based on true events. Some dialogue has been taken verbatim from Jonestown documents.

Some individuals who died on Nov. 18, 1978, among them Jim and Marceline Jones, are referred to by their real names, though they are products of research and imagination. Others are fictions.

IF YOU WANT TO CALL ME GOD,
THEN I'M GOD.

Jim Jones

"The first body I saw was off to the side, alone. Five more steps and I saw another and another and another; hundreds of bodies. The *Newsweek* reporter was walking around saying, "I don't believe it, I don't believe it." Another guy said, "It's unreal." Then nobody even attempted to speak anymore. It was overwhelming. Bizarre."

"I started moving to my left, and I was battered by the smell. It hit me. Went right into my chest. I started to gag, and turned my back. Seeing it, plus the smell … Then, I found if I kept my eyes moving and let my camera be my eyes, I'd never really see it. I shot verticals and horizontals, moving to my left. And there it was. There were piles upon piles of bodies. What do you call it? There's no definition. Nothing to compare it to."

Rolling Stone
January 1979

Watts Freeman
10:05 a.m.
November 18, 2008
San Francisco

KR: Thank you so much for agreeing to this interview, Mr. Freeman. I know our listeners on KBBA, the Black Bay Area's radio station, are very grateful. First, let me do a quick test. Today is November the eighteenth, 2008, the thirty-year anniversary of the Jonestown massacre, and I'm Kenyatta Robinson. Test. Good.

WF: I go by Watts.

KR: Okay, Watts. That tells us something important about you already, and we haven't even gotten to the first question! Just relax; the lapel mike will catch everything. Later, we can edit out all the dead space and mumbling. I'd like you to talk about what strikes you most on this date. But I do have a few questions to start with. For instance, can you tell us about when you met Jim Jones?

WF: I'm a teenager, right? Don't know shit, but I think I know everything. Think I've got the whole scam down cold, but really, I was deeply fucked up. Is it all right, me cussing on tape?

KR: No problem. Like I said, we can edit later. Use whatever language feels most comfortable.

WF: Well, English is all I know. *[Laughter]* Anyway, I was pretty much living on the streets back then. This was in LA, Watts area mostly. I'd come up here to the Bay Area with some friends and we were looking around, thinking about moving since the cops in LA were seriously out of control.

KR: How old were you exactly? And when was this?

WF: Around '68, '69 maybe. I was born in '50. Anyway, that stretch of time is pretty hazy 'cause most days I had a good buzz on. So me and my friends, we're checking out Oakland, scratching around Hunter's Point, and then we're up in the Fillmore, and we see these buses, a whole parade of them, man, coming down Fillmore Street, and they're full of brothers and sisters. Some white folks too but mostly brothers and sisters and they're waving. Waving at us, hanging on the corner, stoned into tomorrow. That was my first sight of Peoples Temple. Didn't see Jimmie Jones that day though. Mind if I smoke?

KR: It's your home, Mr. Freeman –

WF: Watts. Please. But does it bother you? 'Cause if it does, I won't. You a beautiful woman in your childbearing years; how do I know you ain't pregnant?

KR: *[Laughs]* I'm not. You're fine.

WF: You pretty fine yourself. *[Sound of his palm slapping his cheek]* Sorry. Am I making you uncomfortable? Shit. Same ol' same ol' Watts. Jimmie Jones figured me out in about five minutes, but the thing was, I figured him in about four, so generally I was one step ahead.

KR: I hope to hear more about that, Watts. But, to continue where we were, you say you didn't meet the Reverend Jones on that day. So, when did that happen?

WF: 1970. In LA. I was selling dope and doing dope and not much else. My old lady at the time had kicked me out, so I go visit my grandma to get something to eat, and she drag me off to one of them healing services she love. I was too stoned to refuse. She always believing in something, my grandma, something to make her life feel better than it did. God or Jimmie Jones or Jesus or somebody else. So when she found God and Jesus wrapped up in Reverend Jimmie Jones, she was like to be in heaven.

KR: Can you describe your earlier life, growing up in Watts?

WF: And growing up as Watts, right? *[Laughter]* I guess my father was a doper. Never knew him. He died when my mother was pregnant. A dealer too. It was never exactly clear whether he OD'd or got done on the street for ripping somebody off. Doesn't matter. Dead is dead, right? My mother did dope too, and she didn't last long. I moved around, from practically the minute I was born, from one relative to another in Watts, and some of those people weren't in any better shape than my mother. They tried to be good to me; I can see that now. But it was rough, coming up like that. My grandma was working all the time, cleaning houses and such, so I couldn't stay with her. I didn't get to school much, and when I did, recess was where I started doping. I was eleven, but I'd sampled all kinds of shit before then. Every now and again, I did stay with my grandma, but my mama and her didn't get along 'cause Grandma always telling her what she was doing wrong, which was everything, of course, so even though my mama was too fucked up – 'scuse me, too messed up to take care of me herself, she didn't like my being with her mama. So then after some big fight, I'd get sent out to somebody else's place.

KR: Sounds like your grandmother was a source of stability for you.

WF: *[Laughs.]* My grandma, she like every other old black lady in

Peoples Temple. Sweet. A serious backbone for work. At the same time, you could talk her out of anything you needed and decided she didn't. Like money. Stuff to pawn. And I did. Just like Jimmie Jones convincing every one of them grandmas to turn over their Social Security checks every month. Yeah, I'm guilty too, but that was before the Jimmie Jones years in LA. When the Temple finally got its own building there, she would've given every penny in her purse to those collections. Sometimes they had four or five in one service. And her pitiful possessions too, but she died before they could completely rip her off. Before I could, too.

KR: You sound bitter.

WF: Mostly, I'm pissed at myself. I was a nasty character back then. Hope I'm not so nasty anymore. Anyway, my grandma passed from natural causes. She wasn't one of them widows lying face down in the mud, swollen up like a goddamn balloon in Jonestown. I'm not sure if dying of a heart attack in a rat-hole project in Watts is better than that, but at least she got buried proper.

KR: So, did you join up that day? With your grandmother? You were twenty then?

WF: Old enough to know better. Nah, not that day. But Jimmie Jones talking about how he's a nigger like the rest of us, and how the government hates black people. Second part of that is true anyway. He says look at the Japanese. They had money, he says, they owned a chunk of California, and they got put into camps here 'cause they ain't white. Not so long ago either. Like the Jews in Europe. He says, *Don't think it can't happen here.* And he goes on about how the white man wants us to be drunk and stoned and wasting our lives, and how we play right into their pale ugly hands when we get messed up on dope and booze. Asks us who own all the liquor stores in the ghetto. White people, right? He still right. 'Cept now it's mostly Asians. Anyway, he's talking like his skin is brown as yours or mine. Which I think is weird, 'cause the man is white. He ain't mixed, not Indian, like he claim. He a white boy. He got that dark hair from Wales, not no Cherokee Nation. *[Laughs]* Anyway, he's talking about this program they have at the church to get people like me, like a lot of young folk, off the dope and out of jail, to help us be useful in the community. It's not like I never heard what the man said before, but he got a good rap and a fine delivery, and it's penetrating my stoner head. Then my grandma gets on me, and she won't quit razzing me 'til I say yes. Now, I'd done rehab already, and I'd been to jail already, and you know, I didn't have nothing going on that was worth keeping going on. My girlfriend say she don't want nothing to do with me 'cause I'm too fucked up – sorry, too messed up – too much of the time. So, Grandma says I can stay with her if I enroll myself in that program.

KR: So it worked? The Reverend Jones straightened you out?

WF: Kenyatta – that your name, right? Kenyatta, you gotta remember I was young at the time. And dumb. Dumb about dope, 'specially. But it wasn't Jimmie Jones got me off the dope; it was the people in Peoples Temple. Man, they were some fine people. Some very fine people. That's what always trips me up. To this day it does. Trips everyone else up too. All those good people. They weren't crazy like Jimmie Jones. Anyway, the nurses running the program, the other folks helping us get through the first days, like Jim McElvane, the guy everyone called Mac, and Archie, and of course some of the other dopers, like Rufus. They got me through.

KR: Can you talk more about that, about what you call the "fine" people and how you still find it hard to understand what they did, three decades on?

WF: Well, you know how they showed us in the media – not first-hand of course, you too young – but you must have checked out the newspapers and the magazines, and the shit they had on TV.

KR: Yes. I did quite a lot of research for this interview. And I'm probably not as young as you think, Watts.

WF: You way younger than me, that's for sure. *[Laughs]* Good old Watts hit the big five-eight this year, no thanks to Jimmie Jones. A miracle just the same, though. Never thought I'd get to be twenty-eight, much less fifty-eight, not what I was doing back then, the time we're talking about. What I was saying was that the news made out all of Jonestown was psychos and sickos and brainwashed, brainless zombies. So far from the truth, Kenyatta. You know, that group of black people about the most together bunch of people I ever saw. True then and maybe truer today. It was the Reverend himself, as you call him, who was crazed and drugged out and sick. The inner circle, what I call the "white chick circle," though there were some dudes in it too, mostly white – they like slaves to their master. "*Yassuh, Dad.*" Yassuh all day and all night. "*Yassuh, Dad. Whatever you say, Dad.*" He built himself such a bunch of yes men and yes women that if he say night is day they say, "*Yes Dad, that's right: Night is day.*" He say day night, they say, "*Thank you Dad – Day sho'nuff is night.*" You want a cigarette?

KR: No thank you. I don't smoke. But go ahead. It really doesn't bother me.

WF: You sure you ain't pregnant? Maybe you should say you are so I won't smoke so much.

KR: Okay, Watts. Let's say I am then. For the sake of your lungs. *[Laughs]*

WF: You funny. You a funny, smart lady, talking about my lungs. What I already put my body through it don't make sense I ain't dead. Now I think the diabetes gonna kill me in the end.

KR: I read that the Reverend Jones – Jimmie, as you call him – was actually very ill during those last days. Is that true?

WF: Hard to say for sure. He a star hypochondriac for certain. Had his wife checking his blood pressure every five minutes and he announce his fever over the PA, going up one degree every hour on the hour. Make people feel sorry for him. I don't think he any sicker than the rest of us in that Jonestown heat, with the bugs and the worms and the water sometimes giving us the runs. And he did like his dope, especially that last year after his mama died. You study those pictures from November 18th, the interviews he give those press guys he had killed on the runway, and you see a user's face. User's shaky hands. Even his bloated belly in that death picture look like an addict's body. He smacking his lips that whole talk he have with NBC like any cokehead. The media want to make all the black folk crazy to follow him, but he the insane one, not us. Night and day, he attended hand and foot by his private nurses and the doctor – most of them white – all of them revering his ass, and at the same time not helping him at all by giving him whatever drug he ask for: painkiller, sleeping pills, wake up pills, those so-called Vitamin B-12 shots the famous folks like so much.

KR: Who was the doctor? His name is escaping me.

WF: Larry Schacht. The last six months or so I was one of Doc Schacht's heavy lifters, and I saw every pill and potion got delivered to that shed. They call it the Bond down there. Ten thousand doses of Thorazine we had, biggest stockpile in South America. You know what Thorazine is? To make the living dead, especially if they troublemakers. Funny I just called him Doc. Behind his back, me and Rufus call him King Doper. Like us, the man came to the Temple with a serious drug habit, and we all got clean. Which was key, I think, in building loyalty to Jimmie Jones, even if he didn't have much to do with it, like I said before. Larry Schacht was a die-hard Jones fan. *[Laughs]* He die very hard. Me, I didn't get sent to no med school in Mexico. Jimmie didn't see no MD in ol' Watts' future, figure that. Rufus neither. Larry Schacht was a Jew, like a lot of those white people in the Circle. Like the brother and sister Tropp and that crazy Stein family. Anyway, I guess the good college boy fell off his path to doctorland into a patch of Mary Jane, and from there it wasn't but a hop and a skip until the habit riding his back in the streets with people like me. I didn't know him before the Temple, you understand. I'm just guessing. Anyway, after he got off of dope, Jimmie Jones sent him to med school. The King used to brag how the governor of California got behind his application because Dad – yeah, he called him Dad – was so insistent. He just worshipped that dude's ass. And I mean literally, because they did the nasty together on many occasions, and not always in private. Ol' Jimmie Jones, who pride himself on being the only "true heterosexual" in Peoples Temple – those his words – he seriously into getting some dick whenever he could. Pardon my language. So if Jimmie say jump, King Doper say not only "how high?" but "Can I get you anything while I'm up there?" He used to tell Rufus and me dope stories, like addicts do, you know, from the bad ol', good ol' days – you knew he was getting off on the memory – and still craved the dope. He didn't do it anymore, understand, but man he loved to dole it out. 'Specially to Jimmie Jones, who sample every medication ever prescribed in the Western World. He flyin' seriously high above our heads on speed since Day One, which was clear as glass to people like me. *"He has so much energy, does the Reverend,"* the white chick circle always saying. *"Isn't he amazing!"* Hah. He have the audacity to say he wear those sunglasses all the time 'cause he worry he could hurt someone with the intensity of his eyes. No shit. Probably the most creative excuse in history for bloodshot eyes, but the Circle didn't want to see it till the end, and even then, some of them refused to believe dear ol' Dad was just another doper like Rufus and me. The black bottom of the Peoples Temple. The base. The place he got all that Social Security money and collection money from to run the operation – poor old black ladies giving him their last dollars and the ratty houses they saved for all their lives because so-called Dad healed some auntie of cancer or cataracts. Of course those healings all fake. Some people – most people, I guess – believe whatever they want to be true. Not ol' Watts. But in a way, that's what the black folk in the base and the rich white people up in the Circle had in common – they all wanted Dad to be God. For Dad to answer every question they ever had. Me, I never had a father, and I sure wasn't taking on some white preacher to be my pretend Dad. *[Sighs]* Just about kill me, this ancient black man at Jonestown – he a hundred years old, at least – calling Jimmie Jones "Daddy" when he young enough to be his grandbaby.

KR: What do you think accounts for Reverend Jones's success – perhaps that's a strange word to use – maybe I should rather say his ability to convince so many people to stay with him, and in the end, to take their own lives? In all the similar events that have happened since – in Waco, for instance, or Heaven's Gate here in California – we're talking about a few dozen people. In Jonestown, we're talking nearly a thousand.

WF: Nine-hundred-nine at Jonestown, four in Georgetown. Even though he pumping up the numbers all the time – he say he have thirty thousand members in California, a million in the US to impress the Guyanese – it way too many human beings. *[Sighs again]* If I knew the answer to that question, I probably be lecturing at some university, like that asshole lawyer, you know who I mean, who make all this money off every conspiracy theory from Abe Lincoln to JFK to MLK Junior. I know they still people think the CIA did it. Maybe there was CIA down in Guyana. Why not? They everyplace else in the world, and sure fucked up Chile pretty good. They probably in downtown Georgetown drinking Demerara with the Embassy guys – or maybe they are the Embassy guys – but how they gonna make all those people drink poison? Don't make sense. No. I was there. It the people who stayed behind in the States that keep wanting to believe Jimmie Jones some kind of wronged god, some kind of crucified Christ figure or shit like that. Just like he want them to. He say he the reincarnated Christ, or Lenin, or Buddha, or some other leader he think impress people. He think the Soviet Union admire Jimmie Jones and his so-called socialist experiment. White people pretty stupid sometimes.

KR: Do you believe there was racism in the Peoples Temple? I know that about eighty percent of the congregation was black, but as you say, most of the inner circle was white.

WF: Most of Peoples Temple was poor. That most important – the blacks and most of the whites who weren't in the Circle. So living in Jonestown not so bad compared to the States. For some, it was better. Way better. No crime. No worrying about not having enough cash for groceries or what to cook for the next meal. No dog food for dinner. No being afraid of not having money for the doctor when you need one. Or the dentist. Everything taken care of. That especially good for the old people. If my grandma had lived, she be on that plane to Guyana in about five minutes flat – she clear outta Watts for good. You know that Congressman Ryan, he say Friday night, before it all went down, he say something like, "I know that for some of you people, this is the best thing that ever happened to you." And everyone cheer like crazy, 'specially the old black folk. They not cheering 'cause Jimmie Jones tell them to. That applause a hundred percent real. But the rich white folk in the Circle – and I mean the lawyers and the nurses and the PR types – they not in Jonestown 'cause they lives so awful back home. They there to change the world. They there 'cause they think Jimmie Jones the second coming of Marx and Che, Lumumba and Mao combined. He the white Leftist wet dream. So yeah, there racism in Peoples Temple. Like the Supreme Court, you know, white people making the laws for everybody else. Sometimes they let in a token or two. What that line? The exception prove the rule. Archie Ijames in the Circle for a while. Yolanda for a little bit. But them black folk didn't last. They too smart. Yolanda one of the very smart ones got away from Jonestown practically the day she arrive. And Archie – he dead now – Archie with Jimmie Jones from the start in Indiana; he didn't like Jonestown neither. Tried to quit the Temple, but Jimmie Jones knew that wouldn't look good, not to have even one black in the higher ups. Even if it only on paper. So he send Archie and his old lady back to the States. They very happy to go, too. No question Peoples Temple racist, like every other institution. You know one that ain't? But in Jonestown, I mean before it went bad, we having a pretty good time, the black folk and the white folk too. I mean, the white people not in the Circle. It beautiful in Guyana. The colors. The birds. Super-colorful sunsets every night. Me up and sober seeing sunrises every morning. Even the rain felt good.

KR: Do you miss it? Have you ever been back?

WF: I had a wife there. *[Long pause]*

KR: I'm sorry; I didn't know.

WF: Yeah. I don't talk about her much. Think about her every day though. Sometimes every minute, seems like. She and our baby the first to die. She volunteer. Can you figure that? She volunteer to kill the child and then herself after Jimmie Jones say babies go first, 'cause we don't want the enemy – whoever the fuck it was on that particular day – to be torturing the children. Shit.

KR: I'm so sorry, Watts. I didn't know you had a wife or a child there. I don't believe I've read that anywhere. Do you want to take a break? Should I turn off the tape?

WF: Nah. I want to talk about her. About them. You know I done a lot of interviews over the years – all the big anniversaries, the media look up ol' Watts. One-year, five-year, ten-year, twenty-five-year silver anniversary – ain't so many of us anymore, not the ones who in Jonestown, November 18th, 1978, anyway, and live to tell about it. You look up Robert or DeeDee? Almost nobody talk to them, they nine smart black people left that morning; they see what's coming down and they hightail it out of there, right through that nasty scary jungle Jimmie Jones and Mac warning us about every five minutes. They say, "*We going on a picnic, Dad,*"and they gone. I guess since none of them seen the massacre go down, like me, the media not interested in them. But they smarter than me. Mostly parents and their kids. Not like the mother of my kid.

KR: Watts, would you mind talking about her?

WF: Sure. I can talk about her.

KR: What was her name?

WF: She go by Earlene. Earlene Jones. No relation to Jimmie. She from Indiana originally, one of them kids who grew up in the Temple. You wanna talk about brainwashing? Well, the little kids who joined with their parents, sometimes grandparents, they didn't know no other life. Her mother there, three brothers, two aunties, a few cousins. Her grandpa die over there of a stroke a few months before the end. And the baby. I think it was mine anyway. I don't know for a fact. That girl so completely different from me. Earlene only eighteen years old. I was twenty-eight. She thought she reform me or something. Make me see the light. Wanted me to shine beside her in the true gospel of Jimmie Jones. Never woulda happened, even if Jonestown still there. Her mama figure me out, try to tell Earlene to keep away from me. But all the same, she like me. I like her. We have some good times. She the only girl ever pregnant with my baby – my body so fucked up – so messed up, I mean. From the dope. I suppose that could be a sign it wasn't my baby after all, but I just think it was.

KR: How old, then, was the child? If you don't mind saying.

WF: The baby, she three months old. She one of thirty-three babies born in Jonestown, Guyana. We name her Cassava, 'cause we eat so many of them, and they good, and it a pretty name. 'Scuse me. Gotta use the rest room. *[Sound of door slamming]*

KR: We're going to take a break now. Mr. Freeman has disclosed that not only did he lose his wife, but also his child, and that the mother and baby were the first to swallow poison. Apparently, his wife volunteered. I believe this is a scoop for KBBA.

BLACK PEOPLE HAVE BEEN
TREATED LIKE DOGS
BECAUSE OF THE COLOR OF THEIR SKIN.
JEWS WERE MURDERED, AND THEY'RE
SUPPOSED TO BE THE CHOSEN PEOPLE
OF GOD, OF THE SKY GOD.
THERE IS NO SKY GOD.
BUT I AM THE EARTH GOD.

Jim Jones

Six Weeks Before the End
October 2, 1978

"On behalf of the USSR, our deepest and most sincere greetings to the people of the first socialistic and communistic community from the United States of America in Guyana and in the world."

Soviet Consul Feodor Timofeyev stepped back from the microphone to bow, as the nearly one thousand people crowded into and around the Pavilion screamed with approval, applauding for several minutes.

From his seat at the VIP table near the front, Virgil Nascimento looked into Nancy Levine's eyes to gauge her reaction. Like all the ardent Jones devotees, she glowed. Her smile radiated bliss, her satisfaction that years of struggle were today being rewarded in the Soviet diplomat's tribute. Her brown eyes gleamed, her long, dark hair, adorned with shiny barrettes, glittered under the lights. Here in the jungle, the Soviet satellite named Jonestown was thriving, the Agricultural Mission of the Peoples Temple an internationally acknowledged success. Enraptured, Nancy didn't even remember to acknowledge Virgil, he thought, as her gaze went from Timofeyev to Jones and back, as if she were watching a championship match back in her hometown of Forest Hills, New York. She looks at Jones like a lover, Virgil thought, and Timofeyev too. For all he knew, she might have slept with the Soviet as well, his whoring mistress to Georgetown's petty political brokers.

Jones then motioned the crowd to silence and stepped to the podium, embracing Timofeyev before speaking.

"For many years, we've made our sympathies publicly known. The United States is not our mother. The USSR is our spiritual motherland."

Again, the applause was deafening under the metal roof as a sudden splatter of hard rain added to the crowd's appreciation with bullet-like staccato. Virgil was the master of the diplomatic smile, but beneath the veneer his anger was mounting, his pulse accelerating. Nancy was so many people. A different self in every setting, for every occasion. He was only one. The man he had primed himself to be for a lifetime, with two Mercedes in two Georgetowns, two tasteful homes, two attractive mistresses. Only offspring were lacking. But not for long, he hoped. Last night, his American Jewess had announced in bed that her period was late, and this news reinforced his virility and desire for her. He liked her mouth best of all. She had a talent for using it, but that was not going to result in his own personal empire of Georgetown Guyanese bi-continental progeny. His Guyanese wife had failed in that respect. No child of theirs over the decades had ever survived her womb. But with Nancy, who was twenty years younger than either of them, he could fulfill that dream.

Somewhere in the crowd was the black American baby Nancy had adopted with her American husband, one of the handful of emasculated blond boy-men who trembled in Jones's wake as if experiencing orgasm solely from proximity to the Great Man himself. Not unlike Nancy, he mused. He watched her wipe her eyes and hug Sharon Amos beside her, who was crying openly, murmuring something. Was she saying, "*I love you, I love you*" to Jones, who wasn't looking her way? Or to Timofeyev, whose eyes were taking in the vast, adoring crowd? Had that Amos cow slept with the ambassador? Long ago, Nancy had confided to Virgil that Jones told Nancy he would never sleep with Sharon on principle, that he coerced her extraordinary energy by holding out on her while simultaneously hinting that glorious lovemaking was somewhere down the road of

18

their future, after every single member of the Temple had reached the Promised Land, and the first stage of their revolutionary struggle to build a paradise in Guyana had come to an end.

"Ambassador Timofeyev," said Jones, cutting into the applause, which instantly ceased. "We are not mistaken in allying our purpose and our destiny with the destiny of the Soviet Union."

The two men shook hands, then embraced, sparking a mass of embraces throughout the crowd. Virgil wondered if Timofeyev believed anything Jones said. Did Jones believe any of it himself? Did the Soviets really want their destiny linked to that of Jones and his Jonestown Jerusalem? Wasn't Jones too self-interested to be a good fit with the USSR?

The next time Virgil looked to Nancy to gauge her current state of Jones-adulation, her seat across the table was empty. Where had she disappeared to? Virgil did not trust her. Was she looking for her white boy to share the joy? Why had she left him alone? Beside him was the Soviet ambassador's aide. Virgil didn't have a full-time aide. It rankled. Timofeyev had had one for years, but the illustrious Guyanese Ambassador to the United States was always without an attendant whenever he was in his natal country. On his other side was Marceline Jones. She did not appear to be trembling at the edge of rapture like Sharon and Nancy. Instead, she was biting her lip. Still, she clapped along with the others. Noticing Virgil's attention, she quickly smiled at him.

"Ambassador Nascimento, we're so very pleased you were able to be here today. As you can see, it's a big, important moment for our church."

Adjusting his tie, Virgil smiled back and thanked her for the invitation. Always he had wondered about her, the woman behind this extraordinary man, though he personally despised Jones for having slept with Nancy prior to his own meeting with his modern Mata Hari. How did this kindly, motherly woman, she with her enormous "rainbow family" of adopted children, now a grandmother, manage to ignore her husband generously dispersing his sperm among the luscious young women in his circle of secretaries, administrators, and financial officers? True, she had conceived one child with Jones before he began his out-of-wedlock family – the teenaged Marcus, glowering on his mother's right, a carbon copy of Jones but without the bravado.

"You have always been a great friend to us, Ambassador Nascimento, notwithstanding my husband's remark just now about the United States." She winked.

"Of course, my mother country is not yours," he said, pretending to go along with his hostess's intimation that indeed the Soviet Union could offer their group more than the United States. And he didn't believe for a moment that the Peoples Temple would ever re-locate to the cold, barren landscape of Russia, though the Peoples Temple officers in the capital were always giving lip service to it, including Nancy of course, waxing poetic over Russian literature and music. She kept a Russian grammar by their bed in the Guyanese Georgetown and liked to conjugate verbs first thing upon waking, as if to impress him.

The crowd was mostly black, a majority with roots in the humid American South. They were so comfortable here in the jungle, and Virgil couldn't possibly imagine them living in the Baltic region. Apparently some "warm" spot by the Black Sea had been scouted out already for their future home. Jones was lying about the balmy weather to his people. The Soviet Union had no place for a Peoples Temple, with its leader-idol and legions of idolaters.

Months ago, he'd overheard Timofeyev at a cocktail party telling someone that the Peoples Temple's love for the Soviet Union was entirely unrequited. It was true. The Soviets would never want someone like Jones in their midst, a figure who would only interfere with their particular version of hero worship which extended even beyond the grave: Lenin's tomb and its long line of necrophiliacs waiting to show their obeisance. Virgil winced, remembering his Moscow visit decades earlier, the pallid lighting of the corpse's face, the widows' tears streaking the glass coffin cover.

"As you know, Ambassador, we're in love with *your* mother country," Marceline said, gesturing toward the greenheart trees surrounding them, their outlines fading in the dusk as the fluorescent lights of the pavilion illuminated hundreds of faces, black and white, grinning and gleeful, around their table. Marcus Jones's arms were folded tightly across his chest as he listened to his mother. It was hard to discern the meaning of the smirk on his face. Was Marceline being ironic? Did the boy agree with her? Did he wish to be excluded from that *we*?

"Ambassador Nascimento, I'd like you to meet my daughter, Quiana," said Nancy, suddenly appearing behind him. He swiveled as she materialized out of the dense crowd of bodies, her arms around a little black baby, a girl with no hair and a huge toothless smile. Virgil squeezed the baby's hand.

"Pleased to meet you, Quiana." Even to his own ears, Virgil's voice rang horribly false. He knew that Nancy knew his pretend pleasure was all show for Marceline. Virgil wasn't interested in Nancy's adopted daughter and didn't adore adoption the way Peoples Temple members did. Virgil wanted his own blood to represent him in posterity, not someone else's. He had tried to make pure Guyanese progeny and failed. Now he would make Guyanese-American babies. Nancy would forget about this Quiana when she had her own child.

"It is a great pleasure," interrupted the heavily accented English of Timofeyev over the loudspeaker, "to see how happy you are being in a free society which you built with your own hands, developed with your own hands. I am very happy that I saw here in Jonestown the full harmony of theory which have been created by Marx, Engels, Lenin, and the practical implementation of this—some fundamental features of this theory, under the leadership or together with you, by Comrade Jim Jones, and I'd like to thank him for that."

Roaring applause again, which Virgil joined. He clapped like a European. Tastefully, without calling attention to himself. Not like the Americans.

* * *

In San Francisco, Truth was listening to the speech over the short-wave radio. She too was weeping, but her joy was leavened with the frustration of not being there in person to listen to the Soviet ambassador, whom the Temple had been courting for years. Finally, they had succeeded in their quest to bring him to Jonestown, along with the doctor, Nicolai, who had praised their clinic as the best of its kind in any developing nation, Marxist or Capitalist. For months, Truth had been involved with Stateside planning for this, locating primers in Russian for the Temple population and shipping them overseas, ferreting out recordings of Russian songs the group could sing to the ambassador. She had been studying Russian too. Whenever she could. In her spare moments over meals or before bed, humming in the shower. "We are communists today and we're communists all the way. Oh, we're communists today and we're glad."

Whenever the group applauded, her headphones shrieked. Tonight there had been so much applause that Truth was holding the bulky contraption beside and above her ears rather than on them. She had noticed that her formerly excellent hearing was deteriorating from so much radio work.

"Hey Truth. My turn!" Ida said, coming into the room. "You been hogging those headphones for an hour, girl!"

Without a word, Truth handed them over. It was true. She ought to be sharing. Although the speech was being recorded, their broadcasting technology in the San Francisco temple had failed, so they were unable to play the speech over the PA system. Only one person at a time could hear the words live, as they were being uttered at the Pavilion in the jungle, with only a thirty-second delay before they entered the ears of the listener thousands of miles away in the Peoples Temple's last remaining home in the United States.

Truth rose to stretch her legs, walked down the hall and back. It wasn't fair. Ida had been to Jonestown twice already while

Truth had been stuck in the Bay Area the entire time, wanting desperately to join the rest of her chosen family in the Promised Land. But whenever she brought the subject up with Jim, he chided her for selfishness.

"Truth, honey, we got twelve hundred people here who *need*. Do you understand what I'm saying? They need me for strength, they need me for discipline, they need me for love, they need me for food. It takes a hell of a lot out of me every damn day, you understand?" He had repeated this speech, with variations, every month or so when she brought it up on the phone. "So don't complain to me about where you are right now. I need you there, and the Temple needs you there, you and the rest of the good people still in the city. You're making what we have here possible, and as soon as I can, I'll send for you. End of discussion. You know I love you, honey."

Did she know? Did he really love her?

Up and down the hall she paced, looking in on the empty rooms where once staff had lived, in bunk beds two or three or even four to a room, sharing the communal bathrooms as if it were some cramped college dormitory. Truth had begun and quit college so fast she barely recalled her days in a real dorm. Mostly she remembered the unbearable loneliness, how estranged she felt from all the beautiful blond people with their California tans and tales of vacations in Hawaii and Mexico. For a New Jersey girl who'd never even been on a plane before her trip to San Francisco just after her eighteenth birthday, the isolation of her skyscraper dormitory beside Lake Merced was brutal. Her roommate, Patience, made fun of her accent. Not with malice, but the girl's teasing made her feel like a clod. Uncomfortable and out of place in the world. This was a sensation Truth had lived with most of her life. Patience was from a place called Grass Valley, and of course everyone joked about the name of her hometown, puffing pretend joints whenever they said it. But Patience had taken it all in stride, laughing as she expertly rolled her daily doobies, a supply from her boyfriend back home that never seemed to quit.

"Truth?" Ida was calling her. "Something's not right here; it keeps squawking in my ears. I'm getting an earache."

Truth told herself that if she really were a good person, she would explain to Ida how to lessen the impact, how to finesse the temperamental dials, but really, she wanted Ida to hand the headphones back over, so she shrugged and said, "It's hard on the ears, but oh well."

Ida frowned and shook her head. "You something else, Truth. Here. I know you dying to put 'em back on your head." She rolled her eyes at Truth, a familiar gesture, as if to say, "Crazy Truth, there you go being weird again." Before she had joined the Temple, it had been "Crazy Lizzie," or "Wacko Elizabeth."

Taking the headphones, Truth went back inside the radio room, shutting the door carefully behind her, wishing it would lock, but nothing locked in the Temple, except for wherever money was stored. Jim said it wasn't to hide from his own people. He trusted them implicitly, he swore. It was from outsiders, their enemies, and the ever-present traitors. At first, Truth hadn't believed in the idea that those who left the Temple would harm those who remained, but time after time, Jim offered proof of the traitors' vindictive intentions, resulting, finally, in the disastrous *New West* article last year, in which nearly a dozen former members uttered hideous lies about Jim and the Temple, prompting the massive exodus to Jonestown. "People lie," Jim always said. "The press prefers lies to truth." Like a mantra, he repeated it so often that Truth believed it. Just as she believed in Jim, without reservation or doubt.

When she put the headphones back on, she heard Deanna Wilkinson singing "The Internationale." God, that woman could sing. Truth couldn't. Not a note. "Tone stone deaf," her elementary music instructor had pronounced when ten-year-old Elizabeth had tried to play the clarinet. Listening to Deanna's beautiful voice, the tears began to fall, the lyrics eliciting Truth's yearning for a

24

better world, one without suffering or cruel teachers. A kinder, better world awaited her in Guyana.

This time the Soviet ambassador's voice came through without squawking.

"Lenin, when he addressed the youth, he said, 'Comrades, your first task is to study, study, and again, to study, how to build the socialism, how to build the communism.' So our young people, our old people, our middle generation, our teenagers, everybody knows the importance of the knowledge. Because only through the knowledge, through the understanding of the international processes, through the understanding of theory of communism, of the Marxist-Leninist philosophy, of political economy, and some other subjects, you can really become the communist, you can really build the society which is free of exploitation, free of any form of racial or any other discrimination, because you should know the theory, how to build. But not only know it but implement it practically and daily in your life."

Yes, Truth said to herself. The words energized her and pushed her away from her own petty failures. That was indeed what she needed to do more of: to study. To educate herself. Not to hang her knowledge out of some ivory tower window for show, but to use it every day, on the street, with the people, in the bush. If only she could get to the bush. Why Ida but not her?

Tears rose again, and she willed them back down. She could picture Jonestown, the scene at the Pavilion. She had pored over so many photographs of their revolutionary agricultural mission. Recently, a member had shot a blurry film of the latest harvest, full of black and white people waving at the camera, happy to be plucking cassavas and eddoes they had planted and sown themselves. Just like Timofeyev had said: With their own hands, they had grown this life, nurtured it into being. A miracle? No, the hard work of all those bodies out in the fields. She desperately wanted to be one of them, to sweat her dedication into the soil that would in turn produce their food. But not yet, not now, Jim had said. For now, her work was here, in the tilling of papers, the harvesting of positive PR, getting the Feds off the backs of the Peoples Temple in Guyana. Truth had been part of the successful effort against Social Security, who had stopped the elders' funds for a few months, believing the Temple administrators were keeping the old folks' money from them against their will. Without that money, the commune could barely function, but now the paperwork had been reinstated and checks were flowing as before. Jim had praised her for her part. It was small consolation compared to the glory of being part of that jungle dream. She reminded herself that Revolution is slow, full of missteps and mistakes, but at least there was one thing she'd done absolutely right.

Once, just after Jim made Exodus, he said he was thinking of sending Truth to DC to lobby for the Temple. Awed by the prospect of such responsibility, she had meekly told him that she didn't know if she was up to such a task. Someone better-looking and more articulate – a woman and not a man would be chosen for the job, it was clear but never stated – might be a better choice. Jocelyn, obviously, or Maria. Of course Marceline was first choice, but she was needed in so many places in so many different capacities that she wasn't always available for travel. Better a woman without children.

"You're right, Truth," Jim had said in response to her half-hearted objections. "You're always so accurate in your self-assessments. I've always admired that about you. I'll send Jocelyn. Thank you."

Devastated, she'd cried after ending their radio connection. Really, Truth hadn't meant to disqualify herself. She'd only meant to be humble, as Jim was always preaching. Humility was important, especially for white people. She would have done a spectacular job, Truth thought. She would have acquired some conservative-looking clothes at a quality thrift shop, had her hair cut, maybe lost some weight ahead of time. But she'd never be Jocelyn, bright and poised and pretty and brilliant. Jocelyn had a degree in French literature or something. She wasn't a dropout like Truth.

After a lot of static, she heard Timofeyev again: "I wish you, again and again, all the successes in your work, in your difficult task, to build the socialism, to build the communism. Thank you very much."

Applause again, deafening, screeching, scraping her tender eardrums. Abruptly, she removed the headphones and opened the door to look for Ida.

"Ida? The ambassador just said goodbye. I'm exhausted. You want to listen now?"

Arriving at the door with two steaming Styrofoam cups, Ida said, "Sure I do. Brought you some coffee. Want some?"

Shaking her head, Truth said she was going to sleep.

"More for me then." Ida gave her a warm hug. "I'll stay up and monitor for a couple hours. You crash, sister. You need it."

Timofeyev had returned to the table and was speaking Russian to his assistant. Virgil watched their easy communication, the obvious authority Timofeyev had over the younger man, who had his notebook out, taking directions swiftly and without backtalk. Nicolai, the Russian doctor, had joined them and their conversation was spirited following an obviously successful speech. Once, Virgil had been fairly conversant in Russian after his six months in the Soviet Union during his Oxford days, but the intervening years and his immersion in English had displaced that vocabulary.

Timofeyev accepted Virgil's outstretched hand and shook it with vigor.

"*Karashaw, tovarich,*" Virgil said loudly, "*Ochen karashaw.*"

Sure that Nancy would be impressed with his Russian, Virgil searched for her, but she and the child had gone off again. He wanted her beside him. Not in his arms – they didn't do that in public – but next to him, so that he could feel her presence, her sex, that Americanness inside her he had come to possess during the last few years, that idea of possession more and more important as he aged. Yes, she would produce a baby. His baby, one of many. Prudence was too old now. Besides, her life was in London now. She had no room for children.

"Feodor, I must compliment you on your English."

Timofeyev looked gratified. *"Spaciba, Comrade Nascimento. Spaciba."*

After a few more words with Nicolai and the assistant, Timofeyev tapped Virgil's arm. "Are you flying back with us to capital this evening? Or staying here, in this utopian exemplar?"

There was a touch of sarcasm in Timofeyev's tone. Utopian exemplar. Where had he heard that phrase? Did he mean it sincerely? Perhaps, like Virgil himself, Timofeyev knew how to talk the appropriate talk but personally believed none of it. Virgil had seen the Muscovite's home in Lamaha Gardens. One of Georgetown's nicest, as grand and finely appointed as the Prime Minister's. Communism was fine for the masses, as long as you weren't one of them.

"As soon as I find Miss Levine, we will be joining you."

After surveying the encroaching darkness, the blackening edges of the greenheart canopy, Timofeyev said, "We must go now if we are to get out before night falls."

Evidently, Marceline Jones was thinking the same, as she arrived to usher the ambassadors toward the tractor that would transport them the several miles to the airstrip in Port Kaituma.

"I apologize for the primitive condition of our vehicle," she said, pointing to the huge, mud-caked wheels, "but one day, down the road, we'll have better."

Timofeyev insisted that the tractor was perfect, the ultimate rural proletarian vehicle. Virgil fulsomely agreed, though he would much rather be in the Guyanese constable's jeep which at least had shock absorbers, and an intact roof.

Where was Nancy?

As Virgil and the three Russians crammed into the open cab of the tractor, the driver said, "Hang on, *das svedana*." Marceline looked back for Nancy, who was evidently not coming. Reverend Jones's wife was too discreet to say anything aloud, but she knew, like the rest of them, that Nancy was expected by Virgil to accompany him back to Georgetown.

"I believe Quiana had a fever," Marceline said. "I'm sure Nancy will get back to Georgetown as soon as her daughter's better. You should go now, before the light does."

The driver of the tractor introduced himself in Russian. "*Ya loobloo Watts.*" That's what it sounded like to Virgil, who translated the man's sentence as "I love Watts," an American slum famous for burning itself down in protest back in the sixties. Virgil had never quite understood the impulse to destroy one's own habitat to *épater les bourgeois,* but he understood that African Americans of all backgrounds shared the view that skin color was all.

The Ambassador responded in a happy stream of Russian words, but the driver said, "*Da, da.* Whatever. I gotta concentrate on driving now." He turned the tractor around and shortly they were heading back up the hole-pocked lane, everyone hanging onto whatever part of the vehicle they could so as not to fall into the mud. The young man had a massive Afro and a muscular build, and he drove fast, far too fast for the condition of the road, but Virgil knew that the pilot wouldn't wait much longer, and then they'd have to bed down either in the village, which had no hotel, or back in Jonestown, which was far too uncivilized for Virgil's taste. The Soviets evidently felt the same, as he heard the assistant telling the driver, "Hurry, please. We must not miss this plane."

"I'm going as fast as I can, Comrade Tovarich." The fastest he could drive on a road like that in a beat-up tractor was five miles an hour. At that rate, they'd never make it.

Suddenly, the driver braked hard, almost tossing Dr. Nicolai onto the road, but Virgil caught him in time. Why were they stopping?

Running swiftly, running as only an energized very young person could, Nancy appeared beside the vehicle. "Thanks, Watts," she said, giving him her megawatt smile.

Virgil was conflicted. He was gratified that she had made it but was jealous of that smile. He grunted a hello. She held on to one of the upright supports beside him. As the Soviets were deep in conversation, pausing only to ask the driver to go "Faster! Fastest!" Virgil allowed himself to be caressed by his mistress. Nancy's hand boldly reached beneath his suit jacket, cupping him through his trousers. Did the driver wink at him? No, he must be squinting due to the waning daylight, the difficulty in seeing the road clearly.

"It went really well, don't you think?" Nancy whispered as she rubbed him. "I'm so happy. I think Jim is too. I haven't seen him smile like that in a long time." She laughed with relief. Her face was flushed, and she seemed high to Virgil, though he knew it wasn't anything chemical.

Jim was more a father figure than a love and sex object for her. Virgil frowned with distaste when he considered he was the same age as Jones. She was always trying to please her leader in the way children do their parents, frantic that he be proud of her efforts, of how hard she had worked. Bagging Virgil must have netted her an A+. But she didn't seem to harbor the same fatherly feelings for Virgil.

"What's the difference, in the end?" Virgil whispered back, enjoying her hand's steady rhythm. "You're not moving to the USSR, are you?"

Immediately, she stopped her ministrations. "If Jim wants me to, I'll go." Although he couldn't see her face clearly, Virgil knew she was frowning at him, as if he had no right to expect loyalty from her.

"What about the girl? Is she all right?"

"What are you talking about? Quiana's fine."

Mrs. Jones must have invented the fever just to cover for Nancy in case she didn't show. Virgil sighed, wishing his attempt at concern would elicit Nancy's continued caresses, but he remained as before, yearning.

The driver was humming that idiotic Communist song Jones

had sung to Timofeyev over and over, solo and in chorus, as if Timofeyev actually enjoyed hearing it. *"Oh, we are communists today and I'm glad. We are communists today and we're glad. Yes, we are communist today; we are communist all the way. We are communist today and we're glad."*

Nancy joined in for a few rounds. "You have a good voice, Watts," she said to the driver. "Why don't you sing in the band?"

Shaking his head, Watts hit the brakes again as a cluster of spider monkeys scampered across the road in front of them. Everyone tumbled, grabbing whatever was at hand to keep from falling out of the tractor. Reflexively, Watts grabbed Nancy around the waist to steady her. Virgil to want to smash him. He owned her body, and this common black man should not presume to touch her. But he knew if he wanted to get laid later on, he should say nothing.

When they arrived at the Port Kaituma airstrip, their pilot, Joao, was pacing beside the small plane, muttering and drinking from a mug. Rum? Coffee? Both? Typical Guyanese behavior, Virgil thought.

Observing Joao's behavior, Nancy squeezed his hand. "Oh well. It's not like he's never flown like this before. We'll be fine."

Virgil felt a surge of rage. If they'd been alone, he would have raised his hand to her. Did she think he was frightened? Did she dare to assume she knew his mind? These American women had no idea how offensive they were in their pretend strength, as if it were her role to reassure him by being the tough half of the couple. She had described herself as a *"Long Guyland JAP."* She'd had to explain the term to him, as he could find no Japanese in her anywhere. Nancy's upbringing had been so privileged, unlike his own. She'd never worked. Never earned anything for herself. Not until she'd joined up with Jones.

Virgil quietly removed his supply of Demerara from his pocket hipflask and turned away from Timofeyev and his cohorts to have a discreet swig. The shiny sterling silver flask had been a gift from the Prime Minister, who had no reason to question Virgil's loyalty.

Cursing the darkness, the pilot hurried them into the ten-seater, then bustled inside and revved the engines. In an instant, they were off, aloft over the opaque jungle foliage, Nancy behind him squeezing his hand, the Russians on the other side still conversing in their sleepy Slavic tongue. Virgil dozed.

At Port Kaituma's only bar, Watts stopped for a drink before heading back to the compound. Jones was in a great mood tonight, and if Watts had a little booze on his breath, he didn't think ol' Jimmie would notice. The man was riding too high on his visions of grandeur, Soviet-style, that he really was king of the world, Marxist-version. The white chicks would be sure to monitor Watts's behavior, so he resolved to steer clear of them all when he returned.

Watts looked around the handful of patrons at The Last Chance Bar. He was the only American there. Though he'd been in the bar a few times before, with others, he studied the locals carefully. The constable was there, as he was each time Watts had been in, and a few old women were nursing their Demeraras, as well as two Amerindian men drinking by themselves in the corner, speaking to one another softly in their language, which Watts could barely hear, much less decipher.

A young Guyanese woman, pretty, with an infant on her hip, came by to offer him another drink and perhaps something more – herself for an hour? – but Watts declined. He had only a dollar, hard-got, lifted from a stash belonging to a rich black dude in his dormitory. Shaking his head, Watts downed his rum, left the dollar on the table, and trotted out to the tractor.

"Wait, have another!" called the woman, who evidently thought he was one of those Americans-from-money crowding the Peoples Temple's highest rung. Watts let the door swing behind him, juddering in the breeze as night replaced the sweaty, muggy air of another October afternoon in the tropics.

The engine started with some difficulty. Not due to the Demerara, which had glided down so smooth he could hardly believe it was whiskey, but because of the shoddy ignition, which had been rewired so many times. Clouds of dirty exhaust fumes spurted out each time he stepped on the gas, until he got the tractor moving towards the compound, what he liked to call the Peoples Temple Right-of-Way. Rufus had laughed and said it should be called the Left-of-Way. "You know Jimmie Jones about as left as you can get in an American preacher," he had said.

In the cab, Watts watched for moving bodies on the unlit path. Only one headlight was working, and weakly at that, so he needed to be extra careful. If he messed up the tractor, Jones wouldn't let him drive it again. Before leaving, Watts had been warned. Shrugging off that feeling he so disliked of being reprimanded like a child, Watts wished he had a cigarette to keep him company. His wife of three months, Earlene, did not smoke and didn't like his smoking, but whatever she didn't know about her husband was just fine, he assured himself.

Deciding to risk it, Watts left the tractor idling and dashed the hundred feet back to the bar to ask if anyone had a cigarette. No one responded, though most everyone was smoking. Watts wondered if perhaps they hadn't understood his American accent but after a minute, one of the Amerindian guys came over and handed him a pouch of tobacco and some rolling papers. Most of Guyana's indigenous population had long ago been decimated by whites, and the remaining natives who hadn't intermarried into city life lived primarily in the interior, in places like the bush outside Port Kaituma. Watts nodded his thanks, twisted up a cigarette that couldn't help looking illegal, stayed for a light, and took off running.

He felt good, strong in his body and not drunk, not drugged. A million years ago, back in the projects, Watts would never have believed he would so enjoy being straight, being healthy, living a life without dope, booze, or having to steal to support his habit. Jonestown had been good to him. To Rufus too, whom he used to hang with, dealing small change out in Hunters Point before both joined the Temple in 1970. Too bad the others in their group hadn't come along for the ride. Tommy and Jameel were dead, Daquaan and Anthony in prison, and another dude whose name he could never remember was a quadriplegic with a slew of babies from different mothers who regularly mooched off his government checks.

But he and Rufus had been free of drugs and booze – one Demerara didn't change that – and thieving for nearly eight years. Rufus had a nice lady and a little boy, worked as a prep cook six days a week, and seemed to Watts a contented man.

Sometimes Watts remembered life in the States with a peculiar, unhinged yearning, visions of driving fast down Highway 1 with a girl's hand on his thigh, but these were fantasies, based on Hollywood or TV notions of California life. If he thought hard about it, there wasn't anything or anyone to miss back there, except maybe his grandma, and she'd been gone for years.

Earlene loved Watts, and he kind of loved her. As much as he could love anyone, he supposed, but he just wasn't sure about that kid. Doc Schacht said he could do a blood test, but Watts was against it, feeling that it would slight Earlene before their marriage even got off the ground. What did it matter, ultimately? His kid or somebody else's? Watts appreciated the fact that his numerous infidelities were not evident in or on his body in the form of fatherhood or disease. He had no proof she'd been unfaithful, just a feeling. It was better to go forward on hope, he'd concluded.

Without hemming and hawing, for once in his life, he'd made a commitment. He would love Earlene and take care of the baby, though this pledge didn't bear the same onerous weight in Jonestown as it would have back in the States. As long as everyone in Jonestown did their work, they'd have food and shelter and medical care, even trips to the dentist in Georgetown. Maybe the food wasn't great, or consistently filling, but it kept him going well enough. Earlene was happy with him and with her life. Watts worried more about Earlene's very vocal mother. Magnolia had high expectations of her son-in-law. She was an Indianapolis old-timer who believed Jones had healed her sister of cancer and herself of a kidney ailment and probably thought Jones shit gold. Earlene was the same way, only not as shrill. Magnolia kept pushing Watts to rise in the administration of Jonestown, but Watts had no desire for responsibilities. Showing up for work on time was enough for him.

Too soon, he was back in camp. If she'd let him, he hoped to sleep with Earlene tonight. Magnolia warned Watts not to get her daughter pregnant again so soon after she gave birth, but Earlene had told him she couldn't get pregnant since she was nursing and not to worry. She told him often she liked his body, his strong shapely arms and legs, the way he moved inside her. She said he was the first, but Watts found that hard if not impossible to believe.

The compound was quiet. Sometimes, the place looked like a summer camp in the jungle, Watts thought, though he had never been to summer camp and had observed them only on television and in movies: a tranquil, rural world, far from the troubles of urban life. Cabins and boardwalks instead of high-rise projects and broken glass decorating the sidewalks, plus the occasional syringe. Here, the air smelled exotic, a perfume called Tropical Nights or Sultry Midnight. The old people and little ones were all in bed, as were most of the adults, but Jimmie Jones and his circle were still sitting at the main table in the Pavilion, obsessing over the details of Timofeyev's visit.

"How'd it go, Watts? They make it to the plane on time? Any problems?" Maria, the skinny one in big charge, called out to him.

"Fine, all fine." Quickly, he covered his mouth with his hand in case any Demerara fumes escaped. She didn't seem to notice anything, only reminding him to hang the keys on the board in the office.

"Right. Good night," Watts called, pleased to be off the hook, looking forward to finding Earlene warm and waiting in bed. They'd have to be quiet, as she shared her cabin with three other women as well as the baby, but those women worked long hours in the fields and slept hard, or so Earlene assured him.

In the office, Marceline sat at the desk under one dim over-head light, reading through her files. She looked up when he entered. "Hi, Watts. How was the drive? Did the plane take off before dark?" Though her voice was inflected with curiosity, Watts could tell it was forced.

He nodded. "Mother Marcy, you look awful tired. If ol' Watts allowed to give medical advice to a nurse, you in need of some serious sleep."

She laughed. Dark, deep circles ringed her eyes, and she looked old, her forehead lined. She rubbed her temples as if she had a powerful headache and couldn't decide what to do next.

"Those papers ain't going anywhere." Watts pressed his advantage. "Look at 'em in the morning when everything clear. You know what I'm saying?" Smiling, Marceline gave him a pronounced wink. "Very worthwhile advice, Watts. Sounds like something I'd say."

He laughed. "I heard you say it a million times. That's why I know it's good advice."

He didn't know her very well – no one did – but he'd always liked Marceline and sensed her fondness toward him, toward just about everyone, since he'd joined the Peoples Temple. Her kindness made her husband's crude behavior easier to overlook. That's how Magnolia put it, which seemed right to Watts.

"I'll finish up here in a bit. Just making sure all this Social Security paperwork is in order so we don't get behind again."

Watts wondered what she meant, but he was too eager to get over to Earlene's cabin, so he didn't ask. "Goodnight, Mother Marceline. You be sure to follow your own excellent advice, right?"

"Sleep well, Watts. Thanks for being the chauffeur tonight."

Turning from the door, Marceline glanced back at the columns of numbers. When that Stein girl left in the spring, she had told the U.S. Embassy man that the Temple received $65,000 each month from all the checks together: Social Security, SSI, guardianship checks from the state of California and other sources. But that figure didn't sound right to Marceline. Was the girl exaggerating, as she had in her other tales to the press?

Intuitively, Marceline believed Susan might lie about all sorts of things except money. She was good with numbers, always accurate and truthful; that's why Jim had promoted her to the church's top financial post. Over the last few years, she'd traveled to Panama and Switzerland on Temple business, carrying thousands of dollars on her person. Susan had a good brain, and Marceline had always liked her. To her credit, Marceline thought, she was one of the few young women in the Temple administration who was *not* Jim's bed partner. She never had been, as far as she knew. Unlike Nancy, Maria, Jocelyn, Hope, et cetera, et cetera. Why would Susan lie about their Social Security income? Maybe it was Jim who was lying. He said it was forty thousand, not a penny more. He'd convinced Jocelyn and Maria that Susan had come up with that figure to cover her own embezzling, but Marceline had found no evidence of tinkering. For goodness's sake, the girl came from money. Piles of it. Her Jewish mother had given everything she had to the Temple before her death from cancer just a few months ago. At least a quarter million in property and stocks. So why would Susan filch the seniors' checks?

In the old days, in Ukiah and before that in Indy, when the church was small, Marceline had been in charge of all things financial. That was before Jim began sleeping with everything that moved. She had a head for numbers, as her father put it. If Marceline hadn't decided to become a nurse, she might have been an accountant, like her brother-in-law, a successful CPA. Working with numbers was the opposite of patient care, the endless needs and personalities of humans. Numbers were sterile and precise, and she enjoyed their indifference. Before the church had grown so large, the Temple's finances were simple enough to be managed by Marceline alone. And she had worked them well, in addition to whatever nursing and other church business she'd been responsible for during sixty or eighty-hour workweeks. She and Jim had been so alive, so involved with their congregation.

But ever since their move to the Bay Area, with the doubling, tripling, quadrupling of church membership, fundraising, sales of members' real estate, and income from rental properties, finances had gotten too complicated for one person. In San Francisco, Jim had edged Susan into the job, pushing Marceline to the margins. She hadn't liked it, but she'd been afraid to complain. Then they acquired a full-time lawyer, even though there were plenty in the congregation who volunteered their expertise for free. She hadn't found the words to complain about that either.

"Mom, what are you doing up?" Behind her, Marcus pushed open the office door. His tone was sharp, piercing her reverie.

"That's my line," she said, smiling up into her son's dark eyes. Now nineteen years old, Marcus was nearly the same age as Jim when they'd met, long ago in that Richmond, Indiana hospital. Like his father, Marcus was beautiful to look at, kind and sensitive and outraged by injustice. Only lately, Marcus was most outraged by injustices perpetrated by his father.

"Really, Mom. I don't know why you spend your time going over the books. Other people have that responsibility." He ran his hands through his shoulder-length hair, exasperated. "You have more than enough on your mind with the clinic without messing around with the financial stuff." Marcus turned her around in the wheeled chair and pushed her toward the door. "Whoa girl!"

She shook her head to show her disapproval, but she enjoyed her son's antics. He was the only person who could still make her feel genuinely happy.

"Enough already!" Marcus switched off the light and pulled her off the chair and through the door, letting it slam behind them. "Midnight is late enough when you've been up since six."

"Since five," she said, although it was more like four when she'd risen, unable to sleep. Their world in Jonestown seemed to be deteriorating all around them. One defection after another, the growing tension about Sean's custody, Jim's son with the now-estranged Hope, all on top of Jim's increasingly erratic behavior, apparently sparked by his inability to get past his mother's death last winter. But Timofeyev's visit had gone well, she felt, even though she didn't trust the man, nor her husband's blind faith in him.

"Come on, Mom. I have a surprise for you at the cabin." Marcus directed them toward it, circumnavigating the Pavilion, where his father and the various women of the inner circle were still discussing the ramifications of the Soviets' visit.

"Check this out, Marceline," he said, pointing to a small electric burner atop her dresser. A soft smell she couldn't immediately identify hung in the air. Milk. It was cow's milk, simmering in the pot. Her mother used to heat milk for Marceline when she couldn't sleep in childhood, pouring it into a heavy pink mug. It was a private little night-time sacrament between her and her mother, belonging to a prior existence, unshared by sister or father.

"Oh, honey. What a sweet thing to do!" She blinked several times. "Did I tell you about Grandma's warm-milk ritual?"

He snorted, then poured her a cup of the steaming liquid. "Only about forty thousand times, Mom. So when are they gonna get here already? I thought they were coming in October."

For months, her parents had said they wanted to see Jonestown, and for just as long, she'd been stalling. Marceline wasn't sure why exactly, as she generally enjoyed visits with her parents, provided they were rare and short as they had been during the last decade. There were always things to do, places she could drive them, ways to escape Temple intensity and Jim. But here in Jonestown, there was nowhere to go. Once she'd given them the tour of the bakery, storehouses, clinic, nursery, school, woodshop, etcetera, etcetera, then what? Maybe Jim would let them go downriver on *The Marceline*, formerly called *The Cudjoe*. She wasn't sure she liked her name on the prow of a rickety boat that seemed always on the verge of capsizing. She didn't like boats, having a proclivity to seasickness.

"They're coming next month for a few days, honey. You'll go

into Georgetown to pick them up. I'll take them back when they're ready to leave."

"You don't sound very excited, Mom. I haven't seen Grandma and Granddad in a few years, you know. Granddad looked so old last time. Who knows how many more visits we'll even have?"

"You're right, son. I'm just tired." Sometimes she forgot that her freighted relationship with her parents was nothing like the pure joy of the grandparent-grandchild connection. "And this lovely milk is making me sleepy."

"Okay then, Miss Baldwin. Into bed with you." He turned down the covers on her bed and guided her toward it.

"Marcus! Since when do you call me Miss Baldwin? I haven't been that in nearly thirty years!"

"I just wondered how it would sound. Miss Baldwin. What if you'd never met Dad, the great and powerful Oz? You ever think about that? Then we wouldn't be here in the jungle, and you wouldn't be so exhausted every minute of your life."

"Oh, pish-posh! If I hadn't met your father, then I wouldn't have you. That would never do. Not in a million years." She kissed him on the forehead and ushered him toward the door. "Okay, my dear. Out into the night with you. Back to your dorm."

"Oh, Mom! Let me sleep here tonight. Please?"

There was a couch in her cabin that turned into a bed. Numerous times she'd slept on it without bothering to pull out the mattress, reading files until the print blurred, and then she'd wake to the sound of a howler monkey in the middle of the night, her lights still blazing. Jim would chew her out for wasting electricity. Her bedtime habits were always known to him, though she didn't know exactly how.

"You know your father doesn't like it when you stay here. It's taking advantage of your position. You should be in the dorms with the other boys."

She should have stood up to Jim in this respect years ago. Marcus was her own, dear sweet son. What was so wrong with showing her love to him?

Marcus ignored her and opened up the couch, depositing a light sleeping bag that he'd brought with him on the mattress.

"Mom, after I went to all that trouble getting you the electric burner, smuggling the milk out of the kitchen …"

"Marcus! Did you steal that milk? I thought you brought it back from the city today." Marcus had come in with Timofeyev.

"You didn't ask, did you? You took the treat and then you asked." His eyes twinkled, and she laughed.

"Okay, stay." She didn't have much power over him anymore anyway. Not really. She had managed to talk him out of killing Jim the last time he'd gotten so angry with his father that he'd paced her cabin holding a shotgun, calling Jim a bastard and every conceivable foul name he knew. It was a very long list of expletives. They were both hotheads, her men, quick to anger. At least Marcus was also quick to see reason.

Both snug under their respective covers, Marceline allowed herself to stop worrying, however briefly.

"When's your next basketball game, Marcus?"

"We've got playoffs next month in the capital. Maybe Grandma and Granddad could come watch."

"I think they're coming the first week of November. Is that when the game is?"

"No. Later in the month. How long are they staying?"

Wakefulness returned, anxiety beating fast and hard in her veins. She didn't want her parents to come. She feared something bad might happen to them in Guyana. She didn't know what. Something nameless, something awful. She would call and talk them out of it.

"Just under a week, I think. They want to see Brazil on this trip, so Grandad managed to finagle an invitation to some sort of Methodist conference in Rio. That's why they're coming now. I'd rather they waited until things calmed down a little."

Again, Marcus snorted. "Earth to Marceline! Since when have things ever calmed down in Peoples Temple? You used to tell me how much you liked that about your life with Dad. Remember?"

41

She did remember. And she hadn't lied. That was back in the days before the church got so big, and the stakes so high, before dread came to rest in her bones. Her upbringing was so serene she'd nearly died of boredom. But lately, all the back-and-forth with the Concerned Relatives, Hope's custody threats regarding Sean, Jim's generally disintegrating health and his shaky state of mind … she longed for a boring spell, a little serenity. She thought about Laura and her three daughters in an Indy suburb, their cars and houses and expensive but tasteful wardrobes. She'd never wanted a life like Laura's, but maybe a rest, a break, a vacation from all this stress would mend her fraying nerves.

Her parents' imminent arrival heightened her tension. What if they were here when the Concerned Relatives showed up? Marceline had no doubt those vengeful people would make their way to Jonestown sooner or later, with Jim's permission or without it. Maybe she should stay with her parents in Georgetown for their entire visit. That would alleviate most foreseeable difficulties. But her father was keen to visit their agricultural mission, to see the wondrous miracles Jim and the others had wrought. Her husband had talked up the farming achievements of the Guyanese branch of Peoples Temple so much it was hard to distinguish truth from fiction. Her father thought of himself as a good ol' Indiana farm boy. This was a fiction in itself, one he enlarged to include Jim and his presumptive good ol' Indiana farm boy background, the boy from Crete, population 211. Jim came from the country all right but had never grown a houseplant before arriving in Guyana, much less multiple crops to feed a thousand city dwellers.

The anxiety expanded. Her stomach turned. The milk had had a funny smell to it, but she hadn't wanted to hurt Marcus's feelings. The pilfered pleasure was souring inside her. She visualized the curds traveling through her digestive tract, tainting everything inside her. She was exaggerating as usual, something Jim was always accusing her of doing. Sometimes Jim happened to be right.

THE THRUST OF OUR CHURCH HAS BEEN BUILT
ON MY CHARACTER, HUMANISM, AND OTHERS
IN THE NUCLEUS WHO FOUNDED IT …
I PROVOKE THINKING.
THEY EXPLAIN ME AS DEVELOPING
CERTAIN ASPECTS OF MIND …
WE DON'T ORIENTATE AROUND THE FURNITURE
OF HEAVEN AND THE TEMPERATURE OF HELL.
REWARDS AND PUNISHMENT ARE
NOT OUR THING.
I'M PROBABLY SERVING ALL OF MANKIND
BECAUSE I WANT A BETTER WORLD
FOR MY CHILDREN.
I DON'T HAVE THIS SENSE OF BEING
SENT FROM ANOTHER WORLD
WITH A SWORD OF THE SPIRIT OR POWER
FROM THE COSMOS IN MY HAND.
I GET MY FULFILLMENT OUT
OF SERVING MANKIND.

Jim Jones

Virgil Nascimento
9:30 p.m.
Nov. 18, 1981
Washington, D.C.

"How can I live, knowing what I know?"

Voila, my clumsy translation of Camus: *Je veux savoir si je puis vivre avec ce que je sais et avec cela seulement.*

You who read this document, you will attempt to compare me to Jim Jones. Am I as guilty as he? Or just another victim? Americans adore victims. They love seeing themselves as underdogs, as sadly wronged good guys. They who know so little of how the rest of the world lives and works. They who always send their soldiers overseas. Born in Guyana, I have witnessed carnage at home. The decimation of a country by foreigners.

Nancy and the boy sleep in the bedroom beside my study. The boy is my blood but resembles Nancy. His skin is more white than black, conceived sometime during October of 1978. Nancy Levine-Nascimento has been my wife of two years, formerly my mistress, and chief lieutenant in the public relations army of General Jones. Together we made this boy after I divorced my Guyanese spouse of twenty-two years. However, in my mind he is the offspring of Jonestown. Its issue, as the British say. Heir to the throne of Emperor Jones.

Each anniversary, the revulsion returns. The sickness of the act. The horror. In 1979, I wanted to commit suicide but refrained.

In 1980, I wanted to destroy my family, the surviving evidence of Jones and the Peoples Temple, their wrecking of my country; again, I refrained, but this year, all of us: Nancy, former paramour of and true believer in the Bishop Jones, the boy who resembles the Emperor Jim, and myself, estimable and educated bureaucrat, shall be erased. There is no other way.

We are anathema. Myself, my family, my country. My countries.

First, I thought to write this last will and testament on Embassy stationery; the Guyanese Ambassador to the United States makes his Official, Ultimate Statement! But my title, my Oxford degree, my fluency in many languages matters not at all. Jones hated intellectuals as rationalizers, relativists and do-nothings, even though he needed them. I am coming to hate them too, and myself most of all.

But tonight, I will do something.

In the White House, on Capitol Hill, and at the State Department, people ask from where my "beautiful" accent derives. When I say Guyana, one of two answers is possible.

The first: *Isn't that in Africa?* As if my black skin could have its genesis only in deepest, darkest Africa. Perhaps they have heard of Guinea, or Guinée, mythical home of the enslaved dead beneath the waters, those who died in the holds and those who threw their children and then themselves overboard, preferring death to life in the New World. My mother's ancestors traveled those ships, died those deaths.

The second, much more likely: *Isn't that where the crazy guy and all his zombies drank poisoned Kool-Aid?*

What to call it?

Mass suicide?

Mass murder?

The U.S. Congress calls it the "suicide/homicide."

Revolutionary suicide.

Familicide on a grand scale.

The tragedy.

The massacre.

46

The end.

The apocalypse.

The triumph of the CIA.

The revenge of Capitalism.

The nemesis of Marxism.

The sleep of reason.

The death of hope.

The most racist murders of our time.

The most integrated mass suicide.

The end of the Civil Rights movement.

Masada revisited.

Huey Newton's nightmare.

The Event.

What to call Jones?

The Reverend – though revered for what, I couldn't say.

In Guyana, he dubbed himself the Bishop.

Psycho. Devil. Charlatan. Megalomaniac. Monster. Madman. Sociopath. Monomaniac. Ahab.

Messiah. Prophet. Revolutionary.

Christ re-born. Lenin reincarnated.

Guyana's best American friend.

Human Rights Leader, as Indianapolis did in 1960.

Man of the Year, as the Black Press of America did in 1969.

Self-suggested intermediary between the Symbionese Liberation Army and the family of kidnapped heiress Patty Hearst in 1974.

Humanitarian of the Year, recipient of the Martin Luther King Jr. Award in 1977.

A combination of Martin Luther King, Jr., Angela Davis, Albert Einstein, and Chairman Mao, as California State Assemblyman Willie Brown called him.

The homosexual arrested in a Los Angeles cinema toilet for propositioning an undercover police officer.

High school teacher.

Head of the San Francisco Housing Authority.

Friend to First Lady Rosalyn Carter and the Governor of California.

Key vote-harvester for San Francisco Mayor George Moscone and Supervisor Harvey Milk.

Healer of the sick.

Resuscitator of the dead.

Father. Dad.

Monkey salesman.

The man who fucked most female members of the Peoples Temple inner circle.

The man who fucked my wife.

My wife is calling me, asking when I will come to bed.

Soon, I tell her. Soon.

We are anathema. My Guyana. My family. Myself. Three years later, we still reek of the dead. We stink from the stench of a thousand bloated corpses awaiting identification and body bags. Though Nancy and I were far from Jonestown on that date – she was sitting by the radio in Georgetown, and I was thousands of miles away here in DC – everyone smells it on us, even today. They turn their noses and avert their eyes.

Have you ever smelled a body rotting in the equatorial sun? Imagine a thousand bodies, blistered and swollen, a "pornography of power," as someone called it. It beggars the mind, staggers the heart. As Ambassador to the United States, I was immediately summoned home. At the airstrip in Port Kaituma, the bloodstains from the murders of the Congressman and reporters were still visible, and a thousand metal coffins shimmered in a haze upon the tarmac. Guyana violated. Desecrated. I was sick. The smell of my sickness sticks to my skin, despite a thousand washings.

Camus declares in *The Myth of Sisyphus*: "That which one calls a reason for living is at the same time an excellent reason to die."

Camus could have written this essay expressly about the Event, but it was published in 1942, when both the Emperor Jones and I were only eleven.

At that age, I helped my father, a stern widower, harvest and sell cassavas and eddoes. An only child, I was already a bookworm, buried in texts when I wasn't covered in sweat. My father tested me in vocabulary, mathematics, and history while I helped pick the crop. In that same year, the boy Jim Jones was apparently delivering sermons in an Indiana barn, insisting the neighborhood children pay attention to his oratory, refusing to let them leave until he was ready to dismiss them. Perhaps this anecdote is apocryphal, but I believe it. A few years later, he made a study of Gandhi, Hitler, Stalin, and Marx. A harbinger of the man he would become? The "great men" of history rolled into one.

At Oxford in the early fifties, we argued all night long about *Heart of Darkness*. After the Event, literary journalists made the comparison: is Jones another Kurtz? Colonial horror squared, trebled, multiplied exponentially unto a thousand. Conrad placed Kurtz in the Congo, where the darkest heart of all belonged to a white man. I have always believed Kurtz to be a shade of Belgium's mass-murdering King Leopold. Leopold desired diamonds and rubber. What did Jones want from us? What did he get? All our promise, gone.

I thought Camus's essay would teach me to understand. If I memorized the Myth, if I could decipher the Frenchman's melodious philosophy – aren't the French superior to the English? Wiser? Saner? So my West African confreres at Oxford would have me believe – if only I could "get it," as the Americans say, then I would have the answer. The great Algerian thinker and freedom fighter would at last enlighten me. Perhaps I thought I could become him. But it is not possible. Never was it possible. Each time I read his words, I "get" less and less.

In the next room, my wife and child sleep in our bed. Some would say they are innocent. Guiltless of the death of meaning in Guyana. At least the meaning of Guyana as it is perceived here, in the heart of the first world, with its fluorescent darkness. You who read this document will declare they have no responsibility whatsoever. But is their culpability in question? Is mine? The burden of knowledge that Sisyphus bore up and down his mountain was the heaviest and most unbearable weight of all. I do not have the stamina of that immortal Greek. I am not a hero, not even of Hades. Prometheus was brave, Tantalus bold. And surely there is dignity in Sisyphus, shouldering his burden into infinity, as Atlas bore the earth. I hate to say, but I am more like Jones; I cannot bear it any longer.

Information, my father told me, marks the difference between the ruler and the ruled. So he sacrificed all, including his health, to raise me up to the heights of Georgetown society – and the irony of my plush home here in America's Georgetown is not lost upon me – and thence to Mother England, where I would gather all the information I needed, a surfeit of information, about this thing called culture. My cassava and soursop-selling father had more culture in his head, in the way he heard music and parsed power and history, than all the bureaucrats who populate Washington, DC, the city I have called home since 1969.

"How can I live, knowing what I know, and *with only that*?"

To you who read this document, I confess I can no longer. How can anyone? What we know about the world and its brutality will wear any human being with a conscience down to bones and dust.

Americans will say I was not thinking clearly because I was depressed. In Guyana, I never heard that word, and rarely in England. In fact, clarity scalds my brain. Sisyphus was punished by the gods for his failure to heed their warnings. I cannot say I believe in any God, but I shoulder failure as Sisyphus did his knowledge. Nine-hundred and seventeen bodies in Guyana is failure. I don't include the Emperor Jones. My wife and child, sleeping.

What a splendid name you have, my English tutors would say. Virgil Nascimento! The birth of the Latin Epic gestating in my parents' fertile imagination. My mother was descended from slaves and my father from slavers, though the Portuguese and Dutch now make paltry footnotes in imperial history. And the Empire Upon Which the Sun Never Sets shrinks to footnote dimensions beside the United States, the sole deterrent to the Soviet Menace, as Reagan would have us believe. Jones called defectors "Trotskyite adventurists." What would he call me? I, too, was Marxist. Once.

Thucydides wrote everything there was to know about war, yet we learn nothing and war on, as if there were no tomorrow. Tonight I shall finish *Le Mythe de Sisyphe* for the last time, and, indeed, there will be no tomorrow.

My secretary slips me magazine articles about Post-Traumatic Stress Syndrome, called Shell Shock in the first World War, in which my father fought, loyal Briton to the end. Jim Jones *pere* soldiered in that war as well; how odd to think our progenitors might have encountered one another in the rat-packed trenches, fighting on the same side, choking on the same gas.

My secretary worries about me: how I never smile, how brooding I am, how I hate leaving my office, even when it is for home, where I shut myself up here in the study with my books. Charlayne and her husband are kind to us. She brings me sweet potato pie made from her Arkansas grandmother's recipe; she tries to cheer me with cherry blossoms in her five-year-old's hot pink painted vase. In the old days, before children and before the Event, we four would dine together in fancy restaurants, brimming with mutual admiration. Nancy and I would imagine all our children growing up together in an integrated paradise – not in Guyana but here, in this Republic, where two hundred years before, the people threw off the British yoke. We thought we had everything in common: Charlayne and Romulus were descended from enslaved Africans and of their owners, whites of many hues. I was the offspring of Portuguese buccaneers, Dutch surveyors, Amerindians and

Congolese slaves, and Nancy the child of German Jews, survivors of the Aryan attempted genocide. What excellent Americans we would create, we thought. The spawn of freedom, the children of the twentieth-century's greatest liberation movements!

Antelapsarian, that era. Before I acquired such lethal information. How grateful I am that my father is dead, that he did not live to witness what I am going to do.

Before I learned to walk, my mother died of malaria. My father said I refused to leave her body. She had said, "Come to me, come to me, my Virgil, my life, don't go," and then she died. All these years, I have felt abandoned by her. Shall we meet in the afterlife? Even if I still believed, I know there is no heaven for murderers or suicides.

My grandfather named his son, Odiseo, for Odysseus. With typical competitiveness – which I admit to inheriting – my father outdid him by naming me Virgil. What founding epic might I write? On my shelf is a facsimile edition of Sir Walter Raleigh's seventeenth century *Discoverie of the Large Riche and Bewtiful Empyre of Guyana*. Once I aspired to write a history of my Guyana, polyglot country of many rivers and peoples: the Portuguese, the Africans, the East Indians, the Amerindians, the Chinese and the British, a handful of remaining Dutch, all of us commingling, mixing blood and making babies of so many tongues and shades. The meeting of East and West, Old and New engaging in sex and commerce. The native peoples making children with the conquerors. So much possibility, I once thought. Potential. To the end, my father remained hopeful. Though we were a poor country by way of income and export, we abounded in natural beauty, culture, and language. He thought I would embody the post-colonial success story. He foresaw the independent nation of Guyana: prosperous, thriving, the new Caribbean destination of American and European tourists.

He did not foresee the Event, which foreclosed all of it.

From Oxford and Cambridge, my African confreres and I traveled to Moscow. The Soviets invited us to tour the wonders of the Communist heaven-on-earth, where the word of God no longer echoed, and the reign of Marx endured. We were intoxicated with possibility. Forbes Burnham and I saw the future at work in Moscow, the melding and fading of class distinctions. We were gullible, Forbes and me, and so were all the rest; we saw a magic show and believed the sleight of hand. Stalin's Soviet Union shone, the largest shrine to a living person ever built, though we failed to note its secular idolatry. The Muscovites showed us off, not unlike my white American contemporaries here. They steered our group of multi-lingual black intellectuals to Lenin's tomb, to showpiece schools, to state-run industries and farms. Like eager virgins, we yearned for their seduction. We did not understand that we were pawns, expendable pieces in the grand match between new imperial armies.

Nancy in Guyana was like me in Moscow. We both saw New Worlds flourishing, or so we thought. See the children playing with one another without regard to race or class. See the elderly, useful to the end, working in their kitchen gardens. See the happy workers, working. See the magic show.

Forbes is now Prime Minister. Decades later, he and I would again be tricked by a conjurer, this one in Jonestown. Not only us, but other Guyanese elites as well as the United States Embassy team, the white American lawyer of the Black Panthers, who called the compound "paradise," the black lieutenant governor of California and our friends the Soviets, at least on paper, who lauded what they saw in the guarded compound of the man who to the end admired Stalin and Amin.

On my wall is an old Tube poster, bought in some junk shop in Oxford. "Visit the Empire," it reads boldly. Britain's outposts are cross-referenced with names of Tube stops, so we might visit India, Burma, Australia, Malaya, Nigeria, South Africa, and the East Indies simultaneous with Aldwych, South Kensington, Strand, Temple, and Baker Street. Of course, Guyana was too insignificant to note, and had no corresponding station in the breadth of London's subways. The poster proudly showcases the wild animals of each continent and their stolen riches, though the colorful peoples who inhabit these realms are nowhere in evidence. "The Wealth, Romance and Beauty of the Empire" could be realized by the average Londoner on his afternoon jaunt underground.

In contrast, Moscow was bleak. But it spoke louder and more directly to us, resonated with our own soon-to-be independent nations, heralded the potential in a world where the largest wealth of all was the people themselves, those bodies of color so conspicuously absent from my Tube poster. In Moscow, though the bodies were white, we saw only Progress. The British model was the past, the crass American the present, but Moscow was the Future, and ours.

I can laugh at myself as I was then, a naïve and indiscriminately absorbent sponge. Twenty years old. Full of myself and the brilliance I was told so often I possessed, dazzled by the brains and sophistication of my confreres, the chosen young men of the world-to-come. While we marveled through that congratulatory tour of our Marxist Motherland, Stalin was lining his pockets, starving the peasants, and murdering the intellectuals.

"Killing yourself amounts to confessing," writes Camus. "It is confessing that life is too much for you or that you do not understand it. Living, naturally, is never easy ... Dying voluntarily implies that you have recognized, even instinctively, the ridiculous character of that habit, the absence of any profound reason for living, the insane character of that daily agitation, and the uselessness of suffering."

As in melodrama, as in the over-the-top dead bodies covering the stages of my favorite Jacobean revenge dramas, I am moved to commit bad theater. Perhaps it is my snobbery and aesthete's soul that has prevented me from carrying out this deed before. Perhaps I cared too much about reviews, the way the act would be perceived at the Embassy, discussed by the State Department, dissected by *The Washington Post*, dissembled by *The Guyana Chronicle* and *Pravda*. Odiseo would be ashamed of me, not only by my atrocities but by my vanity. I am myself embarrassed by the crassness of my confession.

HEAVEN WAS CREATED BY POOR PEOPLE
THAT WERE WORKING COTTON FIELDS
AND WORKING IN MINES AND LIVING IN HELL,
SO THEY HAD TO CREATE
A GOLDEN CITY SOMEWHERE.
THEY HAD TO DREAM,
BECAUSE THEY KNEW THEY'D NEVER
GET ANYTHING OUT OF THIS EARTH.
SO RELIGION IS A DARK CREATION OF
THOSE WHO ARE OPPRESSED,
THOSE WHO ARE IN BONDAGE.

Jim Jones

Truth Miller
November 18, 1988
Port Kaituma, Guyana

"What's your name, girl?"

Over and inside her, his beautiful accent rolled. He was the black Jim she'd been searching for, the man she'd traveled all this way to find. His sweat dripped into her hair, her ears, puddled in the wells of her collarbone as he pounded. "Harder," she whispered. She didn't want him to talk. *Make a baby. Make a baby. Make Jim's baby.* Part of her was trying to communicate this message telepathically to this black Jim, whose real name she couldn't remember, a rum seller she'd met two hours earlier on the pier when the boat docked in Port Kaituma. But another part was sending the message to Jim Jones, dead Jim in Marxist heaven – an oxymoron, she knew – with the other 912 Lenin-blessed souls.

"What's your name, girl? Haven't you got a tongue?" As if to punish her for not responding, he rammed her harder, but she liked it more; each thrust brought dead Jim closer. "Don't you know English?"

"Truth," she panted finally, though she wanted to concentrate solely on receiving his sperm, on creating this child in a post-Jonestown re-conception of Genesis, the *raison d'être* for her journey to Guyana.

"Yes, the truth. Don't tell me no lies. What is your name?" Then he came, fast, grinding at her to make it last, moaning a little, and kissing her huge, dark nipples before pulling out. "The truth: you're on the Pill, like a smart American girl, aren't you?"

"No. My name is Truth. And no, I'm not on the Pill." Truth exhaled slowly, controlling her breath as he settled beside her on the mattress. She contracted her vaginal muscles, as her book had advised, to contain the sperm as long as possible. Truth pretended to be a statue, as in the children's game, where you had to remain perfectly still or you were out.

It was hot; she was in the jungle, only seven miles from Jonestown. All things were perfect. Just the way she'd planned. He even claimed to have met Jim. "Don't worry," she paused, trying to remember his name. "Don't worry, honey. Everything is exactly how it's supposed to be."

Groping for the bottle on the floor beside the mattress, he asked, "Want some more?" Guyana was famous for its Demerara rum, these days its most profitable export.

Shaking her head and smiling, she felt triumphant. "None for me. Go ahead, though." Never much of a drinker, now Truth would be a teetotaler. For the baby.

He took a long, smooth draught. She liked the way his Adam's apple bobbed as he drank. She put her white hand against his very black chest, admiring the contrast. Her baby would be beautiful, an ideal combination of their complexions: mocha, café au lait, butterscotch. Why were the names for mixed-race skin color always related to food? She loved those flavors. Truth was the kind of person who liked to blend opposites on the palette of taste. Bittersweet chocolate was her favorite kind.

"Why you not on the Pill, girl-named-Truth? You too old to have a child, huh?"

Truth laughed. Everyone thought she was past her procreative years. Her dark hair had turned completely white after Jonestown ten years ago. She was only thirty-six, not too ancient to have a first baby, but strangers judged her to be in her forties. "No, not too old. I just feel fine, that's all. I feel ... pure in Principle."

She didn't want him to know she was trying to get pregnant or to consider the mystical significance of today's date, but she did want to fuck a few more times to make certain she was pregnant.

"I like your titties," he said, fingering them. "You married?"

Again, she laughed. Why had he waited until after sex to ask? It didn't matter one way or the other. He was so good to look at. Tall and thin, rangy without being bony, his hair cut so short his scalp shone in the light of the kerosene lantern. Realizing her plan had been easy. Stepping off the boat, Truth had imagined there would be signs, a marker, something to say that here was the place, ten years ago, where Jonestown and Peoples Temple exploded into world consciousness. It was only half a mile to the airstrip where Congressman Ryan and four others were killed, but there was nothing. Only this man, standing by the ramp as if awaiting her arrival, a strangely familiar grin on his face, as if to say, "What took you so long?"

Shaking her head, she took his right hand and began to suck his fingers, one after the other, before cramming them all into her mouth. "Mm. No, I'm not married." She removed his fingers so she could speak clearly. "I don't want to be married. I like how you taste, Guyanese man. I like it very much."

As Truth had hoped, her mouth around his fingers made him hard again. He was only twenty, maybe twenty-five, she couldn't tell. She guided him back inside her.

"Hey, Miss Truth, I don't want to make no babies with you. I already got two in the city with my woman." He held back but didn't withdraw.

"I'm sterile. You don't have to think about it, okay? Please."

His smile made her giddy. "Okay, American Truth. Tell me no lies, and we float down the Kaituma together. We make pleasure but no babies." He tried to turn her around and onto her knees, but since her book declared the missionary position best for sperm containment, she wouldn't budge. "Like this, I want you exactly like this," she whispered.

59

Finally, darkness pulsed inside the room, and her black Jim was asleep. Outside, the neon blinked "–A–" "–A–" "–A–" as the "B" and "R" were out. The apartment was above The Last Chance, the only café/bar in Port Kaituma, a few hours' walk from Jonestown. She could smell the humidity and hear the birds, toucans squawking. They seemed to say, "Good, Truth. Good."

God, it was beautiful. "Jim," she whispered to the Jim she carried inside her always, even before the implosion of Jonestown. "It's just like you said. It's paradise."

Beside her, Lionel, whose name suddenly returned to her, snored. She wondered if the missing letters of the sign were some sort of portent. Aah. Aah. Aah. The sound an infant makes. Creating a baby as he floated her boat down the river. Envisioning the zygote inside her, she exhaled slowly. Truth wondered if his name was a sign too. Lionel the Lion, king of the jungle. The Rastafarian lion of the Ethiopians. Her child would be a king, a queen, the son or daughter of a Guyanese cousin-in-spirit to Jim Jones, given life in a place he called The Promised Land.

At the dock, the first thing she'd asked Lionel was if he could direct her toward Jonestown. "When I was just a child, I met Bishop Jones," he replied. Lionel remembered the Peoples Temple boat, *The Marceline*, coming into port, everyone on shore waving, and the Americans, black and white, waving back, all smiles on their arrival. That was "before the bloody end, of course," but she didn't want to hear about the end. She wanted to hear about the Peoples Temple Agricultural Mission, the Jonestown-That-Was before the FBI/CIA/INTERPOL/IRS and every other damned capitalist, anti-freedom governmental body killed them all. The beloved community, in Martin Luther King Jr.'s mellifluous phrase. She remembered her beloved community so clearly, its faces of every color, age, and class. Although happy in that moment, Truth's tears rose. Jim would never see his spiritual child, no interracial commune would raise this baby with her, no Marceline would hover over the cradle, humming *My Little Black Baby*. The tears fell. In his sleep, Lionel grunted and rolled over, flinging his arm onto her belly. Both were sweating as if in a steam bath. Truth hoped perspiration wouldn't draw the sperm out of her womb. Of course the notion had no basis in science. Jim liked science. "Empirical" was one of his favorite words. He admired medicine and its achievements. Though the Reverend Jim Jones had practiced faith healing for years, he disliked superstition and folk ideas about the body. The healings were a means to an end, he used to say, to prod the people toward where they could hear his message, to wean them away from the sky god, whom he sometimes called the buzzard god, then coax them to sacred Socialism in its stead. In Jonestown, the staff had built a sophisticated medical clinic.

After the great exodus to the jungle in July 1977, no one missed the faith healings, according to Jim's optimistic letters to their headquarters in San Francisco, where Truth and a few others had maintained their vigil.

Truth had never been outside the United States until three days earlier. Georgetown hadn't looked anything like she'd imagined, dancing visions of a gorgeous tropical town. A little run down, perhaps, but colorful and picturesque, with beautiful black people walking or cycling down the streets balancing baskets of pineapple and fish on their heads. It was a generic Caribbean she'd fabricated, its source in commercials and magazine advertisements.

Instead, Georgetown looked pathetic, the people listless, the streets littered. Deep ruts pocked the roads, and her taxi bypassed more than one accident. She'd demanded the driver stop to help, but he said, "You crazy, lady? It the Georgetown chokehold." She couldn't believe people would fake an accident to get strangers to stop for the sole purpose of robbery. Especially not these people, the descendants of slaves, the socialist workers of the world, the people for whom Jim Jones had sacrificed everything.

She had often been told she was an idealist. So what if she was? She wouldn't let the FBI/CIA/INTERPOL/IRS destroy that crucial part of her, though they had assassinated Jim and the other

912, a third of them children. Truth could conjure no sympathy for the five people killed on the airstrip. That was Congressman Ryan's fault, and the so-called Concerned Relatives and all the other brainwashed capitalist Americans who refused to recognize what Peoples Temple and Jim Jones were truly about: communal living, the care of children and the elderly, and of course the equal sharing of all resources.

In her mind she unreeled what had since become known as the "death tape," the last forty-five minutes of Jonestown, wherein Jim exhorted his people to go quietly, with dignity, so that the fascists outside the gates of the compound wouldn't succeed in torturing their babies and old people. Truth knew the words by heart. By their act of revolutionary suicide, Jim and Peoples Temple had prevailed against their enemies.

It was important to Jim that they not take arms against the GDF, the primarily black Guyanese Defense Force, which might have been coerced by the United States into attacking the commune on false charges: kidnapping minors, for example, or violating the custody order instigated by the number one traitorous defector bitch.

In the morning, Lionel and Truth had sex again, and again, and by the time they parted, Truth was sure she'd achieved her mission. Inside, she felt annealed. The next stop in her pilgrimage was Jonestown itself, where she would pay homage. As they were dressing, she asked if he would accompany her.

"You crazy? We don't go out there. Too many bad spirits. What exactly do you want to see?"

She bit her lip. You had to be careful about anything to do with Jonestown. People claimed Jim was paranoid, but, as they say in New York, sometimes people really *are* out to get you. And in Jim's case, it was absolutely true. "Just curious. You know, some of the people who died were my friends."

Lionel shrugged. "You won't see much. The jungle swallows everything. It's hungry all the time. Like me." He rubbed her ass.

"There's nothing left." Lionel kissed her forehead. "You a sweet girl, Miss American Truth. Now I have to help my mother clean fish. Then I go to work in the bar. Maybe I'll see you tonight?"

Her forehead felt warm from his kiss. It was a blessing from dead Jim through the living black Jim in front of her, though Jim didn't approve of mysticism. It worked counter to Socialism, and he claimed it was no different from the dread opiate Christianity.

"I don't know if I'll be back by then. I thought I might stay out there until tomorrow. To get the feel of it."

Lionel backed out the door. "Don't. It's a bad place. The crazy man himself is still roaming out there. Even white people say they feel him there."

She tensed. "He wasn't crazy." She wanted to add, "He knew the truth about the world," but she refrained.

"Americans pretty crazy in general. When I'm in the capital, working with my cousin, we see them all the time. That's how I spotted you!" He smiled, and Truth tried hard to fix his huge, wide grin in memory: the straight white teeth against the indigo-black skin. Her child would smile like that. Her Little Black Baby. In the back of her brain, she could hear Mother Marceline singing the words to the song she had written herself about her adopted baby, whom they'd named James Jones Junior. Lionel went on: "The Jones people, though, they were the craziest of all. They killed their children! That lady in Georgetown killed her three children with a knife! She slit their throats. Then she slit her own. Don't you think that's crazy?"

Not wanting to argue, she stared at him, preferring to keep their contact as pure and simple as possible, so that she would have only positive memories of the genetic father of Jim's spiritual heir.

"We don't have to talk about it." He kissed her lips this time and massaged her nipples through her T-shirt. "I'll see you tonight, at the bar."

"See you then." It was easier to lie than to persist in telling the truth. Same here as in the US, she lamented.

* * *

Everyone in the village she asked to accompany her to Jonestown refused – even American dollars couldn't sway them. She felt guilty waving greenbacks around to get what she wanted, so she was half relieved when no one took up her offer. She was shown the way, and after eating granola and sipping bottled water, putting extra water and her rain poncho into her knapsack along with her camera and notebook, she set off alone down the muddy road.

Lionel didn't exactly accuse Truth of being crazy but had implied as much. Disappointed but not surprised, she walked away from town, tucking her curls beneath a bandana. It was already stultifying, despite the early hour. Trying to quell the chatter in her brain so that she would be receptive and calm by the time she reached Jonestown, Truth walked slowly, but her internal conversation boomed louder and louder the farther she got from Port Kaituma.

"I'm not crazy. I'm not!" she said loudly, almost yelling. Truth liked the sound of her own voice and talked to herself all the time when home in San Francisco. Generally, it was difficult not to speak her thoughts aloud as she was so used to being alone. But her babbling was one of the reasons people called her crazy. Her own parents did. Her teachers. Co-workers. Everyone but Jim. Jim razored through all the superficial nonsense. It was Jim who gave her the name Truth. "I can see so much good inside you," he'd said to her on their first meeting in 1970. "It's radiating all around you." She was eighteen, lonely, a freshman at San Francisco State, completely lost in every way, and he'd plowed through the morass inside her, plunging straight to the core.

"You're a truth teller. I can see it in your eyes." He gazed into her dark eyes. That was before he wore sunglasses all the time. "You don't like lies. And some people don't like you for that reason."

He was right. She hated lies more than anything. She felt the world had been lying to her since she was born. Her parents, family, school, the news media, religion. All lies. Jim Jones had immediately put his finger on what was most important to her. It was as if he'd known her always. "Authenticity," he'd proclaimed, pointing at her heart. "That's what turns you on."

He'd preached at a church in the black neighborhood called the Fillmore, which she'd never been to before. She was living in the dorms by Lake Merced and had only been in the city a month. Normally, she didn't go to church. Her parents had dragged her to Universalist Unitarian services as a child, and when she'd turned thirteen, she refused to go anymore. But when she saw the flyer on the bulletin board at the Student Union, that yellowing piece of paper now taped to her fridge, she felt something – Jim's invisible hand – reaching out to her, enticing.

PASTOR JIM JONES

Incredible! … Miraculous! … Amazing! …

**Most Unique Prophetic Healing Service
You've Ever Witnessed! …**

Behold the Word Made Incarnate in Your Midst!

**God works as tumorous masses are passed in every
service … Before your eyes, the crippled walk, the blind see!**

**Scores are called out of the audience each service
and told the intimate (but never embarrassing)
details of their lives that only God could reveal!**

**Christ is made real through the most precise
revelations and the miraculous healings in
the ministry of His servant, Jim Jones!**

**This same spiritual healing ministry does not oppose
medical science in any way. In fact, it is insisted that**

**all regular members have yearly medical examina-
tions and cooperate fully with their physicians.**

See God's Supra-Natural Works Now!

So she found herself, alone, on an electric bus making its way from Golden Gate Park toward Fillmore Street. "What you doin' in that neighborhood?" the bus driver asked. He was black, with a Jamaican accent and a flirty eye.

"Going to church."

Shaking his head ruefully, he let her out a block from the address she'd shown him on the piece of paper, now blurred by her clammy hands. "That's all right then. Gal, you take care of yourself. Maybe I pick you up on the return trip."

Lionel reminded her just a little of that bus driver. She'd never forgotten him. She remembered clearly every detail of the day she had met Jim Jones and let him radically alter her life. But did Lionel really look like the bus driver? Or was she just saying that because they both had black skin?

No. They had the same beautiful accent. The height. And the long, smooth limbs. The graceful, tapered fingers. The shining blue-black scalp. And the smile. Her hometown in New Jersey was small and white, as were the public schools she attended, so Truth had never been around black people before, not every day. Her suburb was not far from New York City, but her family rarely ventured there. Her parents seemed fearful. Of what exactly, she was never sure, but they were so afraid of everything, all the time. Mostly, they stayed home and wanted their only child beside them, safe. It was like a coffin, that home in Flemington, New Jersey. A comfortable mausoleum she had to flee.

She enrolled at San Francisco State, as far away as she could get in the continental United States. Her parents opposed the move, but tuition was super cheap, and she had money they'd set aside for her education, which she collected on her eighteenth birthday.

She left the day after. Promising to visit at Thanksgiving, she'd set off that August feeling she could finally breathe.

The road meandered through tall greenheart trees that shut out light but did nothing to diminish heat. Her backpack felt oppressive on her skin. Already she had sweated through the cotton shirt and shorts, and her toes squashed in the swamp of her sandals. Supposedly there were poisonous vipers and tigers in the jungle, but some said later – That Woman who had defected, whom Truth personally blamed for the entire disaster – she said there were no snakes, no tigers, no armed mercenaries hired by the Concerned Relatives roaming outside the compound. She told the press Jim had made it all up to frighten people into staying. That was a lie. If it were true, why were nine members able to go for a picnic on the morning of the last day? Truth wouldn't dignify That Woman with a name. Peoples Temple loyalists spit before they uttered it. Ironically, Truth resembled That Woman. They were the exact same age, height, coloring, build, and people used to mistake them all the time. After Jonestown, Truth was oddly grateful for her white hair, as it distinguished her from That Woman. It separated Truth from Lies, she liked to say.

She coughed and projected the phlegm expertly into the underbrush. Lionel had to be wrong about no one visiting Jonestown. The way would have vanished if it hadn't been traveled in a decade. Hardwood trees stalked beside the road so thick she couldn't see how a body could fit between them, even a child's. Amazing that the Temple pioneers had cleared this place. They'd opened up the jungle! And That Woman, with help from the United States of Capitalism, the John Bircher Congressman Ryan and the supposedly Concerned Relatives – she thought of them as the Unconcerned, for whom truth was relative – they had conspired to do away with the most successful American utopia since the Shakers and Oneidas. History verified her conviction that Jones was a visionary, the latest in a long line, and way before his time. He had named his only natural son Marcus, after Garvey. Jim said black Americans could never have a utopia in their own country, pointing to WEB DuBois, who had ended his days in Ghana, and the former slaves who had made their way to Liberia. California was too compromised by racist capitalism to function as a socialist haven for their integrated church. Hence the migration to Guyana.

In places the road diverged. Perhaps it led to other destinations besides Jonestown? She hadn't even contemplated that possibility. "Don't all paths lead to Jonestown?" she asked aloud, smiling at her joke. Jonestown and Rome: both in ruins.

Her voice didn't carry here, unlike in her railroad flat in the Tenderloin, San Francisco's formerly notorious red-light district. Her three rooms on Mason Street were almost empty. Like Jim Jones, she believed most possessions were unnecessary. Since she worked in the stacks at San Francisco's downtown library, she could get any book she wanted, so had no need for bookshelves. One table with one chair in the kitchen, a futon in the living room which served as couch and bed, plus a lamp, and in the bedroom, which had been awaiting the baby for some time, nothing at all. She'd painted the walls sky blue and added puffy cumulous clouds in the corners. The ceiling was black, with glow-in-the-dark stars adhered to make all twelve constellations of the zodiac. Truth believed that certain realities adhered to the stars, and her planetary advice for the month had predicted certain success with any endeavor she undertook. Truth patted her belly and smiled.

When she came to a fork, she looked left and right and tried to imagine which way Jim would go. Closing her eyes, she listened for his strong, sure voice. "You know what to do, Truth," he would tell her, as he'd advised so many times during her eight years with him. Even when she was just a teenager, he knew who she was. No one had known her properly like that.

"Elizabeth Miller? That's not who you are," he'd responded when she introduced herself after the service that morning in the Fillmore. In those days, Peoples Temple still borrowed churches or halls. They had purchased the temple on Geary Boulevard, but it was not yet opened to the public. That afternoon, Jim's sermon was about how the poor were treated in the United States, and though she wasn't poor or black, as were most of the people filling the pews, she felt the truth of his words permeate to her marrow. She had none of those markers of poverty, but her weirdness had led almost everyone to see her as Other. As lesser. Always, she had known the world's cruelty, intuited the unfairness of the powers that be, but before that day had never been able to articulate the way injustice worked. When Jim explained it, nothing could be clearer or more obvious.

His handshake was powerful. So far from the overly polite, limp-wristed greeting of the minister at her parents' Unitarian fellowship in New Jersey. Shockingly, he had hugged her. It transformed everything. The electricity from his body radiated into hers. It wasn't sexual or even affectionate in nature. Later she would call it Principle. Jim said he lived by Principle, and, of course, he died by it too. In a modest church in September of 1970, Jim's Principle had infused her tired, hungry soul. Something magnetic happened between them; the realized energy of Jim Jones crossed fields with what was latent inside her and lit the potential she had never before been conscious of. Jim had found it. After his long, energizing embrace, he anointed her with a new name and asked if she wanted to volunteer for Peoples Temple as their resident graphic artist.

"But Reverend Jones," she protested.

"Call me Jim," he said, staring her down with that gaze, looking right through to her essence.

"Jim, then." She flushed. "In high school, my art teacher told me I couldn't draw a straight line! She said I had too much enthusiasm and not enough talent. Story of my life." She hadn't felt it coming on, but she sobbed. Again, Jim held her.

"Those days are over, Truth. Your talent and your home are right here, right now in Peoples Temple. What I'd like you to do is design the signs for our new building. That will be your first task."

Remembering that meeting now, eighteen years later, Truth could still feel Jim's charge vibrating her bones. She arrived at a broken gate with a falling-down guard hut beside it, where a welcome sign used to hang: "Greetings. Peoples Temple Agricultural Project." Someone had evidently stolen it. Why? A tourist's curiosity? Some wacko's need for a souvenir? Afterward, Jonestown had been overrun by journalists ransacking the place for clues, for documents, for a "scoop," while the Amerindians and Port Kaituma locals searched for food, medical supplies, any tools they could use.

She'd seen the photographs, pored over the newspapers that gorged on that terrible day. Nothing like it had ever happened before. On the TV, in every magazine, slick and tabloid, the Kool-Aid suicides were splattered, black dead bodies slathered across the pages, Peoples Temple members deprived of dignity in death just as they had lacked respect in life.

It proved Jim right about everything. White America hated black people. Before she joined the Temple, she had been too ignorant to recognize her own racism, though Jim had preached not to hate oneself for succumbing to the brainwashing of the Capitalist State's machinery. Everyone hated black people, he said, even and especially black people themselves, because the press and the government and the fashion industry and the toy industry and Hollywood had manufactured that hatred and flashed it out onto the radio waves, TV sets, movie screens and billboards. The masses bought the message hook, line, and sinker.

"How could we not?" Jim asked. We didn't have the power, the resources, the capital to combat that message. What we had to do was unlearn it, he said, and replace it with the truth. That was one of the many qualities she admired about Jim. He didn't sit around and whine. He *did* something. Already during her first month of college she had felt stifled by her classes: analysis, debate, the endless hairline fracturing of elliptical arguments. Didn't intellectuals ever do anything?

She quit State after a semester and started spending all her time at Peoples Temple. She worked sixty, even eighty hours a week, usually on the newsletter, flyers, and anything that needed artistic attention. At the Geary Temple, she was designated chief designer, and then planning manager after the arson.

Observing the guard hut's remains, she shook her head. Sadly, Jonestown had needed armed guards to keep outsiders out. They weren't there to intimidate Jim's beloved multiracial community. Truth fingered a loose, rusted cable and wished that she'd been inside this boundary a decade earlier, fighting the enemy, the FBI/ CIA/INTERPOL/IRS, though she was glad to be alive with Jim's legacy inside her. She wondered if she would cry.

When all was said and done, Jim had been so right to be so paranoid. That Woman who turned traitor talked about the palpable fear here, lying about how they ate only rice and rice soup, how Jim ranted on the loudspeaker twenty-four hours a day, either on the microphone or on tape. Now, only the unintelligible macaws filled the airwaves. She smelled rain. So peaceful here, so unlike the city. If she'd been here back then, she would have loved it, as they all did. Would have died for it too. If only there hadn't been so many troublemakers.

If only he'd let her come.

For the millionth time, she asked herself why he hadn't let her come to Guyana. He said her skills were needed in San Francisco, as a front-line soldier fighting the PR battle, and that eventually every Peoples Temple member would arrive at the gates of the Promised Land. Still, she could never understand his reluctance. So many of the Geary Temple team had at least visited Guyana. After the carnage, unlike Truth, most were grateful they weren't there. A few turned on Jim and ratted, selling their 913 dead comrades down the river. That's how Truth saw it. She wouldn't do that. Not ever. He had believed in her when no one else did, so she would always have faith in Jim Jones.

Resolved, she entered through the broken gate, picking her way over rubble and foliage. Inside the compound, the road was hard to decipher. Immediately inside the gate, she could feel him. No wonder the Guyanese were afraid. Jim's spirit lingered. A junked backhoe's exhaust pipe poked out from a thicket of liana, guiding her toward the Pavilion. It was three miles from the gate to the center of Jonestown. "It's the power of your spirit," she said aloud, "that frightens them. Not because you're mad or cruel." She waited for a response. Jim was the essence of love. He cared so much for his sisters and brothers, especially the poor ones, those of color, the elderly, and the children. He would never hurt the Guyanese. He had taken them in, given them medical care, fed and clothed them, as it said in Matthew 25, the only lines of the Bible Jim truly liked to quote:

For I was hungry and you gave me food
I was thirsty and you gave me drink
I was a stranger and you welcomed me
Naked, and you clothed me
I was sick and you took care of me
I was in prison, and you visited me.

She heard his resonant voice chanting the verse, which she knew by heart. The words had been printed on Temple letterhead. Since the demise of Peoples Temple, Truth hadn't fed the hungry nor clothed the poor nor done anything to continue the socialist tradition beyond handing dollars to street people. All these years she'd been brooding, reading, studying, until the time was right for action.

Making her way through the bush was hard going. It took an hour to reach the remains of the Pavilion. Here, too, had been a sign: "Those who forget the past are condemned to repeat it." Someone had stolen it too. Although she had her camera, it seemed sacrilegious to take photographs here, where so many of her brothers and sisters had taken their lives, where Jim died of a gunshot to the head. The foliage covered the images that were permanently engraved in her memory. Hundreds of bodies, arms linked around one another's waists and shoulders, the colored shirts and shorts and bandanas resembling a vibrant artist's palette in the aerial photos before the eye discerned the terrible detail.

Some members were angry Jim hadn't taken the poison like the others. They called him a coward to shoot himself. Truth didn't believe he'd killed himself at all. So much would never be known. She had been sure her pilgrimage would give her certainty, but looking around her, she felt none.

The ground didn't speak to her; Jim's chair – some called his throne – was gone. No bloodstains remained, no colored syringes littered the earth. The infamous zinc vat had disappeared. Nature took back everything, the jungle reclaiming its acreage. Only a few bedraggled wooden chairs mingled with the grasses and vines which tendrilled up the supporting beams and across the jagged roof crowned with epiphytes. Perched on the cement steps, she removed her canteen and notebook from her knapsack. She had wrapped everything in plastic to protect it from the damp. The rain began, dropping in syncopated rhythm on the tin roof. The metal was broken in several places, but she remained dry. She felt secure, sheltered by the Pavilion, safe in Jim's metaphysical embrace.

November 19th, 1988.

Jonestown in the rain.

I can feel them in front of me, behind me, all around me, everyone who stood here and sang and laughed and clapped when Leo Ryan said that for some this was the best experience of their lives. The Jonestown Express played music, sang America the Beautiful and people danced, sweated, laughed. At other times, people must have had sex here, too, perhaps in the middle of the night, creating the next generation of Jonestowners. After all, thirty-three babies were born ...

Truth stopped. Babies couldn't drink by themselves. They had to be injected. Or have the liquid forced down their tiny throats. She shuddered. Always, thinking about the infants gave her pause. How had Lionel put it? "*They killed their children.*" But Jim said the babies would be tortured or worse. Wasn't it better for their parents to end their lives mercifully instead? It was like slavery days, or Masada, or the Russian Old Believers. Rather than let the children be brought up by the oppressor, the parents killed them, then committed suicide. A brave act, not one committed by cowards. In Israel, Masada was a shrine, the Hebrew ancestors commemorated as noble patriots. Why were Peoples Temple members regarded as crazy? Duped zombies. Drugged. But no one took drugs in the Peoples Temple: narcotics and alcohol were forbidden. Jim and Marceline had rehabilitated hundreds of drug addicts.

Again, she picked up her pen.

It had to be done. The FBI/CIA/INTERPOL/IRS were waiting. Jim's hands were tied. The Soviet Union couldn't possibly take them (us) after the Congressman was killed. And they (we) couldn't go to Cuba either. Death was the only possible exit. The noble choice, like Socrates, Jim said. The revolutionary's way. The Black Panthers' way.

Something moved behind her, and she startled. A spider monkey. It was hunting for something to eat. Rummaging through her knapsack, she threw a bit of granola on the ground in front of the animal. It looked at her curiously, as if it had never seen a human before. It seemed nervous. Even the monkeys were paranoid in Jonestown, she thought. "Are you a descendant of Mr. Muggs?" she asked.

As if the monkey could understand her, it shrugged, then looked at her expectantly, so she offered more oats. Mr. Muggs was Jones's chimpanzee, kept in a cage at the headquarters in

74

Redwood Valley near Ukiah. Soon after she joined up, the church had moved into San Francisco and Los Angeles. Jim said Peoples Temple could be most useful in the ghetto. Mr. Muggs was found shot, along with some of the dogs. Truth had never understood why the animals had to die too. Did Jim think the Fascists would torture the monkey? Perhaps. As history had demonstrated, they were capable of anything.

Jim had spoken of concentration camps. The German Jews had followed all the rules and laws, and, for their reward, were marched into gas ovens. Were they going to allow that, he would ask the congregation. No! Never! She remembered shouting, fist clenched, along with hundreds of others in the Geary Temple, she one of the few whites who was neither churched nor Jewish, nor poor. In the beginning she felt left out, in a weird way. The blacks and the Jews could testify to persecution. Had persecution woven into their family histories. She remembered Harriet Tropp's strident Jewish voice on the radio: *"We choose as our model not those who marched submissively into gas ovens but the valiant heroes who resisted in the Warsaw ghettos."*

Truth had no history of political intimidation, no poverty, no minority status, except as a woman, and women were the majority of congregants in Peoples Temple.

Jews always used that line about not forgetting the past in order not to repeat it. That's why Israel should have a strong military, they said, why it was important to teach the Holocaust in schools. But in the United States, it was blacks who'd be put into concentration camps. "Or our Yellow sisters and brothers," Jim said, recalling the Japanese internment camps. *"It Can't Happen Here,"* people liked to say, but of course it could. And it did happen. Right here, under the Pavilion. Jim Jones wouldn't be surprised to find that the lessons of Jonestown had vanished from history, leaving only Kool-Aid jokes.

The FBI/CIA/INTERPOL/IRS had harassed Peoples Temple to death. That was the truth. Jim's death by bullet – suicide or murder? – never seemed to fit. Wouldn't he go like the others, his children, and drink the poison along with them? It was better to die in freedom than to live in bondage.

Rubbing her hands over her belly, Truth pretended she could feel the baby already growing, its microscopic cells multiplying and enlarging. She rested her head on her knees and hugged herself.

Were the Peoples Temple dead great American patriots? Truth had changed since then; she wasn't a kid in her twenties anymore. Wasn't quite so hopeful that the world could be fixed if the right person were running the show. The right people always got assassinated anyway. *Look what happened to Martin Luther King! Malcolm X! Medgar Evers!* Jim said. Those great men had worked toward change, radical change, and they were killed. Since he worked for radical change, it was likely he would be killed too. Jim had always been a prophet.

What would Jim say about her bringing a new life into such a flawed and fucked up world? She should have adopted, like Jim and Marceline and their rainbow family, but as a single woman on a low income, no agency would certify her, and in any case the record of her times in the psych ward disqualified her. She had to have her own baby. A Peoples Temple baby. Jim would be pleased her baby would have brown skin.

Rumors that Jim was a racist surfaced from time to time. Not one of his lovers was black. He did like the young, pretty, skinny white girls; it was impossible to deny that empirical fact. But in his sermons, he explained how black women had been raped so many times by white masters that it was impossible for a white man and a black woman to be together without that history stinking beside them in bed like a rotting corpse.

Yet he encouraged whites to be with blacks, blacks with whites, whites to raise black children and blacks to raise white children. Jim was just more sensitive than other white men who got together with black women. Almost everyone on his staff was white, which was empirically true too. Truth hadn't been a member of the inner circle, though. Something always kept Jim at a certain crucial distance from her, kept him from trusting her a hundred percent. She didn't like to remember his sexual distance from her. He'd slept with so many of the women and some of the men too.

The rain stopped. There was plenty of daylight left, and she wondered if she should try to make it back to Port Kaituma and spend the night with Lionel again, just in case.

Why did Jim sleep with That Woman? And not with Truth? Eyes shut, the desire to cry mounted inside her. Jim had said all that jealous, exclusive bullshit was a luxury no one could afford until everyone had enough to eat and drink, proper shelter over their heads and the same high quality of health care and education. The US was no closer to that goal now than when Jim had started preaching in the 1950s. He said he fucked for the Revolution. He openly told of screwing a diplomat's wife in Brazil for five thousand dollars which he used to feed the kids at his orphanage. He hated doing it, he said, but it was a means to an end. Feeding the hungry was worth the dirty feeling he got from that rich white woman, whoever she was.

He'd had sex with almost everyone but her. So what? He *knew* her. Maybe he knew that sex had never been especially meaningful to her, and that was why he stayed away. She had never told Jim about her long promiscuous period in high school. Truth wasn't attractive in any conventional way, but her breasts had grown so fast and so big that guys were all over her when she was fifteen and sixteen. Like Lionel, they admired her titties. In those days, she had indeed been the Smart American Girl on the Pill. Now, her mammoth breasts would feed her child of the Revolution. So much attention was paid to them, yet they were alien to her. She didn't choose a 40D cup. She admired the flat girls, the ones who went braless. The boys and the men suddenly flew to her, wanted her, and for a while it was delicious. There had been some college guys, home on Christmas break, who suddenly noticed her existence, though she'd lived in the same neighborhood her whole life. She liked how her body tingled when touched by a man's hands, liked how full she felt with a penis inside her. Quickly, that pleasure faded. The psych ward visitations happened during her senior year. Breakdown, then recovery, followed by breakdown, then flight. The guys she'd been with were not remotely interested in any element of her as a person. Nobody was. Until Jim.

Truth shrieked as a tapir charged her. It took off with her bag of granola, then vanished into the trees.

As the sudden terror subsided, she realized that Lionel was right: very little of Jonestown had survived the jungle. She liked the feeling of being close to Jim and to the others, but she did not want to be here when darkness fell. She wasn't scared exactly, but she had no more food, and no flashlight. She couldn't write in her journal without light, and where would she sleep? The cottages didn't exist anymore. The only shelter from the rain was right here, under the Pavilion, where everyone had died. Where spirits roamed. Now that she was a parent, she had to be responsible.

WE'RE ECUMENICAL.
WE DON'T HAVE PROPERTY.
WE BELIEVE GOD IS LOVE,
AND LOVE IS SOCIALISM.
WE CANNOT LOVE
UNLESS THERE'S EQUALITY.
THE HIGHEST WORSHIP TO GOD IS TO
SERVE FELLOW HUMAN BEINGS.

Jim Jones

Marceline Baldwin
Mercy Hospital
Richmond, Indiana
1949

Only Marceline wanted to hold the Negro child with the nasty cough, which turned out to be pneumonia. "Aren't you the sweetest thing?" she murmured into the baby's burning ear as she carried her up from emergency to pediatrics. "Aren't you the prettiest little girl?" The infant, whose nametag read Baby Doe, had been left in the lobby, wrapped in a white bedspread, clean but many times mended in crazy quilt style, the intricate crosshatch testifying to the sewer's skill. Whoever left her had bathed and powdered the child and folded a change of clothing into the coverlet, which was promptly tossed in the trash by the receptionist who found her. The other nurses were pretending to be busy around the emergency room desk. Marceline took the girl from Mary Margaret, who was holding the infant as far away from her as possible, breath held.

"Come with me, sweetheart. Let's see if we can cool you down." Always, Marceline had loved the warmth of babies. She relished their fresh smell and their bird sounds. "We're going to get you all fixed up," she whispered, passing the cluster of nurses, all of them older than she by a least a decade. After three years at Mercy, first as student nurse, and now officially three months an RN, Marceline Baldwin, twenty-two years old, could testify to the want of merciful behavior at this institution, though its mission was to succor the poor and destitute of eastern Indiana.

"I'm going to call you Cinnamon," said Marceline as she weighed and measured the baby, then took her temperature with a rectal thermometer. The baby had a coughing fit, which metamorphosed into full-on screaming. One hundred and six degrees. "Let's get her into a lukewarm bath," Marceline called to one of the aides on the children's floor. "Then Doctor Burt can look her over."

A young blonde in a pink assistant's smock backed away. "Nurse Sinclair just asked me to help get a patient out of bed."

"I'll do it," came a male voice. A very young man walked ahead of her into the bathing area, opened the door and turned on the water before carefully taking the baby from her arms. "Nurse Baldwin, will you adjust the temperature? I don't want to get it wrong and burn her."

To the baby he said, in a playful voice, "Now you're one hot little girl, aren't you? We're gonna get you cooled down first thing."

While she checked the water, the boy tickled the baby's tummy. He was white, like Marceline, but his hair and eyes shone brilliant black; he seemed exotic, not only in his unusual appearance but due to his apparent indifference to the baby's skin color.

"Are you new, Mr… ." She paused.

"I'm Jim. Jim Jones. Just started this morning." He smiled at her over the basin, both of them with their hands on the child, he cupping the girl's head gently in his large palm, she splashing water over the baby's toes. Marceline thought the boy would make a good father someday, and she looked up into his eyes. He was studying her face, which she found unsettling and thrilling simultaneously.

"You like children, don't you?" he asked.

Her pale skin reddened, and she looked back down at the baby. "I do. Yes."

"Do you have any?"

"No!" She could feel her cheeks heating up, and wondered if

Jim had intentionally brushed his fingertips on hers as he grazed a washcloth over Cinnamon's belly. "I mean I'm not married."

"Not yet. But you will be. Soon, I think." His laughter, deep and self-assured, forced Marceline to look again into his dark eyes. Was he making fun of her? "I like children too. Like this one." He smiled at Cinnamon. "You are a beautiful girl. Yes, you are." The baby opened her huge eyes and coughed, spitting water into Jim's face.

Marceline tensed.

Again, Jim laughed, wiping his wet chin on his shoulder. "That's right, little one. You spit out that nasty old stuff!" He shook his hair. "What time do you take your lunch?"

"Well, I usually meet my mother in the cafeteria. She works in book-keeping."

His smile vanished. He looked as if he might cry, all swagger and confidence evaporated.

"Oh, why don't you join us," Marceline said reflexively. "Please."

Across his face a wave passed, restoring him. "What time?"

He really was just a kid, Marceline thought. Her half-conscious daydream of running her fingertips through that luscious hair, down his shoulders, feeling his skin on her skin, faded. He reminded her of a young cousin, also named Jim, who did poorly in school and often visited their home seeking comfort. His parents were preoccupied with money troubles and fought constantly and had no time for their children. Jimmy Baldwin was a sweetie, tortured by acne and the girls in his class, bullied by boys for the gentleness that translated as effeminacy.

"Twelve-thirty." She checked her watch. "I'll meet you there."

"How 'bout we go down together?"

How quickly he wanted to know her. She wasn't used to it. From high school she'd gone straight to nursing college, where every student was female, and, as a minister's daughter, her earlier life had been free from male attention. No boy in her father's congregation dared ask her out, and in school she had a reputation for primness, which she had no agency in crafting. "Polly Prude! Polly Prude!" High school boys would taunt her as she walked by the drugstore on Second Street. Just because she was the plain daughter of a pastor. Marceline, who loved her parents and respected her father's work, often wished she could be more "normal." She wanted to be like her girlfriends, who held hands with boys and necked in the back seats of cars. Her friend Sally told her every detail of every kiss and caress, every hand down her skirt, sensations Sally apparently adored.

"It's embarrassing sometimes," Sally confessed one night at a sleepover. "My panties get wet, you know, all over. Soaked! As if I'd showered in my clothes. It feels so good, and I want to do more. More than just kiss and let Michael touch my breasts. But I know I shouldn't."

Marceline also wanted Sally to do more, whatever "more" consisted of, so that afterwards Sally could narrate every delicious moment of it to her. She used to touch herself all the time, at twelve and thirteen. Whenever she thought no one was looking, she rubbed her pubic bone against the wall, the door edge, tucking her fingers inside her then smelling them, finding the odor alien but interesting, unlike any other scent. Her mother walked in on her one day in the bathtub, while Marceline was exploring her vagina, and made her promise not to do it anymore. Mrs. Baldwin said all those good feelings were supposed to wait until God – with Pastor and Mrs. Baldwin's blessing – found her a husband. Because Marceline had promised, she stopped.

Somehow, she managed to turn twenty-two without any man ever finding the courage to lay a finger upon her body. As Marceline looked for Jim by the pediatrics desk at 12:25, she met his eyes staring her down as he walked toward her, his smile radiant with what she thought might be attraction, even desire.

He patted her shoulder. "Hi there. I'm sure hungry. What about you?"

His touch reverberated down her arm and into her belly,

connecting to her groin with a pleasing shock. Flushing, she mumbled that she was, and then that she wasn't. He took her arm – he was so very bold! Part of her liked it, and part of her feared it. It was exhilarating.

At lunch, Mrs. Baldwin quizzed Jim about his life, pleased to learn he was interested in medicine, surprised he was only finishing high school. "And yet you seem so sure of yourself and what you want." She looked sideways at her daughter. "Most people go through some changes before settling down."

"Ma'am, I know I want to help people. If not as a doctor, then it'll be something else. I've been helping people my whole life already. Animals too."

Marceline nodded. She looked from Jim, with his rich self-confidence, to her mother, the pastor's wife. The Minister and Mrs. Baldwin would disapprove of Jim, of his cockiness.

"Well, whatever you decide, you have a lot of schooling ahead. Marcy's already spent four years at nursing college. If you decide on medicine, that's easily ten years before you get your M.D."

Jim's face fell. "Ten years! I can't wait that long!"

Marceline smiled. Her Jim was impetuous. He would become her Jim, whether her parents liked him or not. He had so much energy. Unlike her father, the quiet Methodist rule-follower, Jim would make his own rules.

"There are lots of ways to help people, of course," said Mrs. Baldwin, a petite woman who wiped her lips with the corner of her napkin after each bite of her egg salad sandwich. "You're already doing that here, as an aide. And although bookkeeping has no great merit of its own, I try to do my work so that people's bills are manageable. While being fair to the hospital, of course." Her gray-blond hair in a neat bun perched high on her head, Mrs. Baldwin looked around the cafeteria to check if anyone was listening.

"You've got a bit of the Samaritan in you, I see," Jim said loudly, winking at Marceline.

"Well, of course; it's part of our creed, to help others."

"Which church do you belong to?"

"Methodist," said Marceline, her first entry in the conversation. "My father has the ministry at First Methodist on the East Side."

"What church did you attend growing up?" asked Mrs. Baldwin.

"My family didn't belong to any, so I did my own exploring. Tried all of them in Lynn, Indiana, and Crete, where I was born. My neighbor, Mrs. Kennedy, she took me to her church plenty of times, the Nazarenes. I liked their services. And the Pentecostals, too. So exciting. Not like those sleeping, snooty congregations where no one says anything with real freshness, or that's what it seemed like to me."

Mrs. Baldwin pushed her tray away. "Pastor Baldwin and I have never been to a Pentecostal service. It's possible you'll find my husband's sermons a little too … perhaps too tame for your taste." She bit her lip. "Don't they speak in tongues?"

Jim grinned. "You don't like that idea."

As if they were already conspiring, he smiled broadly at Marceline. Before Mrs. Baldwin could reply, he added, "You'd be amazed at the spirit you find in those churches. I'm kind of a preacher myself. Not like your husband, of course, but I've preached to the kids in my neighborhood since I was a kid. You know, dog funerals and kitten baptisms and such. I can tell when people are listening and when they're just pretending. And boy, those Pentecostals drooling and babbling aren't pretending anything. You have to see it to appreciate it."

Marceline worried that he had gone too far. She admired his rebelliousness, but she wanted her mother to like this boy.

"You know," she said, looking at her watch, "I wish we could keep talking, but I have to relieve Betty upstairs, so she can take a late lunch."

To her relief, Jim rose and extended his hand to her mother.

"A pleasure to meet you, Mrs. Baldwin. I hope to hear your husband's sermon very soon. Maybe this weekend?"

Mrs. Baldwin smoothed her hair and pursed her lips. "I'm sure he would like that. Everyone is welcome in our church." She turned her cheek for Marceline to kiss. "Honey, I'm going to get some coffee and read the newspaper."

Leaning down, Marceline pecked her mother's cool skin, feeling somehow older than she had yesterday at their after-lunch ritual. "Don't rush, Mother. I'll see you later."

Again, Jim rested his hand lightly on Marceline's shoulder, making sure her mother saw. "Goodbye, Mrs. Baldwin. See you Sunday."

On their way back, Jim kept touching Marceline's elbow, opening doors, flashing his wide, powerful grin. "I like your mother," he said. "I think she likes me too."

Marceline laughed. "Oh, you don't know her. She's hard to gauge sometimes."

"I bet she gives all your boyfriends a hard time. But that's okay. She should." Jim whispered in her ear, "You're a treasure."

Shaking her head, Marceline turned away, and announced, in an unnaturally high voice, "There's Betty, waiting for me. See you later, Jim."

All afternoon, Marceline felt glad she had resisted her impulse to always tell the truth, to confess she'd never had a boyfriend, not ever. Sally was now married to Michael with two children and pregnant again. Impatient to "do more," Sally had married her high school boyfriend at eighteen, and in some ways, it seemed her life had ended there, as a mother. Marceline didn't want that life.

"And who's the young man?" asked Betty, a grandmotherly type in her sixties who kept tabs on staff social relations. "I never saw him before."

"He's new." Marceline flushed.

"I see." Betty smiled. "Isn't he a little young for you? I mean, he's awfully handsome, but handsome can be dangerous."

"He's only four years younger!" Marceline retorted, then wished she hadn't.

Betty blinked. "Miss Baldwin, you're both very young people. Don't rush into anything." With a knowing smile, Betty took her purse and left.

Marceline wondered what Betty meant by dangerous. All this is silly, she told herself, as she commenced the afternoon's tasks. It was just this morning she'd met him, this good-looking Jim who reminded her in his earnestness of her young cousin, though he looked nothing like the homely, sad Jimmy she'd always loved and pitied. "Concentrate on your work," she told herself.

Still, she couldn't scrape him from her consciousness. She checked on Cinnamon and was gratified to find her resting, fever down. Marceline couldn't let go of the sweet image of Jim holding this brown-skinned baby, his kindness to a sick child. Warmth filled her as she held the sleeping baby, swaying and humming. Perhaps one day she would have a baby herself, a girl like this one. Playing with the infant's dark tight curls, she thought of Jim's thick black hair, which he wore longer in back than most men, and how she wanted to touch it. The warmth she felt now wasn't centered in her groin but farther up, in a place that sometimes revealed itself in church when her father quoted from the Psalms, or when she read something profound. Where her spirit resided, she thought, though it didn't dwell in one fixed spot, but lodged itself somewhere between her heart and mind. She remembered when Sally insisted she read *Wuthering Heights*, which her friend had devoured for the third time.

"It's so amazing, this incredible love they have for each other, even when they're not together. Even when she's dead!"

"Don't give the plot away," protested Marceline. They were sixteen then, and she found herself appalled by the bond between Heathcliff and Cathy. He was uncouth and violent, but something about him compelled her. Something powerful made Marceline root for him in his quest to win the heart of the upper-class girl, and against Edgar, who, despite his gentleness and obvious love for Cathy, appeared a little boy by comparison. Marceline remembered how she had wished for a love like that in her own life, doubting that such a connection with a man was possible. It still seemed impossible.

At dinner, her mother told her father about the new male orderly and his interest in hearing Pastor Baldwin preach on Sunday.

"What's he like?" asked Laura, Marceline's younger sister, who was already engaged, terribly romantic and impatient to see her big sister in love. "What's he look like?"

Marceline's father waited. "Well, Marcy? Laura and I are curious."

Marceline looked to her mother for help. Mrs. Baldwin shook her head. "You tell them."

Suddenly her soup, Campbell's tomato, seemed especially fascinating, and she probed its red-orange depths, as if seeking an appropriate response therein. She didn't like this feeling of being observed as if she were a cellular organism.

"You're blushing!" shouted Laura, pleased with herself. "Come on, Sensible Sister! Tell us already."

Laura was the pretty one, the boy lure, as her parents called her, a term they'd shortened to "boiler" as a joke. The boiler wasn't interested in going to college or having any kind of career. When Laura had read *Wuthering Heights*, at Marceline's insistence, Heathcliff disgusted her. "What a beast!" she said. "I can't believe Cathy would want to be within a hundred yards of that guy. He's awful!"

"Well, he's got nice eyes," Marceline said finally, more to her soup than her sister. "Big and dark."

"And a good head of hair, too," added Mrs. Baldwin. "I wonder what kind of blood he's got in him. Black Irish, maybe?"

Marceline shrugged. What did it matter? "I have no idea, Mother. He was born in Indiana, like me."

"Tell them how old he is."

She knew her mother's teasing was not malicious, but she couldn't help being defensive.

"What? Is he an older man or something?" Laura asked hopefully.

"No. He's younger than me, that's all."

"He's still in high school!" announced Mrs. Baldwin triumphantly, and everyone laughed except Marceline. She surveyed the room, its well-appointed oak furniture and graceful pewter chandelier suspended over the dining room table. The Baldwins weren't rich, but they were … tasteful, Marceline thought. If she continued to live at home after Laura's wedding, Marceline feared she might suffocate.

"All right, Mother. You've had your joke. So, he's eighteen. We all were, once. Laura's only nineteen, for goodness's sake. I think he's pretty mature, really. I mean, he cares about the world, which you don't find in too many people that age." She glared at her sister, who was winking at their mother and wasn't listening.

Pastor Baldwin sighed. "Okay, everyone. Let's stop making Marcy uncomfortable. I'm sorry, honey. It's just that we've never seen you excited about a boy before. I'm pleased you've met someone you like."

"He seems a fine young man," said Mrs. Baldwin. "He's just a boy, that's all, and impetuous. But I think his heart's in the right place."

Marceline excused herself and climbed the stairs to her bedroom. She loved her family, but sometimes she wished she were independent enough to have her own apartment or that she could share with another nurse. Her sister would go from father to husband; no doubt her parents expected the same from Marceline. While lying on her bed, calculating if her paycheck could support a monthly rental, plus groceries and utilities, the phone rang. When she heard her mother calling, "Marcy! Telephone for you!" she knew exactly who it was.

The heavy black phone rested on the kitchen counter by the door. She was grateful to her mother for leaving the dishes to allow Marceline privacy.

"Marceline? It's Jim."

She liked how he used her full name, not the annoying

diminutive. "I knew it would be you," she whispered, smiling into the phone.

"You did? How?"

"Just knew."

"I was thinking about you, so I thought I'd call. Actually, I can't stop thinking about you." He laughed. "I've never felt like this before."

Breathing in, she felt light-headed. She wanted to say she felt the same but didn't dare.

"Are you there?"

"I'm here."

"You know, after one day at Mercy Hospital, I felt like most of the people who work there don't like Negroes. You were the only person I saw being nice to a colored patient."

"I thought the same thing about you!" This was a safer topic. "I don't understand Mercy. They're so hypocritical, pretending they're there to help the poor," her voice rose, "but when the poor are Negro, they're not so helpful anymore. I'm glad you noticed it too. My mother thinks I'm overly sensitive. But," she lowered her voice, "my mother has a lot of her own prejudices, too. Though she'd never admit it."

"We all do though, you know? Raised in good ol' Indiana, heart of the Ku Klux Klan. My father was a member."

Marceline gasped. "You're kidding!"

"I'm not. I have a lot to atone for in this life, if you know what I mean. He threw me out of the house when I told him I found a Negro ancestor on his side of the family. And he was in the war, I mean the first war, gassing people. He was gassed too, so I guess he got what was coming to him."

For reasons she couldn't identify, Marceline wanted to defend Jim's father. How could Jim speak so derisively of his own blood? "Was he really hurt, then, from the gas? Sometimes we see veterans like that at Mercy. They have so many health problems."

"My old man was a louse before the war. And so lazy. My

mother's always worked. Usually in the factories. She was hardly around when I was growing up, or that's what it seemed like to me. She's from Kentucky, dirt poor, so her family thought she was coming up in the world by marrying James Thurman Jones. They didn't know she'd end up supporting us all."

In her parents' gleaming kitchen in their brick, middle-class home, Marceline felt ashamed of all she had taken for granted. When she and Laura were children, her mother had always been there, keeping their house proper and clean, sitting down with them over tea and cookies after school, checking to make sure the girls did their homework and buying them new school clothes every fall. She'd had an easy life. "Where are your parents now?"

"My father's dead. Mom's still working at the factory. She's head of her union now. I'm proud of her."

Marceline had never known a labor organizer. A couple years back, some outsiders tried to unionize the workers at the hospital, but she hadn't paid much attention. Most of the women were against it, and the effort failed. Often her father spoke against unions, saying they were infiltrated by Communists, and though the intent of the union was Christian, to make sure everyone was paid a decent wage and worked in a safe environment, in practice they were full of crooks. She wondered if her father had any direct experience, or if he was merely parroting what the newspapers said.

"I'd like to meet her," Marceline said, pleased by her own boldness.

"Oh, you will," Jim laughed.

Where did he get such confidence, she wondered. She had never felt so sure of herself in all her life. It couldn't just be that he was a boy – immediately she thought of Jimmy Baldwin as a counter-example – and Laura never let anyone intimidate her. He must have been born with that certainty inside him, she concluded. Like Laura. Not like her.

"I better go now," she said, though no one was asking to use the phone.

"Okay, Marceline. Sweet dreams. I'll see you in the morning. Can we have lunch together again?"

What would her mother think? If Marceline had a real lunch hour, she and Jim could eat some place other than the hospital cafeteria, but forty-five minutes wouldn't cover the walk to and from the nearest luncheonette, plus ordering and waiting for their meal. "Sure. Good night." After she hung up, she found her sister waiting on the bottom stair in the hallway.

"So? Did he ask you for a date?" Laura smiled. "You like him! I can see it all over your face. Marcy's got a date," she sing-songed. "Marcy's got a date!"

Flushing, Marceline dodged her sister. "No. I don't have a date. He just called to say hi. That's all."

"Marcy's got a date! Marcy's got a date!" Laura sang at her older sister until she disappeared into her room.

In bed, waiting for sleep, Marceline kept seeing Jim's eyes, the way they bored into hers, his daring to know her. It was so new. Like Sally, Laura enticed boys. She knew how to flirt, how to play those games which Marceline had never learned. Laura was genuinely pretty with sky-blue eyes and straight blonde hair she wore long. Marceline had always been the plain one, the studious one, the serious one, with a sensible short haircut for her unruly curls. She didn't begrudge Laura her looks. Her sister was always advising her how to "touch up" her appearance, encouraging Marceline to show off her large hazel eyes.

"Between those Baldwin girls," the church women would say, "You'd want your son to date Laura but marry Marceline."

At her old-maidish age, perhaps Marceline had at last found the man – ironically just a boy – who could appreciate her particular qualities, who valued more than pretty eyes and a teasing laugh. Up and down her body she let her fingertips travel, her nipples pushing out the cotton of her nightgown. Would he touch them? She hoped so. She remembered Sally speaking of the torment of holding back when she didn't want to. They were teenagers then.

Did Marceline have to wait until marriage to do more than kiss? Was Laura waiting? Marceline would never ask her sister outright; though she was older by three years, sometimes Marceline felt as if her parents treated Laura as the grown-up. Or was that only since the engagement? Did marriage make you older, and why? Maybe it was sex that made you older. With Jim's good looks, he'd probably had plenty of experience. Though he was younger, she liked the idea that Jim would teach her how to make love.

Beneath her nightgown, under her panties, her fingers roamed, testing to see if she experienced the same wetness Sally had talked about. Yes. Would they kiss in the back seat? He didn't have a car and neither did she. Where would they do their exploring? She couldn't wait. But she would.

IT WILL BE UP TO OUR GROUP
TO BEGIN LIFE ANEW ON THIS CONTINENT.
THEN WE WILL BEGIN
A TRULY IDEAL SOCIETY
JUST AS YOU SEE IT
HERE IN THIS ROOM TODAY.
PEOPLE WILL CARE ABOUT ONE ANOTHER.
ELDERLY PEOPLE WILL BE
MADE TO FEEL NEEDED
AND WILL BE ALLOWED TO BE PRODUCTIVE.
PEOPLE'S NEEDS WILL BE MET
BECAUSE THEY ARE LOVED,
AND NOT BECAUSE THEY HAVE MONEY.
THIS CHURCH FAMILY IS AN EXAMPLE
OF WHAT SOCIETY WILL EVENTUALLY
BE LIKE ALL OVER THE WORLD.
THERE WILL BE AT LAST PEACE ON EARTH.
I HAVE SEEN THIS ALL BY DIVINE REVELATION.

Jim Jones

Watts Freeman
11:16 am
Nov. 18, 2008
San Francisco

KR: This is Kenyatta Robinson, coming back after a break with today's interview with Roman Freeman, or Watts, as he's known to his friends, who was one of four eyewitness survivors of the Jonestown Massacre, which took 918 lives, many of them from here in the Bay Area. Thirty years ago today, Jim Jones and his followers swallowed poison mixed with a fruit drink we've called Kool Aid all these years, though it was in fact Fla-Vor-Aid. Some children and elderly were injected with the poison, or had it squirted down their throats by nurses with syringes, while many others came forward voluntarily to swallow their cupful, as they had rehearsed the act many times with their leader, the Reverend Jim Jones of the Peoples Temple, formerly of San Francisco, Los Angeles, Ukiah, and before that, Indianapolis. Watts, after all these years, can you tell our listeners what you now understand about Jonestown, the wisdom that time and distance have given you on this horrific tragedy? Could it happen again?

WF: It's funny; they ask me that same question every anniversary. You know that famous saying we had on a sign in the Pavilion; every photographer made sure to get it in over the piles of bodies. "Those who forget the past will repeat it," something like that.

What can you say? It happened before, it happened then, and it's happened since. It'll happen again.

KR: Are you referring to David Koresh of the Branch Davidians in Waco, Texas? Or the Heaven's Gate suicides here in California?

WF: Sure, those are the kind of crazy-leader murder-suicide stories that always get compared to Jonestown. But I don't mean only that exact act as what's been repeated, what we repeated, and what will probably be repeated again. *[Harsh laugh]* We were a lot more interesting than Koresh's Bible thumpers or those Nike-wearing woo-woo types in Heaven's Gate, if I can say that without no disrespect to the dead. I don't mean anything nasty by it. In some ways, it's kind of insulting to all these dead people the way every group gets bunched together, when the only real thing those three had in common was a strong leader. The woo-woos, they were all wealthy and white – right? I mean, they were web-designers, or something high-tech like that. Waiting on a comet, I think, to blast them into space. And Koresh was a fundamentalist cracker, right-wing crazy, and they really did have an enemy at the gates, right? The FBI. With tanks and everything. In Jonestown, we just thought we did, or Jimmie Jones did anyway, and convinced a whole lot of folks that guys in helmets carrying machine guns really out there, waiting to torture us. Remember, the Peoples Temple was for poor people, for black people, mostly, so I don't like how the media always put us all in the same box of cults. Lots of groups have crazy leaders – United States does. Russia. China. Most of Africa and the Middle East. Pakistan, Burma – and that's just naming a few, right?

KR: I'm sorry. *[Flustered]* I didn't realize I was in the same category as all the clueless interviewers you've encountered before. Of course you're right that the groups I mentioned have less in common with one another than I realized.

WF: *[Smiles]* Kenyatta, you are nothing like any other interviewer I've ever met or been privileged to lay eyes upon before today. Actually, you're one of the few black broadcast journalists who's talked to me. Most of the media in this country is white, right?

KR: That's the truth. *[Laughs]* Tell me, Watts, if you have another comparison or parallel that makes more sense to you and maybe to other survivors, because it will help our listeners to put the Jonestown Massacre into a different kind of context than the media's been using all these years.

WF: When I say survivor, I don't mean just a survivor of the massacre. I mean anyone connected to the Temple, members who were in the States or in Georgetown, people who'd left before, including the Concerned Relatives, relatives, friends of the dead. A lot of people lost a lot of family in Jonestown. That's gotta be another thousand people. Anyway, about fifteen years ago or so, one of them told me 'bout a book called *Animal Farm*, which was written way before Peoples Temple was even an idea in Jimmie Jones's big fat head. I saw the movie on TV. It was done like a cartoon for kids, but it was real sad. You heard of it? *Animal Farm*?

KR: Yes, but I've never read it or seen the movie. I have read *1984*.

WF: Right. Same dude. He wrote it way before Peoples Temple was even an idea in Jimmie Jones's big fat head. The journalists always mention *1984* whenever they get to talking about Jim Jones. Jonestown was a lot more like *Animal Farm* than *1984*. It was a farm, you know? A kinda jungle plantation for poor black people. Can you guess who were the pigs?

KR: You mean the white leadership, of course.

WF: Yeah, but they always have a token black or two in the inner circle to make it seem like you included. Back in the States, it was Archie Ijames. He passed a while back. They always quote Archie saying, "Jim Jones is God." I never heard him say that. But you know, I figured out that the people on the bottom are always helping the people on top to push 'em down. That story just nailed it for me. That horse, Boxer, he the one who worked the hardest; he busted his butt for that farm, for all the animals, and the pigs treated him like shit. He say over and over, "I will work harder. I will work harder." And then them pigs sell him to the glue factory. Yeah. The brother who sweated and broke his back for the good of the whole farm, they sold him down the river. Lot of people like Boxer in Jonestown, 'specially some of the old timers. "I will work harder." They even used the same words. Not me, you understand. I was more the slacker type. Even before we left California the security team was almost all black brothers and sisters. They were the ones walking around with guns and the crossbows and the cutlasses. They weren't the ones mixing the poison. That was the Doc and some of the nurses, and they all white. But the guards made everyone stay put at the Pavilion. They made it real clear. They didn't use words, you understand, but the way they were standing, and where, and how they held their weapons, if you didn't swallow the bug juice, they were gonna get in your face. They carried the people up to the table where they had the syringes, even the ones who were screaming. I only got out 'cause I figured out how to trick 'em. I knew a lot of those brothers and sisters, and they knew me. Any one of them on the security team could've been me. A lot of us had the same story, whether it was Watts or Oakland or Hunters Point or Detroit. See what I'm saying? They were Jimmie Jones's muscle. The whole mess couldn't have gone down without 'em. You listen to the tape, the one they call the death tape?

KR: *[Sighs]* I have. A few times.

WF: So you know that one sister, Christine Miller, an older woman, she the only one – black or white – who protested right to his face. She just wouldn't back down. And Jimmie Jones, he courteous to her and all, but what happened? The other brothers and sisters shouted her down. They didn't like her talking back. The voices you hear on the tape are all brothers and sisters. I could name 'em for you. One say, "You only have a life to give away because Jim Jones gave you that life," and everybody agreeing, "Uh-huh. That's right."

KR: Why didn't anyone listen to her?

WF: *[Long silence]* I guess they was ready to die. Not so different from the slave days when we looking for rest on the other side. Mac, he one of Jimmie Jones's boys, a black man, he start talking about how it gonna be so peaceful over there, we gonna be happy, not uptight like we'd been for too long in Jonestown. By that time, we'd had so many white night rehearsals; I think a lotta people just ready for the final performance. Then that white dude, I never liked him, Don Sly – they call him Ujara in the tape – had to go knife the Congressman just before he left, even though he didn't actually hurt him. It was probably Jimmie Jones's idea. Ujara couldn't think straight, just like he couldn't knife straight, but I don't know that for a fact. So people were feeling like, let's get it over with. Enough is enough. Everybody was tired. Real tired. And there's Christine saying, "where there's life, there's hope," or something like that, and nobody want to hear it. If they did, they'd all have to stop, you know? Stop the rhythm of the thing, 'cause it was growing. People were ready. Jimmie Jones acting like God telling 'em that somebody's shooting Ryan's plane out of the sky as we're sitting there. Christine was slowing everybody down. Jimmie didn't never carry a gun. He didn't need to. The top guy in all the stories, the pig in *Animal Farm*, that Cambodian dude, or Stalin, or Mao or any of those guys … They all guys, right? *[Laughs]*

KR: Are you trying to pin me with the feminist flag, Watts? *[Smiles]*

WF: Did I use that F word? Sister, you didn't hear me use it. You paranoid, girl! I'm just stating the facts. All these leaders who end up being dictator a-holes, pardon me, they all dudes.

KR: What about Catherine the Great?

WF: I don't know her. What'd she do so great?

KR: She only extended the Russian empire from the Baltic to the Black Sea.

WF: Like I said before, *[Laughs]* the exception proves the rule. Where was I going before you sidetrack me with this F-word stuff? Kenyatta, you and me, we from different generations, but I think I know a feminist when I see one.

KR: Which brings me to another question …

WF: Hang on. You talking to an old man; if I don't finish what I'm on about now, I'll lose it. What I was sayin' was that the dudes in charge, they never do the dirty work themselves. They get a lieutenant-type to do it. Jimmie Jones very smart that way. Always keep his hands clean, so people think he the good guy, the nice Dad, even though he running the whole show and giving orders to the folks who end up looking like the bad guys, only most of them girls. Or women, I should say. For instance, you heard of the Board of Education?

KR: Wasn't that a piece of wood he beat people with?

WF: He never used it, never once. But who did? A black sister. Ruby. She a very large sister, and she carry a lot of weight in the

Temple, in all kinds of ways. Ruby the muscle with the board, not Jimmie Jones, but Jimmie Jones standing right next to her telling her just how to do it, holding the microphone up to the person's mouth so everyone could hear the screaming real good, and the "Thank you, Dad" when it was over. Just like the security forces. He always got the brothers and sisters to do the nasty stuff. And then they got to feeling really important, like they had all this power, 'cause he trusted them to do it. But Jimmie Jones just being one very smart dude, making the enforcement almost all black, while he the big enforcer behind everyone. Kinda like the Godfather or something. *[Laughs]* But he don't mumble like that Marlon Brando.

KR: What's amazing to me is that you can speak about it in such an objective-sounding way. I don't hear any bitterness in your voice.

WF: I was bitter, Kenyatta, for a long time. Many, many years, but it took too much outta me. Too much time. I don't have so much time, not with the diabetes and all. I'm starting to have problems with my eyes, you know? Feet, too. It's all I can do to try and stay a little bit healthy. The bitterness was making me sick.

KR: I hear you.

WF: You? What you got to be bitter about, Miss Kenyatta? You educated, you got a good job, good looks. You never come up how I did, how the poor folks in the Temple did. It ain't in your face.

KR: Do you think growing up in the projects is the only reason a black person has to feel bitter?

WF: Tell me about it. I'm listenin'.

KR: *[Sighs]* This is your interview, Watts. I've noticed that people try and switch the subject to me, just when things start getting uncomfortable.

WF: You pretty smart, Kenyatta. You a very sharp person. I bet your people took good care of you.

KR: Like I said, that's my story, and our listeners are here to hear yours. Can I ask you about the role of women in the Temple?

WF: Now that's a feminist question if I ever heard one. I been asked that one before, you know. Peoples Temple totally run by women. I mean, they did all the grunt work. Everything. What's that line? Women is the nigger of the world? As true in the Temple as anyplace else. The thing that just about killed me was the way Jimmie Jones figure out how to make them feel like they so special and important. Just like how he made the black people doing the muscle work feel like big shots. Like they more important than anyone. Like the place couldn't run without 'em. He made each woman think she the specialest one around, the only one he would trust to do that particular job. Brilliant. So they working eighty-hour weeks. Like Jocelyn and her sister, the nurse, they got a serious high off how hard they worked. And the big man made 'em feel good about it. And then the sex just sweetened the whole thing. He never had sex with his wife, not for a long time, anyway. He hung with Jocelyn all the time, and of course they had that kid, even though he got one of his white dude flunkies to marry her, and he had the other kid with Queen Traitor, the one who jumped ship long before we got to Jonestown. Nobody pretended he was faithful to Florence Nightingale by then. The old folks liked to think of Mother Marceline as some kind of saint, like Mary, 'specially the old ladies who knew a thing or two about their old man runnin' around on 'em. *[Sighs]* I never did figure her out. She smart, organized, together. She could've run a business or something. She was a big deal with the state medical people up in Ukiah, before the Temple moved down here. I guess she a serious masochist to stick around all those years while her old man doing all the ladies in the inner circle, and the occasional dude just to spice things up. Though he never did me, I'll tell you that.

KR: That's one of the things I can't understand. The homosexual part. How could he be gay and then insult gays, like he did in those group therapy confrontations? What did they call that? Something to do with the floor.

WF: Getting called on the floor.

KR: That's it.

WF: Well, Jimmie Jones not gay, but he liked both, for sure. He a hypocrite, and no one said nothing. I mean, here was Mr. Pure, Mr. Anti-Drugs, and by the end he's doping night and day. He talk against people having sex, how sex takes energy away from The Cause, and we don't have enough social justice in the world to get caught up in jealousy and all that exclusivity shit. All the time he's doing whoever he want whenever he want. And nobody says jack. "Do as I say, not as I do." Leaders everywhere the same. Like here when Mr. President gets his healthcare free and cuts it for everybody else. Nobody says nothing. Not the newspapers, not the opposition people, nobody. Like the leaders of so-called Socialist Guyana driving all those fancy fascist cars, like Benzes and BMWs. Everybody just sigh. Like *Animal Farm*. You should read the book. It all about Jonestown. The chief pig, Napoleon, he gets to eat good oats and drink whiskey while the rest of the animals are starving. Napoleon's not working in the fields, you understand, kinda like all us grunts clearing the bush and eating too much rice while Jimmie Jones have his nice roomy cabin to himself with his own refrigerator – with his ladies, of course – and the rest of us stacked up like slaves in the dorms. Napoleon eat the good food, and everyone knows it – he don't try to hide it – and the animals say things like, "Well, he our leader; he need to keep his strength up." Just like Jimmie Jones with his fancy food he keep in his cabin. I wish you'd read it, so you could see what I mean.

KR: I'm definitely going to read it, Watts. You're making me very curious.

WF: Jimmie Jones musta read it. I swear he modeled Jonestown on that farm, but I never saw him with his head in a book. That's what he had the Jewish lawyers for. And those college girls tell him whatever he need to know while he diddling 'em. Oh, man. I'm one crude dude, I know it. And I'm trying so hard to impress you, Miss Kenyatta, and here I am blowing it again.

KR: Watts, you are seriously impressive. You're giving me clarity on something I didn't understand before. I had a lot of facts, a lot of information, but hardly any way to interpret it.

WF: *[Laughs]* So, ol' Watts teaching you something, huh? I'm having a good time talking to you. Before, they always send some old buttoned-up white dude, and I get so bored I have to make shit up to keep myself awake. But I for sure am not bored today.

KR: Me neither.

WF: Kenyatta, you never woulda put up with Jimmie Jones, not for five minutes, and that's pushing it. You too together. But most of the brothers and sisters in the Temple not like you. They had no hope. I know I didn't. What kinda hope do you get in the projects? The one I grew up in burned down in the riots. Some of the old folks couldn't read, could hardly write, they work their asses off their whole lives; what kinda hope they got when the young brothers scare them to death with all the dope and stealing? Young brothers like me. The old folk from the South come to California for something better and find themselves washing clothes for white people just like back home in Georgia, 'cept now they're living in some dirty high-rise far from their people. What kinda hope is that?

So here come Jimmie Jones, and he say he love them. And I won't tell you he didn't, 'cause maybe he did. He say, give me your Social Security checks, and I take care of you. I get a whole crew of people to take care of you, all these nice young people wanting to help; I give you a cozy place to live, protect you at night, get you to the doctor when you need it, look after your teeth. Sound good, don't it? I mean, when you've never had one day's security in your life? No education. No one nice to you. Not even your own young people, who so fucked up themselves they got no respect for the old folks. I didn't never think about my grandma and all she went through before I showed up wanting a meal.

So it ain't no big surprise that there were no educated young black sisters like yourself in the Temple at the end. The ones that got an education at the Junior College up in Santa Rosa, they defected. You know, the famous Group of Eight in 1973? The very first traitors.

Every one of them go to college. They get some time away from Jimmie Jones, start thinking more clearly, reading about the world outside the Temple, and they see. They really see what's going on. See who Jimmie Jones is. Not what he say he is. The rest of us couldn't see. Couldn't see nothing. Too tired, mostly. And the head of that group he become one of the big dudes in the Concerned Relatives. He lost his mother, sisters, aunts, uncles, who knows how many. Jimmie Jones like to say the Concerned Relatives a big bunch of white racists, and the black people with them a bunch a Toms. Not true. He become a dentist, that dude. He do me a good deal on my teeth every year. He ain't the only black one in the group. Half the Famous Eight was black. He sue Jim Jones for a million dollars or something like that.

KR: I know who you mean. He didn't want to be interviewed. Said he'd done too many and he was finished.

WF: So I wasn't your first choice! Now Miss Kenyatta, you leading me on. I feel used and abused. *[Laughs]*

KR: Actually, Watts, you were my first choice. My supervisor wanted me to do several interviews, so we could do a kind of radio magazine about it. Lots of voices. People with different perspectives.

WF: Who else you talk to? You musta left me for last, considering today's the anniversary.

KR: To be honest, I felt I wanted to know as much as possible before I interviewed you; I didn't want to seem ignorant. I thought talking to the others first would help.

WF: You think fast on your feet, Kenyatta. That an excellent explanation for why you leave me dog last. So who else you talk to?

KR: You'll hear tonight on the air.

WE HAVE PASSED BEYOND ALIENATION
AND HAVE FOUND A WAY OF LIVING
THAT NURTURES TRUST –
ONE THAT COULD SPEAK TO A SOCIETY
GROWN CYNICAL AND COLD.

Jim Jones

Marceline Jones
1956
Indianapolis

The phone shrilled. "Is this the nigger-loving Jones home?" asked a male voice with a Georgia accent. Definitely white.

Marceline hung up.

"Jim!" she called to her husband in the front room as she finished drying the breakfast dishes. "Another crank call."

Jim rushed for the phone. "Hello? Hello, you bastards!" His face gleamed with energy.

"I hung up."

"I told you to keep them on the line!" he shouted, as if she were the problem. "We need to get these calls traced, and they have to be connected for at least a minute. Was it the KKK again?"

She looked down. "I don't know."

Again, she had hung up when he wanted her to engage them. You can even flirt, he'd told her. Anything to keep them on the line. Since their church, Wings of Deliverance, on Fifteenth Street had opened several months ago, the calls came daily. Their former church had welcomed Negroes too, but it had been smaller and in a poor neighborhood. Wings of Deliverance was a proper mid-sized church with stained class and arched windows, but it was in a white neighborhood. Next door was the red brick parsonage where they now lived, with more than enough room for her and

Jim and Agnes, the girl they planned to adopt from a parishioner who could no longer care for her.

Usually the calls came in the middle of the night, but lately any time would do. The last caller threatened to burn them down. Naturally, Jim wouldn't knuckle under. She loved that about him. His principle, his willingness to follow his beliefs, no matter what. Her minister father also embodied principle, but he'd never put his life or his family's on the line for it.

It was 6:45 a.m., time for Marceline to head out to Indianapolis General to begin her shift on the pediatric ward. Jim was getting ready to start his ministering for the day, which would include supervising the soup kitchen, organizing the volunteers to transport elderly parishioners from their homes to an afternoon meeting in which other volunteers would help the seniors deal with Social Security and health care problems. Every day, Jim needed to find money to keep it all going, and raising funds gobbled more of his time.

"I told you already. Why couldn't you get me beforehand, like I asked?"

Marceline wanted to stand up for herself, but he never listened. She unhooked her coat from the rack, located her handbag and combed her thick, short hair in front of the hallway mirror. He only harangued her when she deserved it, she told herself. She had to concentrate on what mattered most to the church and to their family. Why couldn't she keep those racist slimeballs on the phone? What was wrong with her?

"I'll stop by the church on my way home tonight, okay?" She smiled lightly and pecked him on the cheek as she opened the front door into a blast of Midwestern winter wind. "And we'll settle the arrangements with Agnes's mother, right? I'll bring the papers."

"All right, Marceline," he sighed. "Go save the babies." Arms around her waist, looking her full in the eyes, Jim kissed her on the lips then shut the door, heading for the telephone to speak with his assistants, prepping them for the day ahead.

At work, the Georgian man's words replayed over and over in her mind as she took vitals, assisted doctors on their rounds and worked in physical therapy with a twelve-year-old accident victim who had lost his right arm and leg.

"Honey, show me how powerful that left arm is," she said to the boy, Peter, who had stopped propelling his wheelchair as sobs racked his skinny frame. "You can do it, sweetheart. Your leg is doing great. We want your arm to be just as strong." She bent down to kiss the wild red curls on the boy's head. He'd been with his mother after she'd fallen asleep at the wheel, ironically after her night shift cleaning at Indianapolis General. She'd picked Peter up from her sister's apartment, where Peter spent most nights, wanting to see him before he went to school. They were on their way to breakfast at the Pancake House for a special treat.

"Mrs. Jones, I can't. I just can't." He cried into her arms now, the two of them blocking traffic in the pediatric corridor. Marceline felt especially close to Peter, wishing he was her son. There seemed to be no division between her heart and the boy's. Maybe she could adopt him as well as Agnes. Instant family, she thought with longing.

"C'mon. Try again, honey. Do it for me." She wiped the boy's eyes with a tissue and grinned. He was so sweet. She ached to make him better. "Do it for your grandma. I know she's coming to see you this afternoon, and she'll be so proud if you can get down the hallway by yourself."

Freckled and pale, Peter finally replied. "All right, Mrs. Jones." He sighed, whistling inadvertently. "I can do this."

She stepped back and tousled his hair again, the long curls inviting her fingers. She loved the way his hair furled back into itself, thick as forest undergrowth. "Good boy. Of course you can."

It was amazing he hadn't been burned, like his mother, whose last act had been to shield his body from the flames.

During her lunch hour, Marceline went to the offices of the State Board for the Welfare of Indigent Children, where she would get the official papers for her and Jim to become Agnes's foster parents. The girl's mother was one of their poorest parishioners and had agreed it would be best for her daughter to stay with the minister and his wife. It would only be temporary, until things improved at home, they all said, but Marceline knew Agnes would be with them always.

The Joneses met the Clifton family at their first Indianapolis church two years ago. Agnes's stutter was so bad that she could hardly be understood. Marceline was sure it stemmed from Mrs. Clifton's nastiness. Agnes's family was like many families the Joneses had ministered to in this city, white and black. Both parents worked, and both parents drank. The father often disappeared on alcohol-fueled binges and would be found, days or weeks later, in another part of the city, without any memory of what he'd done. Filled with resolutions, he would swear off the bottle, come home, clean up, and return to work at the Lily factory. The mother beat and neglected the two children, Agnes more than the boy. Mrs. Clifton was too busy weeping into her beer after starching policemen's tunics at the uniform-cleaning plant on the days she managed to get herself there.

When Marceline suggested fostering the girl, Jim immediately agreed. He supported her one hundred percent in important things, which made her feel deeply loved. The Joneses lived Christ's apostolic life in church and at home, taking in the young and old, anyone who needed help. Marceline hoped to start convalescent care for the elderly as soon as they had enough money to buy a building.

At the State offices, Marceline was surprised that the waiting room was almost empty. The man she had spoken to over the phone was available to see her at once.

"We so appreciate what you're doing, Mrs. Jones," said the man, ushering her into a cramped, windowless office. "There are so many Agneses in this city, and so few families willing to take in a troubled child. Of course, there is a small stipend from the state for her expenses, as soon as we get her declared an official ward of Indiana. It's not much, but it should help with the groceries and school clothes."

"Yes, that will be helpful." Marceline's cheeks burned at the thought of receiving money in exchange for Agnes. "Actually, I'd forgotten about the compensation. My husband and I have our own church now, you know, Wings of Deliverance on Fifteenth and North New Jersey, and so many volunteers are willing to cook meals and babysit and help in all kinds of ways."

"Yes, I've heard of it," said the man, who was bald and bony, his suit threadbare. "I've heard about the soup kitchen, what good food you offer."

Marceline smiled ruefully. "Here we are, in America. It still astonishes me how many poor there are in a world of plenty."

The man sighed in agreement, placing several forms in an envelope before her. "How will Agnes settle with your own children?"

Now Marceline sighed. "We don't have any children of our own. My husband thinks it's selfish to procreate when there are so many kids in need. And I agree with him, though at times I think it would be nice to have a child, my own child, but then I see kids like Agnes, and sometimes the children I work with at the hospital, and I know he's right. We need to take care of who's here already, not bring others into the world."

"I've heard people say that before," said the man, who appraised Marceline in her nurse's whites and prim cap, "but mostly it's just talk. I guess you being a nurse and your husband a minister means you live what you preach, or something like that. But there are plenty of minister couples in this city who don't foster anything except their own bank accounts." He looked away, shaking his head. "I shouldn't say that out loud. I apologize."

"That's all right," said Marceline, wondering if this man himself had foster children at home. On his desk was a photograph of a pair of boy twins. She wanted to ask if they were adopted but didn't.

"Here I am gabbing away, and you probably need to get back

to the hospital." He stood up. "Thank you, Mrs. Jones. And I know Agnes and her mother thank you. You'll have her sign the forms tonight and get them back to me tomorrow? Then I'll get the wheels moving to have your first check in the mail by the end of the month."

Marceline stood up and shook his outstretched hand. "You do good work here, Mr... ." She paused to look down at the nameplate on his crowded desk. "Mr. Jellyby. Thank you for your help."

Marceline arrived at the church that evening after her twelve-hour shift. She heard Jim's voice booming from the office behind the sanctuary. Two white couples, the Beams and the Cordells, were taking notes non-stop, and a large blonde woman sat by Jim's side, head bobbing perpetually in agreement. "Yes, Jim. Absolutely, Jim."

No one looked up when Marceline opened the door. She cleared her throat.

"Hi, honey," said Jim with a big smile. "Come sit down. We're talking press strategy about these KKK threats. Patty here thinks we can get some good publicity out of it for the church. Sympathetic articles might bring not only more members but maybe funds from some of the liberal groups around here wanting to look good."

The group laughed. "What liberal groups?" said one of the men, whose first name Marceline couldn't remember. They were all like-minded, these six people around the table, with Jim as their leader, urging them to do more and do better, partaking of his energy when they were too tired to continue. Jim often said he never got tired, and Marceline believed him.

At the doorway, she remained standing. Sometimes she felt out of place, as if she didn't belong in the circle of Jim's grace. It was crazy. She had started the church with him. Her name was on every document. Everything they'd done together since the day of their marriage nearly seven years before was a mutual effort, and Jim insisted on calling Wings of Deliverance "our" church. Yet the staff didn't recognize her as Jim's equal.

That's your own fault, Marceline, she chided herself. If she were here more often, that wouldn't be the case. But she had to work to support their family and the church. That had always been their plan, mutually agreed upon. Overtime pay at Indianapolis General was especially useful, and since they'd opened their doors, she worked six days a week. Consequently, she was not a fixture at Wings of Deliverance, though she made a point never to miss Sunday morning services. But she always felt comfortable with the congregation.

"Has Agnes's mom showed up yet?" she asked Jim. Instead of joining the meeting, Marceline decided to make herself a cup of tea and wait in the sanctuary.

Jim looked at Patty. "Has she?"

Flustered, Patty mumbled, "I don't know. We've been here for a couple of hours, and I haven't heard anyone come in. When was she supposed to get here?"

Marceline looked at her watch. "Fifteen minutes ago. Maybe she's running late. I hope so. You go ahead with your meeting. I'll be inside."

All heads turned back toward Jim, who immediately returned to the Klan threats, and how they might serve to build the church's till.

As she closed the door softly behind her and went to the kitchen, Marceline pondered the calls again. How did Jim know it really was the Klan? The Georgian hadn't identified himself. His words were harsh, but not bad enough to report to the police. At least Marceline didn't think so. Jim had taken most of the others.

Was he sure the Klan was involved and not just some garden-variety nuts who hated black people and hated whites who treated blacks as equals even more?

Jim still felt terrible guilt over his father's participation in the Lynn, Indiana chapter of the men in sheets. Was it true his father was a participant and not just a sympathizer? Sympathizers were legion in Indiana, where the Klan was said to have its most ardent supporters, especially back then.

She poured herself some tea and left the kettle on low so she could make Mrs. Clifton a cup when she arrived. Marceline wondered why she was questioning Jim's version of his father. His mother, Lynnetta, had confirmed the KKK stories about her late husband. She'd said he was a bitter man after his return from the trenches in France, that he spewed his hatred everywhere. Onto her and Jim, on to the blacks in Lynn and the Jews running the world's banks, et cetera, et cetera. Marceline wished she'd been able to meet James Jones, the elder. She didn't quite trust either of them to offer the straight truth on the subject.

Marceline took her tea into the sanctuary, seating herself in the pew nearest the door, contemplating. She and her sister had been brought up to tell the unvarnished truth. Lying was the worst sort of sin, her parents had repeated countless times in her childhood, and she'd absorbed the lesson well. But Jim had a more pragmatic approach to the truth. He liked to tell stories. Whichever version of a story would get the desired result was the version he told.

For reasons she couldn't quite articulate, Marceline didn't want to believe that her father-in-law could have joined the KKK. Maybe he said racist things, maybe he didn't like Jews, but actually joining the Klan and wearing a white hood, attacking black people? According to both Lynetta and Jim, the man wasn't well; surely he couldn't have participated in cross-burnings and the lynching that had happened outside of Lynn in 1919.

Mrs. Clifton suddenly burst in, a small woman in a light coat, followed by Agnes, a plain girl who looked around ten, her face downcast, dragging a small plaid suitcase.

"Mrs. Jones! He's gone off again! I left the boy with my neighbor till I get back, but I just can't take care of Agnes no more. She too ornery. Doesn't mind me and talks back. I just can't do it." The woman spoke not to Marceline or to the girl but to a place above Marceline's head.

"Please, Mrs. Clifton, sit down. You too, Agnes. I've got some tea warming in the kitchen. Would you like some?"

The girl nodded, but her mother shook her head. "I've got to get back to Earl. You have those papers for me to sign?"

Marceline smiled warmly at Agnes, who was almost twelve – her birthday was next week – though she was small for her age and slumped with straggly hair shielding her eyes. Marceline ached for the girl, who would never measure up in her mother's eyes compared to her adorable tow-headed little brother.

"I'll be right back."

Inside the kitchen, Patty was pouring instant coffee for Jim with the water Marceline had left on the burner.

"Oh, did you need this? I'm sorry," said the woman, her cheeks a bright pink. Marceline was sure Patty was infatuated with Jim. It wasn't unusual for a female staffer to develop a crush on Reverend Jones. He never encouraged them, or so he said, and eventually, the women calmed down. Jim said it came with the job, especially when the woman was also a parishioner he had counseled.

"That's all right," Marceline said. She would get the papers signed and usher Mrs. Clifton out, then she and Agnes could go home and have plenty of tea as well as a good dinner, which she was sure Agnes wouldn't have had tonight or most nights of her lonely life.

Agnes's mother signed the forms with such messy haste that Marceline wondered if Mrs. Clifton knew how to write.

"All right. You be good now, Agnes. You mind Mrs. Jones. Mind her better than you mind me." Mrs. Clifton stood up, still in her inadequate coat, and walked out into the night.

"Would you like to come home with me for some nice meatloaf and potatoes and carrots? I got it all ready before I left for work this morning. I was hoping you'd be having dinner with us tonight."

Agnes nodded. Her eyes brimmed but no tears fell. Her brown hair was unevenly cut around her shoulders, and her dress was too small.

"We'll have tea and cookies for dessert after dinner. Would you like that?"

The girl nodded again.

"Let's go then, sweetheart. I'm hungry!"

As Marceline gathered her things, Agnes finally spoke. "Isn't Pastor Jones coming with us?"

Without turning to face her, Marceline answered, "No, not tonight, honey. He's working. My husband works very, very hard, and sometimes he stays here quite late. So let's you and me go and eat a yummy meal! He'll have his later."

She took the girl's hand and covered it with her own gloved one, vowing to buy Agnes some mittens tomorrow. The wind battered them on the steps of Wings of Deliverance, but Marceline shielded her new daughter from the gusts, whispering into her ear, "Don't worry, sweetie. We'll take good care of you. You're safe now."

YOU DON'T KNOW HOW CLEVER I AM.
ONE THING YOU'VE ALL DONE IS
UNDERESTIMATE ME.

Jim Jones

Virgil Nascimento
11:37 p.m.
Nov. 18, 1981
Washington, D.C.

The last twenty-three minutes of this hateful anniversary lie ahead. Will we live through them? Detritus of Jonestown? Do we deserve to?

Again, Nancy calls me to bed where she lies with the changeling. Again, I put her off.

Dutch Guiana, French Guiana, Portuguese Guiana, Spanish Guiana, and British Guiana, before the name stood alone to symbolize its independence, becoming simply Guyana in 1966. Motto: *One People, One Nation, One Destiny*. It was never called West African Guyana, or Congolese Guyana, where the majority of the population came from as slaves. Then the British began their "enlightened slavery" of indentured servitude and shipped in the lighter-skinned East Indians.

The descendants of those indentured servants are now the majority, but neither has the country ever been called East Indian Guyana. Perhaps only white people have the audacity to name their conquests as they see fit. Like Jonestown. The city of Jones, though most of his followers looked nothing like him, with blacker skin than mine.

Nancy was greedy for my blackness, my authentic Guyanese heritage, my post as Minister in the great Co-operative Socialist Government of Forbes Burnham. I desired her whiteness, her

123

Americanness, and her youth. Though I already had a wife, we had led separate lives for years. Pru preferred to live in our flat in London, rather than the backwater our capital had become under "that fraud Burnham." That was one of her more civil terms for our leader. He was and remains my superior, responsible for all our financial successes, our multiple dwellings, and finely tailored wardrobes.

As the minutes tick by and I remain at this desk, still writing with my Mont Blanc fountain pen, I think we may yet survive this anniversary. But there's an envelope before me, from an acquaintance at the FBI, unopened, though I received it yesterday afternoon.

He has sent me a number of photocopied documents recovered from the ruins of Jonestown. Anything with Nancy's name on it was Xeroxed by his assistant.

"Verge," he said on the phone in his Southern drawl, "there's some upsetting stuff in there, but I figure it's your right to see. If my wife had been involved, I'd damn sure want to know. I haven't screened 'em. Good luck."

I am afraid to open it. Yet it is a wound that needs salt. He does not know I have come to hate my wife, my child, and myself. No doubt he will feel guilt if the information inside is deemed to be the trigger, but my mind is already made up.

You who read this will think that a man of my age and education should understand perfectly well that a fair American girl would have ulterior motives in wedging herself into my life in Georgetown, burrowing in like a termite in wood. And she got what she wanted. Information about Guyana and the World Bank, our relations to the Soviets. Later she pressed me for what we planned to do about the Concerned Relatives, those ex-Peoples Temple types and their family members who had begun to press for congressional interference, for someone to force open the gates of Jonestown and expose Jim Jones as a phony, a Machiavellian Prince or worse. I confess I wanted certain things from her in return for this information, and I got them. She did things Pru would never do, nor would I ever have asked her.

124

She was one of "Jim's political whores." At first, I refused to believe Nancy could be a member of such a group. But after the Event, it emerged that there were other Nancys, inspired by a love of Jim Jones that propelled them to do anything the Bishop Jones required of them. Including offering themselves to multiple members of the Prime Minister's circle to ferret out information that might aid the Peoples Temple.

The woman who killed her children and herself at Lamaha Gardens was the Queen of the Political Whores. Though ugly, she was athletic in bed, apparently. The trick was to make her stop talking.

I refused to include Nancy in that collection of naive female do-gooders who would slavishly follow a megalomaniac like Jim Jones to the foul end of mass murder. Not Nancy.

After the Event, Nancy clung to me as if I were her only salvation. Everyone she loved was dead, she said: the little girl Quiana, her husband, Jim and Marceline, whom she called Father and Mother, though she had and still has a real father and mother here in the United States. I see now she was grieving, not only for those who died, but for a system, a whole universe which had sustained her ever since she'd joined Peoples Temple in 1971, strung out on something or other. A college dropout, she longed to be part of a protest against her rich white heritage. She didn't understand that the campus protestors were rich white kids acting out their idealistic whims while the poor ones, white and black, went off to die in Vietnam.

Jones gave her a job as Temple Administrative Secretary, an impressive title for a girl who couldn't type. He trusted her with secrets, with safe deposit box keys and numbers of savings accounts in Zurich, Grand Cayman, and Panama. No one had ever trusted her like that before, when she was known as a "flaky fucked-up druggie" by family and friends. By the time I met her, she was sophisticated, sober, and multi-lingual, perfectly equipped to charm a Guyanese official out of his pants on our first date.

After the Event, she was desperate to hang onto something,

someone, so I married her. Pru even encouraged me: "I know you want a few little Virgil Nascimentos so they might go on populating the heights of Georgetown society. To send to Oxford in your footsteps. I'm sure she's fertile and would be happy to make babies with you after all she's lost."

Pru got the London flat, the silver Mercedes and of course the shares of bauxite her father had given her upon our marriage, which she has managed so expertly after all these years. We have not communicated since our divorce in 1979. Always, Pru was embarrassed by my excesses, but never was she surprised.

Perhaps if I wait until a new day, until the 19th, the contents of this envelope will not hurt us, but I cannot wait, because I know what I will find within.

Deus salva ela.

Sheaves of letters from Georgetown to Jonestown.

Nearly every day, she wrote him. Neat, typewritten, single-spaced letters dated and placed with when and where she wrote.

After our sessions in bed, she wrote him.

While I was in the shower, she wrote him.

While I was playing poker, she wrote him.

I didn't know the meaning of the word "insecure" until I met Virgil. This country's in trouble if he's typical, which I believe to be the case.

Do I laugh? She calls me insecure? She who needs a man to suck up to or off so that she can remember who she is? She who couldn't live a day without praise from "Dad." Then called on me to fill in – literally – where the Emperor Jones no longer deigned to fill.

My initial desire to do a good job is getting thwarted by the repulsion.

She was repulsed by me. How dare she? She insisted I watch her give birth to that creature, who emerged amid the blood and shit, wanting me to witness that act and she without shame. She who keeps suckling that boy as if he were a piglet. How dare she call me repulsive? I should put this envelope away, or better yet, burn it. These snippets are the tiniest fraction of what she wrote, random phrases which catch my eye as I shuffle the pages and pages of photocopies. I have a mind to shove them in her face, to make her eat her words.

Nancy, you don't understand what repulsive is. That thing you call our son. His cadaverous pale skin has nothing to do with me. The slack, soft hair. How wrong Pru was to imagine a son who'd be my double. He is as white as a ghost, as death incarnate, though I can't deny a resemblance to my father.

Dear Jim: he keeps proposing marriage. I really don't know what to say: encourage, discourage, indifferent. Please advise!

Cons:
not allowed to go anywhere except approved by him
no long distance or overseas calls
severance of activities with PT
jealous possessiveness
non-acceptance of my daughter
not allowed to travel without him
brunt of irrational temper tantrums
possible child

Pros:
contacts with Guy. and US government officials.
Endorsement of PT by union of marriage

She wrote him this list in October of 1978.

Pity we don't have the Emperor's response.

What did he tell her, I wonder? Would he have put "possible child" under "con" as she did, he who made babies with as many concubines as possible? He who practiced Svengali-like control over not one woman but dozens? Let me not forget the men as well.

Only a few months later she was on her knees begging me to divorce Pru and take her back with me to Washington.

"Possible child" indeed. It was she who threw away her pills. She who said she wanted a whole world of babies who looked exactly like me, only she wanted them born in the United States. So they could later choose their own citizenship, she said.

She will die for this, this perfidy, regret with her last breath this "possible child."

How I hate them both. How I want to drink but I shall resist, keeping myself concentrated for the act to follow, lest anyone dispute my intention.

The word "love" doesn't appear anywhere here, though she told me she loved me a dozen times a day. How is it possible I was so conned as to divorce old Pru, who shared my background, my mother country, and an understanding of how things work. How they worked. Before the Event.

Nancy charmed me from my senses. From my pants and from my proper perspective. None of my confrere ministers married their Jonestown whores. Only Virgil Nascimento, the fool who confused his penis with his brain.

Ever since the Ghost was born, I find her repulsive. Heir of Jones. Air of Jones. It was his baby she wanted after all, and his she got.

The destiny of Jones will be hers as well. And the child's. And mine. You cannot separate Guyana from Jonestown anymore.

Since our return to the States, she hates going anywhere, hates being out in the world of American human beings for that very reason, fearing she might overhear someone talking about her lord and leader in disparaging tones. That bastard. Her lover, who initiated her into the upper management circle with his dick.

"That maniac, Jim Jones."

That's what people call him in the aftermath of the Event. Some of the dead probably shared an ancestor or two with me and my mother. Some slaves came south to Guyana from New Orleans, others went to the Deep South of this country, and generations later, headed west to California searching for the good life. Instead, they found Jim Jones. Ended up back in the jungle, murdered by a Marxist white overseer. Some of the overseers were black though. Like Mac. I drank good bourbon with him when I visited their San Francisco headquarters in 1976. The Reverend's right-hand man of color. The one heard insisting on the death tape that a better life awaited in the next world. Reincarnation must have been easy to sell to those old black slave descendants: heaven waiting on the other side of Jordan, the Kaituma river.

Bourbon. I want it. Would it help or hinder? Whiskey would make me feel strong. But I do not want to be a drunken murderer. I must remain sober, despite my reputation as a diplomat who appreciates an open bar more than most.

Since the Event, bourbon doesn't taste as good. After the Ghost was born, Charlayne said I'd start feeling better. She said something beautiful would come of all this. My son. Nearly fifty years old without an heir apparent, and now I have one, whom I refuse to recognize. Not a bastard, though perhaps I created a few of those over the decades, of whose existence I never learned. Charlayne said the Ghost was the spit and image of me. The whiteness in mixed race children is supposed to wear off after a while. She told me they were born light so you could check for jaundice, and then they grew into their true color. But it hasn't happened with the Ghost. White as a pig, as a Ku Klux Klan sheet, as a sarcophagus. Repulsive.

Amongst the circle of whores, only that witch died on November 18th, and not of poison, but by her own hand, her knife, slitting the throats of her three children. I once had a drink with the father of the older girl here in DC. He was one of the Concerned Relatives. Jewish like her mother, though he was a secular Jew. Like Nancy I suppose, though her only true religion has been the worship of Emperor Jones. The poor man had lunch with his daughter on the very day, the 18th, before her mother got the signal from God on the radio to kill and to die.

Will I be any different from that ugly bitch if I kill my offspring?

She had no right to kill those adopted black children. Her own blood, maybe, but again and again, white slaughters black. Not on the killing fields of colonial glory but rather upon a tiled bathroom floor at 41 Lamaha Gardens. Nancy found them. She called me here after she discovered the bodies. She said the word then. Love. She begged me to keep on loving her, despite this terrible thing that had happened.

Before the Event, I was repulsive because I wasn't Jim Jones. But when Jim and his Empire were gone, suddenly she "loved" me. The Empire included the baby girl from Oakland, California, who was a foster child they'd taken along for a monthly check. The foster children were part of the Peoples Temple PR policy, "rescuing" all those poor black people. The lie makes me want to vomit. Father Divine in whiteface. But Father Divine never killed anyone. Father Divine fed the hungry during the Depression. He may have driven fancy cars and lived high on the hog, but he never took a needle to anyone, or forced a poisoned fruit drink down a thousand mouths.

The Emperor sucked the souls from all those black bodies but refused to go down alongside them, as his wife did. He took the easy way, the American-blast-your-brains out way.

Like him, so shall I.

Now I shall be "repulsive" in the same way as the Emperor Jones.

"Mother Marceline" died of poison, but I still ask myself how she, a nurse, and those other nurses and the Jew doctor, the one they were so proud of, how could they do it? They calculated the doses for three different syringes. One color for infants, one for children, another for adults. Not Kool-Aid, but Fla-Vor-Aid. I believe in getting the details right. Which would my son get if he were there right now? Which did Nancy's tiny daughter have forced upon her?

"It's just a little bitter tasting," he says on the tape. They're not crying because they're in pain, he reassures those who are listening to the screams of the dying, but because it is bitter. Just a little bitter.

WHEN YOUR GOD HAS FAILED YOU,
I'LL STILL BE WITH YOU.
I WILL NEVER LEAVE YOU.
I WILL NEVER FORSAKE YOU.
I WILL NEVER LET YOU DOWN.
NOT ONCE.

Jim Jones

Truth Miller
March 16, 1995
Tenderloin District, San Francisco

After reading the letter once, Truth called to her son, Cuffy, who was now six years old, in the next room. "Let's take a ride, babe."

"What kind of ride? A bike ride?" Cuffy had been playing chess by himself while looking out the window onto Mason Street. The sun was out, the street busy, the world inviting.

"Nope. Cable car, to start with. Then we'll go from there."

"But where're we going?" Cuffy was a very precise person who liked to know exactly what his mother's plans were so that she wouldn't deviate from them midway through, which she often did.

"City tour." Truth gathered light jackets for them both, put water and snacks in a battered gray knapsack, the same one she had taken to Guyana when she met the father of her only child, awaiting her on the dock at Port Kaituma. "Let's see. You can take your little magnet chess set if you want. We're gonna take a lot of buses."

"Why? Why can't I ride my bike? It's so nice out." Although Cuffy had lived in this railroad flat in the Tenderloin his entire life, he loved being outside. There were no trees on his block, not one blade of grass, but when he was younger, he had liked running up and down the sidewalk, and now he preferred to bike his two-wheeler back and forth in front of the flat. He didn't mind cold or rain or fog, but Truth did. She was very protective, and unless she also wanted to sit outside and watch him, he had to stay inside.

"We're going too far for it to be a bike ride."

"Where exactly are we going?" Cuffy knew his city geography from the innumerable "city tours" his mother had taken him on over the years. They had no car, but with a Municipal Railway pass, she had shown him nearly every corner of every district in the city, and some of the East Bay too. "Couldn't I take my bike for part of it? I could ride next to the bus while you're on it."

Snorting, Truth raised her eyebrows at him. "Honey, you're out of your mind. You know I wouldn't let you do that in a million years. It's totally unsafe. Okay, here's the plan. We're going to the Fillmore first. And then down to State. After that, I'm not sure. C'mon. Let's go."

Outside, various passersby waved hello to the pair. Cuffy was one of few children on this block, which was populated mostly by old people or prostitutes. In recent years some Eastern European and former Soviet Union refugee families had moved in, living five or more to a room.

"How's chess?" asked Vladimir, the old Muscovite who combed their block daily for aluminum cans and had taught Cuffy how to play when he was barely five. As always, he touched the top of Cuffy's curly hair as if it were a talisman. This gesture irritated Truth. White people always wanted to touch black people's hair. Once she'd asked Vladimir not to do it, but his English was so limited he didn't understand or pretended not to. Though the habit continued to bother her, she let the matter go when she saw how much her son liked the old man. They would sit on the stoop, playing chess for hours while she read beside them, keeping one eye on Vladimir just to be perfectly sure he didn't have any nasty ideas. As a single mother, she was ever alert for men who were "too friendly."

"*Karashaw,*" said Cuffy, who already knew more Russian than Truth. In Jonestown, the Peoples Temple had been studying Russian in preparation for a possible move to the Soviet Union, which of course never materialized. Since Truth had been working at the

Geary office those last years of the Temple's existence, she hadn't learned more than a few words of it. For a time, she did refer to herself as comrade, or *tovaricha*, as did many in the inner circle, even those who stayed in the United States, but after the End, such vocabulary seemed foolish.

They walked down Powell toward the cable car turnaround on Market Street. Even though Truth disliked tourists, she liked to watch Cuffy enjoying the street performers who congregated there to entertain for money. The captive audience of strangers had likely never seen some of the odder San Francisco live shows, like the gilded statue, a person of indeterminate gender who would paint him or herself silver or gold and assume a position for hours on end. Buddha one day, Rodin's "Thinker" the next. The person could remain still as stone for so long that sometimes Truth wondered if it were healthy. Once or twice she asked herself if the performer had figured out some very clever way of substituting a real statue while he or she went off for the day, and the bowl in front of the statue filled to overflowing with crisp and crumpled bills, anchored by heaps of coins in various currencies.

"I wonder who he'll be today," said Cuffy, his grin twitching with anticipation as they neared the turnaround, where a long line snaked up toward them. Behind dozens of tourists, they joined the end of the queue. "Mom, can I go see?"

"No, you cannot." She shook her head. "It's too far from here. When we get closer, you can go look, as long as I can keep my eye on you." She held his hand tightly as they surveyed the people in front and behind them.

She could hear Minnesota accents, French, Texan drawls, and an African language she couldn't decipher emanating from the nearby crowd.

"What's that?" asked Cuffy, listening intently as a man in a turban walked by, speaking to another similarly clad older man. "Indian?"

"There isn't really a language called Indian. It could be Hindi, but I'm not sure."

Cuffy stared after the two men. "I like their hats. Could I get a hat like that?"

"They're called turbans. I suppose they could be Muslims, not Hindus. Maybe Sikhs." Did Muslims speak Hindi? Truth felt ashamed of her ignorance. She ought to know. She had learned in the Peoples Temple of the ever-present and usually subconscious condescension of white people to those of color, especially the assumption that the latter were all the same. She too had grown up in that ignorance. Her parents never tried to correct it. "In Guyana, a lot of people worship the Hindu gods like Shiva and Kali. People who originally came from India."

"To Guyana? But Guyana's in South America!" Cuffy knew a few things about the country of his birth father, information his mother was always happy to share. But she wouldn't say much about the actual man. He didn't even know his father's name.

"Yes, sweetie. But the British, you know, the Evil Empire before ours, they shipped all these East Indians to Guyana to pick sugar cane."

"Like slaves?"

"A lot like slaves. They were called indentured servants, which was basically the same thing. Supposedly they could pay back their ship fare and then be free. Only the plantation owners ripped them off for food and shelter, so they never could get enough ahead of their debts to buy their freedom."

"Like us?"

Truth laughed. "No. Not like us. We're not badly off, honey. Mommy gets health insurance from the city and a salary we manage to live on, right?"

"But then how come you're always saying we can't afford it, whenever I ask for something?"

She messed his hair, which was very like her own, only his curls were tighter and brown where hers were loose and white. "I mean, compared to plantation workers, we're pretty well off. Do you know, when I lived in a commune in the Temple, we had an allowance of two dollars a week?"

His jaw fell. "But that's what you give me, and I'm only in first grade!"

The line was moving now as the cable car on Market turned and began to load passengers. She knew Cuffy would rather wait for the next car so he could watch the performers, and she wasn't in a great hurry. It was Saturday, and the letter in her pocket would surely require multiple readings over the course of this day before she was ready to decide how to respond.

The living statue was painted copper today, standing in a position resembling something from an Egyptian papyrus, shoulders front with head in profile, feet turned in the same direction as the head.

"Wow!" Cuffy walked around the statue-person, thrilled at the new color and enactment. "How does he do that?" he called to his mother, who was now letting other passengers enter the cable car while she retained her place at the front of the line and kept her eye on Cuffy.

"C'mere!" she shouted, annoyed.

Reluctantly, he joined her. "What?"

"First, you shouldn't talk about him as if he wasn't there when you're standing right next to him. It's rude. It's like how people talk about the lousy service in a restaurant right in front of the waiter. And second, we don't know if it's a man. It could be a woman. It's hard to tell."

Cuffy shook his head. "Mom. It's obviously a man. Look at his chest."

"There are women with really small breasts like that. He's so petite. I mean, he or she is so petite."

Cuffy snorted. "Mom, it's not a girl! He doesn't have a shirt on! Can I go back and look?"

"All right. Only stay where I can see you, and don't talk about him in the third person. I mean, don't say 'he' when he's right next to you."

She watched as another child, roughly Cuffy's age, joined him in circling the gilded statue-person. When the other kid, a white girl with light brown hair and eyes, went to touch the statue, Cuffy pulled her hand back and whispered something. She could just imagine what he was saying: "Don't do that while my mom's looking. She never lets me touch him."

Truth looked around for whoever was with the girl, and spotted a middle-aged man perusing the newspaper while he surveyed his daughter. They weren't waiting for the cable car but seemed to be stopping on a walk up or down Market Street. As she watched the girl and Cuffy now running in circles around the statue, she thought she recognized something in that girl, something that reminded her of herself. She wanted to tell the kids to stop running, but she didn't want to lose her place in line, and the street noise was pitched at too high a volume for her to shout. Just then the father went over to the kids and apparently told them to stop, for they did. After Cuffy pointed at Truth, the man came toward her.

"That's your boy?"

She nodded.

"He's a sweetie. They seem to like each other. How old?"

"Six."

"Mine too. Just had her birthday last week." While he paused to read the headlines on his folded newspaper, she studied him. Business suit. Tie. Balding. The kind of guy she used to assume was a racist, capitalist monster on appearance alone. Lately, she had begun to reserve judgment on strangers, a new experience for her, something she was learning from her son.

"What's her name?"

"Anna."

Truth gasped. The name was the same as That Woman's mother, who had died of cancer at Jonestown, before the End, and it was That Woman the girl reminded her of. Hair, complexion, eyes.

She hadn't thought about That Woman in a while, actually, as the life of the Temple receded while Cuffy's life and needs grew larger. But that was silly. Anna was a common name.

"And what's your son's name?"

"Cuffy."

Usually, his name elicited a long discussion. Either she would explain that he was named after the great slave rebel of Guyana in the eighteenth century, and then she'd have to offer that her son was half Guyanese, and then she'd have to say where Guyana was, because everybody thought it was in Africa, and since Cuffy had terracotta skin, they assumed he was African. Which he was, by way of the slave trade to the east coast of South America. Or else she would say it was a "family name," which cut off the questions and was true in a non-blood, chosen-family sort of way.

"Hmm. Unusual. I know that name from somewhere." The man looked into her eyes; he was about her height and age, and behind his wire-framed glasses his hazel eyes searched with sympathetic curiosity. "And what's very odd is that you look a lot like my wife."

"What's odder is I think I know your wife." Truth hesitated. She had never referred to That Woman by name ever since the latter had defected just a few months before the End, and went off to warn everybody, including the FBI and State Department, that mass suicide was planned by Jones and the leadership, though nobody took her seriously, except Leo Ryan.

For years, Truth had blamed her for instigating the suicides, for sending the congressman to investigate Jonestown, which had in turn led to the murder of Ryan and the crew of reporters, which then led to the Peoples Temple membership assuming that the compound would be stormed by the Guyanese military and that it would be more noble to die than to fight, especially since the Guyanese army was black and basically stooges for American capitalist interests. But now, nearly twenty years later, she wasn't so certain of this interpretation of events.

"You know Susan? From the bank?"

Truth laughed. "No. Not from the bank. Is that where she works now? I think I heard that from someone."

"Oh." The man's eyes narrowed. "So you know her from before. Were you in the Temple?"

Truth nodded.

The man sighed. "I'm Alan, by the way. Alan Friedman. And you are?"

She hesitated. "Well, Susan probably remembers me, but I'm sure she doesn't like me."

He shook his head. "She's not like that. Really. She doesn't hold grudges. But I won't tell her we ran into you if you don't want me to." He looked away from Truth and regarded their children, who were sitting cross-legged on the ground near the statue; Cuffy was showing Anna his palm-sized chess set.

"National hero of Guyana, right? Paul Cuffy." He smiled at her.

"You have got to be the first and only person I've ever met not from the Temple who knew who Cuffy was."

"Well, I suppose I'm a member by association. Or former member. Or apostate maybe."

Just as Truth was thinking, "or traitor," Alan added, "Or traitor. I know that's what a lot of people call Susan. You know, she really wanted to save people."

Truth blinked. "But she didn't."

"No." Alan looked into Truth's eyes. "Though not for lack of trying. She lives with a lot of guilt about it every day. She's getting closer to forgiving herself. I mean, she did everything she could to save those people. Were you there? In Georgetown, I mean?"

"No. I never went over. Jim didn't let me." She wanted to say more but stopped herself.

"You're lucky."

Truth didn't respond.

"You know, Susan lost her mother there, a couple of sisters-in-law, or ex-sisters-in-law, and you know all about her brother."

"Yes."

Another cable car rolled down the tracks, and the conductor pushed it with his back and shoulders across the turnaround.

"I know who you are!" He smiled. "Susan's told me about you, mostly because people used to get you two confused."

Truth was surprised. She was used to being taken for Susan but had never considered that others might take Susan for her. Susan had been very high up in the inner circle, at Jim's right hand. That's why her defection had so disturbed him. Perhaps more than anyone else's. And her brother was Jim's sycophantic male adorer, who had pretended to defect with the others on November 18th, only he took a gun into the plane and started shooting, failing to kill anyone because his gun had malfunctioned. Still, he went to prison for years.

"You're Truth."

Truth winced. It sounded a little silly, being called Truth. Who knew what Truth was, anyway? Truth was relative. She had given her son a proud, strong name, a heroic name with a history. Truth was nobody's name, just an idea. An idea of Jim Jones. An idea her eighteen-year-old self thought was terrific. "We're going to take this cable car, Alan."

He smiled. "Okay, Truth. I'm glad we met. It was nice to see our children get along, don't you think? No sins of the fathers for them, huh? Sins of the mothers would be more accurate, I guess."

She frowned. Truth supposed he meant to be funny, but his remark disturbed her. "Cuffy! C'mon, we're going now!" she called as the people in line began to gather their belongings. "Cuffy!"

Alan bowed a little. "Maybe we could get the kids together again sometime. Here's my card. So long." He walked off toward the statue and collected his daughter, who turned to wave at her, and they headed east toward the Bay, hands held. Just as the conductor gestured for people to board, Cuffy arrived by her side.

"You know what that girl said?"

"Anna, her name is Anna."

"Yeah, anyway, you know what she said?"

"What did she say?" They managed to get their favorite seats

141

on the rear right banquette, where no one would obstruct their view of the world.

"She said the statue was magic. That it wasn't a boy or a girl. Like a fairy."

When Cuffy said fairy, he pronounced it "ferry," which always made Truth smile. San Francisco had plenty of fairies and ferries; either pronunciation worked.

"Do you agree?"

Cuffy nodded vigorously. "Don't you? It's the perfect solution!" Then he was distracted by a clown walking by with many balloons and pointed. "Mom! Could I get one? Please? Pretty Please with sugar on it?"

"Saved by the bell," she said, as the conductor rang to signal to the brakeman, and the car lurched into motion. Then Cuffy saw something even more interesting on the sidewalk and promptly forgot about the balloon. She took the letter from her back pocket, unfolded it, and read.

Dear Elizabeth,

We haven't seen you in so long. We haven't seen Cuffy since he was born. We want you to come visit us. Soon. Your mother isn't well, and I'm not doing so hot either. Will you come? We'll buy your plane tickets. It would mean a lot to your mother, and to me of course too. I want to see my grandson again before I die. I'm not saying I'm planning on dying next week, but it turns out I have cancer. And I finally got your mother to the doctor to have that shaking looked at – do you remember? You noticed that her hands trembled when we visited you after Cuffy was born. She has Parkinson's. Growing old is no fun, believe me, but we're not complaining. Anyway, there's some things we want to talk to you about, and not on the phone. It's too complicated to write it all down in a letter. So, please. Make a reservation and I'll send you a check to cover it.

I want to see my grandson again before I die, and of course I want to see you too.

See you soon, Elizabeth.

Your dad.

"Who's that from?"

"Your grandfather."

Cuffy tried to read it. "Why does it say Dear E … Eliza …?"

She folded it back into the envelope, which she stowed deep in the gray knapsack. "You know my real name is Elizabeth. I mean, the one I was born with."

"No, I didn't." He was smiling, excited by his mother's revelation of such a juicy secret.

"I've told you before. You just forgot."

"There's an Elizabeth in my class. She's nice."

Truth grunted. It had taken forever to get people to call her Truth; she didn't want her son to make her name an issue. "Grandpa usually calls me Truth. He must have forgot." She paused. "He's not well."

"What do you mean?"

"He has cancer."

"What's that?"

"It's a really bad sickness. Sometimes it can kill you."

"I wish I had it." Cuffy looked gleeful.

"No, you don't. That's a horrible thing to say."

"I didn't mean it. So, is he going to be all right?"

"I don't know."

"Are they going to come visit?"

"They want us to go to New Jersey." She frowned. "I hate it there."

"Oh please? Can we go? I want to ride on a plane. You've ridden on planes. Why can't I?"

"Honey, it's not so simple."

Above Chinatown, they got off the cable car to wait for an

143

electric bus to take them west to the Fillmore. It was a route they'd traveled many times, when Truth had described what her life had been like before Cuffy entered it. He didn't seem to believe there had even been life before he arrived.

"What are we going to do in the Fillmore? Stare at the place where the Temple used to be?"

"I don't like your tone, Mister. That Temple was very important to me."

"Like, a hundred years ago."

She shrugged. "There's the bus coming."

They got on, and the bus eventually descended from the heights, where wealthy people had fancy flats and freshly painted Victorian mansions, down to the flatlands, where what had once been acres and acres of decrepit buildings were now gentrified co-op apartments. Gay men seemed to be everywhere, always first to move into the inner city and fix it up so that blacks couldn't afford the rents anymore. Truth sighed deeply; the only thing that seemed to have changed since 1978 was that gay people were no longer oppressed. At least in San Francisco.

When the bus driver called out "Japantown, next stop Japantown," they both rose.

"Mom, this is so boring. Can't we go into Japantown instead? I've never even been there, and we're always so close whenever we come here."

She steered him down the stairs and up the block toward Geary. The Temple building had been destroyed in the 1989 earthquake, and low-rise office buildings had taken its place. There really was nothing to look at, but she had to stand there, on the sidewalk where she'd once spent years of her life. She had been so full of purpose, even sleeping there in the days when she worked like a maniac. She closed her eyes, trying to sense Jim's spirit, which sometimes lingered here, but felt nothing. There was no point in hanging around.

"Okay, are you done?"

She wanted to smack him. "Cuffy! This place is part of your history. A big part. You probably wouldn't even be here if not for the Temple."

"Big deal. Can we go to Japantown now?"

"I don't like that place. It's so fake."

"Why? We go to Chinatown all the time."

"I know. But Chinatown is where real people live and have lived for a long time. Japantown is some architect's creation. It's for tourists."

"So what? I heard they have a really neat fountain."

"Who told you that?"

"Midori. Her father has a store there."

"She's probably filthy rich."

"Who cares? I like her. She's one of my friends at recess. Could we go see her? She told me she usually spends Saturdays at the store."

"Do you know which store?"

"Opposite the fountain. Thanks, Mom!"

She smiled ruefully. Cuffy often managed to get his way. She realized she had never been very good at opposition. Not with the neighbor boys who wanted her titties, not with Jim, who wanted her energy, and not with Cuffy, who basically wanted her love. This giving in was different than the others, she told herself; this was appropriate.

Japantown made her eyes hurt. Just as she'd always suspected, it was full of rich people. Not only rich white people, but lots of rich Asians too. She remembered how Jim would talk about how the Japanese had been put into what he called concentration camps – yes, they were concentrations of Japanese people, but they weren't extermination camps like they were in Germany, not what he said would happen to black people in the United States. In Jonestown, he'd terrified the elderly blacks, insisting the KKK was marching down the streets of Los Angeles. She looked around. No black people here except Cuffy, who was running in circles around the fountain, now joined by a little girl who had run out from a fancy store featuring silk kimonos and other shiny articles of clothing. A silver-haired man ran out behind her, yelling in Japanese.

"It's okay," Truth called to him. "They're in school together. Cuffy wanted to say hi to Midori since we were nearby."

The man looked at her suspiciously. "Who are you?"

"I'm Cuffy's mother. They're both in first grade; he and Midori play at recess."

"Okay. You watch them. I go back to my customers."

When he said, "Who are you," did it mean that she couldn't possibly be Cuffy's mother? Or did he mean, who are you, as in, I've never seen you before? Hard to tell.

With her eye on the children, Truth made her way over to his store. It was so expensive there were no prices anywhere, a sure sign of a place exclusively reserved for the excessively rich. She frowned. Yet Midori and Cuffy were playing the chase game like old friends. She wondered if Cuffy, like her, was always attracted to what was different, rather than what was alike. Then again, there were only a few black girls in his grade, and their names came up sometimes, but not as often as Midori's.

An African couple came out of the store with shopping bags full of purchases. The woman smiled at her, pointing to the display. "Beautiful kimonos, no? We can't get these in Togo."

Flustered, Truth nodded, then shook her head. "Oh. I suppose so. I mean, I suppose not. Hello."

The very tall man and woman, dressed in brightly patterned boubous, smiled again and then walked off. Clearly, they had plenty of money and were not worrying about the high cost of shopping at Midori's father's store.

After his customers had departed, Midori's father re-appeared. "Good afternoon. Forgive me for rudeness before. I am Yoshi. And your name is …?"

"Truth. Truth Miller."

"Ah. Mrs. Miller. I am glad to meet you. Midori is always

talking about your son. Cuffy this. Cuffy that. They like each other a great deal, I think."

He, too, was an older parent. So old he looked like he probably had grandchildren. Truth assumed Midori was the product of a late second marriage.

"Do you have other children, Yoshi?

"No. Just Midori. My wife and I try very, very hard without luck, and finally we receive our gift, just after we have given up."

So, Truth was wrong. Again. "Had you considered adopting?"

"Like you?"

She frowned. "No. Not like me. Cuffy is my natural child."

"Ah. I see."

But he looked a little confused. Surely, if he would study their faces, he would see that she and Cuffy had the same eyebrows and nose, but most people saw only skin color. To most, skin color was everything, the only thing. Truth was sure no one ever assumed he had adopted his daughter.

"Excuse me. I have things to attend to inside."

She nodded. Despite persecution during World War II, and the fact that the Japanese had suffered mightily from the dropping of the atom bomb, she had never felt pity for them. The Japanese had joined the Germans, and though they were Asian, like the Nazis they seemed to believe they were superior to all other humans. The Japanese had enslaved Korean women and devastated China, all in the name of their superiority. Sighing, she chided herself for condemning all Japanese people, as if Midori and her father were among the guilty of fifty years ago. They weren't.

"Mom. Watch this!"

Cuffy and Midori were now doing cartwheels around the fountain. Midori was better at them and could perform in perfect parallel to the edge. But Cuffy was more spontaneous and less accurate. His second cartwheel caught his right leg on the low cement wall of the fountain, and before she could yell "watch out!" he was down.

"Baby!" She ran to his side.

"I'm okay, Mom." Cuffy was sitting up, rubbing the side of his leg. "Good thing I was wearing jeans, though."

She pulled up the material; his skin was chafed but not bleeding.

"Let me put something on it," she said, though she didn't have anything with her.

"Nah. I'm okay. Hey, Midori! Can you do three in a row? I can." And he was off again.

Shaking her head, she sat down on the edge of the fountain, hoping her presence there would prevent a repeat injury, and pulled out the letter, re-reading her father's neat print. *Make a reservation and I'll send a check. I want to see you and my grandson before I die.*

Did he want her to feel sorry for them? They were old. They had lived long, healthy lives. She hated the thought of returning to New Jersey. Since she'd left at eighteen, Truth hadn't been back, despising the nauseating sameness of suburbia that had formed her, a monotony she'd spent a lifetime rejecting. Her parents hadn't suffered the way the old people in the Temple had. They were white. They were middle class, though not wealthy, like some of the white families other members had left behind. They weren't educated, like the lawyer and academic types who populated the inner circle. For a moment, she wondered if Jim found her less useful to him for her relative lack of privilege. She'd never thought of that before. Was that why he hadn't slept with her? Because she could offer him nothing of status? Because there was no advantage to her being his lover, in comparison with Jocelyn, for instance? She didn't like that idea, not at all.

"Cuffy! Let's go. We did what you wanted to, and now we're going to State, like I wanted to."

"Mom. Not yet! I'm hungry. I'm thirsty."

Just as she was getting the snacks out of her bag, Midori was pulling Cuffy behind her toward Truth. "Mrs. Miller? Can you come into my father's store? We have plenty of food in back."

Truth wanted to say no. She wanted to get away from here,

from the thoughts she'd been having, but Cuffy said "Please? Pretty please? I like Japanese food. Sometimes I share Midori's sushi at lunch."

"You never told me that."

Reluctantly, she let her son pull her into the store. Separated from the retail area by a silk tapestry was a kitchen area on the left and storage on the right. After opening a small refrigerator, Midori arranged several California rolls on a red enamel tray.

"Yummy!" said Cuffy, rubbing his belly and smiling hugely at Midori.

Truth shook her head. So Cuffy liked to eat seaweed! She never had. She would try it, though, to be polite. It was funny to her that Cuffy had this other life she knew little about, the life of a first grader in a multicultural public school in a big city of the 1990s. It was nothing like the life she had known in 1950s New Jersey, a life she had preferred to forget. Whenever her son asked about her own first grade experience, she had to say, truthfully, that she didn't remember. Truth had willfully suppressed most of her life prior to meeting Jim Jones.

Midori's father entered the room and said something in Japanese to his daughter.

"Can I get you anything, Mrs. Miller? Cuffy?"

She shook her head. "Your daughter is quite the hostess." She wasn't sure she meant it as a compliment, but the man beamed. "Yes! This is very important in our culture. Excuse me. I wish I could sit with you, but I have new customers."

The children were eating sushi off the tray with chopsticks and talking about their teachers and classmates. Truth sampled one and nearly spit it out. If she were alone, she would have said, "Yuck!" but she said nothing and instead sipped the water Midori had set before her. Perhaps she would not insist on going all the way to State after all.

Her new doubts about Jim buzzed in her brain like trapped honeybees. Against her better judgment, she began to list all his lovers, and the status each had brought to him: Jocelyn had the big-deal minister father, whose praise he courted, whom Jim thought would confer legitimacy on the Temple. Sean's mother, the first major traitoress, had an Ivy League lawyer husband, an inner-circle chief who seemed to think Jim was God up until the day he himself defected. Privately, Truth had wondered if Jim really wanted the lawyer but settled for the wife instead. Their child had died at Jonestown. And That Woman, Susan, was a big-deal rich Jew, whose mother, Anna, had given the Temple tons of money. A quarter-million in properties. It felt awful to think this way about a man who had worn thrift-shop clothes all his life and driven second-hand cars when he could have been like the Bhagwan, with twenty-eight Rolls Royces, or Moon, with his mansions all over the world. No, Jim wasn't into money. It was just coincidence, all these women with connections who caught his eye and shared his bed. She flushed, angry with herself for reviving petty jealousies of long ago.

"Hey, Mom. Hello?"

"Don't say hey," Truth said automatically. "It's rude." She wondered where that had come from, then remembered her mother saying it to her, and suddenly she could picture her mother and father and herself at breakfast in their little kitchen, eating eggs and white toast, the room the size of this one, big enough for a table, three chairs, a fridge and stove and that was about all. "What?"

"You weren't listening! I was saying that Midori's been on a plane."

"Six times!" said Midori proudly. "We go to Japan every year to see our relatives. It's a long trip, but I love flying."

"You're a lucky girl, Midori. But you know, flying is expensive."

As she spoke, Truth realized that money was not what kept her from visiting her own family. She was lying not only to Cuffy but to herself. And her father had offered to pay.

"Mom, why can't we go visit *our* relatives? I've never been on a plane," he said sorrowfully to his friend, who nodded knowingly.

"Well, I'd never been on a plane at your age either," Truth retorted. She didn't like how Cuffy was acting like some deprived child just because he hadn't flown by the age of six.

"Please Mom? You said Grandpa was sick. I've never even met him."

"You did meet him. He and Grandma came to see you when you were born."

"But I don't remember! It's not fair. Midori goes every year all the way to Japan. Japan is much farther than New Jersey."

"How do you know?"

"I've seen them on the map. At school we have this huge world map, and everyone writes their names on places where they have family."

"And you wrote New Jersey?"

"Yup. And Guyana too."

She shook her head, amazed by the way Cuffy accepted the circumstances of his life in stride. He didn't judge everything like she did. Truth had always been unwilling to accept the world as it was. She was distrustful and always assumed people were lying. Cuffy must be more like his father, she thought, if trusting people were something that could be passed on in the blood.

"Maybe."

"Maybe what?" Midori and Cuffy spoke simultaneously.

"Jinx!" they shouted.

"Double jinx! Triple jinx! Quadruple jinx!" Both laughed loudly. She loved the way Cuffy laughed, with his entire body. It made her feel good, as if she must be doing something right. She could never remember laughter in her childhood, not her own, not her parents'.

"Maybe we'll go visit your grandparents."

"When?"

"Soon. Maybe spring break."

"That's next month!" Cuffy's eyes sparkled as he looked at Midori. "I'm going on a plane! I'm going on a plane," he sing-songed the words the way kids did when they were excited.

"I guess we're going on a plane," Truth said aloud.

WHY ARE THERE HUNGRY CHILDREN
IF THERE IS A GOD?
WHAT'S YOUR GOD EVER DONE?
TWO OUT OF THREE BABIES
IN THE WORLD ARE HUNGRY …
HE NEVER HEARD YOUR PRAYERS.
HE NEVER GAVE YOU FOOD.
HE NEVER GAVE YOU A BED.
HE NEVER GAVE YOU A HOME.
THE ONLY HAPPINESS
YOU EVER FOUND
WAS WITH ME.

Jim Jones

Marceline Jones
September 17, 1969
Redwood Valley, Mendocino County

"Mama, do I have to go with Dad this weekend?" Marcus asked as Marceline pulled up the covers and kissed his forehead.

"What do you mean?"

"He said he would tell you about it."

Smoothing her hair, Marceline sat on ten-year-old Marcus's bed and felt pain in the small of her back radiating up and out, like a barium treatment flooding her veins. "Honey, you know how busy your father is," she said automatically. "He must have forgotten. What's going on this weekend?"

Her son was a miniature Jim Jones in feature but very like her in expression. He bit his lips, and a blush of embarrassment spread from temple to temple. "Um. He wants me to go to the coast with him."

"Well, he hasn't mentioned it to me." She shrugged, pretending nonchalance. Certainly it wouldn't be the first time he took Marcus off for a day or two, always with other Temple members, usually female. "I'm sure he'll tell me tomorrow," she said brightly, kissing Marcus's forehead again, the pain flowering in her back like a spiky firework as she leaned over. "Good night."

"Wait." Marcus took her hand. "Not just me and Dad. Jocelyn too. He said he wants me to like her, but I don't. He says I need to get to know her."

Covering her eyes with her other hand, Marceline turned away from her son. She didn't want him to see her cry, and already she was letting go.

"Mama. Are you crying? I won't go. I don't want to go."

"No, honey. I'm not crying. There's something in my eye," she mumbled, knowing her son would immediately detect her lousy lie. Although Marcus was only a boy, he already knew too much about adult deception. Mostly from his dad, she reflected, but she had done her part, too, by covering up for Jim. The other kids were also aware, but Marcus seemed uncannily attentive to the lack of truth in his parents' relationship.

With his free hand, he pried his mother's fingers off her face.

Now, she couldn't stop the tears. She tried to remain still, though the other children were all asleep. Jim wasn't there to hear. Working into the small hours, he often slept in the church office. With whom, she didn't care to speculate.

"Mama, don't cry." Marcus put his slender arms around her and hugged. Oh, this was wrong. She knew it was wrong to get comfort from her little boy when the source of the trouble was her husband, but Jim was hardly ever there. Even when physically present, his mind and heart were elsewhere. Always elsewhere. Despising her own frailty, she let Marcus comfort her while she cried, failing to stop the sobs from escaping. He stroked her hair. "Shhh. It'll be okay, Mama. I won't go. I won't." He said it with certainty, the certainty of the righteous child, but she knew that, as surely as Jim got his own way with her, his seductive persuasion woven of words and hugs and brilliant smiles would win Marcus over.

Marceline was exhausted. Her work as a state inspector of nursing homes took her all over Northern California, dawn to well past dusk, and often she was on the road overnight. Sixty hours a week, sometimes more. They needed the money. Though she missed the children and called several times a day, it was imperative to be away from Jim. She needed not to see what he was doing at home, in the church, with his staff. "Oh, sweetie. I'm sorry you're seeing me like this. Mama's just so tired."

"Do you have to be gone so much? Sometimes it seems like Jocelyn's here more than you are. I mean, she's always nice to me and all, but ..."

To Marceline, the boy was a brilliant angel. He'd inherited all that was good in his parents: Jim's energy and enthusiasm, her kindness and loyalty, and had none of their bad qualities. He had Jim's beauty. When still a baby, everyone was already calling him a lady-killer. "Oh, you'll have to watch out with that one. He's a looker. My goodness, how come the boys always get the long eyelashes?" She'd heard that line only four thousand times. Marcus had yet to go through an awkward or unseemly growth period. He grew more and more handsome. She was guilty, as a plain person, of worshiping at the altar of beauty. Marcus was not like his father, who was all too aware of his power, and used it. Marcus did not consider his own attractions and continued to love Marceline, which stunned her. Their connection only amplified as time passed, if that were possible.

"Honey, I'll ask my supervisor not to give me so many overnight assignments. Believe me, there's nothing I'd like more than to stay at home." Was she lying? True, she wanted to spend more time with the children, but not Jim. She liked her nights alone in motel rooms, free to attend to no one but herself. After wiping her eyes with an embroidered handkerchief she had tucked up her sleeve, Marceline's self-control reasserted itself. Sometimes she pretended her home was a hospital, and then she could cope; she could will herself to work hard on little sleep, to be patient with all, to be the good Methodist girl her parents had trained her to be.

On the night table lay a paperback, outspread flat so that its binding strained. "What are you reading, Marcus? *I Will Fight No More Forever*. What do you think of it?" She tried to set the book aright, but its spine had cracked.

"Mama, you're changing the subject."

Though she was perusing the pages of the memoir, she could feel the intensity of her son's gaze penetrate her skin. So like Jim. The power in his eyes. Their nakedness. Their need.

"Sweetie, as soon as I can, I'll stop the road trips. It's just that when you're in charge of something really important, like making sure all these nursing homes are safe and that the seniors are getting the care they need … well, I can't just walk away."

"Like Dad and the church."

"Yes. Like Dad. But your father has even more people depending on him than I do. You know that."

Shaking his head, Marcus sighed. "Mama, I can always tell when you're giving one of your speeches about how hard Dad works." He rolled his eyes. "You always cover for him. It drives me insane."

She flinched. Having such an observant child was often wonderful, but right now, it was excruciating. She could no longer hide her thoughts from Marcus, while she excelled at concealing them from Jim. "I'm sorry honey. It's just that we need the money. We need it for our projects here, and to buy a building in San Francisco for our new temple. You see how much cash everything takes … all the health care we provide for the seniors, especially, and the day care for the babies, the press for our newsletter …"

"Mama! Please don't do this list again."

"Again? When did I do it before?"

"Yesterday. And probably the day before that, too. Mama, I'm trying to talk to you about Dad and Jocelyn, and you're talking about how we need cash. This isn't about money, Mama."

Sighing, she looked at her son. How did he get so mature? "Marcus, there are some things between a husband and wife that should be private. My relationship with your dad is something he and I need to be talking about together, not you and me."

"He tells me things about you. And about Jocelyn. Things I know he shouldn't. Like he told me you can't be a wife to him anymore 'cause your back hurts. You can't do the things a wife is supposed to do. He said it's not your fault. It's because you work so hard."

Marceline bit her lip and felt a rising lump in her throat. She could just imagine exactly how Jim would phrase things, making himself appear the generous, loving husband, while she was cold and stingy with her affection. Jim was always talking about things that should be kept private, but that was who he was, the Jim she'd married. He hadn't changed. For better or worse, till death, et cetera. He wasn't the first husband to sleep with another woman. Sometimes she was surprised it had taken him this long to start cheating on her. All along, she'd known it was coming. Even while focused on Marceline, he noticed the other nurses too, flirted with them, even in front of her. In those days, it hadn't caused her pain. She'd been so grateful for male attention that she reflexively looked the other way, telling herself to concentrate on his goodness. It became a habit.

In church, women were always flirting with him, eying her skeptically all the while. The plain, good woman, the reverend's wife, the do-gooder, the Peoples Temple Florence Nightingale. Her lower back throbbing, she lay on the floor while Marcus continued to talk. The worst was yet to come, she was sure. "Go ahead, honey. Say what you have to say, okay? I won't tell your father, but you know I don't like to speak against him."

"Why not, goddamnit?" He leaned over the edge of the bed to shout at her. He refused to allow her to escape, if only through shut eyes. "Why don't you get mad? You should. I'm mad. I'm super mad. He's so mean to you." He picked up the paperback and threw it across the room, where it knocked down a portrait of Gandhi and his spinning wheel, given to him by his father. "I never liked that picture anyway."

Both of them regarded the cracked glass, which had splintered within its frame, falling face up.

Breathing deeply, she looked into her son's eyes. This isn't right, she said to herself. This conversation we're having in his bedroom, the way he's leaning over me. It's too adult, too husband-and-wife-like. But she felt too weak to get up, too tired to leave. "Don't swear, Marcus. You know I don't like it. Especially that word."

"What word? I didn't cuss."

"God ... you know."

"Mama, I don't understand you." Now Marcus looked as if he would cry, all his anger inverted. The skin on his neck flushed crimson. "Mama, the kids at school – the normal kids – they don't have fathers who do this to their mothers. They don't have to go off with their dads for the weekend with some woman who isn't their mother when their parents aren't even divorced."

She didn't tell Marcus that there were more men like that than Marcus knew, inside and outside the Temple. Of course it was difficult for him. The other children, all adopted, seemed more resilient somehow, as if whatever traumas they'd gone through before joining the Jones family had steeled them for anything. Only Marcus had come from her womb and was uniquely protective towards her.

"Why don't you stand up to him? If he's going to be with Jocelyn, can't you divorce him? Don't you hear what people are saying? Everybody knows. Everyone."

The truth was that she had never been able to stand up to him. Even when he was in the wrong, he had a knack of projecting his culpability on to her. She didn't know how to explain this to Marcus.

"Women always fall in love with their preacher," she heard herself saying, as if in echo of something she'd heard more than once. Had her mother said the same to her and Laura?

"And does the preacher always fall in love with them too? Did Granddad go off for weekends with other women and leave you and Grandma and Aunt Laura at home?"

"Of course not! I didn't say that the preacher loves them back in the same way. I'm just trying to explain that this sort of thing happens with ministers, and sometimes teachers, sometimes doctors, even nurses. People are so grateful sometimes for being helped, for the tiniest bit of attention, that they respond by loving the person who helped them. They can't help it. Sometimes they just imagine it. You know, I've been with your dad for nearly twenty years now. People just adore him. Old women, elderly men, young people too, people off the street … he's changed their lives. Changed them from being lost, being hopeless, to having a purpose. That's an enormous achievement. At ten years old, you might not be able to understand it, Marcus, but it's about the biggest, most important thing anyone can do in a lifetime."

Marcus lay back on his pillow, turning away from her to face the wall.

"I know you're frustrated, Marcus. But it's just not my nature to be angry. You're so lucky to have a dad like Jim Jones. I admired my father so much when I was your age. Other times I know it's a burden."

"Are you comparing Dad to Granddad?"

"Well, they are both ministers. Both have dedicated their lives to helping people."

He snorted. "Yeah, but Granddad helps rich people! He doesn't hang out with drug addicts and ex-cons. He doesn't talk about saving the world, or socialism, or having sex for the revolution. I can't believe you would even put them in the same category!"

Marceline cringed. She'd heard Jim talk about how he had sex to raise money for The Cause, the thousands of dollars he'd begged for the starving kids in Belo Horizonte from the petroleum mogul's wife in Brazil. Only it wasn't true. He told stories; men of the cloth always do. Jim happened to be very good at it. She couldn't cover her children's' ears when Jim started on something she didn't want them to hear. She couldn't expect Marcus to understand the concept of an apocryphal story and she couldn't label Jim a liar. Not to Marcus, not to anyone in the Temple. He told these stories to make a point, to stress that sacrifice was necessary to change the world. Which, of course, it was.

"Granddad and your father are both ministers devoted to their congregations, but you're right that they're very different. My father never gave up his comforts, never went hungry, never defied the status quo. Granddad's church is totally white. He never integrated, even today. He didn't have threats made on his life, didn't have his home threatened with arson. Your father and I have made some extremely difficult choices, more risky ones than Granddad and Grandma. We *do* want to change the world, and that's a noble thing, isn't it? I wouldn't want the life Grandma has, even though I admire how happy my parents are together. My father and mother have been very, very close all these years, and I envy them, really. But you never lived in that house in Richmond, Indiana. You never got squashed into roles like I did. You never got disciplined for asking too many questions, for being curious, like I was. I wanted to give you a bigger life. A better life."

As she rambled, she knew exactly what Marcus was thinking: again, she was avoiding the real subject and making it about something else. Not money this time, but about the nobility of Jim Jones and the Peoples Temple. The sacrifices they'd made. Marceline believed the Peoples Temple was noble, and so was Jim, in his way. Their third-hand beater car, their clothes from the thrift shop. The life they'd rejected: the life of her parents. She had helped make it so, made such idealism possible. Her work and her salary made it continue. "Are you asleep?"

Though Marcus didn't answer, she was sure he was still awake. The breathing wasn't quite regular, and his lips were thin with anger. She turned off the light and left, rubbing her back, deciding on a nice hot bath.

In the tub, she sank down and down, letting the warm water run over her face, her hair, her entire head. She could sink and never resurface. She rose, spouting water like a whale. Death was not an option. Not now. It would come soon enough for them all. Breathing deeply, she rested her neck on the edge of the tub, her head on the baby-blue tiled wall. It had already been ten years since death had come for Stephanie, her second adopted daughter, along with five other Church members in a car accident. At the time, she thought she could never survive such a loss, but she did. Many remained for Marceline to take care of. As well as Jim, she had Agnes, Tim, Ken, and Jimmy Junior, and there were at least three hundred more in the Temple who needed her, or maybe that was an overblown figure. Jim liked to inflate their numbers for PR purposes. Little lies beget big rewards, he said. "If people think you're successful, they want to be part of what you're doing. They'll recruit for us. What does it matter if it's two hundred instead of three? One day we'll have two thousand, three thousand!"

After the group funeral, in a coincidence she could only attribute to God's hand, she learned she was pregnant with Marcus.

Adding bubble bath to the water and then more hot, as hot as she could stand, she looked down at her body. She wasn't fat, but she had no curves, like Laura. No voluptuousness. Nor the flair of Jocelyn, with her quicksilver mind and clever laugh. Jocelyn the intellectual, the revolutionary: everything Marceline was not, and never would be. In a strange way, she was glad he'd chosen Jocelyn to fall in love with and not someone like Hope, one of those people who used their bodies like weapons, like Jim did. Jocelyn was a preacher's daughter too.

"Marcy? You in there?"

Entering the bathroom without waiting for a response, Edith stayed respectfully behind the wall, parking her large bottom on the closed toilet. "You okay, Marcy? It's awful late."

"Did I wake you, Edith? I'm sorry. Go back to sleep."

"Can't sleep, Marcy. Like you, I guess. You okay?"

Edith was one of Jim's first rescue projects, a white widow with a good heart and no money, lots of pride and her own children dead. They took her in in Indianapolis in 1957. She insisted on housekeeping, though her arthritis made most tasks painful, and the results were often inadequate. The peanut butter sandwiches in the kids' lunchboxes were half-smeared against their tin insides because she could never quite get the bread completely inside the waxed paper bag.

"I'm fine, Edith. Go on back to bed."

"Why ain't you in bed? It's nearly midnight, and you gotta get up early for work tomorrow, dóntcha?"

Sighing, Marceline pushed clusters of bubbles up around her breasts, modest even in the presence of their nearsighted seventy-one-year-old housekeeper. How much did Edith know? Though uneducated, she was smart, an acute observer of character and shrewd with money. Surely she knew all about Jocelyn and Jim.

"You know me, Edith. I don't need much sleep."

"That's what you say, Marcy. But you don't take all those pills like Jim do. He practically don't ever sleep. Pardon me for saying you don't look so good these days. You need some rest. Why dontcha call in sick tomorrow, just stay home in bed? I'll take care of you."

Marceline was grateful for Edith's poor vision, as her tears seeped into the lavender-scented water below her temples. Kind Edith. Edith, whose husband had deserted her when their children were babies in the Depression for lack of a job, for guilt at the big bellies of his little boy and girl, swollen with air. "No better than niggers," he'd murmured into Edith's ear the night he left. He told her he couldn't bear the sight of them. Edith repeated the words to Marceline decades later, long after the boy had died from pneumonia, and the girl of septicemia from a trivial cut, both gone before their fifth birthdays. A third death certificate showed up long afterward: her husband was buried in a pauper's field all the way across the country in San Diego, California, where he'd fled on the freight cars from Indy, looking for work.

"You're very sweet to me, Edith. And I do appreciate the offer; you know I do. And so does Jim," she added automatically. "I can't just call in sick. We need the money. I can't walk away from my job."

"Marcy, did I say you should walk away from your job? I said take a day off. You're no hourly. They don't dock you when you're sick, do they? You an educated woman, a registered nurse. Surely they let you take a day off now and then."

Edith was right, of course. "The seniors need me, though. If I don't do my job, how will they be safe, and well fed, and tended to if I call in sick? Especially when I'm not? They won't get anyone to fill in for me, and I have four homes to visit tomorrow. Some of these places, Edith, they're awful. People treat their pets better than they treat their parents."

"I'm sure you're right, Marcy. That don't mean you should lose your health over it. Remember what you said when I got that wicked flu. You told me I wouldn't be no good to no one if I didn't heal myself first."

Practical Edith. "Of course I remember. But I don't have the flu. I'm perfectly healthy. Besides, this bath is curing me."

Sniffing the air, Edith said, "That lavender smells good. Almost like the real thing. Where I grew up, in Kentucky, my mama grew lavender in jam jars. Her one luxury, she called it. Always died. Every year. But she tried. Never gave up on it. 'One year, Edith,' she used to say, 'one year I'm gonna have a big ol' batch of lavender to scent our clothes with.'"

"Tell me more about your mother, Edith. You don't mention her often." The water was getting cool. She should get up and go to bed, her empty bed, but instead she added more hot. This was her one luxury, the bath without end.

"Everyone called my mama a saint, but I knew better. She cried every night after she put us all to bed. My papa worked all the time at the mines."

"A miner's life, that's hard." A familiar guilt washed over Marceline as she thought of her own easy life in Richmond as the child of a prosperous Methodist minister. All the troubles of the world visited on so many, on almost every member of their temple, while she had skated though a middle-class life of middling Methodists. Her biggest problem had been loneliness, while Edith and her children were starving. She would spend her life paying back, giving back, expiating her privileged childhood. She would be the kind of Christian her parents and sister had failed to be.

"A miner's wife's life ... now that's really hard." Edith laughed. She didn't often laugh, and Marceline wasn't sure if the laughter that emanated from her thin, lined lips was sincere or spiteful.

"I'm sure it was hard for you kids, too. Where are your brothers and sisters now?"

Shrugging, Edith said, "I have no idea, Marcy. All I knew was that I was not going to be a miner's wife myself. That was the only thing in my head growing up. And I didn't."

Sometimes Marceline thought of Edith as an alternate mother, the hardscrabble mother with the tough life her own mother hadn't had, her own mother also a middle-class preacher's daughter. Other times, Marceline felt like Edith's mother. Edith needed mothering. Though she'd had one, Edith was like an orphan all grown up. Not unlike Jim, whose mother was still living. Mrs. Lynetta Jones resided down the street in a nice house with more rooms than this one, though she lived alone. A mother who thought her son was fathered by gods instead of a disabled World War I veteran. Lynetta and her fabulous stories. There was one about a vision she'd had while pregnant with Jim, that her one and only child would lead the world to glory. Something like that. No wonder Jim was such a storyteller.

Her mother-in-law worshipped at Jim's feet. She must not make the same mistake with Marcus. She saw how it could happen, how easily the love of a son could become idolatry, especially where the husband was absent. Whether literally or figuratively didn't matter.

"Nope. At least I didn't commit the sins of my mother," Edith said with an exhaustive sigh. "Plenty other sins, but not that one. When my father weren't at the mine, he was at the bar. I hardly ever saw him. My mother didn't see him much neither, 'cept when he came home drunk and went at her in bed. New babies every year."

"Well, at least you and I both managed to stay away from the alcoholics," Marceline said, hearing the ridiculousness of her remark.

Edith snorted. "Sometimes when a man's drunk's the only time you see his tender side. I never saw my father gentle 'cept when he'd been drinking."

Marceline didn't want to hear any more, not right now. Her own troubles were negligible beside the multiple griefs of Edith's family history. If Jim and Jocelyn were sleeping together, what did it matter, ultimately, in the larger suffering of the world? Marceline had been lucky in so many ways.

The year before, she'd briefly flirted with Dr. Persson at the Sacramento Home for the Aged & Infirm. Of course, with his spies everywhere, Jim had heard about it and confronted her.

"Marceline, in case you're thinking of leaving with your Doctor Boyfriend, know that you can't take the kids." Jim had said in a low but charged voice while preparing for a Sunday service.

"I don't have a boyfriend! What are you talking about?"

"That's not what I hear. You're all cozy with him, going out to lunch together and talking shop. Well, if you want that doctor, you can have him. The kids stay with me."

Marceline kept sputtering she had no boyfriend, though she'd found herself daydreaming about Dr. Persson once or twice. So different from Jim, with his kindness and ability to listen.

"You know I got the best lawyers working for me. You'd never win in court." Grinning, Jim had adjusted his robes and strode to the pulpit, never approaching the subject again. But Marceline knew he meant every word.

"I think I'm ready for bed, Edith. You go on. I'll see you in the morning, okay?"

"I'll make your coffee 'fore you get up, Marcy. Sweet dreams."

At dawn, the phone rang, waking Marceline with an urgency she attributed to her sister's will.

"Marcy? You all right? Jim called and said you were in a terrible way."

Rubbing her eyes, Marceline felt in the darkness for the smooth pillow beside her. "Laura? Why are you calling so early?"

"Jim just called and said he was worried about you."

"Really?" She never told Laura or her mother what her life with Jim was like these days. She dreaded their saying "I told you so," or something equally insensitive. Laura's husband, Steve, doted on her and their daughters, of course. Laura had always been vaguely suspicious of Jim – as if she couldn't understand why such a good-looking man would marry a girl like Marceline. She seemed to enjoy flirting with him too, on the rare occasions when they were all in the same place.

"He says you're awfully depressed, what with your bad back and all. Is there anything I can do to help? I could bring the girls out and visit for a while. Help you with all those kids."

The ache in her back started up again. Marceline frowned. A visit from Sister Prima Donna and her three princesses would make everything worse. She chided herself. She missed her little sister in a vague sort of way. "When did he call you?" She squinted in the dark at the clock.

"Just now. From the church. He said your back was so bad he didn't want to accidentally hurt you in the night by rolling over or something, so he slept on the couch in his office. That's sweet of him, huh."

A sharp pain stabbed her spine. "Ouch. My back is killing me."

"You all right, honey? Have you seen a doctor about your back?"

Cradling the phone, Marceline lay down, wondering if she would indeed be able to go to work. Could she talk to Laura? No. There was no one Marceline could tell. No one who would understand. "How's Mother?"

"You're changing the subject on me. Did you see a doctor or didn't you?"

"Laura, I'm a pretty decent nurse, and I know what's wrong and what can be done about it. Back trouble like mine comes and goes. You just have to ride it out, that's all. Back surgery's no guarantee. I've seen patients in worse shape after they've had it. You know me, I'd rather just tough it out. The pain passes. It's not so bad all the time. Just sometimes."

"If it were me, I'd be taking every little pill modern medicine has to offer." Laura laughed. "I bet you don't even take aspirin, do you?"

Marceline shrugged. Drugs were dangerous. She took nothing but baths.

"Well, what do you say to a visit? I could help out. I know you have your hands full with all those kids and your job. Honestly Marceline, I don't know how you do it. Mother never worked a day in her life until we were out of high school, and you've been at it since day one. Didn't even take time off when you had Marcus. You amaze me."

Was this a compliment? Marceline couldn't tell. From Laura's mouth, it sounded more like criticism. Why do you do all that work when you don't have to? Why doesn't your husband provide for all of you? What's the matter with Miss Priss?

"Speaking of which, Laura, I need to get going if I'm going to be on time for my first appointment. I have an hour's drive ahead of me."

"I thought that church of Jim's was doing pretty well, to hear him tell it, at least. Couldn't you switch to part time?"

She hated the way Laura, and her parents too, called the Peoples Temple "Jim's church," as if she had nothing to do with it. Unlike her mother, who saw herself as a church wife exclusively, with no decision-making powers beyond the menus of church suppers, she and Jim believed the church belonged to all of them. To the members, the staff, and to Mother Marceline, as he'd begun calling her after his first visit to Father Divine in 1959. Jim had adopted almost all of Father Divine's organizational structures and financial practices. He never had any assets in his own name.

Having a Mother Marceline beside Father Jim was so important in making the Temple feel like a family, a new and better family for those who'd either never had one in the first place, or whose family was so awful they wished they'd never had one. There was a small group of privileged college kids who were beginning to drive up to Happy Valley from the city, who also hankered after a new family, wanting to flee their prosperous mothers and fathers like a bitter taste they desperately needed to erase.

"You are the Great Mother," Jim had whispered in her ear the last time he came back from Divine's headquarters in Philadelphia. "You're even more important to these people than I am. You literally heal them. You love them unconditionally. My job, like any good father's, is to improve them, teach them, discipline them when it's necessary. Sometimes they're gonna hate me, but you, they're always gonna love. I envy that, Marceline. Being a woman everyone can love, will love, always love. I take all the heat while you get all the goodies."

It was a seductive speech, she remembered, which had led to one of the rare times he'd reached out for her. It always started out slow and tender, their lovemaking, but somewhere along the way Jim got insistent and impatient and then he would ram her fast, and that was the end of that. In the beginning, she couldn't believe this strange roughhousing was called making love. It didn't feel loving in the slightest, not after the first few kisses. He liked to turn her over and get behind her, which she found very awkward but tried to like. She supposed that whichever way he came into her, at least he'd managed to do what mattered most: give her Marcus.

"I like my job. You always seem to forget that. It's not quite the same as Mother's book-keeping. I'll be fine. Thanks for the offer, but Edith helps out plenty. I appreciate your calling."

"Okay, Marcy. But let me know if you need anything, okay? And Mother says she wishes you'd call her more often. I talk to her every day. She sure wishes she could see her California grandkids more."

Marceline wondered if that was true.

170

"I'll let you get to work. Go save the world, Mother Marceline."
Laura hung up.

She was on the road before the children woke. Edith always got
them to school on time, even if their lunches were messy. Driving
down Highway 101, Marceline opened the window and let the
wind ruffle her short hair. Right then, her back didn't hurt, and
she felt free. Jim had called Laura at dawn, but he'd neglected
to call Marceline. He'd told Laura she was depressed, knowing
she'd immediately call their mother. Poor depressed Marcy with
back trouble. Making her out to be the messed-up half of the
couple when he was the one gorging on methamphetamines.
He never listened to her warnings, deaf to the long-term damage
that would result.

"Too many things to do, Marceline. Sleep just gets in the way."

Probably Jocelyn was lying beside him in that fold-out double
couch-bed in the office. Or maybe he was at Jocelyn's house
and lied to Laura about where he was calling from. What did it
matter? Here she was, being useful in the world. That was most
important, not whether Jim was faithful. His heart was in the
right place, despite his fidelity problem. She liked the outlaw
in him. It was immature of her to feel this way at her age. He
loved her, he loved the kids; if he wanted to have nasty sex with
Jocelyn or somebody else, she didn't really care. Staying meant
keeping her family together. She remembered what he had said
if she ever contemplated leaving. He would absolutely deprive
her of the kids. So she would turn the other cheek. Ignore his
dalliances. Mother Marceline was above all that. Jocelyn might
be chief financial secretary or whatever title he'd bestowed upon
her – the titles tended to change rapidly with Jim's favor – but
she was Mother with a capital M. The seniors adored her, as did
the kids in the congregation.

No one gets to have everything, she told herself. Really, when
she looked at the big picture, her life was rich and satisfying.
When she walked into Church in her white robes and sat by Jim's

side, she felt the eyes of the hundreds upon her as well as on Jim. They envied her, being married to someone they called God; they thought her a saint. Marceline was full of flaws and deficiencies, but she had a far more interesting life than her mother's. It was a million times more exciting than Laura's. Marceline smiled and lowered her foot on the gas pedal so she wouldn't be late for her first appointment.

WE WANT THE WORLD TO KNOW
THAT WE WILL EXIST TOGETHER
OR WE SHALL DIE TOGETHER.
THOSE TERMS MUST NEVER BE SACRIFICED,
THOSE TERMS MUST NEVER BE ALTERED.
THAT COMMITMENT
MUST ALWAYS BE KNOWN
IN THE BACK RECESSES OF EVERY PERSON'S
MIND THAT WE ARE A FAMILY.

Jim Jones

Ten Days Before the End
November 8, 1978

Marcus and her parents stepped from the tiny Cessna onto the
Port Kaituma airstrip. Marceline was holding her grandbaby, Sioux
Lee, in a tiny shack to the side, where wrenches and ratchets and
empty bottles shared space with one unevenly footed metal chair
and a kerosene lamp. She hesitated before leaving the shed, as it
was cool away from the sun, which was already glaring off the
white wings of the Guyana Airways ten-passenger plane. Asleep
in Marceline's arms, Sioux Lee opened her mouth and pushed
her tiny fists against her grandmother's chest, then settled back
again into slumber.

Four Guyanese followed her family members off the plane and
nodded to Marcus as they adjusted their hats, then looked up at
the sky to gauge the hour before walking off to their village, a quiet
hamlet many miles inland, far from governmental intervention.
Wearing her straw hat, she stepped forward and grinned. The pilot,
Joao, stood on the folding stairway and tipped his cap to them. In
response, her father fished an American dollar from his pocket.

"Granddad! This is a Marxist country. You don't give people
tips here." Outraged, Marcus grimaced at his grandfather, but the
white-haired, pink-cheeked old man ignored the advice.

"What do you think, sir?" Reverend Baldwin asked the man
in shirtsleeves and a Guyanese Airlines cap, whose arm was
outstretched, reaching for the crisp bill.

"Guyana may be Marxist, but you Americans are not," Joao responded. He smiled and took the bill with a grin. "I accept your capitalist gesture with the most comradely affection."

"You see!" Preston Baldwin laughed good-naturedly at his oldest grandson, his only male descendant by blood.

Dressed in khaki pants and shirtsleeves, Reverend Baldwin took his wife's elbow to direct her off the airstrip. "Marxist or not, everyone likes to see George Washington's old mug from time to time."

Marcus shrugged his shoulders at the pilot. "I guess old habits die hard, Joao."

"Okay with me. I'll get the bags."

"No! I'll do it." Ever conscious of being the Great Socialist's son and heir-apparent, Marcus did not want the pilot to think he, first scion of the Reverend Bishop Jones, Prime Minister Burnham's dear friend and comrade, expected the state airline's captain to act like some sort of flunky cab driver. Marcus rushed back into the plane, from where he expertly opened the rear door and threw his grandparents' copious luggage onto the runway.

"I'll help you, son," Minister Baldwin said, picking up one of his wife's suitcases and her makeup bag.

Still in the open doorway of the shed, Marceline watched the tableau screening before her as if studying a scene in a film. My parents, she thought. My son, and their first great-granddaughter, all together in one, small place, just east of the Venezuelan border. Probably the only time ever.

Marceline shook off the feeling, allowing the baby in her arms to soothe her. For a moment more, she savored the stillness, thankfully free of Jim's frantic energy and anxiety.

"Marcy!" her mother called. At fifty years old, she would never get her mother to use her full name.

"Over here, Mother."

The baby opened her eyes and began to cry.

"Now who's this?" her mother asked, coming toward her, not

bothering about the bags nor thinking about the clash of Marxism and capitalism.

The baby was part Asian. Marceline's adopted middle son, Ken, had been born in Korea. Her mother was Afro-American, as Ken's wife was born to an Alabaman sharecropping family which had migrated to Indianapolis, and joined their first church, Wings of Deliverance, then followed them out to rural California in 1965, to flee the imminent nuclear holocaust predicted by Jim. They stayed on with Peoples Temple all these years, following the Joneses wherever they went, even after the supposed Armageddon date of July 15, 1967, had passed without incident. Arletta Jones (no relation) and her people were among the stalwart black families in the Temple, and Ken and Tina had known one another as toddlers, coming up together in the church. The Jones's rainbow family tradition, modelled for the rest of the congregation what a world without racism might look like. Tina was a lovely girl and a good mother, but Ken had always been so eager to gain Jim's approval, to be the recipient of Jim's effusive praise, that Marceline sensed Ken might have married any girl his father selected for him. Just as Marcus fled his father's embrace, Ken raced toward it, even now in his twenties.

"Isn't she darling?" Marlene Baldwin tickled the little girl under her chin, and Sioux Lee Jones-Jones stopped crying, opened her huge brown eyes, smiled toothlessly up into her great grandmother's pale face, then burped. "Oh, let me hold her."

Marceline handed the child over to her mother. She noticed that her elegant hands now appeared to shake with a slight tremor, something new since she last saw them, on a hurried May weekend in Indiana. Marceline was salvaging Peoples Temple's reputation in the wake of Susan Stein's defection, which had sparked a fusillade of criticism from the Bay Area media. Jim had convinced Jocelyn's father, also a well-known minister, to hold a press conference in praise of Jonestown, to overcome some of the negativity. It had worked for a while. San Francisco's dailies had showcased the minister's effusive tribute to their agricultural mission, calling their utopia a noble success. Why did Jim always go for ministers' daughters? Marceline knew Jocelyn's father's praise was as off the mark as the venomous bashing the California press had spewed two weeks earlier.

"Greetings, sweet Susie, my first great-grandchild in this world."

Was her mother crying? Marceline studied the lined face, the perfectly coiffed blue-ish hair, the ladylike nylons her mother wore for all public occasions, even in the jungle.

"Mother, are you all right?"

A tear fell from Marlene Baldwin's right eye. "Sweetheart, when you hold your first great-grandbaby, I think you'll cry too."

I'll never hold one, Marceline thought, then pushed the notion aside. "I suppose you're right, Mother," she said, feeling sudden affection for this old woman, whose refinement had served her for more than eighty years, a Hoosier among Hoosiers for multiple generations. Supposedly, the Whittaker clan could trace its male progenitor back to the Mayflower, though Marceline never believed it. Her forebears, New World explorers? Too unlikely. What identity would Sioux Lee have? Guyanese? Korean/Afro-American? The baby's maternal great-grandparents were rooted in the Deep South, all the way back to slave days. Before that, they didn't know. West Africa most likely.

"Where are Tina and Ken? I thought they'd be here too."

Marceline frowned, hearing implicit criticism.

"They're working, Mother. Everyone works in Jonestown. I'm taking time off from the clinic to babysit and fetch you."

"Oh, that's right." Her mother looked into the child's eyes again, apparently transported. Marceline marveled that her mother had come this far. She had said nothing about the girl's skin color or made any comment on her name. Of course, she knew nothing of its unusual spelling. Marlene's pantyhose glinted in the sun, her coiffure wilting in the humidity.

"Hello, little girl!" her father called, joining them in the shade while Marcus carried the seven pieces of luggage over to the waiting tractor with the red flatbed trailer.

"Hi, Daddy!" Surprising herself by using that term, Marceline blushed and hoped her mother didn't notice. She hadn't called Minister Baldwin "Daddy" since she had been a small child. She didn't like hearing the ancient seniors call Jim "Daddy." She winced as she recalled one 102-year-old in a wheelchair begging "Daddy" to let him go back to the United States for a visit to see "his people." Jim had unleashed his wrath on the old man, a senile sweetie. "His" people were not Peoples Temple people. That made them nobody.

"She's hardly a little girl, Preston," said her mother. "She's a grandmother, for goodness's sake. And meet our first great-grandchild, Susie."

"That's who I was calling little girl, silly," said her father, kissing Marceline's cheek and making goo-goo faces at the baby. "But you'll always be my first little girl, and don't you forget it." He hugged her hard.

"She was born in September, right?" Marlene asked. "The eleventh?"

"Exactly! You still have an excellent memory, Mother." Her mother prioritized certain facts and ideas and not others. All the wrong ones, Marceline thought resentfully. Her father also refrained from remarking on the baby's mixed race. By this time, nearly thirty years after Jim's and Marceline's wedding, the Baldwins were used to being around dark skin, but usually there was a cringe involved, something unsaid but perceptible to their firstborn. So far, today, no cringe. Maybe her mother had finally relaxed in her ninth decade of life. Was Marlene finally freed from centuries of genteel racism?

"September eleventh, that's the day of the CIA coup in Chile," Marcus said, ushering them all toward the tractor. The driver, Lenny Stein, Susan-the-traitor's big brother, awaited them in his seat, unhealthily thin and pasty, as usual. Once married to Jocelyn, Lenny was one of her husband's chief sycophants, perhaps even his lover. He was the strangest in a cluster of strange, adoring men, another drug addict rescued from one addiction and promptly given another.

"Hey, Lenny," Marcus called. "Could you help with these bags?"

"Leonard Stein, these are my parents: Marlene and Preston Baldwin," Marceline said in her nicest church-wife voice. Her mother carried the baby, her father beside her cooing into the girl's face and appearing, for the moment, extremely content. Inside, Marceline felt uneasy, exhaustion crushing her brain as if in a vice, her gray matter leaching away. Sometimes she felt she was shrinking somehow. Some intangible part of herself, her spirit, perhaps her soul, ebbed daily in the oppressive humidity of the Guyanese jungle.

In spite of the heat and the hairdo, which sank like a cake in an oven, Marlene Blanche Baldwin retained her crisp midwestern matronly composure, a marvel of breeding and upbringing. Laura was exactly like her, except feistier. They climbed aboard, Marcus taking the baby while his grandmother gamely allowed herself to be pulled forward by the sinewy arms of the driver, boosted from behind by her husband.

On the flatbed, which was outfitted with rough planks for benches, and a rickety rail to keep passengers and goods from flying off, they bounced along the road, waving at locals who knew the tractor and its fire-engine red trailer as the major mode of transport for Peoples Temple members from the river port town to the compound seven miles away. The tractor had been shipped from Miami, along with multiple spare parts, when Temple pioneers began to clear the jungle after leasing nearly four thousand acres from the Guyanese government. The vehicle had been patched and welded and soldered so many times it looked like a metallic palette, gilded by sunlight.

"I like your tractor, young man," Reverend Baldwin said to the driver, who either didn't hear or purposely ignored him. Most of the time, Lenny Stein had no interest in anyone but Jim. He and Jocelyn were newlyweds when they joined the temple. Not long after, Jocelyn and Jim hooked up. Then Lenny married someone else selected by Jim, who also found her way to Jim's bed. His wives' amorous lives with Jim did nothing to diminish Lenny's love for his leader, perhaps perversely enhancing it. Marceline pushed away the disturbing thought to concentrate on her mother and father, who were both delighting in the bright yellow toucans calling to them from the crown canopy of greenheart trees along the pot-holed road.

"Jungle life agrees with you, Marcus," said Minister Baldwin, rubbing the boy's full head of thick black hair. "We haven't seen you in a few years, and the last time, you were kind of sickly looking, if I may say so. Your grandmother and I were awfully worried."

Her parents' judgment of her children, on any matter, no matter how picayune, made Marceline tense. Today she vowed not to let their words, especially her mother's, burrow beneath her skin. Five days together loomed, and Marceline wanted her parents to return to the States with the same kind of thrilled approbation of Jonestown that Jocelyn's parents had communicated so articulately to the American press. Of course, Jocelyn's churchy parents were Civil Rights types: anti-Vietnam war protesters, farmworker supporters and ex-con befrienders, nothing like her own parents, whose ministry to the prosperous middle class whites of Richmond, Indiana had never been controversial in any way. No one in that pale-faced congregation had ever gone hungry or suffered race hatred.

"Do you like it here, sweetheart?" Marlene asked Marcus, who paused before answering, surveying his grandmother's now comic blue hairdo.

"I like some things." Marcus did not want to lie. "I like being captain of the basketball team and I really like clearing bush with the dozer. That's probably my favorite thing."

Marceline watched Lenny look into his mirror at Marcus. Whatever they said would get back to Jim.

"And what are your not-so-favorite things?" his grandfather asked.

"Well. Let's see …"

He looked at his mother, who shook her head just slightly. She did not want Marcus to launch into his arsenal of criticism regarding Jim or the way the compound was run.

"I bet lots of pretty girls are after you," Marlene said, "with such splendid muscles and your lovely tan."

Marcus tensed. He hated being talked about as if he were a "ladies' man," the kind of man his father had so odiously become.

"Marcus is so busy with all the building work at the settlement," Marceline said, "that he's too tired for anything but basketball."

"Nothing wrong with that," Minister Baldwin said. "You've got plenty of time for dating in college."

Marcus and Marceline exchanged glances. College was a subject that came up, disappeared, reappeared, evaporated, and returned with a vengeance every few weeks. Marceline wanted Marcus to leave Jonestown, to get his education someplace far, far away, anywhere as long as it was out of his father's reach, but Marcus said he didn't want to leave Jonestown without her, and there the argument rested, unchanged, until the next round.

"Right," Marcus said. "In college I'll be dating like a fiend." He winked at his mother.

"Have you sent out any applications for next fall?" Marlene asked. "Don't you apply in November? My brothers could help with their connections at Purdue."

"Oh Mother, Marcus wouldn't go to Purdue." Marceline couldn't stop herself from protesting, though she immediately regretted it.

"Now what's wrong with Purdue? Most every boy in my family graduated from there, most of them captains of their football team with academic honors, let me remind you."

"I haven't decided yet," Marcus interrupted. "I mean, where exactly I want to go. I'm actually thinking about London. The University of London is supposed to be a good school for economics but without the snootiness of Oxford or Cambridge, and I hear it's pretty radical politically."

This was news to Marceline. How would he know anything about the University of London? Or was this just fodder for his grandparents?

"I suppose that radical label is precisely what attracts you," Minister Baldwin said, laughing. "Oh, Marcus. I can read you like a book, even though it's been far too long. Back then, you were talking about acting school. I'm glad that's out of your system."

Marceline bit her forefinger to stop herself from responding. If Marcus wanted to study acting, what was wrong with that? Her parents probably thought only homosexual men went to acting school. Jim was against it too, but for patently different reasons. He thought no one should be allowed to devote his time to art until the Revolution had succeeded. Marceline was tired of waiting for that. She wanted her son to study whatever would fulfill his desires. Not his father's. For herself, she was too old and tired to start anew.

"Yeah, I might study political science if not econ. Or maybe philosophy." Marcus laughed. "I need some theory to go with my practice, right Mom?"

They all laughed. Marcus was a good tension-defuser, always had been. Everyone regarded one another with affection, except Lenny, whose eyes switched from the road to rear-view mirror with alarming speed.

The baby had fallen asleep again, and all were quiet as the tractor approached the gates of the community. "Greetings: Peoples Temple Agricultural Project." The sign was neatly printed in black block letters against a freshly painted white background. At the guard shack, Elijah stepped out and wrote down their names and the time on his clipboard. His gun remained out of sight inside the tiny building.

Although the Agricultural Mission had existed for five years, its life had been mostly on paper and in Temple members' heads for most of that time. Only a dozen or so people had actually lived here continuously since the first acre was cleared. Some of the troubled youths in the Bay Area had been given the choice of jail or Jonestown. All had chosen Jonestown.

"It's amazing how thick the jungle is here. You can't see through the trees – not even an inch," Minister Baldwin said to Marcus. "And yet you bulldozed how many acres?"

"Over three hundred at this point," Marcus said proudly. "And we're planning a much bigger cassava crop next year. Maybe even exporting some of it. One of the nurses figured out how to use part of the fruit as a wound-salve. Something like that. Right, Mom? Mom could tell you more about it."

Marceline nodded. Jim's nurse had once worked with burn victims and discovered that the inner membrane of the cassava was better than the finest artificial remedy for an antiseptic unguent. But could they really export it? She doubted Jonestown could get that far in packaging and selling a product for profit. The idea was too optimistic, considering how disturbed Jim had become during the last year. His mother's death, Susan's escape, and most recently, Sherry, the other financial officer, had defected just last month, sending him into new realms of derangement. The departure of these last two women from the inner circle were like a fist to the solar plexus for Jim, though the work they had done could easily be accomplished by others.

"Very impressive indeed." Minister Baldwin was nodding. "Marlene, isn't that amazing?"

"What's that?" Her mother hadn't been listening but seemed mystified by Sioux Lee's dark eyes. Marceline reminded herself that her mother was wonderful with infants. Briefly, she remembered Stephanie the infant in her mother's arms, then her funeral in Indy, after the car crash. Had she turned to her parents for comfort back then, or was she already too far removed from their world to find succor there?

It was three miles from the gate to the center of the compound. The Pavilion marked the heart of the mission, where Peoples Temple ate, listened to Jim, argued, sang, danced, laughed, performed plays and music, entertained visitors. Jim reigned there on the wooden chair Marceline had overheard others refer to as his throne. A pitiful throne, with its flaking paint and basic carpentry. He sat there for hours at a time, when he wasn't in his cabin with the rest of his family – the two mistresses and the two children – or talking to Doc Schacht in the clinic about the quality and quantity of his medication regime, over which Marceline no longer presided. Jim didn't walk around Jonestown as much as he used to. He didn't tramp the fields like he once did, didn't tour the grounds unless he was showing some famous person their miraculous achievements.

A Californian screenwriter had visited just after Sioux Lee's birth. Jim was still excited about becoming a grandfather, and for a while the grief over his mother's death subsided long enough for the old enthusiasm to surface. The visitor wanted to make a film about Peoples Temple. Jones was enthused, regarding it as the perfect medium with which to persuade Temple detractors in the United States that Jim Jones had indeed built a genuine marvel, a Jerusalem in the jungle, a city on a hill in the tropics for America's poor, its elderly and dispossessed. Hollywood films took years to produce, but Jim wanted it to happen right now. The writer wasn't bothered by Jim's insistence. If anything, he enjoyed being in the center of Jim's spotlight.

"Look at all these people," the man had said as he watched the mostly black crowd organizing a children's picnic and theatrical performance arranged for his visit. "If they weren't here in Jonestown, they would be in one way or another dead. Either physically dead or addicted or they'd be prostitutes, pimps, in state prisons, mental institutions, hospitals. Some may have committed suicide. In my opinion, you have done the social equivalent of raising the dead."

Jim had lapped it all up, basking in the praise of this erudite intellectual, just as he had in the old days of the healing services back in the city.

"It's a resurrection city. You've done amazing work here, Reverend Jones. I salute you."

"Marceline too, and every single member of this congregation," Jim was quick to add as the three of them toured Jonestown, not wanting to appear to take sole credit for the achievements of a thousand people. Inside, though, he regarded himself the Creator of this world with his name on it. Without Jim, there would be no Jonestown. For herself, Marceline would have been content to stay in the United States, ministering to the elderly and the poor and the sick, rural or urban. Being of service was the same to her wherever she lived. But Jim couldn't stop running. He was bored with routine, with sitting still. It was his need for constant adrenaline that had propelled them across the ocean, up the Kaituma river, then deep into the jungle.

At last, the tractor reached the Pavilion. Plastic smile adhered to his mouth, Jim came out to greet them, having roused himself to play good son-in-law for the afternoon. He had banished the mistresses and other sons.

"Marlene, you continue to be the most beautiful woman in my inner circle, and that's saying a lot." He kissed his mother-in-law on the cheek.

Marlene couldn't keep from grinning at Marceline. "Well, that's a tribute to your wife, dear Jim, because Marcy and I are practically twins."

"Don't I know it!"

Jim put his arm around Marceline's waist, imparting a certain heat that made Marceline light-headed, a sensation she had rarely experienced since her arrival in Jonestown.

"But the real beauty is here in my arms," said Minister Baldwin, carrying the baby over to Jim. "Howdy, Grandpa."

"And howdy to you, Great-Grandpa," Jim said, rubbing his father-in-law's shoulders. "Don't you look great, Preston. You look like a million bucks. Oops. As a Marxist, I guess I'm not supposed to say that."

Everyone laughed except for Marcus.

"A million rubles, perhaps?" As ever, Preston seemed to enjoy Jim. Did he notice the puffy eyes, Marceline wondered, the bloating, the slight slur to his speech? Apparently not. It was amazing how her husband managed to convince everyone in the world of his beneficence and magnanimity. Everyone but her and Marcus. And at times, his own mother. Lynetta was crazy in love with her son, but she always knew when Jim was lying and didn't hesitate to point it out, even in front of other people.

Since Lynetta's death, Marceline had tried to take on her admonitory role, but Jim wouldn't have any of it. She had only ever contradicted him in public once, back in Ukiah. He'd been furious, threatened her with divorce, and even worse, told her he would fix things so she'd never see the children again. He had friends in high places, he warned her, and if she ever dared to criticize him around others again – well she'd better look out. His wrath was not pretty, he said. And though he'd never hit her, he could injure her far, far worse without lifting a finger, he promised. He could call her crazy, declare her an unfit mother, and plenty of medical professionals would agree with the diagnosis, just because he said so. She believed him.

"Aren't you going to show us around?" Preston asked.

"Where will we be sleeping? Not in a dorm, I hope," Marlene said.

Marceline had decided it would be easier to give her parents her own cabin. She could sleep in a dorm for a few nights. The guest house, normally used for visitors, was curiously off limits. Jim said it needed work, that the electricity had to be rewired and the exterior bug-proofed, but Marceline didn't believe him. She'd heard rumors he was keeping some girl there. She couldn't bring herself to walk to the other end of the compound to see for herself. Especially if the rumors were true.

"Marcus, show your grandparents where they'll be staying," Marceline said. "I'll take the baby to Tina in the kitchen."

* * *

Marceline usually only saw her husband at mealtimes and meetings, and not always then, but with her parents there, she felt it necessary to attend to Jim most of the day. His other women stayed out of sight, and the other sons roamed like the other children around the compound. She and Jim had agreed to show them a united front. "It's only for a few days," Jim had said.

It didn't matter, ultimately, what her parents thought about her marriage, as the Baldwins and the Joneses lived on different continents – literally and figuratively – but for her own peace of mind, she wanted her parents to judge her life as good, her marriage worthy, their grandchildren happy. Even if it wasn't true.

Occasionally, it was true. Some days, Marceline looked around and felt her prayers had been answered, that Jesus was still walking on the earth, for she could see His footprints in Jonestown when she watched the seniors working in their vegetable gardens, or sitting on their porches, fanning themselves as their own elders had back in the South, with their extended families all around them. To Marceline, the care of the elders, their feelings of complete safety and security, was their most important accomplishment at Jonestown. Nothing could take that away. Even Jim's paranoia and drug abuse couldn't ruin the simple, daily pleasures in the lives of the eldest citizens of Jonestown, who had their vitals checked every morning by a nurse. They never had to worry again about being robbed or mugged, or fearing they'd have to survive on dog food until the next check, or being swindled by family members or friends for whatever valuables they had. They didn't have to choose between electricity or medication. Here, their lives were far superior to the Fillmore or Western Addition or Watts or whatever public housing project they'd managed to survive in their last years in the States.

As the screenwriter had said, it was a kind of paradise, a city of the reborn.

"Jim, I understand you have lots to teach them," her father said reasonably, "lots of wisdom as well as information to impart, but having the P.A. going at all hours will make them want to shut their ears instead of open them. That thing crackles on and off day and night. It's enough to drive someone crazy."

Marceline tensed. She and Jim were sitting with her parents and Marcus on the deck behind Marceline's cabin. It was late afternoon, and the heat had died down somewhat. A pair of parrots preened on the perch Marcus had built for them, showing off their flashy tropical colors. One had a red body, the other yellow, and both had wings of extraordinary blue, the color of the Caribbean. The parrots mated for life. At least, that's the story Marceline told herself about them. Like her parents, perhaps, who had never spent a night apart in fifty years, save her father's service as an Army chaplain. Did they see her and Jim this way too? While Laura and her husband would surely never divorce, it was Laura who engineered that marriage. She was the life force propelling her family forward. Like the rest of the world, Preston and Marlene both thought Jim orchestrated their marriage, powered it to success. They didn't know how much she'd sacrificed to keep them together. And how, despite all she'd done, she and Jim weren't really married anymore, except in name. They kept up the pretense for visitors, official and otherwise, but the members of their flock knew and understood the way the Jones marriage worked and didn't work.

"Look, Preston. You have no idea how hard it is to keep this place together, to keep it functioning. It's nothing like running an ordinary church, nothing like what you did back in Indiana." He paused to rein in his irritation, plaster the smile back on his grim lips. "Nothing like what I did back in the States either, you understand. Even in the Bay Area, when we had all those communal homes for our members. This here," he gestured with both hands around them, toward the distant crops, the dorms on stilts, the huge Pavilion, "this here is completely new and different. The New World incarnate, the new word made flesh. No sir, you have no idea whatsoever."

Over and over, Marcus was punching his right fist into his left hand, with a smacking sound like a slap to the face. He didn't say a word, though he kept sighing and exhaling loudly.

"What is it, Marcus?" Preston asked. "What do you think?"

Marcus looked to Marceline and then out at the jungle, avoiding his father, who obviously wanted him to remain quiet. "I know people here can't stand it."

"What are you talking about?" Jim rose in anger. "Nobody's told me they hate the public address. Where did you hear that?"

"Forget it, Dad. Just forget it." Before his father could touch him or say more, Marcus got up and jogged toward the Pavilion. "See you later everyone. We have to practice for the game next week in Georgetown." His shoulders were slumped as he fled his father.

Preston cocked his head at Jim. "Maybe you should listen to the boy. Sometimes, you know, we older preachers get a bit set in our ways. We need to hear from the young people, to listen to what they really think, instead of what we want them to think."

Snorting, Marceline shook her head.

"And what's that supposed to mean, Marcy?" asked her mother. "Isn't it true we older people need to listen to the youth?"

"Sure, Mother. I was just thinking about how, back in Richmond, you didn't have any sort of forum where kids could talk to the elders. I mean, there was a youth club, but not any real opportunity for dialogue. Peoples Temple is all about dialogue, between all segments of the church."

"Sometimes too much dialogue," Jim added, and he smiled warmly at her, a real smile. He was surely pleased by her defense of the church, which he took to be a defense of him. Actually she was annoyed by the hypocrisy of both her father and her husband, by the notion that these well-meaning male ministers could actually reflect on their own words and take action to remedy their own mistakes. Perhaps her father could do so now he'd retired. But not Jim.

"I hear what you're saying, Preston. I'll ask my staff about the P.A. It's our only form of communication that isn't face to face; we don't have telephones here in Jonestown, and no mail service."

"I appreciate the logistical difficulties you contend with every day. But it's not like the telephone, where you can have a two-way conversation. When you use the P.A., only the speaker gets to talk." Preston spoke calmly, as he if were reasoning it out for himself, not criticizing Jim per se.

Suddenly, Jim walked off the deck in a manner reminiscent of his son. "That reminds me," he said, turning back to them, "I've got some announcements to make. I'll see you at dinner."

Relieved he was gone for the rest of the afternoon, Marceline sat back in her chair and sipped her lemonade. Her parents' presence overwhelmed her, made her feel as if she weren't a grown up, a grandmother, a woman in charge of her own life. She hoped she didn't do that to her own children: infantilize them even as they made adult decisions, fathered children, willingly became expatriates. Of course, Ken had joined Tina in Jonestown; he hadn't thought to question the move. Jim assumed Ken would follow his leadership, and so he did. He expected it of everyone who loved him, and most were like Ken: only too happy, considering themselves privileged to follow a leader like Jim Jones. As she herself once did. Only now could she see the core of this clay-footed idol, not a great man but just a man. Like any other. It seemed to Marceline that the greater the vision, the more numerous the foibles, the petty horrors.

"So, Marcy? What next?" her mother asked.

"If you don't mind resting for a while and entertaining yourselves, I think I'll go to the infirmary and see how our patients are doing. It's nice for them when I visit every day."

"Of course, dear. We'll be fine."

The pair of parrots squawked at her departure. Did they look fondly on her, or were they mocking? She couldn't tell.

During the remainder of her parents' stay, Jim behaved remarkably well. With his own parents dead, the Baldwins were among the few older people he deferred to, perhaps viewing them in a quasi-parental role, just as he had when he'd met them as a teenager in 1949.

Marceline compared Jim's interactions with her father with his exchanges with Jocelyn's father, who was younger and more liberal. She saw that these two men both had the power and authority to rein in the worst of Jim's excesses. But in their absence, Jim was free to be his worst self.

The day of their departure, Marceline was both relieved and sorry to see her parents go. As planned, she flew with them into Georgetown. She was quiet while her father waxed optimistic about the future of Jonestown. They knew nothing of the suicide drills, the White Nights, which had been going on since Susan Stein's defection, nor of the threat of the Concerned Relatives to get their family members out by any means necessary, nor even of the relatives' recent coup in gaining a U.S. congressman's interest.

"Marcy, why don't you come back with us to the States? You look so very tired. Just for a little while." Her mother was scrutinizing Marceline without mercy, as she used to do when she was getting dressed for church, and everything she saw was wrong.

Marceline sighed. Indiana, its lazy Midwestern flatness, the front porches with wicker furniture. The idea of rest. Of course she was tired, and of course her mother would note it, while her father was better at seeing what he wanted to see.

"Thank you, Mother. It's a very kind offer. I might take you up on it down the road, but for now, my place is in Jonestown."

Her parents looked at one another. Marceline realized the suggestion was not spontaneous. She saw they had a plan and were determined to make it work.

"Really, Marcy. That place seems to run itself," her father said. "You have plenty of dependable nurses to run the clinic in your absence. The young one who came up with the burn cure is very sharp. Plus that Jewish doctor, Shat? Schacht? Anyway, the point is that we're concerned about you."

Marceline found herself weakening. Part of her wanted to get on that plane, to return to the cold, boring Indiana of her youth, a place that remained the same, year after year. Her old room was there, unchanged since she'd left it nearly thirty years earlier for her life with Jim. If she could persuade Marcus to come with her, why not?

"Bring the kids," her mother said. "Any or all of them. Bring Sioux Lee. What a sweetheart. She ought to meet her Great Aunt Laura, don't you think?"

Beside the road to the airport, they passed numerous Guyanese, too poor for cab fare, too impatient to wait for buses that rarely came on time. They were beautiful in their various colors, their humanity, their neediness. Nothing Indiana offered could compare with them, with Guyana, the country and the people she had adopted. Here in this tiny Co-operative Socialist Republic in South America, she had taken on another country's destiny willingly, just as she had married Jim, till death do them part.

"Mom, it's a lovely offer, and I'll certainly think about it."

"No, you won't, Marcy," her mother said curtly, hurt. "I can tell by that stubborn look on your face, the way you've set your jaw."

Marlene read the disappointment in her mother's gray eyes and the set of her very similar jaw. The two women were equally matched in resolve.

"Marcy, it's okay," said her father. "We just miss you, that's all. Moving across the country was one thing but to another continent, well that's been hard on us." He sighed. "We've tried to keep that from you, because we know how much this ministry means to you, but we are, after all, parents. And parents like to see their children. And grandchildren."

"And great-grandchildren," Marlene added. "I'm glad I got to meet Susie, anyway. That was absolutely the highlight."

Whoever crowned her mother's list, it was never Marceline.

"Here we are." The small plane stopped, and they descended the outdoor stairs. Pan Am's jet adorned the runway, its white wings and shiny sleek fuselage looking like something from science fiction after their week in the jungle. It belonged to that other world Marceline had departed. Most of the airport personnel knew her. She greeted them warmly as she walked her parents out to the jet. What an odd bird, she thought, comparing the huge flying machine to the brightly colored pair of parrots she had grown to love. This bird was made by man, not Mother Nature, nor the male sky god her husband loved to deride. It was sterile and ugly and reeked of money, representing a life she no longer cared to live.

"Goodbye, Mother. Goodbye, Dad."

Her mother offered her cheek, which Marceline dutifully kissed. Her father hugged her. Both looked as if they might cry but didn't.

"We'll miss you, honey." Her father gestured for Marlene to mount the stairs before him.

"We'll miss you too, Daddy."

From the base of the stairs, Marceline watched them, two old people who clung to the railing, no longer the god-like adults who had dominated her childhood and adolescence until she married. Had she merely exchanged one master for another, then, in uniting her life with Jim's? Maybe she wasn't so different from Laura, who had married so young without thought of a career, eagerly adopting the role epitomized by their mother that Marceline had so abhorred back then? She was nothing like Laura, Marceline assured herself, though she couldn't deny that the structure of their lives, while superficially contrasting, bore unpleasant similarities. Not one of the Baldwin women was in control of her own life.

From the shade of the hangar, Marceline watched the huge jet taxi to the far end of the runway. Though they couldn't possibly see her, she waved goodbye to her parents. She waved and waved as the plane revved its engines, impossibly loud, and then raced down the tarmac, faster and faster, ungainly and yet miraculously able to fly.

YOU CAN CALL ME AN EGOMANIAC,
A MEGALOMANIAC
WITH A MESSIANIC COMPLEX.
I DON'T HAVE ANY COMPLEX, HONEY,
I HAPPEN TO KNOW I'M THE MESSIAH.
IT'S ONLY A COMPLEX
WHEN YOU'RE CONFUSED.
IT'S ONLY A COMPLEX WHEN YOU
HAVE NEUROTIC COMPULSIONS.
HONEY, I DON'T HAVE ANY CONFLICT
ABOUT IT AT ALL.
I KNOW I AM GOD THE MESSIAH.
THERE WASN'T ANY GOD TILL I CAME ALONG.

Jim Jones

Virgil Nascimento
11:56 p.m.
Nov. 18, 1981
Washington, D.C.

"Ce qui déclenche la crise est presque toujours incontrôlable."

"What sets off the crisis is almost always uncontrollable," writes
Camus, as if he knew me. My comment is solipsistic to the extreme,
yet absolutely true. It is not solely this anniversary and my suppu-
rating self-hatred that propel my hand toward the drawer in which
I keep my beautiful handgun, a Ruger .44 magnum, undeniably
fine killing technology.

Is it because I can that I want to kill?

As I handle my Ruger now, I admire its sleek lines, its under-
stated power. I am mighty with this tool in my hand. Jones
persuaded his followers to swallow cyanide, a dreadful poison
despite its strangely pleasant almond-like smell, which took long
minutes to attain its desired effect, minutes during which his
followers watched one another suffer, yet he took a gun to his own
head. No suffering for me, thank you very much, he must have
said to himself after watching the contorted bodies writhing in
unspeakable pain. His doctor mixed several tranquilizers in with
the poison to ease the suffering, but they took fifteen minutes to
activate and were therefore useless. Like the others, his wife, the
angelic Marceline, took the poison. Did she take it voluntarily?

No one knows. Insane, these women who idolize the insane. But in this era of so-called women's "liberation," the distaff population must not be allowed to shirk its responsibility. Are the followers in fact any less guilty than their leader?

I am ruled by my childhood friend Forbes Burnham, our unholy Prime Minister. I like to blame him for my own excesses, for his ignoble and prodigious example of greed and pilfering. I believe his own models were our confreres in Haiti, Uganda, Congo, and the many African nations who gained their independence before we did, whose leaders grew filthy, excessively, immorally rich from the blood, sweat and tears of their subjects, as the British and French did before them. Surely I am as bad as the PM. I pride myself on it. My idealistic secretary, Charlayne, has no idea that beneath my respectable Oxfordian veneer and "beautiful" accent, I am just another monster. I am the colonial tyrant, but now "post" and in blackface. I am rich, rich as Croesus, and like the good husband I never was shall leave everything to Pru. She can finish her days in London's highest style, as befits a royal personage, the queen she always wanted to be.

I suspect Nancy loved her adopted child more than she loves the Ghost, though she would never say so. Perhaps she loves the dead more than the living. She would not be the first. If so, she is too prudent to state her sentiment aloud. Funny, for she has a written record of imprudence, which my FBI friend so kindly passed on to me.

Once more she disturbs me at the door, wanting me beside her in bed. Again I ask her for time to finish my daily writing. As she speaks, she nurses the Ghost, perhaps believing I find her maternal gesture endearing. It is repulsive.

Nancy is more repugnant than she herself knows. *Marxism is only as good as its leader, and I believe totally in you. I saw myself as an expendable piece of meat.*

Note her use of the past tense. I see her this way still. I cannot imagine selling my body for secrets, as she and Jones's other whores did in the capital. What does she sell herself for these days? Mere survival? (As if survival could be "mere.") She and the Ghost live on while all her people died, including the adopted black daughter she convinces herself she so adored. Quiana. Not long ago, Nancy was on the phone to another Jonestown whore, now a housewife in Los Angeles. Both were mourning their dead, as if the new children, their new husbands and lives, did not exist. Well, dearest American wife, I can and will make that desired end possible. As I note the clock ticking, I wonder if I can delay a few minutes longer to take us into the nineteenth of November, when it is no longer the anniversary of the death of my natal country, the Guyana we once dreamed of.

Nancy Levine-Nascimento knows very little about Marxism, despite her blithe use of the word in her billet-doux to her leader. We are all pieces of meat: Nancy, the Ghost, me. And every leader is Jim Jones, every Marxist a fascist in disguise. In the past, I pretended to be different, but I am not. The secret to gaining peoples' love is to destroy them. Machiavelli wrote that there is no surer way of keeping possession than by devastation. Is that not what we learn from Jim Jones and the demise of Peoples Temple? Hitler's subjects adored him; they did whatever was required to be loved by their Fuhrer, to be beloved as the child craves the love of his parents. They died by the millions for him.

In contrast, what is Emperor Jones? He failed to manage an even thousand. Papa Doc did better. Amin better still.

To you who read this document, you must understand I do not admire Hitler per se. He was a peasant and a bore. But he managed to con millions into believing in him. Purely objectively, one has to marvel at what he accomplished. How he changed the vocabulary of our time, turning ordinary citizens into mass-murderers, all in the guise of persuading them how superior they were to those they annihilated. Pure genius.

I cannot pacify the asshole with reason – he is a raving madman.
I laugh at this, rather than seethe. Does Nancy see herself as
reasonable? Just a few months after writing this, she was on her
knees, begging this "raving madman" to marry her.

If the deed is to be done on the anniversary, I must not tarry.
But what matters a few minutes before or after midnight? In
the morning, our bodies will be discovered by our Polish housekeeper, and the press will write about the post-traumatic stress
of Jonestown, the lingering residue of Jonestown, the aftermath
of Jonestown.

Not far from Georgetown, Guyana, we ministerial types have our
very own shooting range, where Forbes's bodyguards show us how
to use our Rugers. We drive there in our Mercedes Benzes, the car
all dictators worthy of the title love to drive.

Again and again I returned to practice, finding great delight in
obliterating the target. One of the guards was a good caricaturist and
liked to take a pencil to the silhouettes. Each day we killed someone
different. Jimmy Carter, the Queen, once someone's wife. Once,
when he was drunk, this artist-guard took away our targets and
asked us to model while he drew extraordinary like profiles of each
of us. It should be noted that we had drunk our share of Demerara
and joked about switching targets. The Minister of Health wanted
to shoot the Minister of Education, or perhaps vice versa, but in
the end, we all chose our own silhouettes. I remember the shooting
that day was particularly excellent.

Camus declares: "There is no sun without shadow, and it is
essential to know the night." Thus, he invites death. He invites me
to create the night, as the Judeo-Christian god did so that mortals
would know the day. Camus did not commit self-murder, like
Seneca. Neither did he encourage murder like Machiavelli. He lived
without melodrama, his days of violence in the Resistance numbered
and only by necessity. I long for such righteousness but know it
shall elude me always, whether or not I perpetrate the crime I plan.

In one of her letters to the Emperor, Nancy tells him that she hates offering her mouth to me: *I cannot bring myself to do it, but I will if it will make him more accommodating to us.* I am no longer laughing. I am her dupe. Instead of taking a mistress in the capital, I divorced Pru, married this freak American and procreated with her. The two of us colluded to create a monster.

"If God exists, all depends on him and we can do nothing against his will," writes Camus. "If he does not exist, everything depends on us."

And if Camus is right, there is nothing more to write.

Only action means.

WITHOUT ME, LIFE HAS NO MEANING.

Jim Jones

Watts Freeman
12:12 p.m.
Nov. 18, 2008
San Francisco

WF: I'll never forget that smell. Almonds. Almonds everywhere. You'd think it would stink. After everyone was dead, it did. But when the people were lining up and the doc and the nurses were getting everything ready with their little colored syringes and paper cups and all, it smelled good. Sweet. Didn't smell like death. Like what the army guys started calling "Jonestown perfume" later on. Turns out all those military people who came to get the bodies had to throw out their uniforms and every single thing they were wearing 'cause the smell of the dead just wouldn't come out in the laundry. I heard they burned or buried the stuff, and even then, maybe it's just a rumor, but some nights they could still smell it even years later, coming out of the ground in Panama, or wherever that corpse patrol was from.

KR: Didn't you help identify the bodies, Watts?

WF: Yeah. It was fucked though. Excuse me. I mean it was basically pointless, 'cause what we did was write people's names in pencil on these ID tags, right? That's all anybody had to write with. But by the time the military got the bodies into bags, after a couple of days or so, the writing had pretty much faded. It got bleached by the sun, or dissolved from the humidity and rain, so all that effort was for nothing.

KR: Couldn't you just re-write the names?

WF: You ever been to the tropics?

KR: I've been to Jamaica; does that count?

WF: Woman, that's the North Pole compared to Guyana! A couple hours in the sun at the equator, in the nineties or more, and the bodies start swelling up like crazy. No way I could figure out who was who twenty-four hours after doing it the first time. Bodies blowing up, spitting out fluid. Sorry for being disgusting, but that's how it was. The clothes got all raggedy too. And one of the weirdest things was that by the third day, you couldn't tell which bodies were white and which were black, 'cause they all this grayish-greenish color. Everyone except Jimmie Jones.

KR: Really? What color was he?

WF: *[Laughs]* He white. Ghost-white. White as the day he came out of old Lynetta, who liked to talk about how she gave birth to a god or something. Like the bad old Sky God Jim used to rail on come down and made His final point. In that last tape, Jim start talking about God, can't remember what exactly he call him …

KR: The Supreme Being.

WF: Yeah. He say it's the will of the Supreme Being, or something like that, what's going down here. Can you dig that? He deny this so-called Supreme Being for thirty years, and then, on the day of his own damn judgment, he start saying little Jimmie Jones got nothing to do with it; it all the will of the man upstairs. Man.

I'm gonna put a cigarette in my mouth and just suck on it for a while, if you can stand it, Kenyatta.

KR: Watts, it's fine. Whatever you wanna do.

WF: Whatever I wanna do is fine? Hmmm ... I like the sound of that.

KR: Can you say anything more about what he called the Sky God? There's a kind of theology, I suppose, that Jim Jones stood for, and it's hard to get my mind wrapped around it. Sometimes it sounds like Marxism, sometimes Christianity, sometimes both. He quoted Matthew on the Temple stationery and retained the Temple's membership in the Disciples of Christ all those years, and then other times it sounds like one of those seventies encounter groups that used to be so popular, confronting people with their behavior in front of everyone, exposing their sins. I guess they still do that today in some places.

WF: It all those things. Not one thing. Not one theology, as you call it. He just pick and choose from what he need at any particular moment to make people believe him. And sometimes, sin had nothing to do with it. He liked shaming people. Like he call one woman fat, told her she ate more'n her fair share, not like a good socialist. Made her stand naked in front of everybody to show how fat she is. Got everybody, even the kids, to say bad things about her body.

KR: Depriving someone of their dignity like that ...

WF: That's it right there, Kenyatta. You put your finger on it to the T.

KR: Is it true that he threw the Bible on the ground and stomped on it in front of the congregation? That he was mad too many people believed in that book and not enough in him?

WF: I don't know. I heard that story too. Some of the old folks kinda shocked by him going against the Bible sometimes, or him pointing out where it say one thing in one place and another thing in another place. But later on anyway, that stuff about the Good Book didn't matter so much to the old people. I mean, he take care of them, whatever he say about the Bible. He get them a roof and food and a doctor and visits to the dentist. I think with the really old ones, a nurse come every single day to their dormitory just to check blood pressure and whatnot. Just to see how they doing every day, even though nothing particular wrong with them. That why they stay. Not 'cause he stomping or not stomping on the Bible.

KR: Well, that does sound pretty good, I have to say. My grandmother would probably appreciate that kind of attention too. Though I don't know about living thirty to a room, or however many there were. One or two of the reporters with the congressman compared the sleeping quarters to berths on the slave ships, with three or four bunks stacked up and no light and no room and no fresh air.

WF: Yeah, those reporters all white. What they know about it?

KR: Watts, no one alive today, black or white, saw those slave ships themselves, right? I mean, we've all seen drawings or paintings or engravings, things like that.

WF: Yeah, I hear what you're saying, but even so, those reporters didn't get what Jonestown was about. Okay, that one dude did. Guy from the Washington Post. He wrote that it was a pretty amazing place when you compared it to the ghetto in D.C., say, or Detroit.

KR: Or Watts.

WF: Or Watts, yeah. But the rest of them, those NBC guys, they just hammering Jimmie Jones over and over, like banging a hammer down hard on a nail already deep in. I see how the man boiled over. I don't like what happened. Not at all, but those reporters … face it, a bunch of ugly white guys, nothing like you, they just digging at the man, poking at him like with cattle prods or something, like they wanted to get him mad, like men at a cockfight. Not asking fair questions but ones they knew would make Jimmie Jones blow up. They had cameras. They wanted to make him do something dramatic, so they could get it on the TV. Yeah. They sure got some drama, huh, though those NBC guys didn't live to see it on the tube.

KR: The photographer from the Examiner also got killed.

WF: Maybe Jimmie Jones just lump together all those guys with cameras when he told the shooters who to get.

KR: Did you actually hear that conversation, Watts?

WF: Him telling those guys who to kill? Nah. I just think that's what happened. Look at who died and who didn't. The congressman for sure, and the reporters with cameras. The ones with the notebooks didn't get killed.

KR: What about Patty Parks, the defector who got killed?

WF: That an accident, I'm pretty sure. I don't think Jimmie wanted any of his people to die. Even the ones who left. I mean, not die in that way. The whole suicide thing wouldn't have gone down the way it did without that nasty interviewer. Amazing that Patty was the only accident. I mean, those guys sprayed the airstrip with a shitload of bullets. Excuse me.

KR: A number of others were very badly injured.

WF: Yeah, I know. Didn't die though. That what count. That gal with the congressman, Jackie something, she in politics today, still. She got hurt, yeah, but she recover.

KR: You make it sound, I don't know, as if somehow the congressman and the reporters got what they deserved. *[Laughs]* I'd hate to think you felt that way about journalists in general, Watts.

WF: Some journalists, maybe. But I try ... I try not to bunch everyone all together in huge groups like "cult followers" or "the media" and make these big statements about 'em.

KR: Because?

WF: Because that's how you start lying. Like when I said none of the reporters could understand Jonestown 'cause they white, I remember the *Washington Post* guy, a white guy, he kinda got it. So I can't say all of them this or that, because it ain't true. And after Jonestown, I try really, really hard not to lie no more.

KR: I see. It's how you maintain your integrity. I really appreciate that. Watts, I should get back to the station if I'm going to edit this tape for tonight's broadcast. Is there anything else you want to say to our audience, anything we didn't get to that you think is really important? I can try and get it on the air, though I can't make any promises, as I do have a boss who gets the last word.

WF: Only one last word, Miss Kenyatta, and that's death.

KR: I'm sorry Watts, but I didn't quite catch that. Can you face me please?

WF: It ain't worth repeating. It's just weird, you know, how thirty years ago it some big, big deal about all these people offing themselves in Jonestown, like nobody ever heard of such a thing, and now we talk about suicide bombers right and left, every day in the newspaper. Every country in the Middle East make their own, and now they exported everywhere in the world.

KR: Are you saying that what happened in Guyana was some sort of preview of the future?

WF: No. I'm just noticing it. People all over the world these days saying they gonna die for the Cause and take a whole bunch a people with 'em. Not just Muslims neither.

KR: Wasn't it Huey Newton who first used the term revolutionary suicide? Back in the sixties? And then Jones took it on?

WF: Jimmie Jones liked to copy the black man, like he did with Father Divine, 'cept he got it wrong, which don't surprise me. That Huey Newton wrote a book a whole five years before Jimmie Jones notice it. But the man got it backward.

KR: How so?

WF: Did you read that book, Kenyatta?

KR: No, I'm sorry I didn't.

WF: *[Laughs]* You got some homework, girl. Jimmie Jones got Huey all wrong. He wasn't talking about killing yourself like the Peoples Temple did, with poison and everyone going down instead of letting yourself be taken by the enemy, or any of that shit. He talking about living for the Cause. About dying for the Cause if you had to, but through living. Like, through protesting or something, through getting your ass kicked by the cops when you out there on the streets with your fist in the air. He not talking about laying down and giving up. No way. He didn't do that, not any of those Panthers.

KR: I suppose you're right. Now I know I have to read it. I wonder if I can get a copy this afternoon?

WF: Well, funny thing, I found it in the stacks at the downtown library. Dig this, the chick who worked in the stacks that day, excuse me, the woman, I mean, she a Peoples Temple member! Name of Truth, which Jimmie Jones give her, like Father Divine naming people Sweet Delight or Lovely Mercy or shit like that. She crazier than most of the white people in the Temple, but when I saw her again, I guess in the early eighties maybe, she still gung-ho supporting Jimmie Jones, going on to me about the CIA and whatever other shit she read or heard about. Like she thought I'm gonna agree with her. I ask her, "Truth, you know who you talking to? I was there, woman. I was in that jungle, and I walked out of it, left behind nine-hundred-odd brothers and sisters, and you think I'm going praise Jim Jones with you?" This real crude, so don't put this on the air. She must have never got laid by him. The people who did the nasty with him say he a horrible lay, if you pardon my language.

KR: *[Laughs]* Watts, on that note, I have to get going. Thank you so much. You've been very generous with your time. We'll be on the air tonight at eight p.m., 91.9 on your FM dial. Can I call you if I have questions while I'm editing this afternoon?

WF: Kenyatta, you call me any time. Anytime is a good time to hear that beautiful radio voice of yours. Believe this old man. Kenyatta, can I call you sometime? I mean, not for an interview but for something else? A burrito? I wanna talk to you when we ain't on the air, hear what you have to say back to me when you ain't being so professional.

KR: Okay, Watts. You call me. Here's my card.

WF: You an associate producer? Wow! You a big deal, girl. I mean woman. I mean, Ms. Kenyatta Robinson.

KR: I'll see you, Watts. Let me know what you think of the broadcast tonight, okay?

WF: I will do that, for sure. I call you right after. You at the station then?

KR: I'll be in bed by then! But you can leave a message, okay?

WF: Not gonna give me your home phone, huh. What, you got a boyfriend or something?

KR: I'll talk to you, Watts. Soon. Goodbye. And thanks.

I AM PEACE
I AM JUSTICE
I AM EQUALITY
I AM FREEDOM
I AM GOD.

Jim Jones

Truth Miller
April 20, 1999
Flemington, New Jersey

At the kitchen table, Truth was studying *Thought Reform and the Psychology of Totalism: A Study of "Brainwashing" in China* for her exam in Twentieth Century Political History when Cuffy came home from school. As soon as she heard his key in the door, she inserted a bookmark – her grocery list on the back of an envelope from the gas company – and went to greet him.

"Hi, Cuff. What's wrong?" His wide eyes brimmed with tears. Truth felt a chill saturate her body. "What is it? What's happened?"

"Mommy!" He allowed himself to be hugged, the kind of physical contact he'd been resisting as his tenth birthday approached.

She led him to the table, pushed aside her books and notecards, put his knapsack on the floor and took his face between her hands. "Talk to me, Cuff. What's happened?" With her fingertip, she arrested a tear before it slid into his ear.

Cuffy wiped his eyes with the back of his hand, pushing her away. "Didn't you hear?"

She shook her head. "I've been studying all day. No radio, nothing."

"Turn on the TV."

Observing the ghost-trails of tears on his dark cheeks, fear swept over her.

Beside the sink sat her parents' black and white TV, which she allowed him to watch while she washed dishes, but only then. There was no other television in the house. Sighing, she rose and turned it to the major network news station.

The anchorman, a white middle-aged man with a stern expression, said: "The latest on the Columbine High School shootings are fifteen dead, twenty-four wounded, and the gunmen identified as two minors who were students at the school, though their names have not yet been released to the press. They committed suicide as SWAT teams were closing in. We take you live to the high school in Littleton, Colorado, where our Denver associate is interviewing survivors."

The graphic read "COLUMBINE MASSACRE" beneath a characterless modern box-building in pastel colors. For reasons she couldn't immediately articulate, Truth was glad Cuffy would go to a red brick high school, over a century old. A lot of rich-looking white kids, mostly blond, and their parents, were hugging, crying, and pushing away reporters. Truth turned it off.

Cuffy let himself be hugged again while she fingered his hair, cut in a stylish flat top, shaved close on the sides. "Tell me what happened."

He swallowed. "We were having social studies, and the assistant principal runs in and tells Ms. Eldridge what happened. Dr. Sexton was crying. So after the principal left, Ms. Eldridge turned on the TV in the middle of our lesson – we were learning about the three branches of government – and we saw what you just saw, only it was earlier, and they didn't know who was doing the shooting, and they kept talking about pipe bombs and explosions."

"Ms. Eldridge let you watch as it happened?"

"Yeah. She said this was 'history in the making.' She said what we were watching would be a 'milestone in the history of American violence.'" Cuffy shook his head and blew air up from his lower lip, making the hair above his forehead quiver. He did this when he was disturbed.

Truth liked his teacher. Her politics were more liberal than many Flemingtonians', and she kept patriotic propaganda to a minimum. This made her a hero in the overwhelmingly conservative school system.

"What do you think about it, Cuffy?"

He blew air again and said, "I don't want to talk anymore. Is there anything to eat?"

"Okay. But we'll talk later for sure." She usually insisted he get his own after-school snack, but today she fixed it for him. From the fridge she removed a gallon of milk, an apple, baby carrots, and from the breadbox a carton of Social Tea cookies, which she had eaten as a child and introduced Cuffy to when they'd moved back east four years earlier.

After he swallowed two glasses of milk and ate half the apple and four cookies, she asked, "Did Ms. Eldridge have a discussion about it?"

"There wasn't enough time. We had to go to P.E. after that, and then school was over."

"Well, I'm not sure she should have let you see that. It must have been terrifying."

Angry, Cuffy pushed the cookie box away. "Mom! You're always saying how Americans don't know anything, how they never pay attention to what's happening in the world. Why are you being such a hypocrite all of a sudden?"

He was right. She did always say that, but there were good and bad ways of learning what was happening in the world. The American broadcast media were sensationalist, as she had learned too well during Jonestown, whose twentieth anniversary had passed last November. Truth had not attended the media-blitzed memorial service at the collective gravesite in Oakland. "Well, I can see how you may think that. I just don't think it's good to get your information from network news as it's happening. There's no context for anything." To her own ear, her words sounded weak, and Cuffy was not convinced.

"How else are we going to learn about it? That community radio station you listen to isn't going to have a reporter on the scene."

"But why do we need to witness it while it's happening? We don't know any of the details yet … who these kids were, or what was going on with them, or any background at all." Truth didn't like the words leaving her mouth. There was no excuse for students gunning down their classmates and teachers, no matter what. She wondered if perhaps the shooters – that's what the reporter called them – were minority kids who'd suffered racist and second-class treatment by their peers and teachers. But looking at the very suburban white crowd, she had a feeling that was not the case here.

"Mom. I think it's important to know about it while it's happening." He pulled the cookie box back toward him and took out four more. "Everybody at school and on the bus couldn't stop talking about it. It's like the biggest, scariest thing that's ever happened in our lives. And it was kids, kids like us, that it was happening to."

Truth felt vaguely sick. "I just don't know the right thing to say about it. My gut reaction is that it's too violent for you to watch. Even if you didn't see any of the killing." Inside, she was replaying the days of the Jonestown massacre, when they'd kept the TV on in the Geary temple twenty-four hours a day, relentlessly besieged by reporters as facts ebbed out of Guyana. The first numbers released were too low by half, giving them hope that perhaps four or five hundred Peoples Temple members had somehow escaped mass death.

"Mom, can we turn it back on? I want to know what else they've found out."

For the next hour they sat at the kitchen table, watching, the fright in Truth's stomach turning her study-day caffeine to acid. The various networks had different graphics to highlight the Columbine Massacre developing news story. She wanted to use the coverage to show Cuffy how American media distorted reality, but she felt too nauseated to speak. All afternoon, Cuffy was on the phone with his friends Jason and Mikey. When he asked if he could go over to Mikey's, who lived only three blocks away, Truth surprised herself with the vehemence of her response.

"Absolutely not! I want you here!"

He drew back. "Mom? Hello? The thing's happening in Colorado! The boys who did it are dead. I'm not in danger." He rolled his eyes toward the ceiling, shaking his head in his standard "my crazy mother" gesture.

"I know. I just want you here, that's all. I don't have to be rational every minute, Cuffy. It's freaking me out, this thing, this thing they're calling a massacre. I want you next to me, so I know you're safe. You can invite Mikey here, okay?"

After Mikey arrived, and Truth locked the door behind him, she got a second glass for Mikey and more fruit. The carrots remained untouched, as usual. Then she collapsed on the couch, the same one her father had fallen asleep on every night during the last few decades of his life. She had changed little in the house. The biggest alterations were in Cuffy's room, which had once been hers. She'd let him paint whatever colors he wanted and even graffiti the walls. She had been forbidden to express her personality in there. Her parents had prohibited thumbtacks, posters, anything that wasn't neatly contained in proper frames. But here in the living room, with its dull brown sofa and overstuffed armchairs, the Impressionist prints bordered in fake gilt, it could almost be the 1950s again. Except she'd donated the big console TV which had dominated her parents' lives to the Flemington women's shelter.

Truth lay on her belly, hoping she wouldn't throw up. She ordered herself to remain calm; she must be having some sort of flashback. She had to stay calm for Cuffy, who, while upset, was clearly not experiencing his world turned inside out and ass backwards as she was. His first response of fear had passed. It was like a movie to him, these shooting deaths in sunny Colorado, where the scenery looked something like a set from an after-school TV series. The violence was far away and unrelated to his own life. Perhaps that was how Jonestown had seemed to most Americans.

She felt like calling someone. There was no one. Although Truth was cordial in her classes and to her neighbors, she hadn't made any friends. Since the demise of the Peoples Temple, she didn't know how to. In terms of human connection, Cuffy was it. Before their deaths, her parents had grown increasingly necessary to her. She had nursed them as best she could. They died only three weeks apart, her mother first.

Beside the couch she'd stacked her books, but nausea made it impossible to study. She thought about the killings at the Port Kaituma airstrip. One minute, the Congressman and his flunkeys were getting ready to board their plane, and the next, guns were going off everywhere. All these years later, teenagers were using semi-automatic machine guns as well as explosives. How could suburban kids get hold of stuff like that? If she started to cry, she feared she'd never stop.

"Hey, Truth," Mikey called from the kitchen. "Could I ask you something?"

She liked Mikey. He was her son's closest friend. He was a skinny Italian boy with dark features. His father drank too much, and his mother worked two jobs but made it to all their school events and was always kind to Cuffy. "Sure, Mikey. What is it?"

He and Cuffy flopped into the armchairs flanking the sofa and stared at her.

"What?" She knew this would be no ordinary question. Probably Cuffy had told him about Jonestown, whatever version of it he understood.

"Who's Cuffy named after?"

The boys exchanged looks. They were testing her.

"Cuffy knows," she said carefully. "Haven't you told him about Paul Cuffy, honey?"

Cuffy nodded. "But I don't know a lot of details. You said he was a leader of a slave rebellion in Guyana in the eighteen hundreds, I think."

"Eighteenth century. That means seventeen hundreds," Truth interjected. Stating a straightforward fact made her feel better.

"Right, seventeen hundreds, I mean. That's really all I know."

"What I want to know," said Mikey, "is how many people did this Cuffy guy kill?"

She turned red. "I don't know." She cleared her throat. "I never heard any numbers mentioned."

"A lot, right?" Mikey prodded.

"In a rebellion, you have to kill lots of people," added Cuffy. "So why did you name me after a killer?"

"Revolutions are always violent," she said numbly. She wanted to hide from these boys, not to answer their not-so-innocent questions. She paused. "I hope you're not calling this thing that happened in Colorado today a revolution, comparing it to the Guyanese slave rebellion. Cuffy and his people forced the Dutch colonists out of that part of Guyana and governed it themselves for nearly a year. That's pretty amazing, don't you think?"

"Then what happened?" Mikey asked. "Did the slave owners come back?"

She sighed. "Well, it's hard to govern thousands of people, and Cuffy's followers didn't get along, so their rule sort of evaporated. But he was still a big hero in Guyana. Their first brown-skinned leader. When Guyana became independent from Britain in 1966, they made Independence Day the same day as the Berbice Rebellion, which Cuffy led."

"But still, Cuffy must have killed tons of people, a bunch of Dutch, I guess, to be able to take over their government, right?" Cuffy said.

Truth's stomach wrenched, and she ran for the bathroom, but only for a long series of dry heaves. She was dried out, empty, though she wanted to purge the feelings inside her.

Cuffy knocked.

"Mom, are you all right?" His voice rose in concern. "I didn't mean to make you so upset."

Through the door she said, "It's all right, Sweetie. You didn't do anything. I'm just not feeling very good. I think I'll go to bed. Maybe you should have dinner at Mikey's, if that's okay with his mom."

* * *

The next day, after her exam, she followed her professor back to his office. "Dr. Wheeler? Do you have a minute?"

Turning in surprise, Norman Wheeler, a white man in his sixties, pudgy and bespectacled, waved her inside. "Come in, come in. I'm glad you're here. This is the first time all semester you've come to my office, Truth."

She nodded.

"What can I help you with? Are you concerned about the test? I wouldn't be. You've done very well this term."

Shaking her head, Truth looked down, the nausea returning to twist her insides. An ugly moan came out of her.

"Are you all right? Here, have some water." He poured a glass from a pitcher on the windowsill. "You look kind of pale."

In the background, his radio was tuned to the local public station. She kept hearing the words "Columbine Massacre." The phrase assaulted her nerves. "Could you turn that off? Please?"

"The radio? Oh, sure. I forget it's even on. That Columbine shooting is a real horror. I wanted to talk about it today in class, but we had the exam, so next week we can try and put it into context with what we're looking at this semester."

"How can you put it into context?" She looked up at him. "I have no idea. My son's only ten, but they had the TV on in his class yesterday, if you can believe that. I wanted to help him think about it, but I froze. It's just horror, as you said. Pure violence without any kind of rationale. How could there be anything political to it?"

"The fact that middle-class high school boys in the American heartland can equip themselves with enough material to make bombs and hold off a SWAT team for an afternoon ... don't you think that's political?"

She shook her head. "I don't know. All I know is that I'm really, really scared." She looked into her teacher's eyes. "Scared for my little boy."

Professor Wheeler refilled her glass, and she drank it gratefully. She felt calmer, her stomach settling.

"You don't speak up much in class, so I only know you through your essays, and you don't seem to mix much with the other students, but you seem to be seriously invested in learning about these political movements."

"The others are a lot younger."

"That must be hard. And they're not as serious as you are. You seem to care a lot about understanding these ideas and their manifestations. Understanding Soviet Communism, for instance, and how it differs from Chinese Communism."

"My parents were there."

"Excuse me?"

She cleared her throat. "It turns out that my parents were in China during the revolution."

"Really?" He smiled wide as if she'd given him a great gift. He cleared some books from the desk so that his view of Truth could be unobstructed. "That's amazing. Tell me more."

She shrugged. "I didn't know any of this, who they really were, until just a few years ago."

"When you started studying?"

She shook her head. "I started studying because of what I found out. My parents, Dave and Ellen Miller, were really Dimitri and Yelena Gurov. Both were born in Russia in 1913. Their parents were White Russians, who fled with them to China to escape the Bolsheviks."

"And to hang onto some of their money, I would guess." He was grinning. "This is incredible! You have a fascinating history."

"Yes. My parents were toddlers when their parents took them in the middle of the night out of Moscow and headed east, through Siberia, to northern China. They were worried they might be executed. I'm just repeating what they told me. They never breathed one word about any of this until they got sick. I grew up thinking my parents were ..." Smiling, she shook her head ruefully, still amused by her own ignorance. "Finnish. That's what they told me, and I never asked them even one question about it."

"Go on."

"So, the short version is that they grew up in Tientsin, somewhat prosperous. Their parents ran a fancy hotel together; they spent their whole lives together, my parents, from infancy, practically, till death. Got married there when they were eighteen, in the city they call Tianjin now."

"Yes. I've been there. Where the international concessions were located. A kind of international or more precisely European spot in Northern China. It makes sense a hotel would thrive."

"Exactly. So they lived there, made it through the war fine, and were getting ready to have kids when the Chinese revolution happened. They had to run from communism again. They made their way to the United States, somehow to Flemington, New Jersey, of all places." She cleared her throat loudly in a common Flemington grade school joke. "Only first my father spent some time in a re-education camp."

"Did you ask your father about it?"

Truth shook her head. "I didn't know anything about anything. They kept it all secret because it was the height of the McCarthy era. I feel like such a jerk. I'm almost fifty years old, you know? I went to college for one semester when I was eighteen, and then, well, let's say I kind of fell out of the mainstream for a long time. I was involved in a kind of … counter-culture movement, you could say. Some would call it a cult. I don't like that word. Anyway, I was living in the Bay Area before I came back here in 1995 when my parents got sick. I'd never ever been close to them, and when they were dying, they started telling me all their secrets. I felt like the most clueless, dumb idiot in the world. So I decided to go back to school to study what happened. So I could educate my son."

"You're brave, Truth. Your family has quite a story, and I'm sure there's a lot more you're not telling me."

She looked away from him and studied a poster of Che Guevara on the wall. "What I wanted to ask you about, so that I could talk to my son more intelligently, is how to analyze what happened at Columbine, or is it 'just,'" she held up her pinkies to make quotes, "two crazy kids killing a bunch of other kids?"

"What do you think, Truth?"

She shook her head and sighed, looking into her lap. "Dr. Wheeler, I have no idea. Not one."

He looked at the clock over the window. "I have to go soon, but I do have another class in a little while, but we can talk for a few more minutes. To be accurate, we have to acknowledge that we don't know much about the killers yet, but I think we can take race and class out of the equation, as almost all the dead were white and well off. Well, there was one African American young man, but only one."

"I think I heard I heard something like 'trench coat mafia' on the news this morning."

"Me too. It's a provocative term, which I'd never heard before. It's really too early to do any kind of deep analysis. That's probably why you're reluctant to say anything conclusive to your son about it. That's good. We're always jumping to conclusions in this fast-food culture. Give me my explanation, and give it to me now, along with my Big Mac!" He laughed, and Truth joined in, beginning to feel somewhat at ease. She'd always been in awe of Dr. Wheeler, ashamed of her woeful ignorance of American history, although she was the class's oldest student by far.

"I agree."

"Speaking of Big Macs, are you hungry? I need to catch a bite in the cafeteria before class. You're welcome to join me."

She surprised herself by accepting. He was kind and not as imposing up close. His skin was smooth and pale, his eyes gray. He was balding, with a heavy gray beard. He was brilliant but he wasn't vain about it, a quality she disliked in most of her professors. When she was a teacher – her vague plan was to teach high school history someday – she would never act superior to her students.

In the crowded lunchroom, she drank tea and ate her peanut butter sandwich, which she'd made that morning, while he had a Chinese stir-fry and drank coffee, spilling both on his white shirt and apologizing for his messiness.

After they had sat for a while, he asked, "So what was this

counter-culture movement you mentioned? If you don't mind my asking?" He sipped his coffee, grimaced, and checked his watch. "I've only got five minutes, actually, so this conversation may have to wait for another time."

She sighed and smiled with relief. "Saved by the bell."

"I'm interested. My brother was with the Krishna people for a while – you know, the ones chanting at the airport – back in the seventies, so I know a thing or two about cults."

"Another time, then." She rose.

"Walk me to the Humanities Building?" he asked, gathering his things.

She looked at him quizzically. Did he pity her? Did he believe she was crazy and thought it would be an interesting intellectual exercise to probe her craziness? "Okay."

He asked her to come to office hours next week, and she said she would. Somehow, she felt a little bit better.

When Cuffy got home that afternoon, she wanted to talk to him about Jonestown. She wanted him to understand that the media made out that all the Peoples Temple members were wackos, and now they were doing the exact same thing to these two boys. She thought it unlikely they were politically motivated, but she wanted to reserve judgment. But when he came in, he was frightened. Not tearful, like yesterday, but terrorized. He shook. "Mom. I overheard the scariest thing on the bus just now."

"What? Tell me."

He looked into her eyes. He was as tall as she was now, which was only 5'3", but this equality in their height was new and continued to amaze her. "Will you promise not to tell anyone?"

She considered. "You know, Cuffy, when a doctor talks to a patient, she's supposed to respect the person's privacy unless there's danger or possible danger involved, to the patient or to anyone else. Being a parent is a little like that. So I don't want to promise until I know what it is. But I hope you'll trust me."

Shaking again, he let himself be held.

"Oh, sweetie, this is a hard, hard time for you."

"It's not me, Mom." He paused. "I'm not scared for me. But I heard these two seniors on the bus talking about how they thought the Columbine shootings were really, really cool, and they wished they could do the same thing at Flemington."

She blanched. "Are you sure?

He nodded. "Mom, they were right behind me, and they weren't even whispering. It was like they were broadcasting it."

Relieved, she said, "Oh, they were probably just showing off then, wanting to talk tough, as sick as that is. I'm sure they didn't mean anything by it."

"But you don't know these boys."

"No, I don't. Do you?"

"I've known them from the bus since second grade. They're mean, Mom. They're always, always mean. They tried to intimidate me in the beginning, called me the N-word and everything, but they got over it."

"What?" She wasn't sure she heard him right. "They called you nigger?"

Wincing, he nodded. "It's not the first time, Mom."

"Why didn't you ever tell me? When did it happen?" Her voice rose along with her adrenaline. She felt like punching those boys, or worse. Sending them to re-education camp, perhaps.

He shrugged. "Me and Mikey told them off, and they quit hassling me when this deaf girl started riding the bus in third grade. Seems like every year, there's a new kid who gets all their crap."

She slumped into a chair. How could all this have happened without her knowing? Had she been so blind to her son's world while she tended her parents? "Sweetie, I'm kind of in shock. More that you didn't tell me than that it happened."

He sat down beside her. "Mom, that's not important now. It's the thing about Columbine that I'm worried about. I just don't know if I should tell anyone. I mean, I'm telling you, but do you think I should go to the cops? The principal? I mean, you might be right, and it's just talk, but what if it isn't?"

She hugged her knees. "Cuffy. Oh, Cuffy, I just don't know what the right thing to do is. I don't. I never thought I'd go to the cops for anything in my whole life."

He sighed. "But Mom, what if, say, just last week these guys in Colorado were talking about what they were gonna do before they did it, and somebody overheard them and went to the cops, or whoever. Maybe then it wouldn't have happened, and there wouldn't be all these dead kids, including the two boys who did it, and their history teacher too."

She felt tears rise. "You amaze me, Cuffy. You have such good instincts. You're right. Of course you're right." She paused, pushing the tears back down. "Probably all over America, kids like those boys on your bus are talking like that, even though it's totally sick. But in this culture, I can believe it. The question is, how many of all these admiring kids actually have access to guns, and enough darkness inside them to actually do it?"

Cuffy shook his head. "Mom, I have no idea. None. But if I rat on them and if somehow they find out it was me, then I'll be in deep doo-doo. But isn't that better than people dying?"

Rising from the floor, she pulled him to his feet. "Let's eat something first, then figure out what we're going to do."

She ate the carrots while he finished the Social Teas and an apple. The kitchen was quiet. It was bland, but warm in its way, and she liked it.

"What did you say to those boys when they called you … that word?"

He laughed. "I told them my father was a big black prize fighter, and that he'd beat the shit out of them if they said it again."

"You told them that?"

"Yup. Worked like a charm, Mom."

She raised a glass of milk to toast him. "Cuffy, you are a very wise kid. Now, what's our plan?"

YOU WILL NOT GET CHRIST'S BLESSING
IN JIM JONES'S BLESSING
UNTIL YOU WALK LIKE JIM JONES,
UNTIL YOU TALK LIKE JIM JONES,
UNTIL YOU ACT LIKE JIM JONES, UNTIL
YOU LOOK LIKE JIM JONES.
HOW LONG WILL I BE WITH YOU UNTIL
YOU UNDERSTAND THAT *I* AM NO
LONGER A MAN, BUT A PRINCIPLE.
I AM THE WAY, THE TRUTH, AND THE LIGHT.
NO ONE CAN COME TO THE FATHER BUT
THROUGH ME.

Jim Jones

Marceline Jones
October 2, 1977
San Francisco

While in San Francisco on Temple business, Marceline worried about the boys in Guyana. She worried about all of them, her thousand children at the mission in the jungle, but most of all she brooded over Marcus and the way his anger had mutated over the years. Last spring, he had got drunk on his eighteenth birthday and had talked about killing his father if the drugs didn't get him first.

"Marcus! You shouldn't say such a thing. Especially not to me. It goes against everything we believe in." She felt all the blood rise into her cheeks. In her one-room cabin, the two had been celebrating with a clandestine cake shipped in from a Georgetown bakery, and a forbidden bottle of wine. The goodies had been hidden in the gear room of *The Cudjoe*, one of the Temple's two trawlers, which Jim had recently renamed *The Marceline*. She was still unsure how she felt about her name on the side of the Temple's biggest boat. It wasn't especially seaworthy.

Jim's staff had located her as far from Jim's place as was possible in the cluster of dwellings named Jonestown by the Guyanese government, the three hundred-odd acres they had cleared from the three thousand acre-swathe not far from the Venezuelan border. A bureaucrat had given the settlement its name. She had protested, but Jim said that it wasn't worth "fighting city hall" over a name, and besides, it had a certain ring. Georgetown and

Jonestown were sister cities, he said, linked by the Temple, the former representing their urban and political arms, and the latter their agricultural body.

"He tricked us down here, Marceline, and you know it," Marcus spat out, swilling instead of sipping his wine. When he turned sixteen, Marcus began to call her by her first name. That year she went against Jim for the first – would it be the only? – time to grant her son's wishes. He wanted to study acting at the Conservatory in San Francisco. Jim naturally found this to be a selfish diversion from Socialism. But Marceline had promised to make it possible, and she rented him a cheap studio in the Tenderloin near the school and enrolled him in classes mid-year, all without Jim's knowledge. It felt delightful to make Marcus so happy, allowing him to do what he wanted. But it was short-lived. When she thought about how Jim would respond, for of course he would find out sooner or later, a terror seized up inside her, fear sheathing her vital organs. She hadn't anticipated her husband's particularly clever method of enforcing his will, though in retrospect it was nothing new.

One week into classes, Marcus had been summoned out of "Improv 1" by Jocelyn or maybe Maria or perhaps some other woman with whom her husband was currently sleeping, with the urgent message that Jim was on his deathbed in Georgetown, where he'd been laying the foundation for the exodus of the congregation. All night long he'd been asking for Marcus, begging to see his son again, so the women got on a plane that morning to fetch him. They hadn't told Jim what they were doing. His father needed him, they said, tears in their eyes, urging him to fly to South America immediately to speak to his father before he died. It was a stroke, they said, or a heart attack, or something very dire. His father loved him so much, they told him. He needed his only son to know his final thoughts, to aid Marcus's direction of the future of the Temple. That was how they phrased it.

"Here," one of them said, handing him an envelope of tickets and cash and his passport. "You have a red eye to Miami tonight and a connecting flight through to Georgetown first thing tomorrow morning. Go, or you'll regret it the rest of your life."

That night Marcus got on a plane and never returned to the States. She withdrew him from the Conservatory and paid off the lease, mournful but resigned. Of course, Jim's deathbed story was a ruse. He was ill, it was true, but not dying. Exhaustion depleted him, and he had too many drugs in his system all working at cross-purposes, resulting in severe pain and a deathly pallor. Jocelyn's younger sister was his nurse now. He no longer listened to Marceline's medical advice.

Marcus had fallen for the story, and now their son was one of Jonestown's principal members, at times fighting with his dad and at others working against him behind his back. Either way, utterly unable to break with him. Marcus was too like her. She was sure that his talk of murder was just that: talk.

Despite feeling cheated out of his acting school dream, Marcus loved the hard work of building the settlement, driving the 'dozers and working in the hot sun, clearing the jungle. He loved seeing the results of his labors: two years of sweat had made this home to one thousand people, with crops, cattle, a mill, pigs, chickens, a bakery, a medical center, and cottages and dormitories for almost all their flock. Indeed, it was an astonishing accomplishment that she couldn't bring herself to criticize, in spite of Jim's nefarious methods of getting his son back to Guyana.

Marceline was in accounting, perusing the financial ledgers with her keen eye for the occasional error or omission when the first call came into headquarters.

The girls in the radio room, Truth Miller and Ida Bradstreet, immediately put out the alarm to everyone in the Geary Boulevard temple. The speakers with the emotive language that Marceline had grown accustomed to hearing in Jonestown. "Alert, alert, alert." Sometimes, even the female voices sounded like his.

She wasn't eager to hear the details of the latest emergency. Since

Jim had decamped permanently for Guyana in April, and she shortly afterward, he appeared to thrive even more than before on catastrophe, as if only disaster were worth rising for each morning. Crises, conspiracies, and treason comprised his holy trinity. Sometimes he invented situations just to make life more interesting. She forgave him for it because Peoples Temple had plenty of enemies. In this way, Guyana was no different from Ukiah or Indianapolis. The litany Jim had so often recited unspooled easily from the spokes of her memory: "There are always those who hate and fear change," went the tape in her head, and it was true: they had assassinated Martin Luther King, Robert and John Kennedy, Medgar Evers, Malcolm X, and every progressive who stood for change.

It was difficult to tell real emergencies apart from Jim's embellishments, which were subsequently whipped into the highest drama, usually with the help of Jocelyn and Maria and the Tropps. The Tropps were siblings, Jews from New York, children of Holocaust survivors. The brother was a professor and the sister a lawyer, and to Marceline they represented the worst examples of intellectual excess. They lived solely in their heads, surviving on ideas and books. She'd never seen two people so disconnected from their bodies, and for that reason, she felt confident neither had ever slept with her husband.

"Mother! Mother, where are you?"

Footsteps slammed down the corridor, then Truth burst into the office. "Mother, they're talking about ending it all unless Washington calls off the snipers!"

Turning away from the files, Marceline looked into the girl's earnest, troubled face. Like Father Divine, Jim had for a time renamed his followers with whimsical, faith-based appellations. Truth was one of the chosen few. The girl's real name was something ordinary, but it was extraordinary how she had been transformed into a powerful, assertive woman by her new name. Marceline admired her husband's genius at work in the young woman standing before her, who put sixty to eighty hours a week into Temple communications. She wanted to tell Truth to calm down, but one didn't say things like that to any of the gung-ho gals who worshipped at her husband's feet. Whether they venerated any other part of his anatomy was a subject on which she no longer cared to speculate. "Who's on the line with you?" Marceline asked.

"Harriet. She's got a statement for the press. She wants you to call a press conference right away so she can read it over the radio."

Sighing, Marceline rose and went to the door, where Truth was hyperventilating against the jamb. "Honey, lean over and take deep breaths. It's all gonna be okay." She put her arms around the girl and stroked her wild, dark curls. "We've lived through crises before, and we'll live through this one too." She held Truth until she stopped shaking, then trudged down the hall to the radio room, an old janitor's closet, now the nerve center of Peoples Temple communications since the mass exit of the congregation during the summer. It was staffed by exhausted and malnourished young women like Truth and Ida, who didn't know how lucky they were to be here, in cool San Francisco, instead of in the humid equatorial zone with Jim, though Marceline knew how much they yearned to go.

When Marceline put on the headset, however, it wasn't Harriet Tropp's New York accent that greeted her but Jocelyn's quiet, tense voice. "Marcy, it's looking very grim right now. Summons for Jim to appear in court in Georgetown got nailed to the poles in the pavilion. A sniper's been at us for over twenty-four hours, and our people are losing it. It's awful. Do you copy?"

When Jocelyn said "our people," it was never clear if she meant Jim, the congregation, or both, and in what group she included herself and her child. Jim had fathered her son, and everyone knew it.

"Okay, Jocelyn. Tell me, from the beginning, what's going on?"

Jocelyn's rambling made it clear she hadn't slept in a long time. Probably Jim had been on the P.A. all night, urging the congregation on to a further pitch of fear. It always went back to the boy. Not Jocelyn's son, but the boy that Hope, the Queen of the Traitors, had given birth to six years earlier. She had abandoned him almost as soon as he was born, leaving him with the Peoples Temple in Ukiah and now the child was in Jonestown. Jim swore up and down he was the father. After her defection, Hope had denied it. Now Hope wanted her child back. She'd hired a hotshot California lawyer to get the boy out of South America and returned to her, his legal mother. The Guyanese courts had become involved. Despite the significant number of lawyers working for Peoples Temple, many of whom were members working pro bono, Jim had not been able to avoid a summons to appear in a Georgetown court with the child for a custody hearing.

"We won't give Sean up," Jocelyn said, crying. "Everyone's agreed. If they take him, then who's next? Every parent with a kid in Jonestown will be down here, trying to destroy us."

Marceline didn't understand what Hope had done. How could she have walked away from a child who'd come out of her womb? Maybe she realized she had made a horrible mistake in leaving her son behind. Perhaps now, with age and insight, she'd realized how much she needed her child.

Jim said it was just a power play. Hope was vengeful and would do anything, even use her own child, to bring Jim and the Temple to ruin.

Privately, Jim had told Marceline that he had been dragged into the thing, that Hope's husband, an attorney, had begged him on his knees to "sire" a child with his wife because he was unable to. What had he said? If he couldn't do it himself, then he wanted the father to be the most "compassionate, honest, and courageous person in the world," or words to that effect.

"Isn't the Deputy Prime Minister here in the States this week?" Marceline asked, calculating what she'd need to do to prevent this new crisis from reaching its worst possible outcome. She didn't believe the whole community would commit suicide if the summons weren't re-called, but lately she was finding it more difficult to read Jim's intentions. The threat of mass suicide had been Jim's trump card since the U.S. government had begun meddling with their finances.

"Yes, exactly," Jocelyn said. "We've been calling him non-stop in D.C., but apparently, he's in Chicago right now. Could you go to Chicago?"

Marceline sighed. She'd left Jonestown only three days earlier, but geography no longer mattered. Jonestown was inside her, thousands of miles distant, yet close enough to infuse her veins with dread, as if direct from an intravenous line. "Yes, of course I can go. But how will I find him if you can't? And what exactly does Jim want him to do?"

"Jim says that he can stop the court from enforcing the summons. The Georgetown crew is on the phones working on pinpointing his exact location in Chicago. He has family there. We'll find out soon."

"But he's an administrator, not a judge." Marceline bit her lip. She feared Jim's attempts at interfering with Guyanese politics. "He's not in the judiciary at all."

"Jim still thinks he can help us. He says that after the Prime Minister, he has more power in the government than anyone else, and that the judge who signed the summons could probably be persuaded to change his mind if it came directly from him."

"I suppose it's possible. Where is Jim? Can I speak with him?"

"He's resting ... He's been up seventy-two hours straight with all this chaos. He so wishes you were here, but maybe it's good you're there so that you can get to the minister ... Jim says he's always liked you."

Marceline shrugged. Perhaps it was true. She'd never exchanged more than a few words with him on their occasional meetings in Georgetown.

"Are you there, Marcy? Do you copy?"

"I copy, Jocelyn. I'll get on the next plane to Chicago and call from the airport. You'll have more information by then."

"Okay. Is Robert there? Harriet wants to talk to him about handling the press."

"Robert? No, I think he's in Santa Rosa."

"Can you put Truth back on, then? Harriet needs to brief her about the press conference. When Robert gets back, he can take over from her. Can you set that up before you go?"

"I will."

Marceline handed the headphones back to Truth, who was pacing the tiny room behind her, sweating and mumbling as if praying, but Marceline knew Truth wasn't one of the true believers in the church. The elderly blacks were the ones who worshipped her husband as if he were another Christ, a twentieth-century incarnation of their beloved son of God. They needed to think like that to sustain such deep faith.

Truth belonged to the other element of the Temple, the educated white kids, who wanted to save the world and believed they could, via the quasi-Marxist Peoples Temple and its mission to end racism and poverty. She was hopeful and hard-working, despite some strange behaviors, like talking to herself non-stop as if she were a bag lady on Mission Street. She often carried numbers of plastic bags with her, stuffed to overflowing with files of notes and clippings, all ideas to help improve the services of the Peoples Temple. She didn't think Jim was Christ, but Truth probably saw him as a saint in the secular mode, like Mao perhaps, or the undeniably handsome Che.

Robert was unusual amongst the Peoples Temple followers, an educated black man who believed in Jim's message of equality and integration.

After packing a small suitcase, she was driven to the airport by Leroy, a young man who'd once been strung out on heroin and now worked as a mechanic on the Temple's vehicles.

"You hold up, you hear?" she said. "And tell everyone back at Geary that nobody's dying tonight."

"Okay, Mother." He cried into her shoulder before pulling himself together, wiping his eyes with the back of his hand. "You know, my Mama's down there in Jonestown, with my two sisters and their kids. I just don't want anything to happen, you know?"

"Yes, I do know," she said firmly, smiling. "Things will be fine. This will pass." After finding him some tissues in her pocketbook, she breathed deeply, and walked confidently into the terminal.

* * *

Three hours later, she was in Chicago. Her cab driver had the radio tuned to an all-news station, and in the back seat, Marceline heard Harriet's lawyerly voice buzzing from the speakers beside her:

Martin Luther King told his Freedom Riders: "We must develop the courage of dying for a cause." Before we submit quietly to the interminable plotting and persecution of this politically motivated conspiracy, we will resist actively, putting our lives on the line. This has been the unanimous vote of the collective community here in Guyana. We choose as our model not those who marched submissively into gas ovens, but the valiant heroes who resisted in the Warsaw ghettos. Patrick Henry captured it when he said, simply: "Give me liberty, or give me death."

We would rather die than compromise the right to exist free from harassment and the kind of indignities that we have been subjected to. Those who cannot appreciate this can never understand the integrity, honesty, and bravery of Peoples Temple nor the commitment of Jim Jones and the principles he has struggled for all his life.

We do not want to die: We believe deeply in the celebration of life. It is the intention of Jim Jones, and always has been, to light candles rather than curse the darkness, to find and implement constructive solutions rather than merely complain about problems. But under these outrageous attacks, we have decided to defend the integrity of our community and our pledge to do this. We are confident that people of conscience and principle understand our position. We make no apologies for it.

"What a bunch of crazies, huh," said the driver to Marceline, peering at her in the rear-view mirror. He was a black man in his fifties, whose lined face indicated a life of struggle.

Marceline said nothing and looked away at the busy city.

"Lots of traffic tonight, isn't there," she said, hoping not to be drawn into a discussion.

"No more'n usual. But man, those people! You know, I have

a friend from Indy who almost got suckered into going out to California with them. His wife did, though, and I think some other family. Wasn't a great marriage. He drank, and she went to church."

After Marceline failed to respond, the driver turned to a blues station, turned up the volume, and didn't attempt to engage her in conversation for the rest of the trip.

The minister, Dr. Jarndyce, was visiting his brother. It looked like this brother lived pretty high on the hog, Marceline thought, as the cab pulled into a circular driveway in front of a large Colonial-style home on the Lake. A bodyguard stood at attention next to where two Mercedes-Benz cars adorned the entryway.

Marceline added a hefty tip to the cab fare. She felt guilty about how much rice that money could buy in Guyana. The driver looked at the cash and said, "Thanks, lady. I guess you can afford it if you have people in this part of town. Take care of yourself."

Then he released the parking brake and crept forward, admiring the Benzes with a look that reminded her of lust. A guard approached Marceline and asked in that lovely Guyanese lilt if she had business with the Minister.

"Yes, he's expecting me. I'm Marceline Jones, wife of the Reverend Jones."

The guard smiled. "The Bishop's wife. Yes, he told me you'd be coming. The Minister is inside with his brother's family at dinner. He told me to bring you right in."

Dr. Jarndyce was gracious, as was his brother, sister-in-law and nieces and nephews, who were all relaxing around an elegantly appointed dinner table. Their meal was prepared by a trained chef and was served by two East Indian women. Marceline felt deeply uncomfortable.

"Dr. Jarndyce, I hope you can forgive me for disturbing your vacation like this."

He pointed to an empty seat wedged between his chair and his brother's. He patted his mouth with a white cloth napkin before speaking:

"Mrs. Jones. You know I am always happy to help the Peoples Temple and the Bishop. Now, your person in Georgetown told me about the court order regarding your husband and the child, but the connection wasn't very good. She said you were on your way, so I thought you could explain it more clearly in your own words."

Marceline flushed. Within the Temple, everyone understood that Jim had fathered children with other women, a circumstance which by this time seemed almost ordinary, though it didn't please her. Yet explaining the situation to outsiders filled her with trepidation. She took a deep breath.

"Tolly, where are your manners?" asked the other woman at the table. "No introductions? No offering dinner? Mrs. Jones must be famished after her trip." She smiled warmly at Marceline, which calmed her somewhat.

The minister introduced everyone, though Marceline was too nervous to remember anybody's name. She accepted a cup of tea but refused food, saying she'd had dinner on the plane. This wasn't true. She hadn't been able to eat.

"Go ahead, Mrs. Jones." The minister sipped his wine and waited for her to begin, a neutral expression on his kind physician's face.

"The mother of a child at Jonestown wants him back. She's gotten a court order from California as well as a magistrate in Georgetown to schedule a hearing at which Jim and the child need to be present. They served him papers at the mission." She paused to try her tea. She knew she was evading the difficult truth about Sean's relation to Jim, and what stake Hope had in the Temple, but she couldn't bear to be more specific just now. "She abandoned the child after he was born. Peoples Temple is his family. My husband —" She faltered.

"What exactly is the problem with your husband attending this hearing?"

She sighed. "Well, he feels it would be dangerous for him to go into Georgetown at this time. You see, there are a number of people who don't appreciate what the church is doing, who don't like Socialism in general and want to shut down Peoples Temple for good." She hoped she didn't sound paranoid. "Apparently, there have been snipers at the compound today – no one's been hit, though – and Jim doesn't want to leave his people, even for a short trip to the capital."

"And what he wants precisely from me is …"

"My understanding is that you might be able to delay the hearing until things calm down a little."

"I see." He looked at his brother, older and also a doctor, in an identical beautifully tailored suit, who resembled him, though with all-white hair. At this point, the woman and children excused themselves, the servants cleared the table, and Marceline was alone with Dr. Jarndyce and his brother.

"Have you called Forbes?" asked the brother, whose name Marceline couldn't remember.

"I believe our people have," answered Marceline, just as Dr. Jarndyce was saying, "Not yet."

"Excuse me." Marceline flushed, looking down into her tea.

"That would be wise, I think, before I take any action," said the minister to his brother. Then, to Marceline, "I need to make a few calls to Georgetown. Nothing is going to happen until tomorrow. Do you have somewhere to stay tonight?"

"Oh yes," she lied.

"Well, why don't you go back to your hotel while I make some calls and leave a few messages with some people who could help, then we'll proceed when I have more information."

"You're very, very kind to us," Marceline said, rising. "I'm so sorry to disturb you on your vacation. It's just an awful emergency, and we didn't know who else to turn to. I believe our people have been unable to reach the Prime Minister so far."

He put his hand on her shoulder. "Tell your husband not to worry so much. You Americans, you are very nervous, we think." He smiled at his brother. "True?" The brother nodded. "In the tropics, we are more easygoing. Everything will be fine, I'm sure. No doubt you need some sleep. Mrs. Jones. My driver will take you to your hotel."

"Thank you so much, Dr. Jarndyce. We're very grateful."

He waved away her words. "No problem whatsoever. I'll see you tomorrow. Give George your phone number too, please, where you're staying."

Back in San Francisco, Marceline stumbled up the steps from her cab, aching for sleep. She hadn't slept at all the previous night. She wanted only to curl up in her single bed in the third-floor apartment and collapse. Her meeting with Dr. Jarndyce that morning had gone very well, she thought, and the situation was now surely in hand.

But when she opened the door to the Temple, she realized her efforts had been in vain. Truth and Ida were sobbing. Reporters were crawling around, interviewing other staff members down the corridor, and a funereal feeling lingered in the air.

"Oh, Mother," Truth burst out. "They say they're going to commit suicide, every one of them! The summons hasn't been called off. They say they'll die if they can't live in peace."

Close to tears herself, Marceline reminded herself to breathe deeply. Likely this was all just talk. She must avoid falling into crisis mentality herself. Jim always relied upon her for exactly that. Most of the people in the inner circle jumped headfirst into frenzy alongside Jim, except perhaps one or two of the lawyers. But she was so tired she could hardly move, and her mental stamina diminished with each breath.

"What's happened now? I thought I straightened everything out with Dr. Jarndyce."

Truth wept as she spoke, making her words difficult to decipher. "There's been more shooting. Nobody's called off the summons. I swear I wish I were there. Everyone's suffering so much."

Marceline couldn't find the energy to talk Truth out of her despair. As she was deciding what to do next, one of the reporters noticed her. Then the whole group was upon her. She couldn't breathe.

"Mrs. Jones!" called the reporter from the *Chronicle*. "They say they're going to commit mass suicide at Jonestown if the summons doesn't get called off. Is that just an idle threat? Or would your husband really lead his people to their deaths?"

Marceline faltered. "I'm sorry, but I can't speak with you right now. I need to get on the radio to talk to Jim and the staff. I just got off a plane. I'm not yet aware of the latest details. Please excuse me."

Ida and Truth each took an arm and helped her up the stairs to the radio room, though the reporters kept yelling questions at her back.

"Is Jim Jones really the father of Sean O'Neill?" one called.

"Who do you think is shooting at the compound, Mrs. Jones?" shouted another.

"Don't you think mass suicide is … a little extreme?" said yet another, her voice laced with sarcasm.

Finally, she reached the janitor's closet, accepted the headphones from another staff person and heard Jim's voice on the other end, talking to someone beside him. It shrilled in her ears like some horrible shrike. The uneven cadences of his sentences were due to lack of sleep, a condition so ordinary to Jim she sometimes failed to note it. Now, with her own strained exhaustion, and the tension of the last twenty-four hours nearly unbearable, she felt her core of reserve and strength dissipating into nothingness.

"As you know, there's been an order for my arrest … People are conspiring. We're going to have to make a stand. We are prepared to die. Do you copy?"

"Roger Roger."

"The last few days has been nothing but harassment. People shooting at us." His voice was slurred.

"Roger Roger. But can I say just one thing? Give us time to let us work something out. Please," she begged.

"We will give people as much time as we can afford. We've

246

been lied to and deceived. The foreign minister of this country promised us we'd have complete sanctuary. We've also gotten the promise of Dr. Jarndyce. I can't imagine them going back on their word ... but I can be arrested at any moment."

"Roger Roger. But surely they can stop that from happening. Please, please give it some time." Marceline began to cry.

Jim's rejoinder was harsh: "If you don't get control of your emotions, you can destroy the greatest decision in history. We will not allow any of us to be taken. We will die unless given freedom from harassment and asylum somewhere – Tanzania, Libya, even Uganda. That chap seems to be able to stand up for what he believes."

Marceline cleared her throat but could think of nothing to say. She had never stood up to Jim, and now when she really needed to, she was still unable to do it. She despised herself.

"Yes, my good wife," he said encouragingly.

"I just want to say that I am your wife. I've been your wife for twenty-eight years. And I know the pain and suffering you've gone through for socialism, for complete economic and racial equality ..." Why was she speaking to him as if they were on a political broadcast? Why could she not speak the simple truth? Who in their right mind believed mass suicide to be the answer? She remembered the words of her Chicago taxi driver: "A bunch of crazies." The man was right. But how could she get Jim to see sense over a crackly radio thousands of miles away? She needed to get back.

"I missed your copy, darling ... I want to tell you that I've been glad being married to you. You've been a very faithful wife, but most important, you've been a true humanitarian ... I love you very much."

After a moment, Marceline went on:

"I love children about as much as anybody could love children. As much as it's hard for me to be away from everybody there, I wouldn't have them back here. I want them to be with you."

The words were tumbling out of her tiredness. They weren't

even true. She didn't want her children to die. She needed to get back to protect her children. From him.

"They're wanting to die too quickly, some of them. I'm the one that's holding back. Well, we're gonna die if anyone comes to arrest anyone. That's a vote of the people. We'll die because we've done no crime. I offered to go, to make that painful sacrifice, Marceline, but the people said no. The morale would not stand it. I don't mind chains. But it's an illegal arrest order based on an illegal proceeding … Our people have surrounded the perimeter of our property … They have cutlasses and are ready to defend themselves."

Marceline couldn't listen anymore. She passed the headphones back to Truth and left, sobbing, no longer attempting to control herself. She made her way to her little room and fell into bed. Surely this was a bad, bad dream, she told herself, and in the morning, everything would be all right. She had nothing left inside her upon which to draw. It was too much. She wanted to pray but found nothing prayerful inside her, so she pictured each of her children, first Marcus and then Tim and Ken and Jimmy and Agnes, and then every other child in Jonestown, then the old people, then the adults, trying to fix each of their faces in memory, recalling the freckled complexions and the scars, the smiles of some of the toddlers, the gurgles of the newborns, the acne on the adolescents' skin, the elders' semi-toothless grins, hoping that if she could protect them in her mind, they would remain safe on the ground in Guyana. Like keeping a plane in the air while you're on it by sheer will alone. Sleep came to her after she had remembered the last patient in the clinic, Harneitha Franklin, seventy-three, with complaints of unidentifiable intestinal disorder, on antibiotics, bedrest and under close observation. Doc Schacht would be looking after her. At last exhaustion overtook Marceline, and in the depths of sleep, no dreams disturbed her.

WHERE THE EAGLES GATHER,
THERE HAS TO BE CARCASS,
AND WHERE THE CARCASS IS, THE
EAGLES WILL GATHER TOGETHER,
AND I AM THE CARCASS, WILLING
TO DIE THAT YOU COULD LIVE,
WILLING THAT YOU COULD EAT FROM ME
THAT YOU WOULD KNOW
THE DIVINE PRINCIPLE
THAT WILL SAVE YOU AND SET YOU FREE.

Jim Jones

November 18, 1978
Jonestown

Robert isn't woken by the daily Jim Jones harangue over the P.A. Instead, he hears music. Not the Jonestown Express, but classical. He recognizes Vivaldi. It's not "Spring" or "Summer," which were overplayed endlessly in department stores and elevators, in the hope that their cheerfulness would prod consumers to buy. Instead, it is "Winter." As a child, Robert had been a prodigy on the piano, but gave it up in adolescence. Classical music is hopelessly unhip and unblack.

The others in the dormitory are still sleeping. Most of them black like Robert and the majority poor, from hard lives and torn families, nothing like his own cushy middle-class world of San Rafael, California. He'd gladly fled that life on meeting Jim Jones four years earlier. Elijah on the bunk beneath him started smoking pot at ten but had been clean since his family joined the Temple. And Reg on the bed beside him had a rap sheet the Oakland cops liked to describe as "As long as their dicks to the hundredth power," but in Jonestown had found prestige and power as a big wheel on the security team.

"What the fuck?" says Reg, on waking. "What is that shit on the P.A.?"

"Oh man, he's trying to impress the congressman," says Elijah.

Now Robert understands the Vivaldi. Congressman Ryan is still here. Jones hadn't permitted the media to stay overnight, but he'd relented when the Peoples Temple lawyers insisted he let the congressman sleep in the guesthouse, a nicely appointed cabin he'd evacuated swiftly with his latest female conquest, a very young black girl. She was the first black female Robert remembered the Petty Tyrant, as he had taken to calling their leader in his mind, had ever been with. She is only nineteen to Jones's forty-seven. Her black hair is very real while his was from a bottle and looked it. Shanda is one of the recent arrivals. Jones had asked his faithful elderly followers to recruit young relatives to the jungle in a show to the folks back home that Jonestown is thriving rather than dying. It's all make-believe.

Robert looks at his watch: 7:30. Clearly, this is no ordinary day. Usually at 5:45 a.m. Jones himself or his recorded voice was waking them with comradely, inspirational words, plus the latest news from Tass, to start a day planting in the fields or clearing bush or whatever the day's grueling labor might be. In Guyana, work begins at dawn, because the heat makes life impossible after eleven. Civilized people, which is to say, those native to the tropics, usually spent mid-day napping or resting in the shade, but the Petty Tyrant says building a new world takes everyone's energy all day long. *He* never rested, did he, Jones would ask rhetorically. Over and over, they were reminded to be like him.

The field workers are given half an hour for lunch, fifteen-minute breaks once every three hours, and are expected to work till five. Robert's had it. As has DeeDee, who, at twenty-two, was five years younger than Robert but had been in the Temple most of her life.

Back in San Francisco, Robert gave himself completely to Peoples Temple, when they were doing meaningful work in the Fillmore, helping the elderly and the street kids, getting medical care to those in need. But here, after only six months, he can no longer see the point.

On his way to the pavilion for breakfast, Robert smells bacon; Jones is going whole hog to impress Ryan, Robert thinks, laughing at his wordplay. So far, the congressman's visit has gone extremely well. Far better than what the Petty Tyrant had prepared them for. But Robert saw from Jones's expression last night that the Petty Tyrant was still skeptical and unhappy. He hated the press even more than he hated the congressman, blaming them for the demise of his Bay Area fiefdom. Most likely, the reporters were saving their hardest questions for today, before they leave Jonestown for good. That's what Robert had done when he had worked for the Press-Democrat back in Santa Rosa. While Peoples Temple were still in California, Robert had fielded the media attack at Jones's request when the *New West* exposé came out. He had done so faithfully and with heart. He'd believed wholeheartedly that the press really was out to crucify Jones. The article had been highly critical, full of damning testimony from "false traitors," prompting Jones to leave the capitalist states of AmeriKKKa for good.

But once the Petty Tyrant was gone, taking his paranoia with him, Robert had begun to doubt. Maybe it was because he'd been able to sleep on his cot in the pressroom at the Geary temple – really sleep, for the first time in years, early to bed and late to rise.

He should have paid attention to those doubts. When he got here, it was a shock to see DeeDee so unhappy. Not because of their brief romance and subsequent separation of over a year, but due to life at Jonestown. And she was a true believer. He decided to leave. Whatever it took, he would do it. Every day of his six months in the jungle he'd spent convincing DeeDee to go with him. At last, she'd agreed. Now, they're waiting for the right moment to conduct their own exodus.

Everyone on the food line grins with joy at the bacon and eggs breakfast, perhaps the second such meal they've eaten here. Up front, Ryan is chatting amicably with Marceline. The Petty Tyrant has yet to make his appearance. Probably wasted from whatever he'd taken to get to sleep while the meds to wake him up are not yet functioning. A good-looking Irishman of middle age, Ryan observes the group contentedly. His relaxed smile seems genuine, and Marceline is laughing, though Robert can never read her accurately. Is she full of shit, like so many of the women who fall under the guru's spell? Is she a puppet, unable to sustain an original thought? Or is she a Pollyanna craving utopia? Not so long ago, Robert shared the same impaired vision.

Among the hundreds of people eating at the long tables, he finds DeeDee, sitting with her family in their usual spot.

"C'mon over," says her mother, Cora. "Robert, you get some of that bacon? We all very excited that the congressman visiting us this morning."

"Yeah. Hope he stay for a week!" says Deondré, DeeDee's youngest brother, who at fourteen is always hungry. At every meal, DeeDee and her mother give him some of their food.

The boy gets up. "Sit here, Robert. I'm gonna see if they got seconds for us today." He laughs. "Bet they do."

DeeDee puts her hand on his knee beneath the table and squeezes. "Hey babe. How you doing this morning?"

Robert holds her hand and studies her. He nods, then whispers, "Today."

DeeDee's forehead creases with confusion. "Why?" she whispers back. "Things are going really well."

"Exactly. Let's do it while the going's good." He notes Cora looking them over with curiosity.

"What you two whispering about like church mice down there?"

"Nothing, Mama," says DeeDee, slapping his thigh softly to indicate they should stop talking.

Robert likes Cora and wishes she could be persuaded to leave with them, but she's one of the die-hards, so he hasn't even tried. DeeDee agrees it's useless and would only draw suspicion to them both. Deondré also loves Jonestown, where he feels free, has many friends, and is learning how to drive the tractor.

Robert feels a stab of sadness. And fear. A month ago, Jack, one of Robert's dorm mates, had been found at the northern border of the settlement, close to the Venezuelan border, stashing supplies for a future escape. Now he's a zombie in the ECU, the Extra

Care Unit. Robert and others who understand the real function of the place call it the Electrical Cure for Eunuchs. There's no proof electroshock actually goes on there, though it's probably insufficient juice in the power plant rather than want of will. Doc Schacht, the Jewish Mengele, does whatever he wants in the ECU to those who don't go with the program. Jones has threatened Shanda with a stay in the ECU to stop her from leaving him. For Robert, being doped to zombiedom on Thorazine would be the worst fate of all. He's got to get out of Jonestown immediately.

Vivaldi continues to play in the background while everyone eats and talks leisurely, as if they did this every day. Robert and DeeDee drink tea and wait for their unit supervisors to collect the crews for work. They're overseers, Robert thinks. He heard the Petty Tyrant say that if every supervisor had a shotgun, they wouldn't have any problems at Jonestown. The group had cheered. That applause only strengthened his resolve to flee.

It seems today is to be a day of rest. Saturdays are normally like every other workday, and Sundays have gone from full days off to afternoons only.

At last Jones appears, wearing a shiny red shirt and his habitual black shades. He looks like hell, but no more than usual. Instead of Jones, it's Marceline who reads the announcements over the P.A. The press will be arriving shortly from Port Kaituma. There will be more interviews and tours, and then, after lunch, "our guests" will be leaving Jonestown. "I want to say how wonderful it's been to have the congressman here," says Marceline, and everyone claps. Robert joins in because there is always someone watching. With a lift of her eyebrows and the slightest of nods, DeeDee indicates she's ready.

Despite the plastered-on smile, Marceline looks worried. The Petty Tyrant's entourage sits beside her at the front table: Jocelyn, Maria, six-year-old Sean, Hope's son. Hope, the Grand Bitch Traitoress. Maria cares for the boy as if she were his mother, though she's only twenty-three, and so thin Robert doubts she can reproduce. Beside Sean is two-year-old Jamie, Jocelyn's son with Jones. Jamie has the last name of some white flunky Jones had Jocelyn marry just for show. Shanda's nowhere in sight, and Robert wonders if Doc Schacht got her in the ECU after all. Chaikin, one of the Jewish attorneys, is in there. He'd had a serious falling out with Jones and had been hauled off to the ECU after dark. Of Jones's other sons, only Ken is here, along with his wife and baby. The other adult sons are all in Georgetown, playing basketball against the Guyanese state team. He doesn't see Agnes, who is shy and never sits up front.

Pulling the red flatbed full of reporters, the tractor arrives beside the pavilion. This is Robert's signal to leave. "I'm going to straighten up in the dorms," he tells DeeDee and her mother.

"Me too," says DeeDee and immediately follows. They take their dishes to the clean-up area and make their way toward the bathhouse at the center of camp, smiling at everyone they pass, greeting them with "brother" or "sister."

"Meet me at the stash in an hour," says Robert, under his breath.

Robert regards his sparse belongings. He can't take anything that won't fit in his pockets. His most important possession is a photograph of his little sister, who died at eleven from heart disease. When no one's looking, he slips it out of its frame and presses it carefully into his shorts. Hidden in the bottom of his one drawer, is a twenty-dollar bill, which he nestles beside the photo. He thought he had more cash but doesn't worry about it. At the other end of the dorm, Watts, a lanky sweet-talking idler from Southern California, is chatting up some girl in the doorway.

For their trek they need water. With a good breakfast in their bellies, and the prospect of arriving at Matthews Ridge by night-fall, they can probably do without food, but it would be better to bring something they can munch on, as the humidity saps everyone's energy by noon.

The guards' guns are conspicuously absent. Robert nods at Reg as he passes on his regular patrol route, walking the camp's perimeters. As he walks past the old folks' dorm, an argument breaks out. Mac, Jones's right-hand man, is telling a couple of reporters that they can't go in. Marceline is by his side, agreeing.

"Some of these elderly are ill, some are on bedrest, and some of them, frankly, just don't like strangers. They don't want people they don't know invading their living space with cameras," she says as politely as she can.

Mac's more direct. "Look, you folks have been everywhere here in Jonestown. We're not hiding anything, but c'mon, let's show these old folks some respect and not barge into their bedroom with flashbulbs!"

"If you don't have anything to hide, why won't you let us in?" says the bigger one. "It seems mighty suspicious."

Just then one of the expensive Peoples Temple lawyers shows up. He's flown in solely for the congressman's visit. Robert can't stand him. He's one of those white liberal shylocks who puts lots of energy into helping the have-nots while leading a very bountiful life in a four-story Victorian house in the heart of Pacific Heights. His friends are all white, Robert is sure.

The lawyer huddles with Marceline and Mac; everyone's gesturing toward the long low building whose few windows are curtained. Even to Robert, who knows it's only a dorm, the place does look suspicious.

"All right, then," Mac says finally, "but you be very respectful of those old people. They deserve it. If you aren't, I'll take you out."

The newsmen agree, but they clearly don't like this black man with his authoritative tone telling them how to behave.

Marceline knocks, then talks through the door, which finally opens. The cameramen push in behind her. Robert hears cries of astonishment even from his distance on the main boardwalk, trying not to look conspicuous as he fiddles with the lace on his sneaker.

"Jesus!" one of them shouts.

"Why's it so dark in here?" says another.

"It's like a cave or something," calls the first.

"No, it's like a ship it's so tightly packed in here."

"Like sardines."

"Like slaves," booms the big voice of the big reporter.

"All right, that's enough!" Mac says, hustling them out of the building. Mac looks like he wants to punch the big guy, and perhaps if Marceline weren't there he would, but the newsmen, having gotten their dirt, seem content to move on.

Robert makes his way past the baby nursery, where the littlest kids are cared for, but today it's empty and rather forlorn without the laughter and chatter of children. He notes some of the Concerned Relatives talking to their family members at the edges of larger groups and wonders if they'll convince anyone to return to the States with them. He doubts it. Only four of the Concerned Relatives made it to Jonestown. The rest are still in Georgetown, as there had been no room on the congressman's plane to the jungle. It must have been a bitter disappointment to them after all their trouble and expense of flying to Guyana. Today, Robert bets the Petty Tyrant would have preferred a plane full of relatives to the gaggle of journalists he's ended up having to face instead.

A strangeness hangs in the air. A young Italian-looking man who must be Maria's brother is trying to talk to her behind the pavilion, but she keeps walking away. He follows, begging her to listen, but she stalks off again. He removes a pendant from his neck and hands it to her. She shakes her head angrily and tries to give it back, but the brother refuses. Their voices rise.

"Dad wanted …" starts the man.

"Take it."

"But why won't you …"

She throws it in her brother's face and strides back to the Pavilion, where the reporters are clustered around the Petty Tyrant on his throne, a white chair with cushions conforming to Jones's bottom.

DeeDee makes her way along the boardwalk towards him. Carrying nothing, she speaks to those she passes with a smile and a nod, playing the part of happy camper so well, Robert feels fear prickling in his belly.

"Hey!" She kisses him on the cheek.

"Hi."

"I have a great idea," she says loudly. "Let's have a picnic! I already asked Virginia if she could make us some sandwiches."

Hugging her, Robert wants to say, "You are brilliant, woman," but he merely smiles.

He wishes he could watch the interview, which is being filmed by the big guy's cameraman. The reporter asking the questions looks mean, and the Petty Tyrant acts defeated, though the interview has just begun. More and more people come to the Pavilion to watch. It's the perfect time to leave.

He nods at DeeDee, who makes her way toward the kitchen. They can't say goodbye to anyone. Who knows when they'll see her family again? Like everyone who leaves, they'll be called traitors and worse, and the family, even Cora, will have to denounce them, no matter how they feel. He can't believe he's persuaded DeeDee to leave. Her life is here, with this community and almost all her blood kin. Back in California, she has a father she barely knows and a couple of aunts in Los Angeles, who excommunicated Cora from the extended family when she joined Peoples Temple.

Unlike DeeDee, Robert has a home to return to, though he hasn't spoken with his parents in over a year. DeeDee is too country for their taste, but they'll probably let them stay until they figure out what to do.

In the kitchen, Virginia, a heavy woman with a beautiful toothy smile, hands them a bag. "You got four sandwiches, two cassavas, and some eddo muffins my sister baked last night. We figuring out how to make sweet potato pie out of them eddoes."

DeeDee hugs her tightly, causing Virginia to put the younger woman at arm's length. "What you going on about, girl?" She studies her face. "You don't need to cry 'cause I give you some extra sweets. You just like Cora."

DeeDee wipes her eyes with the back of her hand. "Thanks, Virginia. Thanks a lot."

Robert pulls her out the door.

"Sorry," she whispers. "I couldn't help it."

"I think it's okay," he reassures her, wondering if Virginia might report them. She's one of the oldest followers, from the segregated days in the fifties back in Indianapolis, when Jones and Peoples Temple accomplished amazing things, the first church to integrate in a city where the KKK had more sympathizers than the civil rights movement.

They'll just have to hope Virginia's too busy making a fancy lunch to impress the media and congressman.

They head in the opposite direction from Port Kaituma. Matthews Ridge is much farther away, but they can't risk running into anyone from Jonestown on their route. All they need to do is get through a mile of bush to the railroad tracks, which still carry bauxite once a day on an antiquated freight train. The tracks will take them into Matthews Ridge, a dilapidated mining town larger than Port Kaituma. From there, they'll figure out some way to get to Georgetown. In the capital, they'll ask the American embassy for emergency passports. Jones holds all passports "for safekeeping."

Despite everything, Robert doesn't want to rat out Peoples Temple. He has no desire to bring on the CIA and the FBI and the IRS. All he wants to do is to leave. But he imagines it won't be so simple when they get to the Embassy. Just after Robert arrived, Jonestown had been rocked by the defection of Susan Stein. She had memorized the bank account numbers of Peoples Temple funds all over the globe. The Petty Tyrant had gone apeshit and still has not recovered. Defections are becoming more common, even amongst those in the heavenly spheres. Robert is pretty sure the Temple will dissolve naturally before too long; he just doesn't want to hang around and watch. Unfortunately, one can't simply leave; one can only defect. One can only be a traitor, not a well-wisher who simply prefers a different life.

The Stein woman had spilled every bean at the Embassy when she asked for her emergency passport, including details of the suicide drills. Ever since, Peoples Temple has been on "high alert," the let's-pretend-we're-committing-mass-suicide dramas. Jones calls them White Nights, as Black Nights would be racist, apparently. Jones adores crisis; urgency energizes him. Robert dismisses the White Nights as melodrama, part and parcel of Peoples Temple's love of theater.

When they get to the stash, Robert crawls inside a cluster of lianas draping three greenheart saplings. "Shit!" he yells. He tenses at the noise, fearing a guard will rush out and find them, but nothing happens.

"What's the matter, honey?"

"The water's gone!" He's ready to cry. "I put five canteens in here, and there isn't even one left. Someone took them!"

"Don't worry." A quiet female voice calls from behind another cluster of liana-crowned bushes. "It's just Carol and Arlene."

Two young mothers and five children of varying ages, including one infant, appear. "We heard your voices, so we hid," Carol whispers. "We're leaving too."

"Look like de black folk leaving de ship," says Robert in a faux-Southern accent. "We's gett'n out while de gett'ns good."

"You got that right," says Arlene, shifting the baby. The kids, two of them Arlene's, two Carol's, and the infant belonging to Arlene's sister, are all quiet, waiting for the adventure to begin. The older ones carry the canteens.

"How do you know about this path?" DeeDee asks.

"I found it on clearing crew about a month ago," says Carol. "We're not the only ones wanting to get out of here. Let's go already!"

"Want me to carry the baby?" Robert asks.

"When he gets heavy, we can take turns," says Arlene.

"Let's go!" says one of the boys.

"We're gone," says Robert.

* * *

I can't stand how they're talking to him. Why won't they leave him alone? I hate this. I hate them.

"Doesn't it bother you that people want to leave?" asks the large reporter. "Last night, someone passed me this note, asking us to take them back to the States with us."

"People play games, friend," Jim looks down at his lap. "They come and go all the time."

I can see where this is going. They want to crucify him; they do. Do they think it's easy running a community of a thousand people, some of them so damaged by the time they reach the Temple that they can barely function?

What can I do to shift the direction?

"Well, if that were the case, why would I get this note?"

"They lie, they lie, they lie. What can I do about liars?"

"Why do you think they'd lie about something like this?"

I'm so grateful the boys are in Georgetown. How I wish Ken and Tina and the baby were with them. Agnes too. I suppose the boys will see the interview on American TV someday.

Just end it, Jim! Just tell these guys to go away. Everyone standing here watching is probably thinking what I'm thinking: Jim is in pain. Deep pain. They criticize and criticize and never see the value of the work he's done in its best, truest light. I ache for him.

At last. It's over.

Thank you, God or whomever, any and all powers that be.

"Sweetheart, drink some water." I offer him a glass.

If I could only get him hydrated, but he won't drink it. Doesn't even hear me. He won't listen to Jocelyn either. He's very bad, maybe worse than ever.

Thank goodness. They're leaving, all of them.

"If there's anyone else who wants to join us, to go back to the United States, you are welcome," says Ryan, smiling, doing his best to pretend that interview wasn't a complete disaster.

"You can get your things and climb on the flatbed. We have two planes waiting for us in Port Kaituma."

So far, only a few are going: the Parks and the Bogues. A nearly all-white crew. Amazing. The whites keep leaving while the blacks stay because they know he loves them. I love them. And they have nothing better to return to. Despite all the countless problems here, it's still the Promised Land for some. For many.

"I'm taking the kids, and we're going back," says Al Simon, who's standing beside the Congressman, wrenching his youngest daughter out of his wife's grasp.

"You bring my kids back here!" Bonnie's screaming as loud as she can. "Don't you touch my kids!" She pulls the girl back, while her older sister looks confused, staring at her parents one after the other, and the boy stands off to the side as if to say, please leave me out of this. The Simons? I never expected this. Our only Native American family.

This is terrible. I didn't know they weren't happy together. The girls are crying. They don't want to go with him. Or do they? I don't think so. The girls want to be with their mother, and the boy ... well, maybe he does want to go home. Back to the States, I mean.

"Now, I think we can work this out without rancor," says Ryan.

"There's at least two lawyers in a ten-foot radius," says Charles, attempting a smile. "We ought to be able to figure out a solution. Congressman, can they leave tomorrow instead? I know you need to get to the plane right away, so we'll mediate tonight with both parents, and send whoever wants to go on a plane in the morning. If anyone decides to go. How's that?"

"Absolutely. Great idea, Charles." Ryan looks relieved.

Jim, on the other hand, looks broken.

The Simons are walking away, all together. I guess they'll figure something out with Charles. It's a good solution. I didn't want to watch that family break up right here, this minute, in front of everyone.

"Well, we better get going before that runway becomes inoperable," Ryan says. "Remember that wrecked plane we flew over?"

Some of the reporters nod.

Here comes Lenny Stein. What's he doing? Defecting? I don't believe it. It's not possible. Not Lenny.

"I want to come too," says Lenny. "Let me on." He throws his knapsack onto the flatbed, then climbs on. The Bogues and the Parks are looking as confused as I feel. Lenny can't want to go. He loves it here. He loves Jim. Jim saved his life.

Something peculiar is going on. I don't like it.

"Is that everybody, then?" asks Ryan.

One of the Parks is whispering something to Ryan.

"Well, I can't discriminate among you," he says, smiling at everyone including Lenny. "I said anyone can come back with me, and I meant it."

What's Ujara doing over there? What's in his hand? A knife? He's going after the congressman!

What's happening? I can't see! Oh, thank God, Charles grabbed him. But I see blood. Lots of it.

"Let me through! Let me by, please!"

Ryan's shirt is soaked. But it's not his blood; he's not even scratched. Thank God. Thank you, God. But Ujara nicked himself pretty good. I'll get that arm wrapped up right away.

"This man needs to be arrested," says Ryan, who looks frightened now, his movie-star face gone. What will he say about Jonestown now? Ujara's ruined us.

"I'll radio the police in Port Kaituma," says Mac.

"The constable there can take him into custody," says Charles.

"You hold him," Jim is saying to Mac. "Hold onto Ujara until we figure out what's going on here. Congressman, are you all right?"

Ryan is looking down at himself, the red staining his white shirt, shaking his head. "I believe I am, in fact."

"Does this change everything?" Jim asks. I can't tell if he's going to laugh or cry. Did he put Ujara up to this? Tell him not to stab him just to scare him? Or is Jim upset that the Congressman didn't get hurt? I can't tell. Please, God, don't let that be true. We've always stood against violence. Please, Jim, don't change that now.

"It doesn't change everything," says Ryan slowly. "But it changes things. Now, let's get going before anything else happens."

Finally, they're leaving. I count sixteen defectors, over half of them from Indiana. Plus Lenny. What if Jim put him up to something? Does he have a knife too? Or worse? Was he backup in case Ujara didn't do the job properly? Please no. Please, please, let us get through this. I'll do anything to get us through this.

They're gone. I can hardly breathe.

"Thank you, Jocelyn. That water tastes good." She is kind to me.

Now what? Everyone looks terrified. Jim isn't doing anything, just standing there. Dazed. I can't tell what he's thinking.

He wants me to take over.

"Hello, is the mike on? This is Mother. Can everybody hear me?"

Grunts. Yeses. Yes, Ma'ams. Yes, Mother.

"Okay, everyone, let's be calm. I think everything is going to be all right." I breathe and find something like calm buried deep inside. "Let's all go back to our dorms and get some rest. That's what I'm going to do."

Everyone starts moving in the general direction of dorms and cabins.

Here comes Zipporah, crying.

"Sweetheart, Zippy. Don't cry. It's going to be all right. Everything's okay. The Congressman wasn't hurt. No one was hurt."

"Oh, Mother Marceline. I have a horrible feeling inside me. A most horrible feeling." This old, old woman with the sweetest soul, she's shaking, all over. "What's that congressman gonna do to us once he get back to the States?"

"Shhh. It will all be okay. I promise." Poor Zippy. Such a faithful soul. She and her sister have been with us since 1959. From Indiana. The loveliest women in the world. I can't bear to see her so sad. "Just go on back to your dorm and take a nap. Where's

Hyacinth? Go to her. We're all exhausted from this. Every single one of us. Let's take it easy, we'll rest and then eat and we'll all feel better. Then we'll figure out what to do next."

She's walking slowly with her cane. One of the other elders is taking her arm, crying too. I must go on believing we will survive this.

Here's Ken and the baby.

"Ken, honey. C'mere. It's all right. Everything's gonna be okay. Let me hold the baby for a minute, please?" She feels so good in my arms. If only I could hang onto her and make everything else vanish. Oh no. I cannot cry. I will not cry. I won't. "Okay, Sioux Lee, sweet pie, go to your Papa. I'll see you later, Ken."

"See you later, Mom."

"Jim, what was that all about? Why did Ujara do that?" I ask when everyone has left the Pavilion. "It was going so well. Only sixteen people have gone. Out of a thousand. Practically no one. Only two families, really. I'm sure Ryan will speak against the lies the press have told about us. Not one of the people the Concerned Relatives were so very concerned about even went with him. Ryan liked it here; I know he did. He told me so more than once. Or at least he did until Ujara went after him."

Jim shakes his head. "They just won't leave me in peace, Marceline. They won't. They'll never let us be. It's not in their nature. Well, if they want fireworks, we'll give them fireworks."

"What do you mean? What do you mean by fireworks?"

Jim points to the sky. "Look up there, Marceline. In not too long, you'll see a plane go down, and no more Congressman. No more media. No more trouble."

"What? What are you saying? Did you send Lenny to …?"

"It was his idea, Marceline. He wanted to do it. He wants to give his life for us. For Peoples Temple. He's going to take them down."

"What? Does he have a bomb? Jim, no. Please, we've got to stop him!"

"You can't stop this, Marceline." Jim won't look at me. He's looking up at the sign, the don't-forget-the-past sign. "You can't. Once in motion, a body remains in motion. That's physics, isn't it?"

"*You* can stop him, Jim. You know he'd listen to you. Send someone on a dirt bike to get him. Send Mac."

Jim shakes his head. "We're out of fuel, Marceline. The bike won't work."

"Send one of the kids on a bicycle, then. Even a fast runner could catch up with the tractor. Send Deondré!"

"I'm not sending anyone."

He is looking around at the empty Pavilion. Where is Jocelyn? Where is Maria? Mac? Just me and my husband.

I look at this man, the Jim Jones I married who stood for peace and love and brotherhood. Who is he? Not that wonderful man anymore. He is someone else entirely. Someone who won't even look his wife in the eye.

"Jim. Did you send Lenny with a bomb?"

He talks to the sky instead of to me. "A gun. Lenny has a gun. If he takes out the pilot, they'll all go down. Bye bye."

"The pilot? Joao? A Guyanese?"

The Jim I once knew would never, ever countenance this. That Jim's not here anymore. I'll find someone else who can stop it. Mac. Where is he? Mac can stop this. Where are you, Mac? Nowhere in sight. Not in the kitchen. Not anywhere. Please, Mac.

"Marceline, go back to your cabin," Jim says softly as I leave him to search for Mac.

"What?"

"Go back to your cabin, I said. I'm your husband, and I want you to go back to your cabin and lie down. Nothing's going to happen for a while yet. Let's just sit this out and stay calm."

Is he kidding? Stay calm? He's never been calm a day in his life. Yet, he looks bizarrely calm right now. As calm as if he planned it all, and it's going exactly as he wanted. Don't let that be true. I didn't marry a murderer. I did not marry a murderer. A murderer did not father Marcus. A murderer did not raise our beautiful rainbow family. A murderer did not get all these beautiful old people down here to take care of them.

"Marcy? Why don't you go lie down?" From behind Jim, Jocelyn appears.

What does she know? Did she know this would happen? I can't tell from her expression, which looks resigned. Lenin's mistress reincarnated, he once called her. Her face never reveals what she's thinking, not like me. She's always been one giant step ahead of me. Since she came to our door in Ukiah. With Lenny, her husband.

"I'm fine right here. Can you tell me where Mac is?"

"Jim wants you to lie down." She's talking to me as if I'm a child. "Just for a few minutes. Just like you told everyone else to do. It was a great idea. You saved the moment for us. That's what we need right now. Some rest. Some calm. We can figure this out."

What do I do? I need to think. I have to figure out my next step, very, very carefully, and be extremely canny about it.

"All right, Jocelyn. I'll go lie down."

The ceiling is telling me to remain alert. Not to give up one second of consciousness. Not voluntarily. Why? What will happen? Oh please, God that I deserted, Jesus whom I forsook, please come to me now and guide me. What do I do? What is the right thing to do at this moment in my life, in the lives of all our people? For all our people?

No answer.

Of course there's no answer.

Jim will call a White Night. That's his obvious next move. The constable will come for Ujara. Jim won't let him be taken. Ujara should be arrested, even if he didn't hurt Ryan. We can't go around stabbing people we disagree with. We've always been against violence. Gandhi and Martin Luther King are our role models. And Jesus. What would any one of them do now? They'd go to the police and give themselves up, offer themselves up in lieu of their follower who'd done the wrong thing, the violent thing. They would sacrifice themselves. All of them did.

I'll ask Jim to give himself up.

I can't.

I can't face him.

Who is he?

I saw the look on his face when Ryan was attacked. Jim was glad. I know what gladness looks like on that man's face. He glowed with it; he was thrilled. Don't let it be true. I don't think I could handle it. How can I handle it? How will I handle it? I will.

Could I get *myself* to Port Kaituma? Maybe if I turn myself in, it would help. But it wouldn't stop Lenny. Maybe he'll come to his senses and not do it. Wishful thinking. If Jim told him to fly to the moon, Lenny would find a way. Jim said it was Lenny's idea. I don't believe him.

How can I get into town? No gasoline for the Jeep. It's too far on foot in this heat. And by the time I get there, Jim will already have declared a White Night. He'll call it as soon as I leave.

No.

I must stay.

Stay and make him see reason. See that nothing irreversible has happened. Ryan didn't even get nicked. His shirt got bloody, that's all. A minuscule percentage of our people left. None of his women, not Maria, whose brother tried so hard to get her to go. As if giving her their Episcopal priest-father's crucifix would do it. Of course not. No one's irreplaceable. The Parks and Bogues, our oldest supporters … it's sad, but it's not desperate.

If only I could get up. Please, God, help me get up. Help me to do what I need to do. Help me to be certain.

Do I have to kill my husband to stop what he's planning?

Who put that thought in my head?

No.

I cannot kill. I'm a healer, not a killer. If only I could talk to someone. Who can I talk to? Mac? Jocelyn? There's no one. If I told any of them what I was really thinking, Schacht would have me in the ECU in a blink.

I can't talk to anyone.

I have to do it.

Do what?

Kill him?

Maybe I could inject him with a sedative to make him sleep. Just sleep for a long time. By tomorrow, the panic would be past; we'd all get beyond this temporary insanity.

Yes, that's what I'll do. That's the answer.

Marceline, get your body off this bed and over to the Bond.

Feet rise and walk!

No one's here. But it's locked. Of course it's locked. Where's my key? Back at the cabin. I don't know if I have it in me to go back and get it.

There's Maria with Mac.

"What are you doing, Marcy?" Mac asks.

"Um. Just walking."

"Did you want something from the Bond?"

"No. Yes. I have an awful, awful headache, and I thought I'd get some Midol, but I forgot my key." He's looking at me funny. "Don't you have a key, Mac?"

"Marcy, you know only the doc and the nurses have keys. They don't let us laypeople run around with access to drugs. And that's a good thing, huh?" He's smiling. He's trying to make a joke of it.

"Of course you're right." Did Mac ever have drug problems? I don't think so. "I can get my key."

"Let me walk you back to your cabin. You probably just need some rest. And food. I bet you'll feel better after dinner."

Beside him, Maria is nodding. The Yes-Woman. The Yes-Girl. Where's Sean? He's usually with her. "Definitely. You'll feel better with food in your belly," she says. She who looks as if she hasn't eaten in years.

Dinner. Are we going to have dinner? That sounds so odd, so normal, so not-of-this-moment. Maybe it's a sign that we'll get through. This too shall pass, like all the other crises.

"Yes, Mac. You're right, Maria. But I can walk back myself."

"It's my pleasure, Marcy. I always enjoy my time with you." Mac says, and Maria heads off toward her cabin. Their cabin. The cabin she shares with Jim and Jocelyn and the boys.

Mac is carrying a gun. All the guards are walking around with their weapons visible. A very bad sign. I wish I could talk to Mac. Beautiful Mac. I always thought he was so level-headed. But I can't. He'd turn me over to Schacht as quick as any of them. Just play along.

"Here we are."

"Thanks, Mac. I'll see you at dinner."

"Right. Have a good nap, Marcy."

I have to think of something else. The sedative idea won't work. Mac will have somebody guard the Bond to prevent me from getting in.

What next?

Around me are the photographs of all my children, the one I gave birth to, the five we adopted, and so many other Temple children, from Indiana and California and the ones we picked up all across the country on our bus trips. I don't want it to end, our family, our beautiful multicolored family. But Jim wants to end it now.

He'll never listen to me. Did he ever listen to me? I'm sure he did once. How long ago did he stop listening? When Jocelyn showed up? When we moved to California? He won't reason with me. Is he beyond reason? That strange gladness in his eyes when it looked as if Ryan had indeed been stabbed. He wanted Ryan dead. The power glutton has taken over the man I married, the non-violent lover of humanity. He's gone.

I was always afraid it could happen, but I wouldn't let myself believe it.

"Alert. Alert. Everyone to the Pavilion immediately." A voice on the P.A.

Who is that? Harriet? I must go, must gather all of my abilities and strength and smarts and cunning to stop this White Night from happening. He'll do it this time. That's why Mac didn't let me in the Bond. The poison is there. That shipment that came in a few days ago on *The Marceline*. Of course Mac has a key. So does Maria. They all have keys.

"Marcy! Come sit with us," Jocelyn says.

Her calm face looks like his now, that resigned-to-the-end face. I knew she would join the death march with Jim, and Maria, and Harriet and Dick and Mac and all those idea people who believed their legacy should be history instead of flesh, beliefs instead of children.

Help me save the children, Jesus.

Help me.

Come to me now though I forsook You so long ago I do not deserve You but ask You anyway for Your mercy, to help me save the children, not me. The children.

"… how very much I've tried my best to give you the good life."

What's he saying? I can hear it already in his voice, the resignation. This isn't his *let's-fight-the-bastards* tone. This is his farewell.

"… but in spite of all of my trying, a handful of our people, with their lies, have made our life impossible. Not only are there those who have left and committed the betrayal of the century, some have stolen children from others, and are in pursuit right now to kill them, because they stole their children."

He's not even making sense, but everyone's nodding. Where's their fight? What happened to everyone?

"It is said by the greatest of prophets from time immemorial: 'No man may take my life from me; I lay my life down.'"

Please Jim, you can lay your life down, but not the lives of others, not the lives of babies. Go off and lay it down, Jim.

Lay it down alone.

"So to … to sit here and wait for the catastrophe that's going to happen on that airplane … it's going to be a catastrophe. It almost happened here. Almost happened. The congressman was nearly killed here. But you can't steal people's children. You can't take off with people's children without expecting a violent reaction."

Everyone's agreeing. They're with him. Why are they with him? Why don't they want to live?

"The world is fueled by selfish violence, and the violence will take it by force. If we can't live in peace, then let's die in peace."

Now is the moment to speak. I need to tell Jim that death isn't the answer. I need to ask him why are we all sitting here as if you're talking sense? Look at them yessing you, black and white and young and old, male and female. Why are they agreeing? What are they agreeing to? I don't want to die. I will if I have to, but we can't take babies with us. We cannot. We cannot kill.

Don't cry, Marceline.

If you cry, he'll denounce you, like he did on the radio during the siege.

Get a hold of yourself.

"We have been so terribly betrayed," Jim intones.

No. We haven't. Sixteen people leaving out of a thousand is not a betrayal. And Susan and Hope and all the others who've left already … we survived their going. We've survived just fine, so what are you doing? Why are you saying this?

You want death.

You want to stop fighting.

At last. I never thought you'd give up. It's the drugs. The drugs have killed you. And I let it happen. And now you want to take everyone with you.

No.

I can't let you.

I won't.

The people are clapping. Why are they clapping?

"But we've tried, and as Jack Beam often said, if this only works one day, it was worthwhile."

They're applauding like crazy, each and every one of them.

We've had so much more than one day. How can they think he's right?

We've had hundreds of days, years of days, even decades where we've lived just how we've wanted to live, done what we wanted to do. This kind of talk doesn't make sense.

One day only? It's such a pessimistic notion. We can have many more days, so many more.

If I try to seize the microphone, they'll take it away from me: Mac and Jocelyn and Maria. They're all on his wavelength, all on his team. And I'm not.

Have I ever been?

"Thank you," he says, in response to the applause. "Now what's going to happen here in a matter of a few minutes is that one of those people on that plane is going to shoot the pilot. I didn't plan it, but I know it's going to happen, and down comes that plane into the jungle. We better not have any of our children left when it's over, because they'll parachute in here on us. So my opinion is that we be kind to children and be kind to seniors and take the potion like they used to take in ancient Greece, and step over quietly, because we are not committing suicide. It's a revolutionary act."

How can he think taking poison is kind?

Kind to whom? Jesus, Jesus, Jesus. Help me. Why can't I open my mouth? If ever there was a time to speak it's now. I'm defeated before I even start. How can I oppose him? I need to think of an alternative.

They love him, these people. They'll do what he says. They'll even kill their children; I know they will.

Maybe the only ones who wouldn't are the ones who've left.

"Anyone who has any dissenting opinion, please speak. Yes. You can have an opportunity, but if our children are left, we're going to have them butchered. Yes, Christine?"

Thank you, Jesus. Christine-named-for-Christ is making a stand. How can I support her? How can I let her know I'm behind her without Jim's people carting me away as if I'm hysterical?

"Why can't we go to Russia?" she asks.

Good Christine, good for you for thinking. Of course. We can go to Russia. We can go anywhere. Just not back to the States.

"It's too late for Russia. They killed. Otherwise I'd say, Russia, you bet your life. But it's too late. I can't control these people. They've gone with the guns. And it's too late. If one of my people do something, it's me. They said deliver up Ujara, who tried to get the man back here. Ujara, whose mother's been lying on him and lying on him and trying to break up this family. And they've all agreed to kill us by any means necessary. You think I'm going to deliver them Ujara? Not on your life."

Ujara? Are we going to die for Ujara, all of us?

Ujara's a pig. He's always been a pig. I never liked him, from the minute we met back in Ukiah, but Jim's always been attracted to him, for reasons I've never understood. He's a white thug. Maybe he appeals to the white thug in Jim. And now we, all of us, all the children, are supposed to die to save Ujara? A murderous thug?

Not me.

Not me, Jim. I won't.

Listen to all of them shouting: *No! No, we won't give up Ujara.* They've all gone crazy. Nothing will happen to Ujara if we give him to the constable. He'll go to prison for a while. So what? He's been there before and survived. Why doesn't anyone else see what is so very obvious? Oh my Lord, I despise myself for not speaking up.

Who's that? It's Ujara! He's offering himself up. Good for you, Ujara. I'm sorry I thought nasty things about you. Jim was right about you after all.

Thank you, Jesus.

Now this madness can stop.

"You're not going. I can't live that way. I cannot live that way. I've lived for all, and I'll die for all."

Jim should offer himself up. If Ujara is man enough to do it …

Will he die like Jesus?

Jesus died alone. He didn't take children with him. If I had half an ounce of courage, I'd speak up and support Christine. What's he saying? He's answering her.

"I've been living on a hope for a long time, Christine. You've always been a very good agitator. I like agitation because you have to see two sides of one issue, two sides of a question. But those people will make our lives worse than hell. When they get through lying. We are done-in as far as any other alternative."

"Let's make an airlift," she says.

Yes, Christine. You can say it. If I said the same, he wouldn't listen.

He's not interested in a solution. When he sets his chin like that, no one can get through to him.

"How are we going to airlift to Russia?"

"What about the code? You said there was a code we could give the Russians, and they would help us."

Oh, Christine, God bless you.

"No, they didn't," he's saying. "They gave us a code that they'd let us know on that issue, not us create an issue for them. They said if they saw the country coming down, they'd give us a code. Otherwise we die. Death is not a fearful thing. It's living that cuts you."

No, Jim. It's not living that cuts you. It's the drugs and the pills and the blind adoration and the power hunger that cut you. You cut you.

You have taken all these good people down this path which they'll follow to that end you want so much, the one you've wanted all along, though I never wanted to believe it was true.

I thought all that death talk was just more drama, just theater.

They're applauding again.

"I have never, never, never, never seen anything like this before in my life. I've never seen people take the law in their own hands and provoke us and try to purposely agitate murder of children. Christine, it's just not worth living like this."

They're cheering, all of them, ready to die for him.

All of them except Christine.

Why can't they hear the insanity of what he's saying? *They're trying to agitate the murder of our children.* No, it's you, Jim, who wants to murder the children.

Christine, you're so brave I want to cry. Why aren't the rest of us strong like you?

"Not enough people left for this extreme response to make any sense," she says, and she's right.

"But what's going to happen to us when that plane goes down?" says Jim.

She's confused. "Why would that happen?" she asks.

Now I understand. She thinks he's talking about the plane with us in it bound for Russia. She says they wouldn't kill us all, not even if we were going to Russia. She's saying Americans wouldn't do that.

"You think Russia's gonna want us with all this stigma? We had some value, but now we don't have any value."

My God. No value? A thousand souls, all of us beloved, how can he say that? Our beloved community. How can you put a value on a single soul, never mind a thousand. How dare he say that?

Christine is disagreeing. She's the only brave soul among us. She's shouting to be heard over the multitudes telling her to shut up.

"As long as there's life, there's hope," she says. "That's my faith."

Yes, Christine. What she says is true.

Why isn't every person in this crowd agreeing with her?

"Someday everybody dies. I haven't seen anybody yet didn't die," he says in a horrible flat voice. "And I'd like to choose my own kind of death for a change. I'm tired of being tormented to hell, that's what I'm tired of. Tired of it."

Christine's not tired of it. I'm not tired of it. We can't be the only ones.

"Twelve hundred people's lives in my hands. I certainly don't want your life in my hands. Christine, without me, life has no meaning."

How dare he? How dare he assume it? It's monstrous.

They're cheering as if he'd announced the Second Coming. Please Jesus, the Jesus I prayed to until I met Jim Jones.

Please save us. Save us from Jim.

"I'm the best thing you'll ever have. I'm standing with Ujara. I've always taken your troubles right on my shoulders. And I'm not going to change that now. It's too late. I've been running too long. Not going to change now."

They're cheering and cheering, as if he were saving them instead of killing them. Are Christine and I the only ones who want to live?

"Maybe the next time you'll get to go to Russia. This is a revolutionary suicide council. I'm not talking about self-destruction."

He's not even making sense. A council of revolutionary suicide. What does that mean?

Like everything he's ever done, Peoples Temple council says amen to whatever Jim decides.

"I'm not ready to die," says Christine. Me neither, Christine. "Not afraid. But not ready." She holds her head up. "I look about at the babies and I think they deserve to live, you know?"

Oh my God, who I have forsaken, yes, Christine. Yes. Surely Jim can attest to that. Someone could take the children to safety – not me. It's too late for me. I am pathetic. Someone else could take them. That's the answer.

"I agree," he says. It's another of his lies. "But don't they also deserve much more? They deserve peace."

What does he know of peace? He's never known peace for a

day in his life. He's never wanted it. He's wanted drama, wanted fame, wanted people looking at him every minute, praising him or hating him, but not peace. He thinks peace is death. That's all he can imagine.

"We came here for peace, all of us, says Christine.

"Have we had it?" he says, like he's holding some kind of trump card. "We all know we've not had a moment's peace since we arrived in this place. I tried to give it to you. I've practically died every day to give you peace." Another lie. "And you still don't have any peace. A person's a fool who continues to say that he's winning when he's losing. That plane won't take off. It's suicide. That traitor has done it. Him and Hope. He has done the thing he wanted to do. Have us destroyed."

No, Jim. It's you destroying us. But I'm nodding my head, puppet that I am because I lack the courage to speak out. Christine's still talking back.

"When we destroy ourselves, we're defeated. We let them, the enemies, defeat us."

Why aren't I brave like her? I'm shaking with fear.

She's so right, so exactly right. I'm Mother Marceline, the one who's supposed to save the children. Everyone's shouting at Christine to stop talking already. They want to get on with it. I don't have the gumption to make a stand like her.

Now Mac jumps in. "Just hold on sister, just hold on. We have made a beautiful day, and let's make it a beautiful day. That's what I say."

They're all cheering again, cheering and cheering for death, as if they just voted for a picnic party. Jim's takes the microphone back.

"I cannot separate myself from the pain of my people. You can't either, Christine, if you stop to think about it. You can't separate yourself. We've walked too long together."

He wants her on his side. He can't abide naysayers. He doesn't understand she can't be conquered.

"I know that," she says. "But I still think, as an individual, I have a right to say what I think. What I feel. And I think we all have a right to our own destiny as individuals."

Where did her courage come from?

Ken isn't talking back.

Agnes isn't talking back.

I'm not talking back.

Of course Maria and Jocelyn aren't.

Only Christine.

"Yes, Christine. You have a right to say what you think." But he's looking around for someone to shut her up. He won't let her go on. The more she talks, the more likely it is that someone in this mad crowd will listen.

Someone, Mac or somebody, will make her shut up.

She's got the mike again. "And I think I have a right to choose mine, and everybody else has a right to choose theirs. I think I still have a right to my own opinion."

He's making that *mmm* noise, like he's pretending she's said something reasonable.

You do have a right to your own opinion, Christine. You're speaking here for Jesus. In a way I never ever dared to. Me the quiet saint, the saintly fool. I am going to die hating myself.

"Christine, you're only standing here because he was here in the first place," says Mac. "So I don't know what you're talking about, having an individual life. Your life has been extended to the day that you're standing there, because of him." He's so aggressive. How can he speak to her like that?

Because of Him. That's one of our songs, on my favorite record. I can hear the Peoples Temple Choir singing it …

Because of Him.
Because of Him, this world has hope again,
Because of Him, this world has got a good Friend,
A Friend that will dedicate
His whole life to humanity,

Helping each race and creed
To meet their need
So that all may see
That it's so wonderful to care,
To love, to give, to share,
Oh let us start today
To live the same way …

Someone else says, "You've saved so many people." She has a catch in her voice, as if she's about to cry. Is she supporting Christine? Or is she throwing herself at Jim's feet? That's where he likes people to be.

"I've saved them," he says. "I made my manifestation, and the world was not ready for me. Paul said, 'I was a man born out of due season.' I've been born out of due season, just like all of us, and the best testimony we can make is to leave this goddamn world."

They're cheering again. Everyone but Christine and me.

Jocelyn is smiling, as if she wanted the end as much as he did. How can she, with her child beside her?

Now that woman – who is it? Cora? She's saying that we must prepare to die.

No. Still Christine won't let go.

She's shouting: "I'm not talking to her! Would you let her or let me talk?"

Jim is gesturing at Christine to continue. He hates to let a potential convert go, can't stand to let her keep her opinion. He'll smash it out of her or make someone else do it while he looks on as the benevolent father.

"Would you make her sit down and let me talk while I'm on the floor?" demands Christine.

He doesn't like demands.

The crowd is getting angrier. They're simmering, like a swarm of wasps.

"Lay down your burden. Down by the riverside," he says soothingly to Christine, then he turns to the crowd. "Shall we lay them down here, in Guyana? When they start parachuting out of the air, they'll shoot some of our innocent babies. I'm not lying, Christine. But they gotta shoot me to get through." He points to a mother in the front holding a baby. "I'm not letting them take your child." He gestures at another with a toddler on her lap. "Can you let them take your child?"

Now everyone's yelling and it's hard to understand anything at all.

Jim keeps watching them all, my preacher-husband, calculating his next rhetorical move.

He's got them now.

Christine can't stand against him, not alone.

Someone says something about Sean.

"Do you think I'd put Sean's life above others? If I put Sean's life above others, I wouldn't be standing with Ujara. Sean's no different to me than any of these children here. He's just one of my children. I don't prefer one above another. I don't prefer him above Ujara. I can't do that. I can't separate myself from your actions or his actions. If you'd done something wrong, I'd stand with you. If they wanted to come and get you, they'd have to take me."

Cora shouts: "We're all ready to go. If you tell us we have to give our lives now, we're ready. At least the rest of the sisters and brothers are with me."

Oh, Christine. Don't give up.

"I've tried to keep this from happening. But I now see it's the will of the Sovereign Being that this happen to us. That we lay down our lives in protest against what's being done. To protest the criminality of people, the cruelty of people. Who walked out of here today? Mostly white people."

They're cheering him again. What he's just said is true. White people left. Only one black girl went. The girlfriend of one of the Bogue boys.

What's he doing invoking the Sovereign Being?

The Sky God he's been denouncing his entire life?

Jim Jones the hypocrite.

I am a hypocrite too.

I want God.

I want Jesus.

Now.

"Mostly white people walked. I'm so grateful for the ones that didn't. We are born before our time. They won't accept us. And I don't think we should sit here and take any more time for our children to be endangered. Because if they come after our children, and we give them our children, then our children will suffer forever." He looks directly at Christine. "I have no quarrel with you coming up. I like you. I personally like you very much. You had to be honest, but you've stayed, and if you wanted to run, you'd have run with them 'cause anybody could've run today. What would anyone do? I know you're not a runner. Your life is precious to me. It's as precious as Sean's. What I do I do with weight and justice and judgment."

Christine says she's finished talking. Sent by Jesus. Like Jesus, no one listened.

I listened. Now there's no one but me. To try and stop them. To try and fail.

They're all talking again. What am I going to do? Grab the mike. Grab the children.

Mac gets there first. "Everyone," he says in his booming voice. "Be quiet and listen."

Have I lost my chance?

Mac pushes a woman to the front and gives her the mike. "At one time, I felt just like Christine," she says. "But after today I don't feel anything … It broke my heart, to think that all of this year the white people had been with us, and they're not a part of us. So we might as well end it now because I don't see …" Amos runs in and whispers in Jim's ear.

He gets that gleeful look on his face. "It's all over," he says. "The congressman has been murdered."

Ryan is dead. Look at my husband. He's glad. He wanted it. He ordered it. Lenny wouldn't pee without asking Jim first.

Oh my Christ, oh my Jesus.

It really is the end of us.

All the best security shooters are trooping in now from the flatbed. I hadn't noticed they were gone. A whole load of shooters, gone to do his bidding.

I am numb with the horror of it all.

The crowd is in a frenzy. They'll die for Jim. For Ujara, for Sean.

"Well, it's all over," Jim is finding it hard to quell his excitement. "What a legacy, what a legacy. They invaded our privacy. They came into our home. They followed us six thousand miles away. Red Brigade showed them justice. The congressman's dead."

"Do it now! Do it now!" shouts a woman from the crowd. She wants to die. To kill. What difference does it make? What can I do in the face of this frenzy?

Jim turns to Schacht and the nurses. "Please get us some medication," he says, as if he's asking for an aspirin. "It's simple. There's no convulsions with it. Just please get it. Before it's too late. The GDF will be here, I tell you. Get movin', get movin', get movin'!"

The medication.

The poison.

The medication is the poison.

"Don't be afraid to die," he says soothingly. "They'll torture our people. They'll torture our seniors. We cannot have this. Are you going to separate yourself from whoever shot the congressman? I don't know who shot him."

The crowd are screaming their agreement.

Jesus, You are not here after all.

You are nowhere.

Amos whispers something else to Jim.

"How many are dead? God Almighty, God Almighty," he says,

as if finally realizing that being isn't him. "Did they kill everyone on the airstrip? They killed Patty Parks? Did they kill all our people? All the reporters?"

"Some of the others who endure long enough in a safe place can write about the goodness of Jim Jones," shouts a woman from the crowd. Delusional, like so many of the others. Does she think the members back in San Francisco will write glowingly of my husband?

He'll be the Anti-Christ.

"I don't know how in the world they're ever going to write about us. It's just too late. The congressman's dead. Many of our traitors are dead. They're all layin' out there dead."

Where's Christine? I don't see her. I can't see her.

Adoration is written all over their faces. They love him. They've given him their power. "I appreciate you for everything," calls one of his zealots. "You are the only … You are the only … You are the only …" She can't think of a word suitable enough to encapsulate his wondrousness. "And I appreciate you …" They're all clapping, erasing her voice with the with violence of their agreement.

If anyone's with Christine, they're quiet about it.

Like me.

Jim is telling them to hasten, hasten with the medication, with death.

He sent that team of shooters out after the defectors to kill them. In case Lenny failed. My husband the antichrist.

What does that make me?

Complicit, that's what.

"There's nothing to worry about. Everybody keep calm and try and keep your children. They're not crying from pain. It's just a little bitter tasting."

No pain, he says, when there are people convulsing with pain all around him. If Jim Jones says there's no pain, then it must be so.

Marcus and Tim and Jimmy Junior will survive this. Maybe this very minute they're in the midst of their game.

Their father is in the midst of his game too.

"Sit down and be quiet, please," booms Mac the Enforcer. "I used to be a therapist. And the kind of therapy that I did had to do with reincarnation in past life situations. And every time anybody had the experience of going into a past life, I was fortunate enough through Father to be able to let them experience it all the way through their death, so to speak. If you have a body that's been crippled, suddenly you have the kind of body that you want to have. And everybody was so happy when they made that step to the other side."

Jim's smiling. He's loving how Mac backs him up.

"It's the only way to step," adds Jim. "But that choice is not ours now. It's out of our hands. It's hard only at first. Living is much, much more difficult."

I sit here mute even though I hear the first screams.

Phylicia, one of the first children born in the church in Ukiah, has the mike.

"This is nothing to cry about," she croons. "This is something we could all rejoice about, something to be happy about. I wish you would not cry. And just ... thank Father."

They're clapping and cheering.

They don't want to be here anymore, and I don't blame them, really.

I don't want to be here anymore either.

Phylicia again: "I've been here one year and nine months. And I never felt better in my life. Not in San Francisco, but until I came to Jonestown. I had a very good life. I had a beautiful life. And I don't see nothing that I could be sorry about. We should be happy. At least I am. That's all I'm gonna say."

Why stop living that beautiful life?

Why deny it to your children?

She doesn't have children. That's why she's denouncing all the crying mothers. The mothers are crying, but they're going up to the table anyway.

Someone else this time. Another young one: "Good to be alive today. I just like to thank Dad, 'cause he was the only one that stood up for me when I needed him. Thank you, Dad."

She doesn't have children either. Christine had a daughter who was murdered in L.A., but she doesn't want to give up.

Yet another: "I'm glad you're my brothers and sisters, and I'm glad to be here."

Jim's getting twitchy.

"Please. For God's sake, let's get on with it. We've lived as no other people have lived and loved. We've had as much of this world as you're gonna get. Let's just be done with it. Let's be done with the agony of it."

I've watched him nearly thirty years and said nothing. *Now's the time to act, Marceline.* When he started fooling around, I did nothing. Any other woman would have left him when he started up with Jocelyn. If I'd done that, there would be no Jonestown. No murdered Congressman. No dead children. No frenzied suicides.

"It's far, far harder to have to walk through every day, die slowly, from the time you're a child 'til the time you get gray, you're dying … This is a revolutionary suicide. This is not a self-destructive suicide. They brought this upon us. And they'll pay for that. I leave that destiny to them."

It's everyone else's fault this is happening.

Not his. Never his.

The Reverend Jim Jones has nothing to do with it.

"I don't want to see you go through this hell no more. No more, no more, no more. You'll have no problem with this thing if you just relax."

People are taking their turns at the mike: "The way the children are laying there now, I'd rather see them lay like that than to see them have to die like the Jews did, which was pitiful anyhow. And I'd just like to thank Dad for giving us life and also death. And I appreciate the fact of the way our children are going. Because, like Dad said, when they come in, they're gonna massacre our children.

And also the ones that they take captured, they're gonna just let them grow up and be dummies like they want them to be. And not grow up to be a socialist like the one and only Jim Jones. So I'd like to thank Dad for the opportunity for letting Jonestown be, not what it could be, but what Jonestown is. Thank you, Dad."

That man has no children. No one loves him but Jim Jones.

The children lie dead, and I do nothing.

I do what I've done all my life. I watch. I watch and help or watch and do nothing.

"It's not to be afeared. It's a friend. Sitting there, show your love for one another. Let's get gone. Let's get gone. Let's get gone. We tried to find a new beginning. You can't separate yourself from your brother and your sister. No way I'm going to do it. I don't know who killed the congressman. But as far as I am concerned, I killed him. You understand what I'm saying? I killed him. He had no business coming. I told him not to come."

Ryan lies murdered on the airstrip, yet Jim's blaming him for this horror. His fault that around us our people, our black women and men and children and the whites that are left, the harem and the eunuchs, they're swallowing poison like it's Jim's bullshit, which we have all swallowed all these years. I am complicit. These people writhing in their death throes believe, but I've known all along it was bullshit. I swallowed it anyway. Like I'm going to swallow the poison. I know it's wrong, but I'm going to swallow it anyway.

Jim's even lecturing his acolytes on how to die: "With respect, die with a degree of dignity," he says. The hypocrite. He's never been able to stand pain.

"Don't lay down with tears and agony," he continues. "There's nothing to death. It's like Mac said, it's just stepping over into another plane. Don't be this way. Stop this hysterics. This is not the way for people who are Socialists or Communists to die. We have some choice. Look, children, it's just something to put you to rest. Oh, God." His voice catches. Has he finally understood what he has done?

* * *

Watts's heart aches. Earlene and the baby are dead. She'd been one of the first. To prove her loyalty. He's trying to process what it all means when Christine rushes for the vat of poison. Jones wails over the P.A.: "Please, please, please. Don't … don't do this. Lay down your life with your child. But don't do this."

The guards block her. Four of them, including Elijah and Reg, each holds down one of her limbs, as if rehearsing some bizarre dance move. She's struggling, but she's down.

The guards are grim-faced as they keep her pinned. Doc Schacht hands a needle to a nurse, who approaches Christine as if she were a wild animal, rather than a woman pinned down by four burly men. She prepares a clean injection site. Watts would laugh if it weren't so horrible. What good is hygiene to a corpse? Christine's eyes are wide open, but Elijah's covering her mouth. The crowd watches as her struggles come to an end.

Watts shudders. He heads toward the edge of the crowd, dutifully in line for their cupful of deathly Fla-Vor-Aid. Some are crying but resigned. Those who can't drink get a syringeful down the throat. There were a lot of needles prepped in the clinic yesterday, but a thousand is a lot of people. There's a logistical challenge in killing so many. Injection is the Doc's last resort.

Watts sees his moment. He leaves the Pavilion and calmly walks toward the clinic. He stops to hug a little boy, who is the picture of bewilderment, looking up at his crying mother. He looks behind him at Doc Schacht, dispensing poison as if it were medicine. Or Kool-Aid on a hot afternoon. Some of the nurses are checking the dead for pulses.

"Where you going, Watts?" Shit. It's one of the guards.

"The Doc needs me to grab him another stethoscope."

She looks him over.

Without pausing, Watts extends his arms to hug her, taking care to avoid the cutlass hanging from her belt. "Goodbye, Sister. Goodbye."

He can't see Jones from the doorway but can still hear his voice on the P.A., summoning the spirit of Martin Luther King, Jr.: "Free at last. Peace. Keep your emotions down. Keep your emotions down. Children, it will not hurt. Mother, Mother, Mother, Mother, please."

Watts hears Jones and wonders who he's talking to. Are some mothers resisting? Is Mother Marceline resisting? He grabs the stethoscope in case he's questioned again. He heads to the back door of the clinic, which leads to the far side of the Pavilion. He's going full throttle on hope. "Free at last," says the man. "Amen," whispers Watts under his breath, but he doesn't want Jones's kind of freedom. With utmost care, he inches the door open and peeps outside. No one in sight. On the P.A., Jones's voice booms as Watts flees.

"It's been done by every tribe in history. Every tribe facing annihilation. All the Indians of the Amazon are doing it right now. They refuse to bring any babies into the world. They kill every child that comes into the world because they don't want to live in this kind of a world. I don't care how many screams you hear, I don't care how many anguished cries, death is a million times preferable to ten more days of this life. If you knew what was ahead of you, you'd be glad to be stepping over tonight. Death, death, death is common to people. And the Eskimos, they take death in their stride. Let's be dignified. I call on you to quit exciting your children when all they're doing is going to a quiet rest. I call on you to stop this now if you have any respect at all. Are we black, proud, and Socialist, or what are we? No, no sorrow that it's all over. I'm glad it's over. Hurry, hurry, hurry, my children. There are seniors out here I'm concerned about. Hurry. I don't want to leave my seniors to this mess. Only quickly, quickly, quickly. Good knowing you. No more pain now. No more pain. No more pain. Have trust. You have to step across …"

His voice dies away in Watts's ears as Watts puts more distance between himself and the horror show he's left behind. He steps lightly across the open green to the thicket of liana and greenheart trees, a welcoming arbor, despite the supposed tigers and vipers awaiting all who dare to imagine an escape from Jonestown. He hasn't had much in the way of schooling, but he's pretty sure there aren't tigers in the whole of South America anyways. Howler monkeys make their eerie human cries at him as he enters the shade. He stops to breathe and to listen. No one is chasing him. He forces himself to look back. No one. He has no water, nothing but a stethoscope in his hands.

Watts remembers Doc Schacht reciting the physician's rule number one to him, "First do no harm," as he lorded over him and Rufus.

Quiet descends as he moves through the jungle. There's a path somewhere to his right if he can only find it, but the foliage is so thick it's hard to make any progress without a machete. The howler monkeys stop screeching; even the macaws fall silent. He can't hear any more from the Pavilion. The road into Port Kaituma is close by, but he can't risk it. The guards might be checking for escapees. Or for the snipers that exist only in Jones's deluded imagination.

The image of Earlene, baby in arms, walking up to the Doc to take the poison first … the smile on her face will haunt him forever. He hadn't tried to stop her. She was way out of reach. Besides, Schacht would have stuck him in a flash. The man loved the thrill of his own power.

It takes so much energy trying to part the branches and vines that Watts decides to wait where he is until he can make his way to Port Kaituma. They'll all soon be dead, he reasons. Once in Port Kaituma, he'll figure out what to do from there. Slapping flies, he waits, feeling his thirst. He checks his own heart with the stethoscope, which beats loud and fast. Powerfully. No reason for Watts to die today. No reason for any of those people out there, except the Monster himself.

Jones had said he wanted to see his people go before him. Did he plan to stay alive? Watts wouldn't be surprised if the bastard escaped to another country with a million dollars in a suitcase, maybe with one or two of his women. Skipping away from a pile of corpses. There's a bunch of cash in Jonestown somewhere. He's heard rumors of a safe in Jones's cabin, hidden with the harem.

The quiet is ominous. No movement anywhere, not even a dog. He hears a shot. Another shot. A few more shots. Watts is stunned. Maybe they've run out of poison.

Schacht is the man behind the curtain, thinks Watts. Jones is just a cheerleader. Schacht didn't have to put real poison in the vat. Could have put Demerol in to make everybody sleep. Imagine that, thinks Watts, who is getting delirious with thirst. They could have lain down to die, then woken up the next day, full of joy at the miracle. Like Jesus on Easter Sunday.

Two more shots ring out.

For reasons he can't name, Watts knows that's it. There will be no more. After forcing himself to wait – he doesn't know how long – he finally creeps out, holding the stethoscope as if it were a weapon.

The dead. Oh my Lord, the dead. Piles and piles of bodies, one atop the other, all his sisters and brothers. He spots Rufus, his arms around his woman on one side and his child on the other, the bottoms of the kid's sneakers pointing skyward. Absurdly, Watts thinks of putting the stethoscope to Rufus's chest. He throws up, heaving and heaving until nothing comes out.

A strange smell of almonds hangs in the air. Cyanide. The smell of death is sweet. But that'll change. Night is coming, but the heat remains heavy. The bodies are already beginning to swell and will soon burst into unrecognizable shards.

He wants his passport, and he wants water. Nothing else. Maybe Rufus would have come with him. But when Rufus's woman joined the line, Rufus couldn't bear it. Watts wonders if something's wrong with him. His wife and his child – maybe his, maybe not – dead in front of him but he'd had no desire to join them. He knows where their bodies are, but he doesn't look. He doesn't want to see them swollen with death. There is no other side, no beautiful reincarnated life like that shit Mac was spouting. Dead is dead.

Picking his way over the bodies, he breathes, "Get the passport. Get the passport and get the fuck out of here."

There's Schacht and the nurses, dead on the ground. The guards who'd murdered Christine. His dorm-mates, dead. No Mother Marceline.

From a distance, he sees the brilliant red of Jones's polyester shirt, raised up around Jones's stomach, his ugly white belly poking up at the sky god. But there's blood beside his left temple. Shot himself, or somebody else did it for him. Yellow-bellied hypocrite.

A dead dog lies in the middle of the path to the office, also shot. Killing the animals. What the fuck for? So they wouldn't give up their secrets to the GDF? He sneers. That fucker Jones. The animals are spared the suffering that's heaped on the people. What kind of love is that? Watts has done some bad loving in his life, tons of it, though he's been better to Earlene than to any other woman. He got into women's pants, tired of them fast and left, sometimes saying goodbye, sometimes not. Over and over he's done the same thing, too many times to count. Earlene was different. Maybe his grandma had been like Earlene as a child in Georgia, a rural girl who loved her Jesus more than anything or anyone. Instead of Jesus, Earlene had Jimmie Jones to die for.

He's close to the office when he sees more blood. Jones's nurse, shot in the temple, a gun beside her. Did she do it? Some fucked up mercy killing to spare Jones from the convulsions that even the babies suffered? Wedged into the locked office door is a folded piece of paper, which he opens. The scrawled handwriting is blurred in some places:

We, the undersigned mothers, have been shown a dream. We left our homes to follow it. Now we fear that it is about to turn into a nightmare. Dad, we beg of you, don't finally embark on the step that you have spoken of. Please spare our children. If we must die, let them live. There is nothing noble in dying, nothing fine in killing children.

It's signed by a number of names. Names he knows. What's become of them? All the mothers, dead. He folds the paper back in the door for someone else to find. He slides the window up and crawls inside.

The drawer full of passports is open, as if rifled through moments before. Perhaps he isn't the only one to run? No one else came through the window, so it must be someone with a key. Someone in the white chick circle.

Has Jocelyn or Maria escaped? Did they kill him and split with the kids? The calculation of those in power … whites for sure … makes him feel sick again.

Under "F," he finds his passport with his given name, Roman Freeman. There are a number of other Freemans at Jonestown, none of them related to him, but all with Southern roots, like his grandma, his mother's mother, whose name he's taken. He doesn't know his father's name.

He pockets the passport then goes to the kitchen and fills a canteen with water. Then he runs. He runs down the road, past the red tractor and red flatbed, past some spread out bodies toward the outer cabins and dorms. What about all the old people who couldn't walk, couldn't get out of their beds? Schacht would have taken care of them somehow. Watts doesn't want to imagine how.

He runs as fast as he can, though no one is chasing him. The humidity makes it hard to breathe, but he runs anyhow. It's so eerie, this empty place, the quiet of a world with a thousand cadavers. A pair of parrots squawks beside the gate, as if saying goodbye. There'd been at least a thousand people in the Imperial Projects in Watts, the high rise he'd lived in as a child. Then the city tore the buildings down. Implosion, they called it. Here, it's as if some biological weapon fell from the sky and wiped out every single one of them, including the pets. What the fuck for?

A stitch in his side forces him to stop. He can't keep running like this. He'll die of a heart attack.

He reaches Port Kaituma at night. At The Last Chance bar, he finds the lights out and the door locked. This is very peculiar.

"Hello," he calls softly, knocking, feeling afraid.

"Who's there?" calls the Guyanese constable. He points a gun at Watts, who puts his hands in the air.

"It's Watts," he stammers. "Watts Freeman from Jonestown. I don't have any weapons. Nothing."

The older man comes closer, still pointing his rifle, which looks at least thirty years old. He smells of booze, which makes Watts want to drink. Drink for a thousand days until he's satisfied.

"You from Jonestown?" says the constable.

"Yes."

"You know what happened here today? There are injured people inside the bar. Got shot up on the runway today. You know anything about that?"

"Can I put my hands down? I'm so tired. I don't want to hurt anybody, and I don't want to get shot."

"Okay. Put your hands down. But I got my gun on you."

"All right."

"The folks inside are worried the gunmen from Jonestown are gonna come back and finish the job."

Watts sighs. "Nobody's left to finish them off. Everybody dead."

The constable looks him over. "What you talking about? They got one thousand people in Jonestown."

"They're dead."

"So why you not dead? You kill them all?"

Watts finds himself laughing. Sick, toxic laughter makes him sound like a howler monkey. Then he's rolling on the ground, laughing and crying and groaning and not knowing what he's doing, only that he has to do it, to get the awfulness outside of his body. He heaves up the water he'd drunk on his way into Port Kaituma, and then he's spitting air.

"You want a drink, boy?" says the constable gently.

Watts's head spins.

"You delusional. You come with me. I got me a nice chair in back and a bottle of water. Rum too."

The constable's name is Gordon Luckhoo. He tells and re-tells Watts his version of what happened on the runway that afternoon, though he hadn't been there. Five dead, as many or more wounded, and some fled into the jungle. No one knows where they are. The U.S. Embassy man finally radioed the capital, but no planes can land till morning. The wounded just have to sit tight till dawn. From time to time, Luckhoo gets up to patrol the building, sees if the people inside need anything. He tells Watts to stay outside with him. The people inside are so scared the shooters will return. Word is that the Guyanese Defense Forces will arrive at Jonestown by morning after marching all night from Matthews Ridge.

"They ain't gonna find anything but a bunch of dead black people," Watts tells the constable, who shakes his head. "And some of the higher-ups. The whites."

"Mr. Freeman, maybe you drugged. Never would a thousand people kill themselves. Why would they do that?"

Watts shrugs. How can he possibly answer that question? He's calmer now. He's had a short sleep but woke to the murmur of Gordon Luckhoo's lovely voice, a little slurred as he sips his Demerara. Watts sips water, though part of him craves the oblivion that drink offers.

Not long after dawn, Watts wakes to the sound of a plane landing at the nearby airstrip. Gordon Luckhoo is snoring loudly, so Watts gets him up.

The wounded are loaded into the plane. Those who can walk make their way up the stairs, and those who hid overnight in the jungle walk out, tired and frightened but otherwise fine. Some know Watts. They nod at him but say nothing. The survivors propel themselves toward the plane, looking in every direction for more shooters.

The Embassy man asks Watts if he wants to go to Georgetown on the plane.

"You're gonna need me to identify the dead. Before it's too late."

"They're identified already. Congressman Ryan, the three newsmen, and Patty Parks," he says. He's a fair white man who's been burnt by the sun so many times his skin is a permanent unnatural red. His eyes are pink with lack of sleep.

"No. I mean at Jonestown."

"What are you talking about?"

Watts makes his story brief.

"Get out of here," says the man from the Embassy. "That Stein woman said they'd do it, but ... no. I don't believe it. Not a thousand people."

"Let's get our asses over to Jonestown and I'll show you what I'm talking about.

YOU CANNOT STAMP ME OUT.
I'M HERE TO STAY.

Jim Jones

Watts Freeman
8:31 p.m.
November 18, 2008
San Francisco

Watts wakes to the murmur of the radio. After Kenyatta's departure, he'd walked all afternoon around the city, feet aching, revis-
iting the corner on Fillmore where he'd first seen Peoples Temple
buses thirty-eight years ago, maybe more. Exhausted, he'd slept
all afternoon. He looks at his digital bedside clock. He's missed
half the program already.

"Damn it!"

Rubbing his eyes, he shakes himself awake and turns on the
radio.

It's Kenyatta: "Following is a clip from my interview with the
Miami newsprint photographer who was one of the first reporters
allowed into the Jonestown compound. Since then, he's covered
various wars, school killings, and other horrors around the world.
Here's what he had to say."

"When we arrived, the bodies had weathered a few days of tropical
heat," begins a hoarse male voice with a Latin accent. "Hundreds and
hundreds of bodies. There were shoes in the mud and on the grass
and in the fields. Some were children's shoes, sandals no bigger than
the palm of your hand. I was there to do a job, but I couldn't bring
myself to photograph those shoes. Those little sandals are etched in
my brain, even more powerfully since I became a parent myself."

Kenyatta again: "I asked him if he'd been surprised by the fact that the majority of the bodies were black. Here's what he said."

"I cover stories all over the world, so I'm used to corpses of all shades and hues. What I wasn't prepared for were the infants and the toddlers. And so many elderly, some still in their beds. I suppose they'd been injected with syringes, as there weren't any little paper cups in the dorms. They were scattered all over the ground around the tub of Kool-Aid. So, to answer more directly, for me – my mother's Cuban, my father Irish, my wife Brazilian – I didn't note race as much as age. At Ground Zero, of course, there were hardly any bodies at all."

Watts gropes for a glass of water, reaches for his pack of cigarettes but thinks again and pushes it away. He lies back, wide awake now, and stares at the ceiling, thinking, as he has before, that the stain on the plaster reminds him of the outline of South America, another world he knew long ago.

"My last interview is with Hope Garcia. Ms. Garcia," says Kenyatta in an official voice, "thirty years after the death of your son, is there any sort of message you have for our listeners, anything you want to express today, perhaps a new or deeper insight into what happened?"

After a pause, the woman says, "Never give up on your child. That's all I can say. I was so young when I left Sean with the Temple in Ukiah. I left him with good people, some very good people in the organization, but it was the greatest mistake of my life. When I came to understand how stupid I'd been, it was too late. I've been lucky. I married again, I have three wonderful kids, but there isn't an hour that passes without me wishing Sean was here."

Watts hears her clearing her throat. Her voice cracks.

"In retrospect, I should have done *anything* – illegal or otherwise – to get him back. I could have kidnapped him while he was still in the States, or gotten someone else to do it, a deprogrammer, anyone I could've paid or bribed. Whatever it took."

The original Queen Bitch Traitor Hope is speaking. Watts feels a wave of pity for her. He remembers the hatred directed her way in Jonestown, even on the last day.

"Some people blame you for sparking the disaster, for having the summons served on Jones over custody of your son," says Kenyatta in an even tone. "How do you feel about that now?"

Hope sighs and laughs simultaneously. "Guilty. Guilty as charged. I just wanted my son back. I didn't want anyone to die. Jones was out to make the end he chose for the Temple possible by any means necessary, and I'm quoting Malcolm X deliberately. Jones craved a place in history. If his spirit is anywhere, it's probably thrilled to hear us talking about him three decades later, and on that note, I'm done."

"That was Hope Garcia, whom I interviewed in her Marin County home. Listeners should know that many of the Jonestown survivors I spoke with chose not to participate in today's retrospective. Some have been burned too many times by the media over the last thirty years. Not once or twice but dozens of times. Fortunately, as you heard earlier from Watts Freeman and a few other Temple members, not every survivor feels that way. I hope KBBA has done them and their history justice."

In a less journalistic tone, Kenyatta adds, "Peoples Temple loved music and singing. The Peoples Temple Choir recorded a number of albums, most of them right here in Oakland. We're going to finish this hour with one of their songs, not from an album but rather a song that cropped up spontaneously in a meeting, recorded during a White Night, that is, a rehearsal for mass suicide, about five months before the Temple's implosion."

"I want to thank for speaking with me on the program Jim Jones Junior, Marcus Baldwin, Watts Freeman, Elzaveta Gurov, known in her Temple days as Truth Miller, her son, Cuffy, Carol McKnight and Arlene Thompson, and their children, who walked out of Jonestown the morning before the end, photographer Alejandro Machado and Hope Garcia.

"Here's Peoples Temple member Zipporah Edwards, a woman in her eighties, singing. Then you'll hear Jim Jones, as well as hundreds of Temple members joining the chorus, most of whom perished thirty years ago today."

Watts turns up the volume and sings along with Zippy, whose cracking voice indicates she might cry at any moment:

All the days of my life
Ever since I been born,
I never heard a man speak like this man before.

[Syncopated clapping begins]

I never heard a man speak like this man before,
All the days of my life,
Ever since I been born,
I never heard a man
Speak like this man before.

Watts hasn't heard this song since Jonestown. Swallowing hard, he bites his lower lip, knowing what is to follow.

Jones shouts to his congregation: "C'mon sing it! You can sing like socialists. Louder! Louder!"

Everyone sings, Jones's baritone loudest of all.

I never heard a man speak like this man before
The days of my life
Ever since I been born
I never heard a man speak like this man before.

Extended applause follows for what seems like several minutes.

Jones laughs, then adds, "Wherever in the hell it's brought us, it brought us on principle, it brought us on courage, and it brought us to the right place, and if we hold on, we'll make it."

Epilogue

Kenyatta Robinson
6 a.m.
Nov. 18, 2018
Evergreen Cemetery, Oakland, California

As Kenyatta steers the van around the bend in the cemetery road, she sees the graffiti: three-foot high letters, legible and neat. JIM JONES = KILLER. She parks, grabs her video camera, and goes the rest of the way on foot to the Jonestown Memorial site, filming the letters as they grow larger and larger in her viewfinder. Her long legs glide easily along the pavement, her graying Afro bobbing in the slight breeze. Black spray paint shines in the dewy light, as if still wet, and Kenyatta wonders if the artist might be lurking somewhere, hoping to gauge first reactions. Several oaks provide possible hiding places, but Kenyatta doesn't see anyone.

Beyond the word "KILLER" is one more phrase: EXPUNGE HIM. On her clipboard, retrieved from the giant canvas satchel she carries everywhere, Kenyatta notes the particular word choice: not "expel" or "remove." There are many who believe Jim Jones should not be memorialized along with the other 917 dead on November 18, 1978, in Jonestown, Guyana. But there he is: James Warren Jones, sandwiched between James Arthur Jones, one of his grandchildren and Jesse Weana Jones, an elderly black woman from Louisiana, no relation. The names are inscribed alphabetically on four granite markers installed in 2011.

Today, Kenyatta and her assistants will film the forty-year anniversary ceremony for her documentary production company, IDA B. FILMS, which she incorporated after leaving KBBA. Once immersed in the stories of Jonestown, she could not extricate herself from that murky moment of particularly American twentieth-century horror. Kenyatta has finished three unrelated projects during the last decade, but this one endures: *Paradise Undone: A Documentary of Jonestown.* It has no end date in sight.

The black letters stand in stark relief against the stubble of yellow lawn. She tries several angles and settles on filming from above, where the camera captures all the graffiti at once. A drone will do the job. She texts her two assistants to hurry, then she climbs the sloping bank up to the four plaques. The artist – or, some may say, the vandal – has blotted out the three parts of Jones's name with black spray paint, carefully sparing all others. Spattering the few inches of black are drops of glistening red nail polish, representing blood.

The Jonestown survivors are split into two camps: those who want Jones's death to be documented along with the others, and those who say it's akin to including Hitler's name on a Holocaust memorial.

Since these four stones had been laid, every November 18th until today, two separate commemorations have been held: one in the morning led by the minister, and the other in the afternoon, directed by the inclusion promoters. That way, the twain need not meet. But this anniversary year, when media are expected to flood the scene, the Jones's family group is going first, at 9 a.m.

Her team's UC Berkeley van pulls up beside the graffiti, obstructing it.

"Hey, you two," she shouts to the young people who descend, coffee containers in hand. "We have to get some clean shots of the graffiti before all the vehicles block the view. Then you can film the responses as people arrive."

Addison, an Asian woman in her mid-twenties attending

Kenyatta's investigative reporting class, nods. "I'll move the van back down behind yours," she says.

"You set up the drone and get the giant letters as well as the paint on the plaque, where Jones's name is blacked out and spattered with fake blood," she says to Keith, an African American man around the same age as Addison who attends her graduate film seminar.

Keith nods. "Excellent."

A golf cart pulls in silently beside Kenyatta at the curb. Two older men, one white and one black, are wearing pressed coveralls labelled *Evergreen*. They're deep in conversation. Kenyatta looks at the sky. It's warm for November, though typical of drought-plagued California these last few years.

Upon seeing the graffiti, the white man yells, "What the fuck!"

"Jim Jones equals killer," says the black man, reading the words in an even tone. "Expunge him." He shakes his head. "They mean from that stone up the hill."

Kenyatta nods. "Go see. It's already done."

The white man pulls out a cell phone. "I'm calling the cops. This has to be documented for the insurance."

The two men survey the letters. One touches the paint, perhaps to gauge its age. His finger comes up dry.

"I'm guessing it was an art student," the black man says.

"Why?" asks Kenyatta.

"Look how neat the letters are! Perfectly even, each the same width and height as the others. Ordinary folk are just not that good with a spray can."

Addison and Keith release the drone, which hovers briefly near the two men. "What the fuck is that?" asks the white man.

"I'm filming the ceremony today for a documentary," says Kenyatta, offering her free hand. "Kenyatta Robinson, on the journalism and film faculty at Cal."

The man looks her up and down. "I'm Al Goodman, here for the owner today, who's in the hospital." He takes her hand.

The black man comes forward. "Thomas McKnight. Grounds director." They shake hands.

"How many people are you expecting today?" Kenyatta asks.

Keith appears behind her and introduces himself. The men nod.

"No telling," says Thomas. "Some years about forty or so, but on the big anniversaries, like the 30th, we had a few hundred."

As if on cue, a large truck pulls up, dwarfing the golf cart. It's marked with Art Deco letters: *Oakland Events Planning*.

The driver gets out and approaches Thomas. "We're ready to get started."

"You setting up the wheelchair ramp too, right?"

"Yup."

The man yells toward the passenger side of his truck. "Let's get going!"

Two well-muscled young black men descend from the cab, open the back of the truck, and start moving racks of chairs, canopy poles and canvas, speakers, sound equipment, and, last, a podium.

As the sun climbs the Oakland hills to the east, Kenyatta roams, admiring how the memorial site rises above the rest of the cemetery, offering a view west, toward the bay. While a few trees offer shade, canopies will be needed today for shelter from California's merciless light.

The young men and their boss efficiently arrange a rubber walkway up the slope to the podium. Kenyatta asks their names and if they mind being filmed. One flexes his biceps for her, flashing a grin.

"So, what do you know about this memorial?"

"Jonestown? That's where all those black people died from drinking poisoned Kool-Aid. I know because I was here last year too. Lotta wailing and that preacher woman yelling Jim Jones was the devil. She say he kill twenty-seven members of her family."

"So do *you* think his name should be memorialized with the others?" she asks.

"I don't know. I heard both sides of it last time, but I haven't made up my mind yet." He smiles again. "Sorry, Professor, I gotta work."

Folding chairs stretch in rows forming a semi-circle before the podium. Around fifty seats are unfolded so far, though more remain in the truck. Oakland Events Planning will spend the entire day on site, monitoring the size of the crowd and making adjustments as necessary, ready to tackle any sound issues that might arise.

Two cops arrive in a squad car. "Man, I can't believe the nerve of this crook!" says Al.

One officer looks over the letters and shakes her head. "Well, it sure is giant, this graffiti, but you know it's not exactly damage since it won't be permanent. Eventually, the grass will grow over it. Someday, anyway."

"Well, you gotta see what they did to the stone." Al points up the hill. "That's real damage. Paint's so sunk in it'll take a grinder to get out. The letters will have to be re-inscribed."

"Show us," says the other officer, and the group ascends the black rubber ramp, heading for the stones.

When Marcus Baldwin arrives, he heads straight to Kenyatta. "I'm guessing you already got a good shot of the graffiti." He shakes his head. "Amazing. All these years without incident, and someone does this just in time for today's media infestation. Smart cookie."

"Who are you expecting?"

"I know the *Chronicle* will be here, the *Tribune*, ABC and NBC, KQED, KBBR. I'm sure there'll be many more."

"You still going with the schedule you emailed me yesterday?" She consults her clipboard. "Intro, then your sister, and then the videocast from Georgetown, with you finishing up, all in less than an hour?" She laughs.

Marcus looks tired and old, Kenyatta thinks. Not the robust, handsome fifty-something she remembers from last November.

"Well, you never know what's gonna happen." He walks over

to the podium to deposit a folder, then taps the microphone. "Test, test, test."

His voice booms in the still air.

"Too loud?" He looks at Kenyatta. "Probably good for the old folks."

By nine o'clock, parked cars line both sides of the road as far as Kenyatta can see. Vans and SUVs occlude the graffiti, its effect evaporated. Who would spend so much time on such a fleeting protest? "Expunge him," she whispers, as if one could eliminate Jim Jones simply by willing it.

The broadcast media make themselves conspicuous with their satellite trucks. Once a member of that crowd, she sighs with relief, happy to be teaching and making films, no longer participating in the daily rat race of deadlines and scoop-seeking.

Marcus taps the microphone, and the swelling crowd collectively shudders at the volume.

"Sorry about that. I know it's loud."

"Wha'd he say?" shouts an old woman from the back row.

People laugh.

"Welcome everyone: survivors, friends of Peoples Temple, sympathizers, and critics. You are all welcome today, the fortieth anniversary of the Jonestown tragedy, the deaths of 918 people."

Kenyatta films the crowd while Addison focuses on the speaker and Keith prowls the perimeter, searching for surprising angles and unusual details, which, according to Kenyatta, define the art of documentary.

"917, not 918!" a woman shouts.

"I said 918," Marcus says patiently, "because my father, Jim Jones, is among the dead. But let's put that aside for now. For those of you who don't know me, I'm Marcus Jones, the only biological child of Jim and Marceline Jones, both of whom died that day in the jungle, my mother from poison, my father from a shot to the head."

Some in the crowd are shaking their heads, frowning, accusatory expressions forming grimaces.

"Put that aside? Who's he kidding?" shouts the same woman.

"I'll leave my remarks until the end," Marcus adds, "as I won't be attending another memorial."

That gets people whispering, murmuring, tapping their neighbors on the shoulders, asking, "What?" and "Why?"

"On today's program is my sister Sue, who's going to speak about my mother, Marceline, who's always overlooked, both in life and in death, too. After Sue, we'll have something quite extraordinary: Gwendolyn Nascimento, the widow of Virgil Nascimento, the Guyanese ambassador to the United States during Jonestown, wants to talk to you, to us. She's very old and frail. Never spoken publicly before. She said she had some important words for us and wants to communicate them before it's too late. She also sent us a crate of cassavas, and so over in the refreshment tent, you'll find fritters to eat, courtesy of two of the ladies who were at the dentist in Georgetown that November day, Opal and Sharlene. They cooked them up just the way we did in the jungle, and there's cold water to drink. A typical Jonestown meal."

The crowd looks at him, surprised, curious.

"After Mrs. Nascimento, I'll say a few words, my last address to you and the world on the subject of Jonestown."

In the audience, someone asks loudly, "What's the matter, Marcus? You sick or something?"

"What's going on?" says someone else.

Marcus hears them but doesn't respond. "Sue?" He looks in the first row for his sister. "Your turn."

A heavyset white woman in her early sixties makes her way to the podium with the aid of a cane. Despite her weight, she appears somehow fragile, unbalanced, and Marcus adjusts the mic for her much shorter stature.

"You all don't know me, most of you," she begins, patting her temples with a trembling hand. "I was one of the rainbow family members, that multiracial bunch of adopted kids that grew up in the Jones home, long before anybody ever heard of Guyana." She pauses and looks at Marcus, who's taken her place in the front row. Her brother smiles and nods his encouragement.

"I didn't make it to Jonestown because I ran away, long before. I ran away from Jim Jones so many times, soon as I figured out who he was. But I always came back because I loved my mother, Mother Marceline."

She pauses to sip from a glass of water. Unlike Marcus, she does not have a file to look at. No notes whatsoever. The words flow easily, spilling out of the speakers in a sacramental cadence.

"Forty years ago today, my sister Agnes died in Jonestown. And her son, and her husband. My brother Lew and his wife and child. Two of my sisters-in-law, both pregnant. My adoptive father, Jim Jones, either put a bullet in his head or had someone else do it. Likely his private nurse, so-called, because he was too much the coward to drink the poison himself. But Mother, she drank it up like all the mothers did. She couldn't stop the children from being killed, couldn't stop the slaughter of innocents.

"My mother was not a saint. I loved her, but she let me down. She let us all down. Because she stayed. Staying is a kind of consent, don't you think? I mean, she stayed with Jim from the well-intentioned beginning until the bitter end, long, long after he turned into a drug-crazed monomaniac.

"But I'm not here to talk about Jim Jones, who I always knew would come to a bad end. I didn't know he would take all of Peoples Temple with him and most of my rainbow too. In part, I blame the mother I loved, and still love, Mother Marceline.

"Back when we were still in Ukiah ... I was already running away in those days because I recognized the power-hunger in that man. I could see the way he disrespected my mother, starting with Jocelyn, building up a harem right there in front of her eyes, as if she couldn't see, as if it didn't matter. Oh my, did it matter.

"She suffered, my mother did, from Jim sleeping around in plain sight. She agonized, for years, until she met a man at one of the State Health Administrators' conferences she attended for work, a wonderful man: a doctor, a real healer of people, not a fake healer like Jim Jones. That man loved my mother. Genuinely. He recognized her true heart and beauty and goodness and begged her to come with him back East, where he lived.

"In case you're wondering, I didn't know about this when it was happening; I wasn't in Ukiah then. I'd run away here, to the Bay Area, though she and I wrote each other letters. She didn't come right out and tell me, but I detected a change in those letters. She was happy! She was vibrant in a way I rarely saw, had never seen since we'd left Indiana.

"I didn't know what it was about until last year, when I read a new history of Jonestown. My mother wanted to leave Jim and take all of us with her. Every one of us. Jim refused. He said get yourself out of here if you want, but you're not taking one of my children with you. I'll have you in court so fast your head'll spin, and your joke of an M.D. won't have a patient to call his own 'cause I'll make such a hullaballoo in the press. Won't they just lap that up? A doctor fooling around with a minister's wife.

"All of you know how convincing he was. Marceline loved her children. She loved us all without limits. She couldn't put herself first. It wasn't in her nature. She couldn't leave us alone with Jim Jones, so she stayed. The doctor returned east without her. And you know how the story ends."

She drank some more water and wiped her mouth with the back of her hand.

"I want you all to understand that Marceline Baldwin Jones was a woman made of love and strength, but when it came to Jim Jones, she was weak. Just like everyone else, it seems, everyone who lost every iota of common sense if they lingered in his orbit for long. She was afraid to cross him, even when it meant her life. And the lives of others. And for that, I blame her.

"Before the Joneses adopted me, I lived with my biological mother and father in a shithole in Indianapolis, and my dad used to beat my mother. My mother beat me. They drank, both of them. There was no love in that house, and when the Jones clan took me in – by then there was a handful of kids in the family, including Marcus – well, then, I thought I'd died and gone to heaven. All that love, flowing out of both parents and among and between us kids. It was beautiful. At first, anyway. But you know, that man, the Reverend Jim Jones, he was just as bad as my birth father. He didn't beat Marceline with his fists. He did something I came to see as worse because it was less honest. He destroyed her with his words, his scorn, from morning till night, sometimes all night too, putting her down, belittling her every chance he got, until she had no self left. It was domestic abuse of the worst kind, leaving deep scars, only they're invisible. No black eyes, no bruises you could see, but I promise you, she was the walking wounded. I think it started in California when he became the famous star of the Peoples Temple. He got too big for his britches.

"What I want to leave you with, to offer you, is the peace I've managed to make with Marceline, who was the best mother to me I could have had. My peace acknowledges her one big flaw. She allowed Jim Jones to cow her. I don't know if she ever had any physical love with that doctor. I sure hope so because she got no love back from Jim Jones. I believe that if she'd stood up to him back in Ukiah, sic'ed a lawyer on that megalomaniac when he made those threats, a good lawyer who would've made sure she got all the kids … What judge would award Jim Jones the custody of six kids? I mean back then, before he became the rock star in sunglasses. Then we wouldn't be here today, none of us.

"But there's no going back. I just want to ask you to pray for Marceline's soul. Thank you for listening."

The large screen behind the podium was uncovered by one of the Oakland company men; a canopy had been erected to block the sun's rays from infiltrating the broadcast image. In the front row, Marcus spoke into a laptop, and an image appeared, filling the screen. An elegant, ancient black woman spoke into the camera. Her white hair rested loosely in a chignon atop her head, and a strand of pearls anchored her delicate collarbones. She was visible only above her shoulders.

"My name is Gwendolyn Nascimento. My husband was Virgil Nascimento, the Guyanese ambassador to the United States during the time of the Peoples Temple infestation of my country. My husband left me in 1977 for a young woman in your institution, one of the women who Jim Jones prostituted, to learn everything he could about the goings-on of the Guyanese government. Some of you might have known Nancy Levine, from New York City. They married and had a child together. Then … my husband, my ex-husband, I should say, he murdered Nancy and the child and then killed himself on the third anniversary of Jonestown in 1981."

The woman's voice was steady, hard. Even cruel, Kenyatta thought. She was the kind of woman who'd been raised among the black elite of Guyana, who went to school in Oxford or Cambridge, who knew who she was and what she merited.

"I wanted to talk to you about what your Peoples Temple did to my country, Guyana. The ones with power in your group died in 1978, but there are still those today – I read their words online, here in Georgetown – those who believe in Jim Jones even today, in 2018, who believe in the mission of Peoples Temple, believe in the promise of Jones's so-called utopia in our jungle."

Some nodded in the crowd, some shook their heads. Some just bit their lips.

"You are colonizers. Do you recognize that? Do you understand that?" She turned away to sip from a teacup, blinked, then stared into the camera.

"You came to my country and used it, used it for your pleasure, like a white man uses a black whore. That's what you did. And your stay in my country has made us anathema to the rest of the world for a long, long time. I'm not sure if we'll ever get past the damage you inflicted. Totally unasked for, one hundred percent destructive.

"We survived the British, who used us first for their pleasures and profits, though they at least left behind a few worthwhile institutions for the Guyanese to make their own.

"What did you leave behind?" Her old eyes bore into the crowd. "A rotted carcass of a settlement, that's what. And murder, mass murder, the only murder of a U.S. congressmen in the history of your country. And where did it happen? Guyana. My home.

"What is your legacy to us?"

The connection was abruptly cut from the Guyanese end. Marcus attempted to renew it, but after a few tries, he gave up. After the microphone and podium were put back in place, he stood, waiting for the attention of the crowd. Everyone in the audience was shaking their heads – whether in anger or agreement with the Guyanese woman's words, Kenyatta couldn't tell. Perhaps both.

Marcus tapped loud on the microphone.

"I didn't know what she was going to say." Marcus's voice shook. "She's certainly entitled to think what she pleases. I'm pretty rattled, but at the same time, I'm glad we got to hear her."

"Do you think she's right?" A male voice boomed from the crowd.

Kenyatta recognized the man from ABC in San Francisco. His cameraman was filming right beside Addison.

"I'm not going to comment on what she said. Neither will I give my opinion on what anyone has to say any more about Jim Jones."

The reporter began to speak, but Marcus stopped him. "No more questions now. I just have a few things to say before I turn the microphone over to Professor Kenyatta Robinson."

Shocked, Kenyatta nearly jumped. She had never talked to Marcus about addressing the crowd. What was he doing?

He opened his folder and glanced at his notes. "I have been diagnosed with Parkinson's disease."

The crowd responded in murmurs and muffled exclamations of sorrow.

"I don't tell you this to get your sympathy. I'm just explaining my decision to step away from everything that has to do with Jonestown, for the rest of my natural life, however long it happens to be, and I hope it's a long time."

Kenyatta shook her head. His words made sense of his sickly appearance.

"I'm changing my name. To what, I'm not telling." He laughed and smiled for the first time. "I've spent forty years being the son of Jim Jones, the face of the Peoples Temple, for better and for worse. Mostly for worse, I think. The face and voice of the 917."

"That's right, 917," called the woman who'd spoken earlier.

"For forty years, I've endeavored to do the right thing by those 917, by my mother, and all of you, including the media, historians, religious studies scholars, American Studies people, psychologists, journalists, and on and on and on.

"I did not procreate because I didn't want Jim Jones's blood to continue in this world. I have my own rainbow family, six children my wife and I adopted from various places in this country and internationally. I have grandchildren now.

"I hope you'll respect my decision. Everything that Jim Jones ever did reverberated through me both before and after Jonestown. I have never had a life of my own, and so now, at fifty-nine, given this diagnosis, I want the life I never got to live, as my own man.

"My wife and I are moving to an undisclosed location out of state. We'll see our children and grandchildren and participate in the world as we see fit, but no longer in the shadow of Jonestown. Do you understand? Don't try to find me."

He addressed the reporter from ABC. "Don't seek out my children or grandchildren. They're all off-limits. But my surviving siblings have nothing to do with my own decision, and if you want to speak with them, ask them. I know Sue is finally willing to talk at last. Talk to her. Talk to my brother Jim, who was instrumental in getting these stones laid, these pieces of granite with my father's name among the dead.

"And by the way, though it's up to the good people of Evergreen and not to me, I think you should leave the black paint and the fake red blood on his name. It will fade away, eventually."

He switched off the microphone and strode away, down the hill. Everyone in the audience sat frozen, watching him leave, while various camera people filmed him from behind, including Keith, who followed all the way to his slamming of the car door.

Kenyatta blinked several times, then walked to the microphone, switching it back on. "Well, I'm as surprised as the rest of you by Marcus's words. I had no idea of this diagnosis. My name is Dr. Kenyatta Robinson, and I teach at UC Berkeley, in the film and journalism departments. My two assistants, Addison and Keith, and I are working on a documentary about the Peoples Temple, about all of you and your experiences. We're *not* making a film about Jim Jones, just so you know."

A few elderly people shouted "Amen!"

"If you could speak with my assistants, or me, candidly, about anything you want to say, anything you feel has not yet been heard – and I bet there's a lot you want to say – we're going to be here all day. Please do seek us out."

Kenyatta paused. "Oh yes." She raised her forefinger. "I wanted to ask if the graffiti artist is here, and if he or she wants to speak." She put her hand over the microphone and looked to Sue, mouthing, "Is that okay?"

Sue shrugged.

Kenyatta uncovered the mic. "You can talk to me, privately, Graffiti Artist, if you don't want to address the group. Or just look me up at Berkeley at another time. I'd like to know why you did this today.

"And by the way, Marcus did not talk to me previously about speaking, so I have nothing prepared. I'm just grateful to all of you for letting us be here. It's a privilege to be part of your narrative. Thank you for allowing us to share your stories as best we can." She switched off the mike.

Immediately, media people rushed Sue in the front row. She remained cool, her cane planted in the ground before her, managing to keep some space between herself and the reporters. Some in the crowd made their way to the refreshment canopy to try the cassava fritters. A couple who ran the Jonestown Institute at San Diego State were talking to an old black man in a wheelchair, who seemed familiar. She realized it was Watts. He looked a hundred years older.

She made her way toward him, but someone grabbed her elbow.

"Professor Robinson, can I talk to you?" The high, tentative voice belonged to a young white woman with a half-shaved head, the other half draped in green dreadlocks. Her skin was covered in tattoos, including her face. She was very young. No more than twenty.

"You're the graffiti artist," Kenyatta.

The girl nodded.

"Can I film you?" Kenyatta asked.

The girl considered. "Yes, but only if you don't name me or show my face."

"It'd be easier to do that in the studio," Kenyatta told her.

"Okay, then just my voice. No film."

Kenyatta set her camera down and fished her recorder from her satchel and tested it.

"Go ahead," said Kenyatta, putting the recorder before the girl's spider-web tattooed chin.

The girl covered her eyes for a second, composing herself. "I just found out from my grandma this year that I'm the grandniece of Edith Roller, who died in Jonestown."

"She was the chronicler, wasn't she? She wrote the journals."

The girl nodded. "A professor, like you. An English prof at San Francisco State. I never knew her, never even heard of her until my grandma was dying last summer. At the end, she decided I should learn something about Edith because I remind her of her big sister. I was even named after her, which I just learned, because everything about my aunt's existence had been expunged from our family story until a few months ago."

"You want to expunge Jim Jones, just as she was, from your history," Kenyatta said.

The girl nodded. "I'm a writer, like my great aunt. She was twenty years older than my grandma. So she was kind of a mythical figure to her, even before she went to Guyana. Jim Jones deprived me of my namesake. Everyone here has been deprived of the people they loved. Since my grandma died, I've read everything I could find online that my great aunt wrote. Even now, forty years after she died, I can tell we're kindred spirits."

Kenyatta nodded. "I'm glad you finally discovered her."

The girl shook her head. "I guess it's better late than never, as they say. I'm still angry at my grandma for pretending my aunt never existed. It's like Edith Roller was the person I always wanted to be, growing up. A true rebel."

"I understand. I'd love it if you would participate in my documentary down the road. Edith's journals are part of the historical record, and so is the graffiti you did this morning. And so are you."

"I want to write a book about her," the girl said, looking down.

"I think you should. Are you staying for the afternoon service?"

The girl looked up. "I'm part of it now," she said.

"Yes, you are." Kenyatta turned off the recorder. "Come with me to meet Watts. He escaped Jonestown on the last day. He knew your great-aunt. He'll have some stories about her."

Annie Dawid has been writing about Jonestown for many years. Sections of the book published earlier include:

"Jonestown, Japantown," published electronically in *Joyland: San Francisco,* 2016

"Jonestown: Thirty Years On," published in *Best New Writing 2015,* finalist in the Eric Hoffer Awards

"Knowing What I Know," published in *Driftwood: A Literary Journal of Voices from Afar,* prize winner of the Abroad Writers Contest, 2006

"The Last Day of Mrs. Jim Jones," published electronically in *Rowayat*, an international magazine based in Canada, 2023

"Long Before Jonestown," published electronically on *Fictive Dream* and in *The Jonestown Report,* 2017

"Marceline Baldwin Meets Jim Jones: Indianapolis 1948," published electronically in *The Jonestown Report,* 2021

"Not Drinking the Kool-Aid," published electronically in *Half and One*, an international magazine based in India, 2023

Acknowledgements

First, I want to acknowledge everyone who lived and died in the Peoples Temple during its long career as a movement that began as an institution for social change in the 1950s and ended so horribly in the Jonestown agricultural project in 1978. Many have said, "The only thing wrong with Jonestown was Jones," and I wrote this book to honor those human beings who worked toward that Utopian ideal of a just society for all.

Joe Sam, I appreciate your willingness to allow your powerful drawing to grace my cover. Those people, so long submerged in the crowd behind their leader, are the subject here, whose lives I have tried to illuminate in my novel.

I want to thank Fielding McGehee and Rebecca Moore of the Jonestown Institute, who have been staunch supporters and resources all the way from the genesis of the novel in 2004. After a reading at the University of North Dakota Writers' Conference, where I mentioned Jonestown in an unrelated story, Jim McKenzie told me, tearfully, about colleagues who had lost family members in Jonestown. A month later, his sorrow for his friends informed my decision to spend my sabbatical writing about Jonestown instead of the hippie communes in Southern Colorado, which still await a future novel. Years later, I would meet those colleagues, Mac and Becky, who inaugurated my writer/artist retreat in Silver Cliff, Colorado, Bloomsbury West. They have helped enormously in every way.

Thanks and love go to friends and family who've cheered me on all these years, believing in the book, despite hundreds of rejections from publishers, as well as the 17 times *Paradise Undone* made it

323

to the finalist stage of contests, ultimately not receiving the prize of publication. I am grateful to Sally, Brooke, Leslie, Kathy, Carol, Paul, Reg, Daryl, Linda, Gayle, Kathy B, Karen, Elizabeth, Vette, David, Baba, Mark, Marcia, Irvin, Sam, Ben, Gail and so many others of longstanding connection for never giving up on me. I thank my departed parents, Heinz and Jeanette, for their gift of unadulterated stubbornness.

Cathy, I am humbled by your enthusiasm for this project. Thank you for saying YES.

Finally, I am grateful to my son, Isaiah Max, for living much of his life with this project in its unfinished state and then blossoming as a college graduate and Parisian grad student when it at last appears in the world at the end of 2023.